About the author

Phyllis Bischoff is a teacher of modern languages and has spent time in Germany and Austria. Her interest in the history of Nazi-dominated Germany and, particularly, the situation in Austria following the annexation by Germany in 1938, inspired her to write *Lilac Time*, which is her first novel. She lives in rural Kent.

First published in Great Britain in 2014 by

Flanders Oast Publishing
Flanders Oast, Reed Court Farm, Hunton Road
Chainhurst, Tonbridge, Kent TN12 9SX

ISBN 9781502590947

This book is a work of fiction. Names, characters, businesses,
organizations, places and events are either the product of the author's
imagination or are used fictitiously. Any resemblance to actual
persons, living or dead is entirely coincidental.

Edited by Nick Moon
Designed and produced by Sue Pressley

Cover photo acknowledgements: Lilac © shutterstock/aboikis.
The image *Central Vienna spring 1945* is in the public domain.
Every effort has been made by the publisher to contact the
copyright holder.

Printed and bound in England

LILAC TIME

Phyllis Bischoff

**FLANDERS OAST
PUBLISHING**

CHAPTER 1

Ida is running. The sound of her footsteps echoes through the deserted moonless streets. Her chest is bursting and the cold air burns her lungs as she gulps it in. She is afraid. She knows she is not supposed to be out here tonight, everyone has been told to stay indoors, but she must warn them at the factory.

Suddenly, the silence is broken by a crash, followed by the tinkle of broken glass. After a few seconds, there is a roar of jubilation in the distance. She knows it is too late for warnings now. There is another series of splintering thuds in quick succession, as window after window shatters. It sounds as if the whole city is exploding around her.

The noises are no longer just behind her, but all around her, getting closer. There is no escape. Now she can pick out individual voices from the crowd. Hands are grabbing at her. She tries to fend them off, but in vain. As suddenly as it started, the noise fades away and all is quiet again.

When she comes to, familiar anxious faces are peering down at her. She recognises Mrs Johnson from next door, and Mrs Singh from over the road. What can they be doing here? She tries to sit up, but a wave of pain engulfs her, making her almost pass out again.

The neighbours had raised the alarm when they noticed her milk hadn't been taken in for two days. Eventually the police had been called. They were forced to break the glass in the front door to gain entry. Ida was discovered, where she had fallen, at the bottom of the stairs. She had been there for nearly twenty-four hours. She had missed her footing on the second to last step, and the cup of tea she had been carrying splattered the walls of the hall. The house is hot, airless, and the curtains are still closed, although it is past midday. A drowsy bluebottle hovers overhead.

When the ambulance men arrive, they truss her up skilfully in a blanket and manoeuvre her onto a stretcher. By this time, her daughter, Anna, has arrived. Ida is severely dehydrated and very confused. When they get to hospital, she is disorientated. She calls out repeatedly in German. Anna cannot remember ever hearing her mother speak German before.

'Wo warst du? Ich habe auf dich gewartet, und du bist nicht gekommen!' Anna doesn't understand.

Ida lies on a trolley in casualty for hours. Eventually X rays are taken. At long last the doctor comes. He tells Anna that her mother's pelvis is broken. This is Ida's third fall in the past year. Much later Edward, Anna's brother, arrives and they discuss what is to be done.

'One thing is certain; Mother cannot continue to live on her own. She is barely able to walk now. She wouldn't be able to look after herself.' Anna is decisive. Edward is less so.

'We have a spare room now that the girls have left home but I don't think Marion would agree to her living with us,' he says cautiously.

Anna, knowing Marion, agrees, albeit silently. So it is arranged that Ida should enter a residential home and her house is to be sold. Anna must give her mother the news. Ida is distressed. She had hoped to leave her house to her children, but now it must be sold to pay the fees.

She is mainly left to her own devices in the huge, impersonal London hospital, but a physiotherapist does come round a couple of times a week to try to get her on her feet again. Physically, she makes a reasonably good recovery and, after a couple of weeks, is able to walk a bit with the support of a Zimmer frame. Mentally, however, things are a little different. The fall seems to have knocked her off balance, taken away her self-confidence and filled her with unaccountable anxiety. She's consumed by it, plucking at the sheets and rocking rhythmically. Sometimes she mutters in German. Anna is worried, but tries to remain positive.

'This is for the best, Mother. The Cedars is a friendly place, and it has beautiful grounds. You will soon make friends.' Even as she speaks, she knows this to be unlikely. Even when her mother was younger, she didn't make friends easily; now, in her extreme old age, she doubts that her mother has any capacity for friendship left. Still, it has to be done. Things cannot go on as before.

***

The Cedars turns out to be aptly named. In the middle of a wide, velvety lawn, the spreading branches of two large and ancient Cedar trees provide shade for those who are capable of walking the short distance from the front door to the benches, bequeathed by the grateful relatives of departed residents. The building itself is a one-storey L-shaped construction, which has been extended as increased demand put more pressure on the accommodation. As there is no upper floor, there is no need for stair lifts. It means, though, that the corridors are very long and narrow, causing the staff to complain bitterly about the distance they are required to walk, and the bottlenecks caused by the ubiquitous walking frames. Wheelchairs aren't allowed.

Ida and Anna arrive on a Friday morning. Mrs Piggott, the care manager, greets them. Anna is startled to hear that she immediately addresses her mother by her Christian name. It must be the modern way, she thinks, but somehow it seems to rob her mother of her dignity.

'You will soon feel at home here, Ida. Everyone is very friendly. I will just call Gloria to show you to your room, while I have a little chat with your daughter.'

Ida shuffles down the corridor after Gloria, and Anna goes with Mrs Piggott into a tiny office.

'Now then, your mother's eighty-six, Mrs Simpson. And German, I believe?'

'Austrian, actually.'

'I see. And what is her religion?' Anna hesitates. 'Officially Catholic, but she doesn't go to church anymore.'

'And does she have any hobbies?' Anna thinks hard. "Hobbies" seems such a childish word to describe her mother's interests. It brings to mind stamp collecting.

Finally she says, 'my mother's great love was always music, but she's a little deaf now.'

'Ah well, we have regular performances here. You know, music hall turns, comic songs, that type of thing. And of course hymn-singing on a Sunday afternoon.'

Anna feels unwilling to start explaining that her mother's musical tastes lie in a different direction. She smiles weakly and nods. Mrs Piggott seems a genuinely kind woman, and the rest of the staff that she has met so far seem pleasant and cheerful. Perhaps it won't be so bad. She just wishes that the atmosphere was not underlaid with the smell of urine. That and stale cooking. A particularly repellent combination.

The interview with Mrs Piggott over, Anna goes to see how her mother is settling in. The corridor seems never-ending, and her progress is frequently impeded by tea trolleys. She forces herself onwards, dreading having to face her mother again. What has she done to her? How would she like to be consigned to this enforced institutionalised cheerfulness in her declining years? But what is the real alternative? Could she have taken her mother in herself?

She dismisses the idea, thinking of the cramped two bedroomed flat in Bloomsbury. The second bedroom is always occupied by Charlotte, Tony's daughter, during the school holidays. And then she and Tony are out all day at the university, and her mother now needs constant care. How about Edward, then? It is true that he is retired now, but Marion would never wear it, and it's hard for a man to do the intimate things that his mother would require. She sighs. She passes large airy sitting rooms, some with televisions blaring. It's strange, she thinks, however much is done to provide a pleasant environment, and to encourage activity, the residents, or inmates, as she thinks of them to herself, still end up sitting in armchairs staring into space, waiting to die. Finally, she reaches her mother's room. It seems to be at the end of the world. Small, chintzy, with a wardrobe, bedside table and armchair. Lavatory along the corridor. At least she isn't sharing.

Ida is sitting on the bed. She looks small and sad. Anna feels a stab of pity.

'Well, Mother, what a pretty room. I'm sure you'll be very

comfortable here.' She speaks brightly.

Her mother looks up but does not answer.

'I'll help you unpack, if you like.'

She opens the old brown leather suitcase. Ida's clothes, though old-fashioned, have a certain chic. An indefinable quality sets Ida apart from the other residents, too. Unlike the regulation stiff iron-grey perm favoured by the other residents, Ida's hair is smooth, pure white and still thick. She wears it drawn back from her face in an elegant bun. Her skin is fine, though criss-crossed with lines, and her figure is still elegant, though brittle with old age. No, thinks Anna, I can't see her joining in the communal singing or taking part in a beetle drive. From what she has seen, most of the others are typical South Londoners. Many are bulky with inactivity and stodgy food. There seems to be camaraderie among them which she feels will never include her mother. Women outnumber men by about ten to one.

Suddenly, Anna cannot wait to be out of the stultifying atmosphere of the home and heading back into London. But Ida has now started to rock backwards and forwards in her armchair. Anna feels a rush of panic. She kneels beside her.

'Mother, what is it? What's the matter? It's bound to seem strange at first, but I'm sure you'll soon get used to it.'

As she hears the stream of platitudes pouring from her lips, she despises herself. Ida's rheumy eyes fill with tears. She speaks at last.

'Where's Jude? Doesn't she know I'm here? Have you told her, Anna?'

'Of course she knows, Mother. Don't worry, I'm sure she'll be up to see you as soon as she has time.'

Anna is not sure this will happen. Jude is not assiduous in visiting her mother. It is a pity, because she is Ida's favourite child.

'Mother, I have to go now. I'll come and see you tomorrow. Edward may come too.' She squeezes Ida's arm as she leaves.

***

When Anna has gone, Ida leans back in her chair and closes her eyes. Eventually the present drifts out of reach, and she is back in the warm safety of her early childhood. She returns here ever more frequently. Although there were great hardships, it was a happy time, she thinks, or is this just how it seems now, looking back? Home is a small flat in the Zieglergasse, near the Opera in Vienna. They don't have much money. After the first war, money is desperately short and people are almost starving. Some children are sent to Holland because of the food shortages, but her mother won't send them away.

'We sink or swim together,' she says. Ida is only two when her oldest brother dies in the influenza epidemic of 1920.

Scenes from her childhood run through Ida's head. Running downstairs and along the road to the Zuckerbacker to buy *Topfenknodel* or *Buchteln*, when there is a little extra money. Sunday afternoon walks in the Vienna woods or listening to a band in the Volksgarten. Occasional trips to Schonbrunn and, once, skating on the Danube when it froze. Such clearly defined seasons, not like the year-long murk that is England.

She thinks of her brother, Ernst. A clever and athletic young man, he was popular with his schoolmates and adored by his parents. Dead in the snows of Stalingrad. What a pointless waste! He died before his life had really begun, whereas she has lived too long, outlived her usefulness.

***

Before Ida can continue her reverie, there is a knock on the door.

'Hello my darlin'. I've come to take you down for your lunch.' Ida flinches at the sudden jolt back to reality. Gloria bounces into the room, quickly dispelling all notions of old Vienna. She is huge and very black, her pale lilac Cedars uniform stretched over her enormous bosom, the cap perched precariously on her tight curls. Ida stares, bemused, at this vision in mauve.

'Have you unpacked your things yet, sweetheart? You need some ornaments and photos to make it seem more like home.' She is arranging the things on Ida's dressing table as she speaks.

'Was that your daughter, then? She seems a nice lady.'

There's a silence, then 'Yes, yes, that was my younger daughter, Anna. She's been very kind.'

'Well, I'm going to take you down and introduce you to your table companions. You've got very special table, you know, right by the window. You can watch the birds havin' a bath!' She laughs loudly.

'Oh, by the way honey, do you need night time pads? I'm only axin' because a lot of the ladies here have them.'

'No thank you,' replied Ida coldly. 'I'm quite capable of taking myself to the lavatory.'

***

Ida is not very mobile after her accident. She struggles to get up from the armchair, and Gloria has to help her. There is a special way of doing this. Ida must put her arms around Gloria's neck and walk forwards out of the chair, whilst Gloria walks backwards.

14

Gloria manoeuvres her skilfully onto the Zimmer frame. They make slow progress along the endless corridor. The trouble is that everyone is converging on the dining room at once, and there is a traffic jam. Some residents are confused.

'I've had my lunch, I'm going to bed now.'

'No, no, dear, it's lunchtime now.'

'What time is it?'

'It's nearly one o'clock, my love.'

Ida is to find this question a constant refrain. Time takes on the utmost importance when there is literally nothing to do but wait for mealtimes. That and death, Ida thinks grimly.

Finally, they make it into the dining room. It is a large, airy room, the tables attractively laid with mauve tablecloths and posy-bowls of flowers. Gloria leads Ida to a table by the open patio doors. Like the other tables, it is set for four. The patio doors open directly onto a small paved area, containing a fishpond. As promised there is also a stone birdbath on a pedestal. It is late summer, and the day is fine and warm, the sun not too strong.

The other occupants are already ensconced as Ida approaches the table. A man and two women. Introductions are performed. There is Grace, a large, mild-mannered old lady. She makes some attempts at conversation. The talk is of their families, the houses they have had to leave. The other woman, Ivy, is thin and ill-tempered. She has a pronounced South London accent.

'You ain't English, are you?' she says curiously, after a pause in the conversation.

'No, I'm Austrian.'

'Austrian, is it? What you doing here then? Why ain't you in Austria?'

'My husband was English. I've lived here for fifty-five years. My youngest child was born here.'

There is a pause, while Ivy takes this in.

Then she says, 'The Austrians was with them Jerries, weren't they? The ones wot bombed us in the Blitz. Every night we spent down the Underground, me and me brothers and sister. Bloody murder, it was.'

'Yes, well it wasn't exactly a picnic in Austria either, especially in Vienna.' says Ida shortly. 'Still, it's all a long time ago now.'

Ivy is silent, but she continues to shoot evil looks at Ida.

The only male occupant of the table, Albert, has said nothing up till now. At this point he enters the conversation;

'Where did you meet your husband, then, Mrs McFarlane?' His mode of address is formal; he has the air of an old soldier.

'I met Ernest in 1945. He was sent to Vienna to do an intelligence job for the Allies. He spoke fluent German, you see.'

'I thought you said you was Austrian, not German.' puts in Ivy. Ida is non-plussed for a moment, then she understands.

'German is spoken in Austria as well as Germany. The accent is different, that's all.'

'Well, that's funny, I thought they spoke Austrian.'

Ida smiles faintly. Ivy is not alone in her misapprehension. She tries to change the subject, to talk about the Cedars, the garden, anything but the horrors of post-war Vienna. But Albert is determined.

'What kind of intelligence work, Mrs McFarlane?'

'I really don't know, it was very hush-hush, you know.' Ida fiddles with the edge of the tablecloth.

She doesn't want any more food and would like to leave the table, but cannot do so unaided. Albert presses inexorably on.

'You said your youngest child was born here. Does that mean

you were married before?'

'Yes, my first husband was Austrian.'

'And what happened to him?'

'He was killed on the Eastern front.' says Ida shortly. She looks round desperately for Gloria or another care assistant, but they all seem to have vanished. Luckily, Albert now wishes to talk about himself. He tells them how he started off fighting in the desert, 'Under Monty, y'know', and ended up fighting his way through Italy in 1945.

Ivy is impressed. 'Was you a desert rat, then?'

'That's right, Ivy. Best time of my life, that was. My son's in the regular army now, you know, the Royal Fusiliers.'

The meal finally ends and Ida is helped back to her room. They try to persuade her to sit in one of the big sitting rooms and watch the television, but she is adamant. She is exhausted and can only think of lying on her bed.

***

Once back in her room, she slips effortlessly into her childhood again. She is a good student. She enjoys school, and either she or her best friend, Esther, is usually top of the class. Ida is better at German and history, Esther at maths. They sit side by side in class; are inseparable in the playground. Esther lives in the same apartment block as Ida, although Esther's family has a much bigger flat. They play together in the little communal courtyard or in the street. Esther's father is a psychiatrist. Ida's father works at the paper factory.

Ida and Esther run hand in hand down the Zieglergasse. It is a sultry afternoon, and the city is sweltering in temperatures of over thirty degrees. There is not much sun, Esther and Ida are skipping.

'*Eins zwei zusammen, drei vier auseinander.*' Esther's twin brothers, aged five, want to join in, but they won't let them. The boys are too young to skip properly; they are only a hindrance. It is getting late, and Esther must go. It's Friday, and she must be back before sunset. Ida knows she will not see her again until Sunday now.

Ida is curious. She has never been inside her friend's flat, but she knows there are lighted candles and a special meal on a Friday. She has seen a sort of box fixed to Esther's doorpost. Esther tells her it is a Mezuzah, containing their special prayers. Esther's family attend a synagogue in a different part of the city. The prayers they say are different from the prayers in Ida's church, and they are in Hebrew, not Latin. When Ida asks her mother about it, she is vague.

'They are Jews,' she says; 'they are different.' and Ida must be content with that. Sometimes, she hears Esther's family talking together in a language which sounds familiar to her, but which she cannot quite understand.

Ida's family attend the Augustinerkirche every Sunday. It smells of damp and incense, and the priest wears a long flowing robe. Ida is often bored, except when there is a sung mass. The music, Haydn or Schubert, soars into the rafters of the church and transports her.

Ida cannot understand why the priest speaks a language they cannot understand. Again, she asks her mother.

'It has always been so.' she says.

One day, Esther and Ida compare notes. It seems they have the same God after all! But then, Ida learns something dreadful. The son of Ida's God was killed by Esther's ancestors! Ida is shocked.

How can this be? Esther says that her people do not believe he was the Son of God. They are still awaiting their Messiah, it seems. Ida is puzzled. She thinks about Esther's family, who are always kind to her. They do not seem like murderers.

She remembers one particular day, when she was about nine, she and her brother Ernst decide to go to the Volksprater, the amusement park on the outskirts of the city. They are desperate to go on the giant Ferris wheel, although their mother has expressly forbidden them from going. She says that unsavoury types frequent the park and that, anyway, it is too far. When they get there, though, they find that they do not have enough money to go on the wheel. It is more expensive than they thought. They are about to turn round and go home, when they meet a man their father works for, a Mr Reuben. He is surprised to see them such a long way from home. When they tell him they can't afford the Ferris wheel, he insists on paying for them to go on it. Ida can remember how her heart raced as the wheel soared high above the ground. It is the most wonderful, yet most terrifying experience of her life. She feels she is on top of the world: the views of the city are stupendous. She can even see their own street! Far in the distance, the Danube shines dully, like a steel band marking the boundaries of the city. She wants it never to end.

It has to end, of course. She and Ernst set off on the long walk home later than they had intended. On one occasion they lose their way, and find themselves in an unfamiliar part of the city. Suddenly, they hear a distant rumble of shouts. As they walk on, the din gets louder. Before they know it, they are in the middle of crowds of men, pushing and jostling, some throwing stones. They are terrified. The men seem so angry, and they are caught in the middle, their homeward path blocked. Suddenly, amidst the hubbub, they hear someone calling their names. They look up and see Mr Reuben again, calling to them from an upper window on the other side of the road. It turns out to be the Reuben family's house, a very grand, baroque building. Thankful but overawed, they take shelter with the Reuben family until the men, weary of their protest, begin to wander off home. Mr Reuben explains that they have been trying to storm the Palace of Justice in revenge for the killing of some of their comrades. Ida and Ernst do not really understand but, as soon as the riot is over, they thank Mr Reuben and set off for home again.

When they arrive back, much later than expected, their mother is desperate with worry and fear. She has heard the riot, and imagines them trodden underfoot. They have to tell her about going on the Praterstern, and how Mr Reuben paid for them. A curious expression crosses their mother's face.

'You had better not tell your father about that.' she says.

'But why not, Mother? Mr Reuben was very kind and besides, Father works for him.' says Ida.

'Your father may have to work for him, but he would not like you to accept charity or hospitality from him, of that you can be sure.'

Ida is about to ask further questions, but her mother angrily cuts her short, and sends her to wash her hands for supper.

Ida has replayed this scene many times in her head. The memory has stayed with her over the years, especially her mother's displeasure. It is the only time she could remember her being so angry.

Ida's reminiscences are again interrupted by a knock at the door. This time, it is Mrs Piggott. She comes in and seats herself on the armchair.

'Well now, Ida, I've just come to see how you are settling in.'

Ida struggles to sit up.

'Oh, please, don't get up now. I don't want to disturb your rest. I just wanted to see if you are all right. All our new residents feel a bit strange at first but it soon passes. I just wanted to make sure that you know all about the activities we have here. Do you play cards, by any chance? We have a whist drive tonight. You might like to join in.'

Ida shakes her head.

'Well, perhaps you would like one of the girls to take you out in the garden for a while. That can easily be arranged, and it's such a lovely day.'

'Well, yes, that would be nice. I miss my garden so much, you know.'

'Yes, I quite understand. A lot of our residents feel the same way. I'll call Kim and she'll take you out while the sun is still shining.'

Mrs Piggott smiles kindly. 'Don't worry Ida. You will soon feel at home here, believe me.'

CHAPTER 2

'Dan, are you there? If you're not doing anything, darling, can you give me a hand to unload the shopping?'

There is no reply. Jude feels sure he must be there, because the back door is unlocked and the television is on. He's probably on the wretched computer again. Once he starts, that's it; he can be incommunicado for hours. His bedroom is at the top of the house, two floors up, and he is capable of staying cocooned in his own world for hours on end. Jude sighs. The day is muggy, and her skirt is sticking to her. Sweat runs between her breasts and under her arms. She lowers her considerable bulk onto one of the kitchen stools, deciding to cart the bags in after she's had a cold drink. The phone rings; Jude picks up the receiver of the cordless phone and clamps it to her ear as she fills a glass with orange juice. She decides to treat herself to a doughnut as well. After all, she has struggled round the supermarket single-handed, shopping for five people and a dinner party.

It's Anna. Jude is not pleased. Phone calls from Anna usually involve some harassing news about their mother; she's aware of her mother's latest fall, and that Anna has been checking out care homes. Now it appears that a suitable one has been found. The conversation is short and to the point.

'I can't possibly visit for the next few days, Anna. I'm far too busy…Yes, yes, I'm aware that she is unsettled but, from what you say, it sounds as though she is in good hands…I really can't help it if she has been asking for me. I have a home to run here, and I'm entertaining clients of Gerry's tomorrow night. Yes, of course, I'll go as soon as humanly possible.'

Jude hangs up. Of course she feels guilty but, really, she has a far busier life that her brother or sister. Anna only has a tiny flat to look after and a sinecure of a job at the university, and as for Edward, well really, she cannot imagine what he does with his time now that he is retired. He does not appear to have any interests, and neither of his children lives at home. Well, it's just bad luck that her mother seems to want to see her rather than Anna or Edward. If she is honest, she cannot imagine why. Anna has always done far more for her mother than either she or Edward. She sighs again. Life is never straightforward. Just when things seem to be running smoothly, some new obstacle presents itself. She will have to go soon, of course. Streatham isn't so far from Bromley. She will probably wait until the twins have gone back to university, and then go.

By now, she has dragged the bags in from the Range Rover. Dan wanders downstairs.

'Hello, darling. Be a love and take these cases of wine to the wine store.' Dan pulls a face. He is twenty and doesn't see why he should participate in household tasks, although he is very happy to enjoy the goodies that are always abundant in his parents' house. Moodily, he grabs a case in each hand and slouches out.

Jude calls after him brightly, 'Have you heard from Kate? Will she be back for supper this evening?' Dan stops in his tracks and thinks.

Finally he says, 'Um, there was a phone call. I think she said she'd be back about seven.'

His twin sister has a job during the vacation, serving in one of those huge new pubs in the town centre. Dan doesn't have a job. He had a brief look in the paper at the beginning of the summer, but nothing grabbed him.

'Never mind, darling', Jude had said, 'something will turn up.'

But the summer has worn on, and nothing has. He is at Oxford. The shorter term has made his vacation longer than Kate's, who is at Bristol.

Jude moves heavily around the limed oak kitchen, putting the shopping away. So, if Kate is back tonight, that makes four for supper, or five, if Hugo decides to turn up. Just then, the phone rings again. This time it's Gerry's secretary, June.

'Hello, Mrs Fairbrother. Mr Fairbrother has asked me to tell you that he'll be late home tonight. The President of United Holdings has arrived unexpectedly from New York, and he has to take him out to dinner. He asked me to tell you not to wait up for him.'

Jude slowly replaces the receiver. She is half-relieved. If Gerry is not coming home supper can be a scratch affair. Pizza perhaps, or pasta. On the other hand, he's been getting June to ring up rather a lot recently, and returning very late.

She wonders idly if he's having an affair. Jude decides she doesn't really care. If he is, though, she's determined to leave him this time. After all, Hugo is more or less off their hands now, and the twins have only one more year to go at university. He'll have to pay for them, of course. If it comes to it, she'll make sure she comes out of it all right, too. The more worrying thing is Gerry's drinking. She can't help wondering how long he'll keep his job. If he loses it, they really will be in the shit. She knows he often gets back from the office after lunch a bit worse for wear. People notice things like that, especially the Americans. She tries to put these thoughts aside, and looks at the kitchen clock. Only five o'clock. There's time for a shower and a potter in the garden before she need even start thinking of supper.

She stays for ages in the large, walk-in shower, trying to wash away the aggravations of the day, but for some reason she keeps thinking about her mother. Why can't she be satisfied with the attentions of Anna, who seems only too willing to shoulder most of the burden?

When she emerges, she dries herself off and digs out an old pair of jeans, which she wears exclusively for gardening. Damn, they won't even do up now. How long ago was it that she wore them? It could only have been a month or so. Surely she can't have put on more weight in such a short time? She scrapes her blond hair back into a wispy ponytail, and glances unhappily at her round, flushed face in the mirror. She has not inherited the effortless grace which her mother possesses, even in old age.

Eventually she goes downstairs again and decides to attack the rose beds. She collects the secateurs from the shed at the side of the house, and walks round the back to the rose garden. The house is large, mock Tudor, with a sweeping gravel drive at the front and extensive grounds to the rear. She starts to deadhead the roses and to cut away spent branches. The sun is low in the sky by now and the rose bed is already half in shadow. It is, after all, nearly the end of August. Although she is superficially absorbed in her task, her thoughts drift constantly back to her mother. She is a proud woman, and will not wish to be cared for by strangers.

From a very early age, Jude is aware that her mother is unlike her friends' mothers. She remembers being embarrassed by her, wishing she were more like them. For a start, she sounded different. She is often asked by other children why her mother 'speaks funny.' In the early 1950s, foreigners aren't such a familiar sight in Britain. And then, her mother looks different. Post-war Britain is a grey place; everything is drab, including the women's clothes but somehow, Ida manages to look what – faintly exotic? God knows, they had no more money than other families, possibly less. The war is still such a raw memory for people, and Ida is often not well received. Not that she makes much effort to fit in. Her grasp of English is still limited and, with hindsight, Jude imagines she is still traumatised by her wartime experiences.

Food is not in short supply, but it is monotonous. However, Ida makes unusual and delicious dishes from what is available: dumplings, goulash and, later, when more varied food is available, Wiener Schnitzel and Sachertorte.

They live in Harrow. Her brother, Edward, five years older, is a silent and withdrawn child. He's not much different as an adult, come to that, thinks Jude. Anyway, he's not much fun to play with. When Anna is born, her father is enraptured by her from the start. Ida always loved Jude best, though, perhaps to compensate for her father's lack of interest.

Her father is distant but never unkind. He works at the Home Office. Jude is not a good student, and often gets into scrapes at school. Anna, on the other hand, is brilliant. Their father cannot conceal his delight in this. Jude is jealous.

'Jude has the personality, though, Ernest.' says their mother.

Later, as they grow up, Anna passes her exams with flying colours; she goes to university. Not such an automatic progression from school as it is now, thinks Jude, much more of an achievement in those days. She, on the other hand, is more interested in boys and pop music. In the 60s, she throws herself into the swinging London scene with enthusiasm. She is vivacious and quite pretty, and soon has a little following of admirers, including Gerry: they get married in 1970. He is already well on his way up the company ladder and her parents are pleased, especially her mother.

The wedding is rather a grand affair, and it's only when they are compiling the guest list that Jude realises how small her family is compared to Gerry's. There are her parents, of course, and her brother and her sister, who is a bridesmaid. Apart from that, though, there's only her father's brother. There is no one at all on her mother's side.

'Doesn't your mother have any relatives, then?' asks Gerry, and Jude has to admit that she doesn't know. Gerry is incredulous.

'Doesn't she ever go back home to visit anyone?'

In fact, Ida has never returned to Austria since she left in 1950. It is only at this point that Jude really thinks about it at all. When she does, she decides that it really is rather odd. When she questions Ida, she is told that there are no living relatives. No, she says, she has no desire to return to Austria, not even for a visit.

Jude is soon distracted by her wedding preparations, and gives no more thought to it, at least until she's putting the invite list together. After all, she might have cousins that she has never met. And then why has Ida never spoken German at home? Edward did it for a while at school, but his mother showed no interest and he soon gave it up. The only other member of the family to speak German is, of course, Kate, Jude's own daughter. She is reading German at Bristol but, as far as Jude knows, she has never spoken German with her grandmother.

The sun has now almost set, and there is a damp chill in the air. Jude gathers up the garden debris and deposits it on the compost heap. She goes indoors to prepare the meal.

***

Although Waterman & Gresham is a relatively small investment bank, it has some major clients. In the last few years, it has acquired several important accounts from the Middle East and now, today, there is real cause for celebration, because they have netted Grossman's, one of the biggest companies in Israel. Hugo's department is cock a hoop. Hugo himself feels that he has contributed to this success in no small way himself. He has been working on the account under his manager, Richard, and now there are congratulations all round.

'Well done lads,' he says. 'This calls for a real celebration. Hugo, book a table at Giovanni's for the whole department.'

The table is booked for nine o'clock. Hugo remembers that he has half promised to go home this evening. Well, too bad, they will have to manage without him. As he leaves the office, he rings home on his mobile, but there is no reply. He leaves a short message.

The evening's celebrations start with several bottles of Bollinger. Giovanni's is unobtrusive but exclusive, in the heart of Mayfair. The cuisine combines unusual ingredients, piled high in the centre of the plate. It is more filling than it looks. Hugo is halfway through his meal when he spots his father.

He is with a woman, dark-haired, attractive, youngish. Their heads are bent together in intimate conversation. This is clearly no business meeting. Suddenly, Hugo is not hungry any more. He is aware that his parents are not getting on, but he didn't think it had come to this. He wonders briefly if he should say something to his mother. His father and his companion leave without noticing Hugo, no doubt seeing only a group of boisterous young men.

The party, by now in high spirits, adjourns to a club. Richard produces coke, and they all do a line. In fact, Hugo isn't keen on drugs. He fears he will pass out, become ill. But he cannot refuse, especially as it's his boss. In spite of the alcohol and drugs, his spirits remain obstinately low. He thinks of his father from time to time. In contrast to the crowd he hangs out with, he's an insecure young man, still attached to his family.

Finally, at about three o'clock, the party begins to breaks up. Hugo and Alistair, his colleague and flatmate, hail a taxi and return to their home off the Fulham Road. Hugo falls into a disturbed sleep, in which he dreams that his father brings the dark-haired woman home to live with them.

**

The Barchester Arms, near Chislehurst, is open from ten o'clock in the morning until twelve o'clock at night, seven days a week. It attracts a mixed crowd – shoppers, workmen and even pensioners in the day, and from mid-evening onwards, a young, raucous clientele out for a good time. At night, the background music is replaced by a DJ who plays something more hardcore, along with strobe lights. It is a cavernous place, serving mainly cold beer and inferior wine and, at lunchtime, various fried and battered dishes, always with chips.

It is the second year running that Kate has worked there. She works alternate shifts, one day, one night. She far prefers the day shift. The place is usually empty when she arrives, and then a few customers start to straggle in at about eleven o'clock for morning coffee or even beer. In between serving drinks and wiping down tables, she sometimes even manages to read a few pages of her book. There is never any trouble in the day. The evenings, however, are a very different matter. From about nine o'clock, the customers at the bar are eight to ten deep, all jostling and shouting to attract her attention. By the time they have had a few pints, they are often spoiling for a fight, shoving, and accusing each other of pushing in. Fortunately the two hefty bouncers who man the doors from early evening are on the spot immediately, and soon put paid to any trouble. Kate works alongside two other girls and two young men. Although her appearance is distinctive, here she attracts no particular attention. Her hair is short and spiky and very black. 'Barmaid black,' her mother calls it.

'Oh well, it's appropriate, then.' she retorts. She always dresses entirely in black too, apart from a large silver-coloured metal belt. She has a nose-stud and was about to get her eyebrow pierced as well until her parents, showing a united front for once, threatened to ban her from the house. Although she cannot wait to leave home for good, she can see how inconvenient this could be at the present time. The pay at the Barchester is not good – she gets the minimum wage – but it provides the money to buy the books and CDs she wants, and to finance a trip to Germany a couple of times a year. Fortunately her boyfriend, Christoph, has at long last finished studying, and now works full-time for a charity for the homeless in the Kreuzberg district of Berlin. This means he can come to England more frequently to visit. He usually comes to Bristol during term-time, and stays with her in her tiny shared flat. It's cramped, but preferable to having him to stay at her parents' house, where the atmosphere can be uncomfortable. Next week, however, he is coming to stay for one night in Bromley on his way to a meeting in London.

Kate plans to move to Berlin to live when she has taken her finals. She likes Berliners, the young ones, anyway, with their idealism and lack of materialism. She finds them a refreshing change from some of her compatriots. She has not yet mentioned these plans to her parents, knowing they will not be pleased. Dan knows, though. In spite of their vastly different lifestyles and aspirations, there is still sometimes a sort of subconscious connection between them. Yet they have grown apart, almost completely. Even when they were still at school, they had different interests, different friends. Now that they are at university, there is a huge gulf between them. Dan is his mother's favourite. He is also gay. Not that his mother knows that. Kate knows she would be horrified. He is reading computer science at Oxford, and looks set for a first and a glittering career. Her future is likely to be very different.

Today, Kate is working the daytime shift, and intends to return home for supper. She has rung Dan to that effect. She suddenly remembers that Aunt Anna was looking for a suitable residential home for Gran after her fall. She wonders if one has been found. Really, she thinks, it is not right of her mother to refuse to help with this. After all, she doesn't work, and Aunt Anna has a demanding job at the university. Kate feels sad that her grandmother has to give up her house and the garden she loved, but she supposes it must be for the best. She is fond of her, always has been, and has happy memories of visits to her house when she was younger. There was always *Sandkuchen* or *Apfelkuchen* with cream, and coffee for the grown-ups, at four o'clock. Mozart or Bach would be playing in the background. She and her grandmother would chat about all kinds of things; she was very knowledgeable and always seemed to have time for her, unlike her parents, who were always busy. Sometimes, Kate would ask her about Vienna. Although she always answered her questions, she never went into great detail, and was inclined to change the subject.

Kate barely remembers her grandfather. He died when she was still quite small. Kate has always felt drawn towards Austria and Germany. The first time she visited Germany was a school trip when she was fourteen. It was to Bavaria, and she immediately felt strangely at home there. Even her first sexual experience was in Germany, with a local boy on the carousel at the village fair. Kate has never forgotten it. Most of her subsequent boyfriends, of whom there have been quite a few, have also been German, though she has been with Christoph for the last eighteen months. Since then, she has gone on to read German at Bristol. She reads German history voraciously, and is particularly fascinated by accounts of the Third Reich. She has visited many different places, although not yet her grandmother's hometown.

By the time Kate arrives home she is tired and irritable. She grinds out her cigarette underfoot, then remembers that her mother does not appreciate stubs being left on the drive, so she half buries it in a flowerpot. She bangs the front door behind her and throws her bag and jacket in a corner of the hall.

The house is in semi-darkness. The only light glimmers from the half-open kitchen door. She can hear the tinny jangle of Capital Gold from her mother's transistor radio. Jude is standing over the stove, feeding spaghetti into a pan of boiling water. She looks round as Kate enters the room.

'Hello darling. You're late. Have you had a good day?'

'Not particularly.' says Kate, flopping onto a kitchen stool. 'Bloody awful, in fact. What's for supper?'

'Spaghetti.' says Jude superfluously, stirring the pan.

'Well yes, I can see that. What's with it, I mean.'

'Bolognese sauce and salad.'

'I hope there's no meat in it.'

'Oh damn, I forgot. Sorry.'

'Don't worry,' says Kate. 'I'll just eat the spaghetti. I take it we've got some Parmesan.'

Just then, Dan comes in. Kate glances at him.

'Oh, hello. Einstein's arrived. Had a hard day?'

Dan is untouched by sarcasm. He goes to the fridge and takes out a half-full bottle of Sancerre, and pours himself a glass. He doesn't bother asking if anyone else wants one. He too sits on a stool and takes a sip.

'Sebastian and I are working on a new programme. If it takes off it should make a fortune.'

'What is it then?'

Dan is mysterious. 'It's very specialised. We don't want to say too much until we market it.'

'Well, let's all hope you can patent it. You wouldn't want to get your hands dirty doing anything menial like me now, would you?'

'Now Kate, that's not fair,' puts in their mother. 'The vacation is the only opportunity Dan has to work on these projects. They're very important for his future.'

' Yeah, right.' says Kate. She lets the subject drop.

There's a silence. Jude moves around the kitchen, setting the table and opening the jar of sauce.

'Isn't Dad eating with us?' asks Kate eventually.

'No. He's out with clients tonight.' says Jude shortly.

There is another silence.

Then, 'How about Hugo? I thought he was coming tonight.'

'He left a message. It seems they've got an important new account, and they're all going out to celebrate.'

'Ah. Just the three of us, then.'

'Right,' says Jude. 'I think we're ready.'

They sit down at the large oak kitchen table. It's already completely dark outside and Jude pulls the blinds.

'Oh, by the way, Mum.' Kate suddenly remembers. 'Have you heard from Aunt Anna? Has anything been found for Gran?'

Jude pushes her chair back and goes to the fridge to fetch a bottle of mineral water.

'Yes, I have actually. Anna rang today. She's got your Gran into a home in Streatham. It sounds very nice. It should be, too, the amount of money it's costing. Honestly, I just don't know how they can justify the fees they charge in these places.'

'Yes, well I expect Gran's worth it. I should have thought that was the least of our worries. The main thing is that she's comfortable and well looked after. When are you going to see her? Tomorrow?'

Jude looks evasive. 'Well, I can't go tomorrow as it happens. Your father's clients are coming to dinner. I'll be busy preparing the meal.'

'Oh for God's sake! I can't believe you, Mum. What's more important, sodding clients or your own mother? I'd go myself, only I'm working. I'm definitely going at the weekend, though.'

Jude reddens.

'Don't speak to me like that, Kate. I've told you, I'm very busy over the next few days. I'll go when you and Dan have gone back to college.'

'What? That's a couple of weeks away. How can you, Mum? You know how fond Gran is of you. She'll be desperate to see you.' She pauses. 'Anyway, how did Aunt Anna say she was?'

Jude is vague. 'Oh, not bad, not bad. Obviously it takes a while to settle into these places.'

'Well, if I were Aunt Anna, I wouldn't be very pleased to be left to do everything by myself.'

Up to this point, Dan hasn't spoken. Now he says, 'What about Uncle Edward? Has he been to see her?'

'Oh Edward.' says his mother scornfully. 'I shouldn't think so. He's completely useless, can't make up his mind to do anything. I expect everything will be left up to us, as usual.'

'Well, at least he used to visit Gran regularly when she was living in Latymer Road.' says Kate.

'Anyway, Dan, why don't you go and see her tomorrow. You haven't anything else to do.'

'Nothing else to do? My project is nearing completion, I'll have you know. Sebastian is coming over tomorrow, and we're going to go through the final stages.'

'Oh well, if Sebastian's coming over we'd better put everything on hold, hadn't we.' says Kate nastily.

'Kate, I swear you've been wearing that jumper all week.' Dan changes the subject.

'So what? At least I go out and work all week. Not like you, swanning about in your ivory tower.'

'I'm not sure that one can actually 'swan' in an ivory tower. I should have thought one did something more static. Meditate, for example.'

'Oh, stop it, you two.' says Jude. 'Look, I'll tell you what. We'll bring Gran over for lunch soon, with all the family. How about next Sunday?'

'Well, I'm going to see her before that, even if you're not.' says Kate moodily. 'Anyway, Christoph will be here then. I told you, he's coming next weekend, on his way to London.'

'Oh God! The Kraut punk!' Dan sniggers. His mother sighs. She does not want any more confrontation with Kate.

After supper, Dan retires to the sitting room to watch television, while Kate helps her mother load the dishwasher.

'Mum, did Gran ever talk to you about when she was in Vienna, during the war I mean?'

'No, not really. All I know is that she met your grandfather while he was stationed there.'

'Yes, I know that bit. I was just thinking about the time before that. It must have been pretty horrendous. I just think it's rather odd that she never talks about it. Perhaps it was so traumatic that she's blocked it out.'

'Yes, maybe she has.' Her mother is already thinking about something else, planning the meal for the next evening. When the kitchen is tidy, Kate goes up to her bedroom. She lights a joint, and sits smoking it by the open window. As she stares out into the dark garden, she tries to picture the chaos and destruction, and the fear which her grandmother must have felt, when she was not much older than Kate is now. It is almost unimaginable.

CHAPTER 3

Anna is on her way to visit her mother. Although she and
Tony own a car, they hardly ever use it, living in the centre
of town. This time she must take it, though, to travel out to
Streatham. It is a Fiat Uno, not very new. Traffic is heavy all
the way. She is so absorbed by her thoughts that she hardly
remembers which bit of the journey she has done, and is surprised
to find herself already at the top of Brixton Hill. She wonders
constantly if she has made the right decision about her mother.
Jude and Edward have been less than helpful. Edward means
well, but he is indecisive and vague. Jude, frankly, seems not to
care. After last night's phone conversation, Anna is sure of it. She
wonders if her mother will ever settle down at the Cedars. The
events leading to her move there – her latest fall and the spell in
hospital – seem to have made her confused and anxious, even
depressed. She supposes it must take time to settle after such an
upheaval.

The drive has taken her over an hour. The Cedars car park
looks full, but she manages to find a space. It is Saturday and
there are lots of visitors. They, and those they have come to see, sit
under the trees or walk around the grounds.

Anna must make a great mental effort to get out of the car and walk into the building. The journey is one thing, arriving is quite another, and she dreads what state her mother may be in. Ida is not in the garden. She must therefore be in one of the lounges or, worse, in her room, by herself. As before, progress is slow along the narrow corridor. Occasionally it widens to provide a sitting area, and she sees groups of people drinking tea and chatting. There are even small children running around. As she passes the lounges, she peers inside. Her mother is not in any of them. Surely she won't be sitting alone in her room with so much activity going on. She passes a care assistant, who smiles and says hello.

'Could you tell me where I would find my mother, Mrs McFarlane – er – Ida?'

The girl, for that is all she is, says 'Oh yes, of course, Ida. She's just joined us, hasn't she? She's in her room just now, but she was sitting in the garden for a while, before lunch. I'll take you to her, if you like.'

Anna follows her. She feels humbled by this young, cheerful girl, who must work with the old people day in day out. Putting them on the commode, changing their soiled sheets and underwear, feeding them. And always with a smile. Sitting with them while they are dying, or, unexpectedly, finding them dead in bed one morning. She knows she could never do it. She finds it hard enough dealing with her own mother, her own flesh and blood. Yet this is just an ordinary girl. Not especially well educated, but with an instinctive warmth and kindness that could never be taught. She wonders if she goes clubbing on her evenings off, if she talks about her work with her friends.

The girl knocks on Ida's door and goes straight in. Ida is sitting in her armchair, half turned towards the window. The view is of the back garden and the road beyond it. It is only a side road, though; there is no traffic noise and little activity. Ida is wearing a dress that Anna does not recognise. It is shapeless, too big for her. Not the type of garment that her mother would have chosen for herself. She doesn't turn around as they enter. Anna has to go right up to her and touch her on the shoulder before she turns and sees them. She starts and mutters to herself. The girl raises her voice. 'Hello Ida. I've got a visitor for you. Your daughter.' Then she smiles and disappears discreetly.

'Hello Mother. How are you feeling today?'

Her mother stares, uncomprehendingly for a moment. Finally she speaks:

'*Wo warst Du, wo warst Du? Ich habe so lange gewartet.*'

Anna sits on the bed. 'Mother, it's me. Anna.'

There is a long pause. Ida plucks at the blanket on her knees. Finally she says 'I keep forgetting where I am. I never used to forget things, but now I do all the time. My head is full of cotton wool.'

'Don't worry Mum. I'm sure when you've been here for a while you'll feel better. It just takes time to adjust.'

Eventually, Ida says 'It doesn't matter where I am. I shan't be here much longer, anyway.'

'What do you mean? Of course you will,' says Anna, panic-stricken.

'No, no, you don't understand I've had enough. I've lived too long.'

Anna takes her mother's hand.

'Please don't talk like that, Mum. I can't bear it.'

Ida looks at Anna and seems to make an effort to recollect herself. She almost begins to sound like her old self. 'How are you, my dear? It's a long way, you know, you don't need to keep coming to see me. And how is – Colin?'

'Tony, Mother. It's Tony. He's fine. Working hard, of course, as usual.'

'Ah yes,' says Ida. 'Tony'. She pauses. 'What happened to Colin? I used to like him.'

'We were divorced, Mother. Five years ago now. I've been with Tony for three years.'

Ida sighs. 'I can't remember these things any more. Life is so complicated now.'

'It's quite simple really, Mother. Tony is my partner. He has a daughter, that's Charlotte, you've met her, she comes to stay with us in the school holidays.' She feels irritation mounting. Her feelings towards her mother have always been like this. A mixture of love, guilt and irritation. Now irritation has the upper hand.

'It's a pity you had no children of your own, Anna. They are such a joy.'

Here we go again, thinks Anna. Her lack of progeny has always rankled with her mother. It is hardly as though I've deprived her of grandchildren, when Jude has three children and Edward two. She decides to change the subject, to try to think of something that will interest her mother. She tells her about the new research she is undertaking, based on the discovery of some Norman French documents. They throw new light on the events leading up to the signing of Magna Carta and, at one time, Ida would have liked to hear about this. She then tells her mother about the ever-increasing numbers of undergraduates she has to teach, and how their general knowledge appears to be decreasing in correlation to the increase in their numbers, year on year. Tony is finding the same thing in his faculty, Chemistry. For this subject, entry requirements are sinking ever lower, and this at a prestigious university. What can it be like in the new universities?

Ida seems to be barely listening. Anna despairs of finding a topic of conversation that will elicit some response. Finally she decides on another approach.

'Mother, when I first arrived, did you know you spoke to me in German?'

'Did I?' says Ida, surprised. 'I don't remember.'

'It's just that I've never heard you speak German before. You never spoke it to us when we were children.'

'I don't like to speak German,' says her mother flatly. 'If you tell me I spoke it, then I must accept what you say, but I don't remember. When I left Austria, I spoke only a few words of English, but I promised myself that once I learned to speak English properly, I would not speak German again. And up to now I haven't.'

'But when you first met Dad, did you speak German?'

Her mother hesitates, seems confused. At last she says, 'He was a friend of my brother, Ernst. They used to play together in an orchestra. He played the violin and Ernst played the clarinet.' Anna realises her mother is speaking not of her own father, but of her first husband. She doesn't bother to correct her, though, not wishing to interrupt her mother's train of thought.

Ida continues: 'One day I went with my brother to a concert. It was the Clarinet Concerto – Mozart – you know it, don't you Anna? A sublime piece of music.' Anna nods. 'After the concert was over, Ernst introduced us. A few days after that, we went to another concert together. This time it was at the Hofburg. They were playing the Faure Requiem. I remember it as if it was yesterday.' She smiles wryly. 'The trouble is; now I can't remember what did actually happen yesterday. Afterwards, he took me to a restaurant for *Erdapfelgulasch* and Heurige wine. I was at secretarial college by then, and I had no money of my own. I was not used to eating in restaurants, it all seemed very sophisticated. I must have been eighteen or nineteen. Horst was working already, so he had money. We used to go to the theatre, to concerts and always to coffee houses. I always used to eat Obers with Strudel. You know what that is, Anna, don't you?'

'Yes Mum, you used to make them for us when we were small.'

'There was always music playing wherever you went in Vienna at that time. Later that changed, though. We would make our coffee last as long as possible, so that we could stay and listen. Sometimes, we would walk along the Danube or in the Vienna woods. We first met in the summer, and the weather always seemed to be fine. A couple of times we even swam in the Danube.'

Anna does a quick calculation. She knows her mother was born in 1918 and she was eighteen when she met Horst. That would make it 1936. There must have been intimations of what was to come by then. The Anschluss, the annexation of Austria was, after all, only two years later. Yet her mother's memories seem untouched by any political unrest. Anna tries to move her reminiscences forward.

'How long were you together before you got married?'

'We were married in 1938, on the twenty-first of September.' Ida is precise.

The year of the Anschluss! Surely her mother must have been aware of the turmoil going on around her.

'Mother, do you remember German troops marching into Vienna, the year you got married?'

Her mother frowns. 'Yes, yes of course. Who could not remember?'

'And what did you think when you saw them enter the city?'

'Well, you know, most people welcomed them. They felt, somehow, that our destiny was bound up with that of Germany. That we would be safer inside the Reich than outside it.'

'And your family and friends. Did they become party members?'

Ida becomes agitated, plucks at her blanket. 'No, not all – well – some. I never became a member of the *Frauenschaft* – the women's organisation, though. Even though many of my friends did.'

'And what about Ernst and Horst?'

Ida becomes more agitated. 'You don't understand how it was then. You cannot. Life was dangerous. The party was everywhere; you always felt there were eyes on you. We were more concerned with our wedding and honeymoon, though. We went to the Tyrol and stayed in a chalet in the mountains. It was autumn, and the days were clear and blue, but the nights were freezing. After that, of course, we had to find a flat, and that was not so easy at that time.' She smiles at the memory. 'We got one, though. Not far from my parents. Three rooms, a kitchen and a shared bathroom. We were considered very lucky.'

'What about that friend you used to talk about, Esther? Did you still see her? She was Jewish, wasn't she?'

Her mother looks up in surprise. 'No, all the Jews had gone by then.'

'Gone? Where had they gone?'

'They had left, emigrated.'

'No Mother, that can't be right. They hadn't all emigrated by 1938.'

'Yes, yes, Esther's family had gone to live in the United States a couple of years before. They got visas, you know. And other children I was at school with went, too. It was the official policy at the time.'

'And what about Mr Reuben, the one you mentioned, who was my grandfather's boss. Had he left, too?'

Ida seems short of breath. She plucks at the blanket. 'I don't know. I don't know. I can't remember everything.'

Anna knows they had not all emigrated. She dares not continue questioning her mother, though. She can see she is getting agitated again, rocking rhythmically in her chair, her breathing rapid and erratic.

Just then, there is a knock at the door and one of the girls comes in with a cup of tea for Ida. Seeing Anna, she asks if she would like one too. Anna does not particularly care for tea, but she accepts, to keep her mother company. Ida quietens down as she drinks her tea, and Anna tries to keep the conversation going on neutral lines. When her mother has finished, Anna takes the cup from her and places it on the tray. She is about to leave when her mother grasps her arm. Anna pauses, kneels down beside her chair.

'You cannot imagine what life was like then, Anna. We were so afraid. Yes, when the Germans first arrived, we did think things would get better for us. But after a while, we realised that we dared not disagree with anything or we would be made to suffer, or our families would be victimised.' Anna nods slowly.

'I do understand, really. Today we have the freedom to make moral choices. It is a luxury. It has not always been so. Try not to think about it anymore, Mum. It was all a lifetime ago.'

'But now I can think of nothing else. Sometimes I remember specific things, and sometimes just how I felt. Guilty and helpless. It seems to have taken over my mind. When I was looking after you children and running the home, there was always something more pressing to do. Now there is nothing else to do but think about it. You asked about Mr Reuben. Of course I remember what happened to him. How could I not? He had been kind to us.' Anna waits. She does not speak.

'First there were some isolated incidents. The windows of the factory were smashed, then the windows of his house. After the Anschluss, though, things became much worse. His factory was confiscated. It was taken over by an Austrian. My father continued to work there, but the new boss was not fair like Mr Reuben. The wages went down and my father struggled to pay the rent. But that was nothing compared to what happened next.'

Ida pauses, then she continues: 'Mr Reuben and his family had to wear the Star of David stitched to their sleeves. He had three children, two of them would have been teenagers, maybe thirteen and fifteen, and then he had a little one, Josef, who would have been five or six.' Ida is silent for a minute or two, plucking at the blanket. Then she continues, her voice almost a whisper. 'One day, I was going to work early and I saw a big crowd of people, laughing and pointing. When I drew near to see what it was they were looking at, I couldn't believe what I was seeing. Mr Reuben and his wife were on their hands and knees scrubbing the pavement – with toothbrushes! Someone had painted anti-Hitler slogans, and they were being made to scrub them off. Mrs Reuben was wearing her fur coat. SS men were standing over them with rifles, forcing them to do it. But the awful – the really terrible thing was, their little boy, Josef, was standing nearby, watching. He was crying, and when he tried to run to his mother, one of the SS men hit him with the butt of his rifle. The poor child lay in the snow, bleeding, and no one would approach him.'

There is a long silence. Ida puts her face in her hands and rocks silently. Anna puts her arm around her mother's shoulders.

'What a dreadful thing for you to have witnessed,' she says.

'I did nothing to help that little boy. I was afraid, you see. Afraid for myself, afraid for my family. But it was unforgivable.

These sights became commonplace. Everywhere you looked Jews were degraded and humiliated and worse. In the end, you became so used to it you hardly took any notice any more. Shortly after that, the whole Reuben family disappeared – to the East. The only way you could escape was by going home and shutting your front door on it. Ernst used to come round in the evenings, and he and Horst would play Mozart, Bach, Haydn. It would allow us to forget the horrors for a while.'

Ida tilts her head back in her chair and closes her eyes. She appears to be asleep. After a while Anna gets up and leaves, closing the door quietly behind her.

***

Outside the door, she hesitates. Her mother has never spoken like this before. Why now? She wonders. It's as though the upheaval of the last few weeks has unlocked some deep memories. She decides to have a word with Mrs Piggott.

Mrs Piggott is in the hall, talking to some visitors. Anna sits down to wait. When she has finished with the visitors, Anna follows her into her office. She explains her concerns about her mother's state of agitation, and Mrs Piggott is immediately comforting. 'This often happens when our residents first come in,' she explains. 'You must understand that it is an enormous change for them. Very often they arrive following a fall, or something of the kind, so they may well have had a spell in hospital, like your mother. It disorientates them. Then they will often have had to give up their house. That in itself can be very traumatic. Old people live increasingly in the past, you know. So, if they have lived through any particularly dramatic events, they are likely to come to the fore.'

When Anna tells her that her mother seems confused at times but very lucid at others, Mrs Piggott is again reassuring. 'That should pass once she settles in. Again, it is quite common with newcomers.' She looks up Ida's file. 'Yes, as I thought, when she was assessed, she showed no signs of senility.' She smiles kindly. 'Try not to worry too much, Mrs Simpson. I'm sure your mother will feel more settled in a couple of weeks.' She gets up and Anna is aware that the discussion is over. She rises too. Suddenly, she is dying to breathe in some fresh air, after the cloying, slightly fetid air of the Cedars.

CHAPTER 4

As Anna steps outside, she notices that a light wind has arisen, of the kind that sometimes precedes a storm. It is a welcome antidote to the heavy sultriness of the afternoon. As she gets in the car, she hears thunder booming dully in the distance. After a few minutes large, isolated splashes of rain start to appear on the windscreen. For a minute or two, she needs not put on the windscreen wipers. Although it is only half past four in the afternoon, it is preternaturally dark, and headlights are needed. When the storm finally breaks in all its intensity, the traffic slows almost to a standstill. Rain batters the car and it seems that its flimsy frame will not withstand the attack. Lightning repeatedly illuminates the road in front. She shudders. Armageddon.

Soon, water is swirling in the gutters and pedestrians, mostly caught out without umbrellas on this August afternoon, crowd together under the awnings of shops and in doorways. One or two brazen young men saunter under the full force of the rain with bravado, clad only in tee shirts and jeans. After about twenty minutes, the intensity of the storm gradually decreases, the thunder begins to recede and the rain becomes less frenetic, easing to a steady downpour. The stream of traffic moves a little faster. When Anna eventually arrives at the flat, it is still raining, and she has to run from her residents' parking space to the building, her light jacket pulled up over her head. She runs up the stairs. The flat is only on the second floor and she rarely uses the lift. She turns the key in the lock and enters the narrow hall. There is a light at the end of the passage and she can hear the muted sound of music, so she knows they must be in.

In spite of the short distance from the car, the hem of her cotton dress is clinging damply to her calves and her feet are squelching in her open- toed sandals. In the larger of the two bedrooms, which she shares with Tony, she changes into a pair of cord trousers and a shirt, and puts her slippers on. She runs a comb through her wet, greyish blond hair. Then she goes into the sitting room. Charlotte is lying on the settee watching MTV. Although she is nearly thirteen, she is small and slight. She looks younger than her age. Her hair is short and dark, and she is wearing hipster jeans — although she has no hips – and a top, which is cut off, above her navel. She looks up as Anna comes in.

'Hi,' says Anna, 'what horrific weather. Have you been out in it?

'No. We got back before it started,' she replies, switching off the sound on the TV. 'I met Dad at work and we went for a burger. I've just been watching TV this afternoon.'

Anna is fond of Charlotte. After all, the child has spent her holidays with them for the last three years.

The flat is small, though, only really big enough for two people, and she sometimes finds herself guiltily looking forward to the end of the holidays, when Charlotte will go back to school and she and Tony can have it to themselves again.

'How was your Mum? That is where you've been, isn't it?

'It is indeed. Well, actually, she's finding it all very strange at the moment. But I expect she'll get used to it soon.'

She glances at the empty crisp packet, the coke tin, and the sweet-papers scattered on the coffee table. She resists the temptation to pick them up and put them in the bin. She knows Charlotte will do it herself eventually. Anna finds it hard to relax, though, if there's a mess.

'Where's Dad? Working?

Charlotte nods and Anna goes into the second, smaller bedroom, which is their study in term time, but which has to double up as Charlotte's bedroom while she is staying with them. Tony is sitting at the small desk, working at the computer. He looks round as she comes in and smiles. He is dark, with a thin, intelligent face and slightly hunched shoulders. He wears steel rimmed glasses, which add to his professorial air. Anna puts her hand on his shoulder and peers at the computer screen, which is covered in incomprehensible symbols and figures.

'What on earth is all that? She says then, quickly, 'no, don't tell me. I wouldn't understand if you did.'

Tony puts his arm round her waist.

'How's Ida? He asks.

Anna sighs. 'Really not good. Would you like a drink?

She goes into the kitchen and prepares tall glasses of gin and tonic with plenty of ice. Tony joins her. The kitchen is a comfortable room, painted yellow, with a small, round table, where they normally eat. There is a back door, leading to the fire escape. Just then, a shape appears outside. Anna opens the door and Henry walks in, furious, dripping wet.

'You silly cat, how long have you been out there? Anna gets a towel and dries his long black fur. Henry meows throatily, but doesn't seem to mind. Anna fills his dishes with his special dry cat food and milk.

They sit down at the table. 'This should hit the spot,' says Anna. 'So, tell me,' says Tony.

Anna recounts her visit to her mother, and Tony listens intently. The only thing Anna leaves out is her mother deliberately forgetting Tony's name.

'Do you know, she was wearing a dress which wasn't hers. It was a horrible dress, something she would never have bought.'

'I expect that with that number of people it's hard to keep track of what belongs to whom. Perhaps all her stuff needs to be labelled.'

Anna admits that he's probably right. Her mother was always so fastidious. It seems appalling that she should now be reduced to wearing other people's clothes.

Just then, Charlotte appears in the doorway. 'What's for supper? She asks.

Tony looks at Anna. 'Shall we go out to eat?'

'That's a superb idea.' Anna is relieved not to have to start thinking what to cook. 'Where shall we go?

Charlotte wants Chinese, Tony Indian. In the end they decide on Italian – neutral territory. This is the great thing about London, thinks Anna. The flat may be small and poky, but within walking distance there is every kind of restaurant, cinema, theatre, concert. And London is so anonymous, nobody cares who you are, what you look like. She would never wish to exchange it for suburbia, where everything is closed by midnight and, if you want to go out for a meal on a Saturday night, you have to book a week in advance. And dress up, in case the neighbours see you. And then if you want to go to the cinema in the suburbs, the only films showing are American blockbusters and, if there is a theatre, it's probably showing the Pirates of Penzance by the local amateur dramatic society.

When they come out of the restaurant, the rain has finally stopped, and the night is clear, though starless. The air feels fresher after the storm. They walk the short distance back to the flat. Anna feels calmer, more relaxed, after the meal and the bottle of Chianti they shared. When they get home, Charlotte goes to her room to watch a film in bed.

'Do you think we should check what she's watching? It might be something wildly unsuitable, says Anna anxiously.

'If it is, I'm sure it's nothing she hasn't seen before,' replies Tony. 'Twelve year olds are more sophisticated now than I was at twenty one.'

'I'm not sure that sophisticated is exactly it, brutalised, might be more like it,' demurs Anna.

She goes to the kitchen to make coffee. Henry is ensconced in his basket in a corner of the room. He clearly does not intend to venture out again for a very long time, after his dousing.

Anna and Tony take their coffee into the sitting room, which is now cleared of Charlotte's debris. It is a comfortable room, containing two wine-red settees and a heavy oak coffee table, under which scientific journals and historical publications are stacked. On the walls there are a couple of original French landscapes, picked up during a recent holiday, and a Bonnard print. A huge bookshelf completely covers one wall.

Anna puts on a CD. It is the Haydn string quartet, the first movement in D minor.

'Mum used to say it's music for all seasons,' she says. 'You can put this on any time, it doesn't matter how you feel. Not like Mozart.'

She sits on one end of the settee and tucks her legs up beside her, coffee cup clasped in both hands.

'I keep thinking about what Mum said this afternoon,' she begins. 'It was so disturbing, and so sad for her. She's obviously plagued by self-recrimination. But, after all, what could she have done different? She was only a young girl, who had just got married.'

'I suppose it's the classic question we all ask ourselves,' replies Tony. 'Would we have made a stand at the risk of endangering our families, and ourselves or would we just have kept our heads down and tried to keep out of trouble? I think it's like trying to imagine what you would do if you were in a plane that's about to crash. Until you're in that situation, you just don't know how you'd react. Anyway, at least she wasn't actively involved in any of the persecution.'

'No, that's true. She wasn't. But when I asked her if her brother or her first husband were in the Party, she didn't answer, evaded the question. She assured me she wasn't in the female branch of it, though.'

'And did she really never talk about any of this when she was younger, when you were children?

'No, hardly ever. She may just have mentioned a school friend of hers, who was obviously Jewish. But apart from that, no. In fact, she told me today that it's only now that she can't get it out of her mind. Now that she has time to think, I suppose.'

'Yes. That's the trouble. When you get old you have too much time to think, and a tendency to relive the past.'

'She's very confused, as well. She almost seems to be in a dream some of the time. When I asked her about my own father, she started telling me about her first husband, Horst. I had a word with Mrs Piggott though, and she said that it's quite common, and should pass.'

'It's hard to imagine what life must have been like in Vienna when she was young. There were all sorts of factions fighting it out, weren't there?'

'Yes, right through the early thirties there was conflict between the Socialists and the government. It must have been an alarming time; street fighting, shootings, road barriers and endlessly scary headlines. Dollfuss was in power at the time, and he was very nationalistic and Catholic.'

'I thought your mother was a Catholic.'

'That's the strange thing. She used to be an avid churchgoer in her youth but now she virtually shuns the church.'

'My grandfather was Jewish, did I ever tell you? He escaped from Poland before war broke out. When he first came to this country, he deliberately settled in a non-Jewish area, because he used to say that wherever there are groups of Jews living together, you get pogroms.'

'Yes, I suppose that's true, but it's inevitable that any groups of immigrants flock together and form ghettoes. It must be a self-preservation thing. I was thinking, isn't it amazing that Jews dominated so many spheres of public life in Austria, and Germany, for that matter. The law, the press, banks, business, you name it.'

'They're so gifted. Even now they're over represented in so many areas of life: the arts, the sciences, politics, medicine, the civil service, even entertainment. You've only got to look at the titles at the end of a film, for example, to realise how many names are Jewish. I often wonder how much human talent has been lost forever; what the human race might have achieved if so many had not been lost. You never know, we might have a cure for cancer, by now.'

They are silent for a few minutes. Then Tony says, 'apparently, the Final Solution was not considered, even by the elite of the Party until 1940. Of course, people were being sent to concentration camps, but that was slightly different. A lot of people don't realise the difference between those and the extermination camps. I read something about this recently. There were only four extermination camps, and they were all in Poland, within a two hundred mile radius of Warsaw.'

'But what about places like Dachau and Auschwitz? Millions of people died there, as well.'

'Yes, but there was a difference. Horrific as they were, they at least offered a slim chance of survival. They were mainly for slave labour and – yes – they did have gas chambers and crematoria and mass graves but, at least, there was a chance of getting out alive. The extermination camps were different. That was their sole purpose and, in fact, only eighty-two people survived them. Those camps all existed only for a short time and, afterwards, they were obliterated by the SS.'

'How do you know all this?'

'Well, having a Jewish grandfather, it kind of gives you a terrible curiosity. As I say, I've read quite a bit about it.'

'Why do you think there's this confusion in people's minds between concentration camps and extermination camps?'

'Well, very few people survived the extermination camps to tell the tale, for a start, and then those that did, I should think, were pretty unwilling to talk about it. Also, there's a sort of universal reluctance to admit they existed. People just don't want to believe that industrialised murder like that could happen.'

'Why do you think they were all in Poland?'

'Well, Poland was a pretty anti-Semitic country. Also, at the time – and I suppose still now – it had a lot of remote areas. They could be easily isolated.'

'Do you know how many Jews were murdered there?

'Apparently two million. A third of those were children.'

They are silent again.

At last Anna says, 'I suppose that's really the aspect that beggars belief. The children. So many murdered, and with such cruelty. How unbearable for their parents Even if you were about to die yourself, your only desire would be to save your child. And, of course, they couldn't.'

'Getting back to Ida, When did you say she got married?'

'It was in the autumn of 1938, so it must have been just after the Anschluss. I think it was in the March. And the Austrian Kristallnacht, when the windows of the Jewish businesses were broken, was actually in the autumn of the same year, so it would correspond almost exactly to the time she got married.'

'What a start to married life that must have been. No wonder she said they just wanted to go home and shut their front door. And, I suppose that was nothing compared to what happened during the course of the war, and just after, when the Russians arrived.'

'Does Edward remember any of that? After all, he must have been about five when the war ended. He should be able to remember something.'

'Well, he's certainly never spoken of it. But then, he never says much about anything. I'll ask him again, though, when I next see him. Dad never said much about his spell in Vienna, either. He was doing some kind of intelligence work there, just after the war. That's how he and Mum met. He spoke fluent German, you know, although I never heard them speaking it to each other.'

'What did your father do when he came back to this country?

'Oh, he started working at the Home Office, and he did that until he retired. They lived in various different parts of London, and they didn't settle in Streatham until just before I married Colin. Dad and I used to talk for hours about all sorts of things, but that's one period of his life he never mentioned. I never thought to ask him at the time and now, of course, it's too late.'

'You and your father were pretty close, weren't you?

'Yes, I loved him very much. We had a sort of affinity that I think used to irritate my mother. But then, of course, Jude was always her favourite.'

'And what about Edward?

'Oh, Edward was a strange one. He was so quiet, withdrawn, it was almost a pathological state he was in. He couldn't really relate to anyone.'

Anna looks at her watch. 'God, it's one o'clock. We'd better go to bed. I've got to give a lecture tomorrow at ten o'clock.'

She picks up the coffee cups and takes them out to the kitchen. After giving Henry a quick stroke, she follows Tony to bed. He is sound asleep already, but she lies awake for a long time. Her head is full of images of evil. Could such a thing happen again? Certainly it could, and has done already, if not on the same scale. She thinks of Pol Pot, the massacres of Kosovo. No one has really learnt any lessons from the past.

***

Anna rings Edward. He's not there though, and Juliet answers the phone. Juliet is Edward's younger daughter. Her father has gone to visit his mother, it seems. Anna is relieved, delighted. This is to be the pattern from now on. First, there's relief once she knows someone has visited her mother. Then there's a period when she can bask in the knowledge that she's done her duty for a while. After that, the whole thing gradually looms again. So the fact that someone else has been, is an unexpected bonus. It puts off the moment for at least a couple of days. It also means that her mother gets to see someone different. That in itself may be a useful topic of conversation when she next sees her. Anna likes Juliet. She is a violinist in a well thought-of orchestra.

Anna is surprised to find her at home. Apparently she has some time off before embarking on a European tour. Anna can never understand how her brother and his wife have managed to produce Juliet, for she is everything that they are not. She has a friendly, sympathetic manner, unlike her father, and a generosity of spirit, which she has definitely not inherited from her mother. There is bitterness about Marion, Edward's wife, which Anna finds hard to fathom. Admittedly, marriage to Edward cannot have been easy. Her resentment seems to extend to the whole of Edward's family, though. Anna gave up visiting the house long ago, and now simply speaks to Edward on the phone about matters concerning their mother.

She sometimes meets Juliet for coffee when she is in town, and sees Amanda, Juliet's elder sister, from time to time. Juliet wants to know all about Ida. What the home is like, whether she has settled in and whether she is happy. Anna thinks that happiness is a tall order, when you are eighty-six. She does not say so, though. Juliet is keen to visit Ida, and says she will go during her week off. Anna is grateful. She hopes that a visit from a young person may help to lift Ida's spirits. They chat for a while, and Anna tells Juliet that her next job must be to clear Ida's house, with a view to putting it on the market. It seems a shocking and final thing to do, but it is necessary. Ida will clearly never live in it again, and the proceeds are to go towards the Cedars' fees. Juliet immediately offers to help. She has no plans for the coming week, she says, and would be glad to assist. Anna accepts the offer with alacrity. She has been dreading the task, knowing that she is unlikely to receive any help from either Edward or Jude. They arrange to meet on Tuesday, when Anna has a free afternoon. Juliet will then go and see her grandmother towards the end of the week.

Ida's house is a nineteen thirties semi, off Streatham Common. Thirty years ago, this was a middle class area, considered desirable in comparison to Clapham, Balham and, especially, Brixton. Now the tables are turned. Clapham has been taken over by affluent young people, working in the West End or the City. It is full of trendy wine bars and restaurants, and house prices have rocketed accordingly. For the last few years, Streatham has been going downhill. The once quiet, respectable roads, with well-tended front gardens have become seedy and noisy. Old bangers are parked nose to tail along the pavements, and many of the houses, which were once family homes, have become rooming houses, with a transient population. There is a general air of decay about them. No one has a vested interest in maintaining the exteriors, and the paint is flaking from doors and windows.

The McFarlane family lived there from the late sixties onwards, and Anna's father died in the house in 1990. Although Anna only lived there for a few years before leaving home, her memories of the place are mainly good. She used to come back regularly on visits, particularly during her father's last illness, when she practically moved back in. She feels profoundly sad as she turns the key in the lock and enters the house. Is this what it all comes to then, in the end? The furniture and ornaments, so carefully chosen over a lifetime, are now simply to be disposed of. They are, after all, really no use to anyone else. However much significance they may have had for their owners, however much they may evoke our own childhood, in the end we have to get rid of them. We have our own furniture, which we have chosen for our own homes, and our own ornaments and pictures, which go with them. Even though we may choose one or two items as keepsakes, everything else must be sold or given away. And the books! Favourite volumes, read and re read, must be parcelled up and given to Oxfam. We have no room for them, you see, much as we might want to keep them.

Anna thinks of some of her own treasured mementoes. The mounted shard of Berlin Wall, acquired during a trip there just after it came down, the glass phial of coloured sand from Petra, the carved donkey from a Christmas Eve visit to Bethlehem. All this will be destined for the junk shop, or worse, when the time comes. She sighs, sits at the dining table. She can almost see her father carving the Sunday joint. A gentle, ascetic man, conciliatory, some might say weak, but basically fair. Unable quite to conceal his preference for Anna, although always treating them all the same. Her parents' marriage was conventional and strangely passionless. They treated each other with respect, though, as was the custom amongst people of the so-called professional classes in those days. Anna could not remember ever hearing them raise their voices. Ida would sometimes make barbed comments, though, to which her father would respond mildly.

Anna starts to make a list: cancel the gas, electricity, water and telephone: arrange for a house clearance agency to come and give an estimate; contact estate agents, parcel up Ida's clothes. She stops. It seems almost as though her mother is already dead. Just then, there is a knock at the door. It is Juliet. They kiss, and Anna goes to the kitchen to make coffee. As they drink it, they decide which jobs are to be tackled first. Whilst Juliet telephones the services, Anna makes a start on Ida's clothes. She already has some of them with her, but Anna is surprised at how many are left. Ida has kept them immaculately, all the suits together, all the skirts and jackets. The drawers stacked with freshly laundered jumpers and underwear. The poignancy of it makes her want to cry. With an effort, she starts to fill the suitcases, which she has brought up from the cellar. She cannot imagine how the single meagre wardrobe and the narrow chest of drawers in Ida's room at the Cedars will ever accommodate all these clothes. Still, she will have to worry about that later.

They start to pack up the books that fill shelves both in the sitting room and on the landing. Juliet has managed to arrange for the house clearance people to come on Friday, when she will be able to let them in. The food in the kitchen cupboards must also be boxed up, as must the contents of the bathroom cabinet, and of the airing cupboard. The work seems never ending. After several hours, though, the end is in sight.

There are only a few more personal effects to be packed. There is a large mahogany bureau in the dining room, which is full of documents, personal papers and photographs. They decide to make more coffee before tackling it. Anna needs to think about what to do with the contents. Eventually, it is decided that Juliet will ask her father if it can be stored in their loft. There simply isn't room in Anna and Tony's flat. With this in mind, they start to sort it into piles: important documents in one pile, family mementoes in another and a third pile to which they designate the rubbish. There are birth and marriage certificates, building society books, bank statements, share certificates, ancient electric bills, personal letters, newspaper cuttings (Edward and Anna receiving their degrees), exam certificates and photographs. They work carefully through the pile. There are several loose photographs. The McFarlanes did not keep meticulously annotated photograph albums, like some families. In fact, Anna does not remember them even owning a camera, when she was a child. There are, however, one or two school photographs of herself and her brother and sister, and even some of the grandchildren as babies.

As she is decanting them into the envelope, she comes across a small buff coloured envelope. It has something written on it in German, in Gothic script. She opens it and takes out some small black and white photographs. They are square with jagged edges, of the type that would have been taken with a Brownie Box camera. There are five of them. They are all of mountain scenery but, in the foreground of one, are two smiling young men, their arms round each other's shoulders. They are wearing SS uniform. Anna turns it over. On the back she reads, 'Ernst und Horst. 1939.' Quickly she pushes it back in the envelope. Juliet, however, has caught sight of her studying the photograph, and asks what it is her aunt is looking at. Anna hands them to her without speaking. Juliet stares at the photograph, then turns it over.

'Ernst und Horst,' she reads. 'Who was Ernst?

'He was your grandmother's brother,' replies Anna.

'And Horst, I know who he was,' says Juliet, 'he was my grandfather.'

CHAPTER 5

It is six o'clock, and there is a pale light round the edges of the curtains. Ida has slept badly. She has been unable to find a comfortable position, and her lower back and groin are aching dully. At about four o'clock she rang the bell for the night staff. After what seemed like aeons, one of them appeared and gave her some painkillers. After that she dropped off for a couple of hours, but now she is awake again. She moves her legs cautiously, and feels darts of pain shooting down her thighs. Then she becomes aware of something distinctly clammy. At first she can't identify it. Then the horrible truth dawns. She has wet the bed! She feels helpless and humiliated. She struggles to look at her bedside clock. It will be at least two hours before the day staff come round to help her to get dressed.

What to do? Should she ring the bell again now, and wait until someone appears? Alternatively, she could try and get up by herself. That way she could at least change her wet pants and nightdress, even if she cannot do anything about the sheets. She decides on the latter course of action. With a great effort, she pulls herself to a sitting position, and throws the bed covers back, with difficulty. She then attempts to swing her legs over the side of the bed, onto the floor. This is more difficult than it sounds, though.

Her legs do not seem to want to obey her. Eventually, she manages to get one leg over the side of the bed. She grabs the other one with both hands and lifts it over as well. Now she is sitting on the edge of the bed. She tries to slide down towards the floor. The bed is higher than her bed at home though. The distance to the floor is greater than she expects, and her legs do not take her weight. She misses her footing and tips forward onto the ground. As she falls, she tries to grab the arm of her chair, but does not manage to save herself. She sprawls on the floor, the pain in her pelvic area making her lose consciousness for a minute or two.

When she comes round, she is unable to move. The call button is situated over her bed, out of reach. She lies awkwardly, the pain coming and going in waves. At times she forgets where she is, imagining that she is a little girl again, at home with her mother, or that she is walking in the woods or in the mountains, picking wild flowers. The images rush through her head, sometimes interspersed with darker ones of bombed buildings and soldiers.

Then again, she imagines she is in a house she does not recognise, running up a long shallow flight of stairs, the curtains at the long windows billowing in the breeze. She is being pursued by someone or something. . She is filled with terror, cries out in anguish. The creature catches up with her, grabs her from behind, nearly knocking the air from her lungs. She gasps and cries out again. She hears voices, realises she is being lifted bodily. One voice is louder than the rest, but curiously calming. She hears her name being called repeatedly. 'Ida, Ida, try to keep still darlin.' We're going to get you up on the bed in no time.

Just try to relax.' Ida feels herself lifted up and placed back on the bed. She is unutterably weary. She lets out a deep sigh and closes her eyes. When she awakes, she is wearing a fresh nightdress and the bed is clean and dry. She feels calm, clear-headed. There is a knock on the door and one of the girls comes in with her breakfast on a tray. This is the usual procedure at the Cedars; breakfast is served in the rooms, and lunch and supper in the dining room, unless any of the residents is too ill to leave their room.

'Here we are, Ida. A boiled egg and toast, and a nice cup of tea. Shall 1 help you to sit up, darling?'

'Thank you,' says Ida. She wonders why everyone calls her darling here. No one ever has before.

With the girl's help, she struggles to a sitting position.

'I'm not very hungry, actually.'

'Well, you must try and eat something. You need to keep your strength up. You've just had a very nasty fall, you know.'

The girl is busy plumping up pillows and straightening the bedclothes.

'How are you feeling, now?' She asks. 'You mustn't try to get out of bed by yourself again. That's what the call bell's for.'

'I know. It was foolish of me. What's your name, dear?'

It's Kim.' She smiles and opens the wardrobe door. What would you like to wear today, Ida?'

Ida shrugs. 'You choose, dear. I really don't mind.'

'You was so smart when you first come in,' says Kim. 'You've got some lovely clothes. Go on, tell me what you'd like to wear.'

Kim clearly has been trained to encourage the elderly residents to maintain an interest in their appearance. Suddenly she says,

'You're not English, are you? Where do you come from?'

'No, I'm not. I'm from Austria,' says Ida mechanically.

'Austria.' Kim gives some thought to this. 'How long have you lived in England, then?

'Oh, a very long time. I came to live here long before you were born.'

Kim is silent again. As she takes out a cream silk blouse and a grey pleated skirt from the wardrobe, she says, 'why did you decide to come and live here?

'It was after the war. The Second World War, you know. I met my husband in Vienna. He was English and we came to live here because his job was here.'

'Wouldn't you have liked to stay in Austria? Didn't you miss your Mum and Dad, your family?'

'Well, yes,' says Ida slowly. 'But Vienna was not a very nice place to be just after the war. A lot of buildings were destroyed, and it was occupied by foreign troops.' She pauses. 'Anyway, I only had one brother, and he was killed.'

Kim thinks about this.

'That must have been awful for you. I know if I had to go and live in a foreign country, I'd miss my Mum and Dad so much.' She pauses. 'There's ever so many foreigners in England now, isn't there? My Dad says there's far too many of them.' She stops, blushes, realising what she's said.

Ida is unperturbed. 'Yes,' she agrees. 'There certainly are people of every race and colour now. It's very different from when I first came here. Then you hardly ever saw a foreigner, let alone a black person.'

Kim is made bolder by the fact that Ida clearly hasn't taken offence.

'Do you think it's right that we've got so many foreigners? My Dad says they're taking our jobs, and that they're nothing but scroungers. Not you, of course,' she adds hastily.

The xenophobic sentiments are expressed lightly, almost

mechanically, not just by Kim but by so many people. In the end, they start to have their effect even on enlightened individuals, thinks Ida. It's no wonder, then, that Kim and her Dad are swayed by the hackneyed arguments. The trouble is, even those that propound them, in the press and elsewhere, have no idea what it can lead to if they are unchecked, or if someone with populist appeal were to take them up and use them as a rallying cry.

Ida knows, though, only too well. She knows how generalisations of that kind, inflammatory statements can take hold and poison people's minds, so that insidiously they begin to see their neighbours in a different light. Then, before they realise what's happening, it's too late. It's official, and the persecution starts in earnest. Too late then for second thoughts, too late to moderate the language.

Everyone, then, is caught up in it. Children that you went to school with: segregated, at first, then locked up, sent away. Where to? And their parents. Respectable, law abiding, patriotic, even. Publicly humiliated. They think it could never happen here, she thinks bitterly. After all, this is a free country, a democracy. A half-remembered quotation flits across her mind. 'For evil to flourish, it is enough for good men to do nothing.' Something like that. But perhaps the very fact of doing nothing, the turning of a blind eye, is an act of evil in itself. Ida realises that Kim is waiting for an answer. Now, what was the question? Ah yes, she remembers now.

'It's no good asking me, dear. I'm a foreigner myself.

Kim is such a good, kind girl. Her whole life is devoted to caring for the elderly. And yet, if it came to it, where would her allegiance lie? How would she act? Would she join in a witch-hunt, influenced by her father's views, or would she act heroically, saving those of her charges who were threatened? Or would she choose the third way, and cross over to the other side of the street, mind her own business? It is to be hoped she won't ever be put to the test. Ida allows Kim to help her slowly, painfully out of bed and to dress her in the clothes she has chosen from the wardrobe. This is what her life has come to, now. No more decisions to be made not even about what clothes to put on. Perhaps she should be grateful.

Ida sits dozing in her chair after breakfast. She feels more comfortable now, but she is still sleepy after her disturbed night. She is getting used to the confined space of her new home. So much so, in fact, that she is unwilling to venture out of it, even for meals. This, however, is frowned upon. The staff encourage her to leave her room regularly, dutifully collecting her and assisting her along the interminable corridor to join the throng at the entrance to the dining room.

Gloria arrives to check on Ida following her fall. She tells her that the doctor is to visit her later that day. When Ida protests that she doesn't need to see the doctor, Gloria informs her that this is standard procedure following any kind of accident. Gloria pulls up Ida's skirt and examines her legs for bruises. The skin on her shins is very thin, and dark patches are already appearing on them. Ida has noticed in the past that her legs bleed occasionally for no apparent reason. Gloria finds one of these abrasions now, and bandages it expertly. As she is finishing off the dressing she says.

'I think you'd better have some night time pads darlin', just until you're fully recovered, you know. I'll get one of the girls to bring a commode in for you too, then you won't have to go traipsin' down the corridor every time you want to go to the toilet.'

Ida realises she must accept this. It is, after all, only one more step on the road to complete dependence. She nods, resigned.

'It's Sunday tomorrow,' continues Gloria. 'The priest comes round on the afternoon to see all our Catholic residents. You can even take communion, if you want.'

Ida shakes her head vehemently. 'No, I don't want to see him. I'm not a practising Catholic now.'

Gloria looks surprised. In her experience, most people do not abandon their religion in old age, even if they haven't been very ardent when they were younger.

'Well, it's up to you, dear. It could be a great comfort to you though.'

'I do not wish to see the priest, tomorrow or ever,' repeats Ida, her voice rising.

'All right, you don't have to do anything you don't want to do. It's just that he's a very nice man. He sometimes comes and has a chat with the non-Catholics too. They look forward to it.'

Ida feels a little ashamed of her outburst.

'Thank you. It was a kind thought, but I haven't been to mass for years, and I'm not going to start now.'

'That's OK darlin'. Just as you like.' Gloria smiles and departs.

Ida's decision to stop attending church goes back many years. As a child she had attended mass every Sunday, never missing a week. Her mother had seen to that. Ida's mother had been a deeply religious woman. It had been the most important thing in her life. Until Ernst died, that is. After that, she never set foot in a church again. As a child, though, and through to adulthood, Catholicism permeated every aspect of Ida's life. She runs through the film of her first communion in her head. The church, packed with family and friends, she and some of her classmates, pristine and tense with excitement in their white dresses and veils. Money was in short supply, and her mother had had to make sacrifices to afford the material. There were no corners cut, though. It was of the best quality and the veil was sewn with tiny seed pearls.

She had married Horst in that church, too. It had been a wonderfully uplifting occasion. Ernst had been Horst's best man. They had made a dashing pair, both in uniform by then. The Handel Oratorio had filled the church and Ida was filled with joy. Afterwards they had gone to lunch in their favourite restaurant. They had for a while managed to forget the menacing atmosphere in the city. After that they had left for their honeymoon. When they came back, however, it was to a city with scarcely a pane of glass intact, at least not in the Jewish quarter. Ida was overwhelmed when she saw the destruction.

The following year Horst and Ernst went on active service. Ernst was eventually killed at Stalingrad, and when the news came back of the appalling suffering of the German troops, Ida's mother was inconsolable. In spite of Ida's efforts, she never really recovered from the devastation of losing her only son, and in such horrific circumstances. For Ida, the loss of her own faith came later and for different reasons.

Kim arrives to take Ida to lunch. Ida would prefer to eat in her room, but it is not to be. She is helped onto her Zimmer frame, and hobbles laboriously along the corridor. She meets Grace at the dining room door.

'How are you my dear? She enquires. 'I hear you had a nasty fall. I do hope you haven't done any serious damage.'

'No, I'm just a bit bruised, that's all,' replies Ida. 'It was my own silly fault for trying to get out of bed by myself.

'Well, just as long as there are no broken bones.'

Ivy and Albert are already seated at the table. They are discussing the menu.

'It's that bloomin' awful scrag end again,' says Ivy. 'It gets stuck in me false teeth.'

'It's not scrag end, Ivy,' says Grace mildly. 'It's actually topside, I believe. What do you think of it, Ida?'

'I don't know, I'm really not very hungry,' says Ida.

'S'pose you're used to fancy foreign food,' says Ivy nastily.

'No, no, not at all. It's just that I don't have much appetite at the moment.'

'When you've survived on the rations we had during the war, you don't turn your nose up at anything,' puts in Albert tartly. 'I don't suppose there was much to eat in Austria, either, Mrs McFarlane?'

'No, that's true, there wasn't. It was particularly bad when the war ended. There was virtually no food at all at that time.'

'Serves you right,' mutters Ivy.

'Ivy, really,' admonishes Grace. 'The war was a very long time ago. We must forgive and forget.'

'Well, I can tell you, when I was in the desert we were on iron rations. A small tin of bully beef had to last us three days. Trouble was, it was so hot, when you opened the damn thing, half of it ran away. It was the jelly, you see. Turned to liquid in the heat. Still, all in a good cause. As Churchill said, before Alamein we didn't win a battle, afterwards we hardly lost one. It was the turning point, y'see. Gave Rommel what for. He soon turned tail and beat it back to Germany!'

'I really don't think these constant references to the war are very appropriate,' says Grace, glancing at Ida.

'It's a free country,' says Ivy. 'We can talk about what we want.'

The girls bring the plates to the table. The quality of the food is really quite good, although there is little fresh fruit, but Ida pushes

71

it around her plate, then sits back wearily. Kim, who is on dining room duty, notices this, and comes over to her.

'What's the matter, Ida? Not hungry?

'No, dear. Not very. I'm very tired, as a matter of fact. Do you think you could take me back to my room?

'Yes, of course I will. Just let me clear these plates and I'll be with you.'

Grace leans across the table and puts her hand on Ida's.

'Don't' worry. I'll pop in and see you at tea time and we can have a nice chat.'

Ida smiles at Grace, touched by her concern, but all she really wants is to be back in the seclusion of her room, far away from these strangers.

***

Once back in her room, Ida asks if she can lie on her bed. Sleeping in bed in the daytime is discouraged, but Kim can see that Ida is exhausted after her fall, and helps her up, covering her with a blanket. Ida lies in the foetal position, face turned towards the wall. After a few minutes she is asleep.

She dreams she is in the Hofburg in Vienna. She is wearing a shimmering ball gown, and she is doing the Viennese waltz with Horst. Round and round they whirl, under the huge sparking chandeliers. As the music rises to a crescendo, they spin faster and faster, until Ida is dizzy. Horst holds her tight, though, and she does not lose her balance. He swings her round so that her feet leave the ground. Suddenly the music comes to an abrupt stop. The double doors to the ballroom swing open, she hears shouting and suddenly there are soldiers everywhere. People are screaming, trying to run away. She looks round for Horst in a panic, and suddenly she sees him. But now he too is wearing uniform. He is one of the soldiers, rifle cocked, ready to shoot into the crowd. Ida nearly swoons in terror and tries to find a hiding place. Finally she slips behind the floor length brocade curtains, and stands very still. Now everything is quiet. Just when she thinks they have gone and she is safe, the curtains are roughly pulled back, and she is staring at one of the soldiers, his face distorted with hatred. She tries to scream but the sound sticks in her throat. Then she awakes, sweating, her heart thumping with fear.

Gloria is standing by the bed and just behind her stands a bespectacled man, attache case in hand. Ida tries to think where she is. Then she remembers. She is at the Cedars. And this must be the doctor.

CHAPTER 6

'No, no, Simon, start that line again. You've got the stress wrong. Simon sighs. He starts again.

'In such a night as this, when the sweet wind did gently kiss the trees and they did make no noise, in such a night....

'That's better.' Gerard claps his hands. 'Right, everybody, we'll go back to the beginning of the scene.'

Everyone troops back to their original positions. Clara, the girl who is playing Jessica, opposite his Lorenzo, smiles at Simon. 'Gerard's hard to please today, isn't he?'

Simon shrugs. Gerard has always been a demanding producer. He does end up getting the best out of people, though.

'I thought you played that line right the first time. Where you put the stress, I mean,' continues Clara.

'It's quite a subjective thing, I suppose. It's how he sees it, and he is the producer,' says Simon.

Clara thinks it's wonderful, how self-deprecatory he is. He's a superb actor, in her opinion, always getting his timing just right, never fluffing a cue. On top of which he is extremely attractive, in a haunted sort of way. She knows he finds it difficult playing the Merchant, and admires him for his ability to disregard some of the more anti-Semitic lines. Actually, Simon doesn't disregard them at all. He finds it ironic, to say the least, that he should be playing Lorenzo, seducer of Shylock's daughter, when really he should be playing Shylock, except that he is much too young and good-looking. Every time he hears the lines 'Hath not a Jew eyes? Hath not a Jew hands, organs, dimensions, senses, affections, passions?' he is moved almost to tears. He finds the anti-Semitism almost unbearable, yet it is also one of the most beautiful and lyrical of the plays.

The rehearsal is finished for the day and, as they return to their dressing rooms, Tristram, who is playing Bassanio, comes up behind him and puts his arm round his shoulders.

'Coming to the 'Whig' for a drink, Simon?'

Simon looks at his watch. He has promised Juliet that he will pick up some food on the way home, as she is rehearsing late. 'Well, just a quick one, then,' he agrees.

There are a few of the other members of the cast already in the pub when they arrive. Clara and a couple of the other women wave as they enter, and beckon them over. A look of contrariety crosses Tristram's face. He had been hoping for a quiet intimate hour with Simon. Simon has always had this effect on the people he works with, men and women alike. Clara, for example, has been chasing him for ages and, although she knows he lives with Juliet, he has never totally discouraged her, always giving the impression that things could be different, that the situation is not completely hopeless.

Tristram, too, although he must assume that Simon is straight, feels that there may be some underlying ambivalence in Simon's sexuality, and he finds this exciting. He has the feeling that if he could only pick the right moment, Simon might change his allegiance. Simon knows this. He is aware of his power, and it suits him to play this game. He needs it, at some level, just as he needs the security of a permanent relationship. He has an actor's desire for admiration, both on and off the stage, and he can never unequivocally turn down the attentions which his looks and air of inner pain elicit in both men and women. When he is talking to someone, or rather listening to them, he has the knack of appearing totally absorbed in what they are saying. It is very compelling. At that moment, his mobile rings. As he expects, it is Juliet. She wants to know if he has done the shopping. It is the interval, and she has another hour's rehearsal to go. He moves over towards the door, to mask the sounds of the pub, but it is too late, she has heard.

'You're in the pub, aren't you?

'Well, yes, I'm just having a quick drink and then I'm off to Tesco.'

'Honestly, Simon, couldn't you just go straight home for once? By the time you get the food and we cook it, it's going to be ten o'clock!

'OK, I'm just leaving. It's been a pretty stressful day, it's just nice to unwind a bit.'

Simon can hear the orchestra being called to resume their positions, and Juliet cuts him off. He sees Tristram looking anxiously over at him and he smiles, putting his mobile back in his pocket.

'I'm going to have to split now,' he says apologetically. Tristram looks disappointed. He knows that tomorrow morning the first part only of act two is being rehearsed, and that Simon won't be in until the afternoon. Simon lifts his hand in farewell to the rest of the cast and saunters out into the moonless London night.

Juliet is walking to the tube station. The rehearsal is over, and her head is filled with the melodies. The first part went well tonight. She felt at one with the music, removed from her anxieties for a while. Why had she decided to ring Simon during the break? It had ruined her concentration in the second part and, a couple of times, she noticed that the conductor was watching her. She had been vexed that Simon had gone to the pub. Perhaps, in retrospect, it was unreasonable of her. He had tried to disguise the fact, so she presumed he felt guilty about it. That in itself worried her. Did he have reason to feel guilty?

She has met some of the cast of the play he's in, and can quite see why he finds their company appealing. She feels a niggle of jealousy when she thinks of Clara, the girl who plays opposite him. She is obviously interested in Simon, and makes no effort to hide the fact. Anyone would be flattered, and she knows how susceptible to admiration he is. She hopes that he is home now and has started cooking.

She walks quickly, her head bent against the drizzle that has started to fall. As she approaches the tube station, she feels the gust of warm air emanating from it laden with its unmistakable odour. She pushes her ticket into the machine, and goes down the escalator in the sickly glare of artificial light. The train is packed, and she has to stand all the way, swaying in the jolting carriage. At one point the train comes to a complete stop in a tunnel for about ten minutes. The straphangers, motionless now, stare silently at the row of advertisements in line with their gaze.

The events of the last few days run through her mind. She has still not got over the shock of finding that photograph in Gran's house. It was so awful when she realised who it was. Who would have thought that her grandfather and great uncle were both members of the SS? She can still hardly believe it. She knows that her grandparents would have been in Vienna before and during the war, and that her grandfather was killed, but she had somehow never considered the possibility that he might have been involved in the Party. Her grandfather, of course, was not her cousins' grandfather, nor was he Aunt Anna's father. Aunt Anna and Aunt Jude's father was Ernest, the gentle man she remembers visiting as a child. She has always known this, that her own grandfather was Austrian, but it has taken the discovery of the photograph of him to bring it home to her.

Her grandfather, a member of the SS! She wonders how much Gran knew about his activities at the time, how much she turned a blind eye. And then, of course, there is Simon. His entire family was wiped out in the holocaust, except for his mother, who escaped to England on the *Kindertransport*. Juliet knows what an effect this has had on Simon, and she tries to make allowances for him.

She knows that much of his insecurity must be rooted in this fact. Perhaps, then, his family were the victims of crimes perpetrated by hers! She cannot bear to pursue that line of thought. On the other hand, maybe her grandfather was just a young man caught up in events beyond his control. After all, there was tremendous pressure on the people to join the party. Come to think of it, she seems to recollect being told that he was killed on the Eastern front. Well, that was it then, he was just a soldier, nothing to do with the atrocities. If only Simon's fear of rejection were not so strong. If only he could put the past behind him, but he cannot do that, and nor can she. Yet it was all so long ago, almost a lifetime. People move on, forget, and so they should.

Should she tell Simon what she has discovered? Would he be able to bear her presence any longer if he knew? But surely he cannot hold her responsible for the sins of her grandparents, whatever they may be. Simon is difficult enough to live with as it is. Yet she loves him, can't stand the thought of losing him. But does he make her happy? In truth, probably not. Their relationship is too like that of mother and child: Simon always trying to get away with things, hoping Mummy will not find out. Juliet hates that, but seems to be unable to break the pattern. She wishes they could be more equal, more like partners.

The train gives an enormous jolt that sends people flying against their neighbours, then moves on. Finally it arrives at Clapham Common, and Juliet is swept out on a tide of people. They swarm up the escalator and out into the night. Clapham Common has been fashionable for quite a few years now. However, the road in which Juliet and Simon have their flat is far from the common, and its cafe bars and trendy eateries. The flat is in a long, rather shabby street, lined with narrow semi-detached Victorian houses. They have the ground floor of one of these. Juliet trudges along the street and lets herself in to number 158.

The kitchen is at the end of the long hall, and she can hear the clatter of dishes. Good. That means Simon is back and has started on the meal. Juliet is ravenous. She realises that she hasn't eaten anything since her lunchtime sandwich, eight or nine hours ago. As she hangs her coat on a hook in the hall, she can hear Simon talking on his mobile. As she enters the kitchen, he quickly ends the conversation. She resists the temptation to ask who he was speaking to, and sits down wearily at the kitchen table. Simon looks at her speculatively, clearly wondering if she is still cross with him.

'Good rehearsal? He asks eventually.

'Yes,' she replies. 'It's coming on well. We seem to be working together now, rather than in competition with one another. The Largo is sounding particularly good, now.' She yawns massively and takes the clip out of her hair, so that it falls round her shoulders. Immediately she looks younger, more attractive, Simon thinks. He is struck again by how much she resembles her grandmother. He has only met Ida once, but he remembers that she has the same wide, low brow, high cheekbones and full lips. Simon, on the other hand, is dark, with a thin ascetic face. They could not be more different. Simon is reminded of his mother's surprise and mute disapproval, when he first introduced Juliet to her.

'How did yours go? She enquires.

'Oh, you know Gerard. Some days he's just never satisfied. He had us doing act five scene one about five times today.'

Juliet knows the scene well. It is the one where Lorenzo makes love to Jessica. For God's sake, she tells herself, don't be so stupid. It's only a play. And they are hardly likely to be up to anything with the rest of the cast looking on. Simon is a Shakespearean actor, after all, not some Hollywood star.

'I just find so much of the play hard to stomach,' he goes on, 'although I admit there are some fine lines in it.' He thinks for a moment. 'Like this one, for instance. You'll like this, Ju.' He frowns in concentration. 'The man that hath no music in himself, Nor is not moved with concord of sweet sounds, is fit for treasons, stratagems and spoils' he quotes. As he speaks these lines in his exquisitely melodious voice, Juliet is moved by the appositeness of them. She feels oddly emotional, near to tears. How can beauty and ugliness exist side by side like this? It is almost as if they are different sides of the same coin. You cannot have one without the other.

Simon takes a bottle of red wine and pours them both a glass, then they sit at the kitchen table and he serves the food. As they eat and drink, the tension between them starts to ebb away. After they have eaten in silence for a minute or two, Simon asks Juliet what she has been doing during the day. She tells him briefly about helping Anna to clear out Ida's flat. Simon looks up.

'Did you find anything interesting? He asks.

'No, not really. It was mainly a matter of disposing of furniture and sorting out junk.'

'No skeletons in the cupboard then? He smiles.

'No, why should there be?' says Juliet a shade too quickly.

'I don't know. I just thought there might be something relating to her past. You know, letters, documents, that kind of thing. She was always cagey about it, you said.'

'Yes, it's true she never spoke much about the past, but there was nothing like that. I really went to help Anna. I think it's most unfair that she's been left to do everything. My Dad's so ineffectual, you'd have thought he could have done something to help and, as for Jude, well she's just selfish. All she ever thinks about is herself. Anna's had to do everything. Not that she was complaining. She just gets on with it.'

'Are you going to visit your Gran?' asks Simon.

Juliet hesitates momentarily.

'Yes, yes I think so, I've got a couple of weeks off before the tour starts, although we're rehearsing almost every evening.'

'Where are you going exactly this time?

'Mainly Eastern Europe. Heidelberg first, then Berlin, Warsaw, Budapest and Vienna.'

Juliet hates the idea of going away just now, although usually she loves going on tour. Although not usually particularly intuitive, she has a feeling that she should be staying at home this time.

'What will you do while I'm away?' she asks.

Simon gets up to clear the plates.

'The play will have started by then. There won't be much time to do anything else.'

After supper, Simon says he's tired and decides to go straight to bed. While she is finishing tidying the kitchen, Juliet puts on the Mozart Requiem. It suits her mood. Then she gets ready for bed herself. When she gets in beside Simon, he has his face turned away from her and appears to be asleep. She puts her hand on his shoulder and runs it tentatively down his body. He doesn't stir. His breathing is regular, but she is not convinced that he is asleep. She sighs and puts out the light. She lies awake in the darkness for a while, thinking about him, wishing she were not in thrall to him. Eventually she drifts into a heavy, dreamless sleep.

***

There are two lounges at the Cedars; one at each end of the L-shaped passage. Both are large, light rooms, with a double aspect. In the lounge in which Ida has been installed, there are chairs all round the walls and a double row down the middle of the room, back to back. Desultory snatches of conversation ring out in the otherwise silent room. The venom of some of these is shocking.

'That's my blanket you got there.'

'No it ain't. Shut up.'

'I wish you were dead.'

A stranger would hardly believe the spite of which some of these old ladies are capable. Fortunately Ida can't hear much of it. Other exchanges are just futile and repetitive.

'What's the time?'

'Half past five dear.'

'No, it can't be half past five, we haven't had our tea.'

'No dear. Tea comes round at four o'clock.'

'Well you said it was half past five. What time is it then?'

And so on. In between, silence. Most do not say a word. They doze, heads nodding at awkward angles, thin legs thrust into carpet slippers. Not awake or really asleep. Juliet tries Ida's room first and, finding her absent, asks a member of the staff where she might find her. She pauses at the door of the lounge, her eyes raking the room for the familiar face of her grandmother. The trouble is, at first glance, most of the occupants of the room look alike, and she is embarrassed to look too hard, particularly as many of them are staring at her curiously, her arrival providing a point of interest in the interminable afternoon.

'Who are you looking for, dear?' enquires one of the more articulate old ladies.

'I'm looking for my grandmother – Ida McFarlane.'

'She's over there, dear, by the window.'

Juliet looks over toward where she is pointing. Ida is leaning back in her chair, a blanket over her knees. Her eyes are shut. The old lady next to her nudges her.

'Your granddaughter's here dear.'

Ida opens her eyes and looks around. Juliet is shocked at her appearance. She remembers her as being always meticulously turned out, her hair impeccably arranged. Now her baggy dress appears to be wrongly fastened and her hair is pulled back into an untidy bun. She looks thinner, and her skin has a yellowish tinge, as though she has been deprived of fresh air. Juliet approaches her chair.

'Hello Gran. How are you?' She is uncomfortably aware that her every word is being taken in by an eager audience. Ida looks up, startled. 'It's me, Juliet, Gran. Edward's daughter,' she adds, as Ida does not seem to recognize her.

'What? What time is it? Are we going home now?

'No Gran. It's me, Juliet,' she repeats. 'I've come to see you.'

'I'll just get my things, then I'll come with you.' She turns to the woman next to her. 'You see, I told you I'd be leaving here soon.'

Juliet is panic-stricken. 'Gran, I haven't come to take you home, I've come to visit you.'

At last Ida's mind seems to clear.

'Ah, Juliet. Yes, yes of course.'

Juliet perches on the upright chair beside her grandmother. This is awkward, because she must bend her head right down to speak to her. She tries to think of something anodyne to say. At last she asks Ida if she has seen Edward, knowing full well that her father visited last week.

'No, I don't think so,' replies Ida. Juliet decides not to argue the point. 'And how about Aunt Jude?' she says, feeling sure that Jude will not have been near the place.

'No, no I haven't seen her either. No one comes to see me.'

The conversation continues for a while in this stilted fashion. Juliet is constantly aware of the curious faces around them. Suddenly she has an idea.

'How about a walk in the garden, Gran? You can walk a bit, can't you?'

'Well, only a short distance. But sometimes the girls take me out in a wheelchair.'

Getting Ida ensconced in the wheelchair is quite a performance. Juliet has to summon one of the girls, then Ida has to be manoeuvred onto her Zimmer frame and steered to the garden door. Once there, she is lowered into the wheelchair. These are kept for this purpose only. The corridors within the building are too narrow to take them. At first it seems strange, pushing the chair. It is surprisingly hard work, too, especially on the grass. Ida is nervous, grips the arms of the chair, fearing she may fall.

When they eventually reach the benches under the Cedar trees, Juliet is out of breath. She adjusts the wheelchair so that it is sideways on to the bench, so they can talk. She sits down. It is very hot. After the cool wind and showers of the previous week, they are having an Indian summer. Juliet has come out in a T-shirt and jeans. She takes her sunglasses out of her bag. Ida asks about her music. Since they came outside the change in her is dramatic, she suddenly seems clear-headed, on the ball. Juliet tells her about the preparations for the coming tour. She describes the progress that has been made with the Verdi, and talks of the technical difficulties with the Prokofiev. Ida listens intently. When Juliet has stopped speaking, she says

'You take after your great Uncle, Ernst, you know. He played the clarinet marvellously. I think he would have played professionally if he had lived.'

'And what about my grandfather?' asks Juliet. 'Was he musical too?'

'Oh yes, he played superbly too. At least their talent was not completely wasted, if you have inherited it. So, tell me where you are going on this tour. It sounds very exciting.'

'Oh yes, it is. We are going to Heidelberg, Berlin, Warsaw,

and Vienna.

Ida is silent for a moment.

'Vienna,' she says at last, 'how strange to think of you going there.'

'It will be my first visit there. Would you have liked to see it again, Gran?'

'No, I don't think so. It would be too full of ghosts.'

'You must tell me where you used to live and I will try to find it.'

'The Zieglergasse, near the Opera. At least, that was where I lived as a child. I don't suppose the building is there any more. It was very badly damaged in the war.'

'Gran, tell me about my grandfather,' says Juliet suddenly.

'He was a fine man. We were very happy together. But happiness like that doesn't last, does it? There is always the counterpart, the downside.'

'And what was the downside in your case?'

Ida is silent for a while.

'Well, the war broke out. And even before that, dreadful things were happening.'

'What did he do in the war?'

Ida plucks at the blanket across her knees. 'He was in the army,' she says at last.

'Where was he sent?'

'To Poland. He was always in the East.'

'Is that where he was killed?'

Ida rocks back and forth. 'Yes.'

Juliet puts her hand on the grandmother's arm. 'Please Gran, don't get upset. I just needed to know.'

Juliet is horrified to see Ida's face crumple and tears start to run down her cheeks. They are caught in the network of lines, and run off at odd angles. Juliet gets out a tissue and dabs at her grandmother's face.

'I loved him so much in the beginning,' she says at last. 'And when I heard the news that he was dead, I just wanted to die too. But I had Edward by then, and I had to keep on for his sake.'

'How was he killed, Gran?'

'The news that came back from the East was so confused then, and always bad. I never really knew the details. The terrible thing is, you love someone, you think you really know them, but then you wonder if you knew them at all. So many fearful things were happening at that time, Juliet. In the end, you became kind of anaesthetised to the horror. You couldn't allow yourself the luxury of feeling, somehow. And then there was the endless pressing need to feed yourself and your children.'

Ida has stopped crying. She looks infinitely sad. Juliet tries to move to a happier topic.

'You must have felt happy again when you met Ernest.'

Ida gives a slight shrug.

'He was a kind man. He was always good to me. I suppose you could say we had a good life.' It is clear from this that Horst had been the one. Ernest came a very poor second. Juliet thinks of her own relationship with Simon. Maybe that, too, will not last, and she will end up with someone safer, but ultimately less exciting. As though reading her thoughts, Ida says

'What about you my dear. Do you have anyone special?'

'Yes I do Gran. His name's Simon Levin. He's an actor.'

'Levin? That's a Jewish name, isn't it?'

'Yes. His family is from Poland, I think.' Juliet does not elaborate. 'We've been together for about six months.'

'And does he share your love of music?'

'Oh yes. It's one of the things that brought us together.'

There is a pause. Juliet thinks about the pressures her grandmother must have been under when she was only about the same age as she is now.'

'How did you meet Ernest?' she asks.

'It was just after the war ended. He was sent to Vienna to assist the Allies. In particular, the Americans.'

'What was he doing exactly?'

Ida is vague. 'I'm not quite sure. He was dealing with prisoners of war, I think.'

'Were there many prisoners then?'

'Oh, thousands and thousands. And so many displaced persons. They were all in camps. They had different camps for different categories of people.'

'What were the categories?'

'I don't know. Just different categories.'

Juliet does not persist. After a while, Ida continues.

'Life was so hard, then. You have no idea. We had literally nothing. Towards the end of the war, the bombing got really bad; we were lucky that our apartment was not destroyed. Another family in the flat across the corridor was wiped out. I managed to get something cheaper to rent after that, and I lived with Edward in one room for the next couple of years. I really wanted to go to the mountains, but it was not possible. I wanted to go to the place where we had our honeymoon, in the Tyrol. I would have felt safe there. I had so few possessions but, even then, someone broke into my room and took my bedding and china. People would steal literally anything they could get their hands on. Luckily, friends lent me some blankets and crockery.'

'Were you working then?'

'Yes, I had a job in the paper factory where my father used to work. But unfortunately the factory closed, and we all lost our jobs. That was probably the worst time. We were so hungry. I used to travel out to the outlying farms with Edward and pick apples, or scrounge food from the farmers. It was a constant battle to feed ourselves. It was a struggle to keep warm, too. In the winter the temperature fell far below freezing, and there was no fuel. My main fear was for Edward's health. He always looked so pale, and he was always so cold. Then when he was four he got TB. and nearly died. He pulled through in the end though, thanks to Ernest. It was just about the time we met. He gave me food and clothing coupons, and I was able to swap some of them for medicine on the black market. I got another job about that time, too. Working in the kitchens in the American H.Q. Things got a little better after that, and Ernest was helping me a lot by then.'

'It must have been so hard Gran.'

'Yes, it certainly was. It teaches you never to take anything for granted, though. The thing I could not accept was the hypocrisy of people. Some of my neighbours had been so ecstatic when the Nazis came. I even remember my mother's friend going out in the street shouting *"mein Führer, mein Führer!"* Then, when the Americans came, she couldn't wait to rush up to their headquarters denouncing this person and that person. It made me sick.'

Ida sighs and leans back in her chair. Juliet can see that she is exhausted. She cannot get over the fact that Ida has recalled so succinctly the events of over fifty years ago, yet she struggles to remember where she is. She gets up.

'Come on Gran. Let's go and find a cup of tea.' More confident now, she pushes the wheelchair back towards the building.

The next day Juliet returns to the house in Latymer Road. She has offered to be there for the house clearance men, and to pick up the box that is to be stored at her parents' house. She has borrowed her father's car for this purpose. As she nears the house, she sees that the estate agents have already put up the 'for sale' sign. Although she knows that the house is to be sold, she feels a jolt of surprise when she sees it. It feels very final.

She lets herself in. The house already feels cold and unoccupied. The silence is almost palpable. She looks at her watch. She's early. The men won't be here for at least another half an hour. She wonders if the gas has been turned off yet. Fortunately it hasn't, so she is able to boil a kettle for coffee. She searches in the packed boxes for the jar of coffee. There's no milk, of course, but she doesn't mind too much drinking it black. She wishes she had thought of bringing something to read.

She wanders from room to room, remembering visits to her grandparents as a child. She and her sister would help with lunch, whilst her father and Ernest sat in the living room, watching television and exchanging the odd remark. Where was her mother on those occasions, she wonders now? She cannot remember her ever being there. The memories are poignant; they underline the ephemerality of the seemingly permanent anchors of one's childhood. Her grandparents' house seemed a real bastion of security – especially as the atmosphere in her own home lacked warmth. Now Ernest is long gone, and Ida is in a home. This is a memento mori, even for Juliet, aged twenty-eight.

Suddenly, she remembers the box of documents, and has a sudden desire to look again at the photograph of her great uncle and grandfather in their uniforms. She carefully picks off the tape, which seals the box, and starts to look through the contents. She remembers that the photographs were right at the bottom. As she rummages through, she comes across a file marked 'Ernest McFarlane – personal' which she had not noticed before. She is suddenly filled with curiosity. She opens it and leafs through the neatly divided sections, marked "bank statements", "insurance", "certificates" and so on. Some of the papers relate to his work and, as she works her way to the bottom, the papers get older and yellower.

Almost at the bottom, a newspaper cutting, thin and brown round the edges, flutters out. She picks it up. The lettering is in the now familiar gothic script. There is a picture of Ernest at the top, underneath the heading *"Neuer Leiter für Entnazifizierungsprogramm."* Underneath this is an article, which Juliet cannot understand at all. She can understand most of the headline, though. So that is why Ernest had been in Vienna at that time! He was involved with the Denazification Programme! No wonder Ida was cagey about his reason for being there. He could well have been investigating members of her own family although, of course by then, both Ernst and Horst were dead.

Just then there is a knock at the door. Hurriedly she puts the newspaper cutting and the photograph in her bag and lets the men from the house clearance in. She reseals the box and puts it in the back of the car, ready to deposit at her parents' house at the next opportunity.

CHAPTER 7

The dinner party had not been a success. Gerry had had several whiskies before the guests arrived and, as the evening progressed, he had become very drunk. At the beginning, he had been good company, amusing even but, as he hit the red wine, he started to go too far, letching over his business associate's girlfriend, making innuendoes, which were not well received by their guests. There is something prudish about some Americans, thinks Jude. She cringes with embarrassment as she remembers some of the lewd comments he had made.

Vernon Mathews, the head of Corporate Holdings, is a man of about their age; his new partner is nearer Hugo's age. Not only is she glamorous in a very American way, but she is also brainy, a high-flier. She is the company lawyer. Vernon has already dumped two wives. The first, Jude remembers, was a woman of about her own age. She had rather liked her. She wasn't a career woman, more of a homemaker type. They had had more in common. With this new one, Jude had struggled to make conversation. She felt the woman looked down on her. She had asked Jude what she did and, when she said she was a housewife, the woman had turned her attention straight back to the men. The third guest was the company secretary, whom she and Gerry had met previously on a trip to New York. The woman, Charmaine, had been wearing clinging black velvet with a plunging neckline. Each time Gerry filled her glass, he put his other arm round her shoulders and leered down her cleavage. Really, thought Jude, it was too sordid. On one occasion, Charmaine had got up from the table abruptly and gone to the bathroom. Jude guessed Gerry had been pressing her thigh with his own or, worse, groping her under the table. Jude felt humiliated.

The Americans had left quite early, pleading an early departure the next day. After they had gone, she and Gerry had exchanged some bitter words. It wasn't exactly a row. It's hard to have a proper row with a drunk. Anyway, Jude was too tired, and Gerry wasn't listening. Jude knows that Gerry has always been jealous of men of his own age with young partners. It used to make her feel inadequate, unwanted, but now all it makes her feel is tired. In the end Gerry stumps off to bed and immediately falls into a drunken sleep. Jude is left to clear up the debris.

Now it is Sunday morning. Amazingly, Gerry was up by eight and has already left to play golf. Jude cannot think how he does it. She knows he shouldn't be driving, but she doesn't care. She empties the dishwasher and pours herself a cup of coffee. She wishes she had not promised to have her mother to lunch today. She's tired and depressed; would really like to go back to bed. Then she remembers that Kate's boyfriend, Christoph, is here as well. He and Kate had gone out the previous evening before the guests arrived. They must have come back very late. She didn't even hear them come in. Just then Kate appears. She is wearing an oversized shirt, clearly one of Christoph's, and her feet are bare. She sits at the kitchen table and lights a cigarette. Jude wishes she wouldn't smoke in the house.

'Any coffee going?' she asks. Jude passes her the jug which she has reheated from the previous evening. Not much had been drunk then. The Americans were not keen on coffee before bedtime, and Gerry was too far into the red wine to bother with it.

'How's Christoph?'enquires Jude. She hasn't seen him yet.

'Oh, he's fine. We didn't get home until about four this morning. He's still asleep.'

Jude loathes the thought of starting in again preparing lunch, and for so many people. Seven, if Gerry decides to put in an appearance. Just lately though, he has taken to staying longer and longer at the golf club.

'Where's Dad?' asks Kate, as though reading her mother's thoughts. 'Surely he's not gone to golf already?'

'Yes, he went at about eight o'clock,' replies Jude.

'Honestly, doesn't he ever do anything else? Oh, by the way, how was last night?'

'The usual thing. Superior Americans, and your father drinking too much.'

Kate feels suddenly sorry for her mother.

'Look, I'll help this morning. Show me what vegetables we're having and I'll do them. Then I'll go and pick up Gran. Christoph can come with me. He'll enjoy the ride.'

'Thank you, Kate. That would be a great help.'

Just then Christoph appears. He is tall and thin, and his hair is very black, like Kate's, short and spiky on the top, but long at the back, tied in a ponytail. He goes up behind Kate and hugs and kisses her, burying his face in her neck. Jude is embarrassed at this public display.

'Good morning Christoph,' she says stiffly. 'Would you like some coffee?'

Christoph too lights a cigarette. Really, thinks Jude, I bet he wouldn't do that in his parents' house.

'And what are the plans for today?' He asks, when he has exhaled his first drag.

'I'm going to give Mum a hand, then we're going to pick up my Gran from the home she's in. She's coming to lunch.'

'Oh, is your Gran ill?'

'Well no, not exactly ill. She had a fall, and she can't move around very well. She can't look after herself anymore.'

Christoph looks surprised.

'And she needs to be in a home for this?'

'We thought it was for the best,' says Jude shortly.

'This would not happen in Germany' says Christoph.

'Oh, what do you do then?' asks Kate, interested.

'We have – er – houses for those people that come out of hospital. To get better, you understand.'

'Oh yes, convalescent homes,' says Kate. 'But what if they just can't look after themselves anymore?'

'If they have children, then the children usually look after them,' replies Christoph.

Jude looks uncomfortable.

'Yes, well it's not like that here.'

'I don't see why it shouldn't be. Some people do it. I don't know why Gran can't live here with us, Mum. She'd be much happier. After all, the house is big enough.'

'Yes,' joins in Christoph. 'You have many rooms here. What would be the problem?'

At that moment, Dan comes in. He walks straight to the fridge and gets himself a glass of orange juice.

'Good morning Dan,' says Christoph heartily. 'How are you,

my friend?'

Dan grunts, hardly glancing at Christoph. He coughs exaggeratedly.

'What time's lunch, Mum?'

'About two I should think, by the time Kate's picked up your Gran.'

'Alright if Sebastian stays? We're working on something pretty important at the moment.'

'I bet you are,' thinks Kate. She doesn't say anything, though.

'Yes, OK darling.' Jude suppresses a sigh. Oh well, probably one more won't make much difference.

Dan saunters out of the kitchen.

Kate and Jude make a start, peeling a mountain of potatoes. Eventually it is finished, and Kate goes to join Christoph upstairs. Jude hates the idea of them sharing Kate's room, where there is only a single bed, but she supposes she is just being old-fashioned, prudish. She pours herself another cup of coffee and sits down in the now empty kitchen. She dreads the arrival of her mother. Anna has told her that Ida is much changed, since being in the Cedars. Jude has not seen her since before her fall. And then there was that conversation with Christoph! Honestly, trust a German to be so outspoken! Jude knows she could never have her mother living with her. It would simply never work. Apart from anything else her marriage is so shaky, goodness knows how long she will even be living in this house. How awful it would be if she moved her mother in, then she and Gerry split up and she had to sell the house. Kate is too young to understand all the implications.

***

Kate is about to take the Range Rover to pick up Gran, when Christoph points out that Gran probably will not be able to get in it. She consults her mother.

'You'd better take the Golf then. It's got four doors, so your Gran should be OK.'

Kate is a good driver, confident and fast. Too fast, her mother thinks. They whiz through the quiet Sunday streets. The leafy suburban sprawl soon gives way to older, more densely packed buildings, as they approach Streatham. Christoph looks out of the window with interest.

'And this is all London?' he says, amazed.

'Well, Greater London, I suppose you'd call it,' replies Kate.

'It is so vast. And so old. We have not such old buildings in German cities. Berlin, for example. It is nearly all rebuilt.'

'Yes, well this part of London wasn't bombed much in the war. I believe it was mainly the East End.'

'So there wasn't the pressure to rebuild it. I suppose it's a pity, in a way.'

'What, that it wasn't bombed? How so?'

'Well, I mean at least you started with a clean slate, so to speak. Perhaps it gave you the impetus to rebuild, and now you have the benefit of brand new cities.'

'But many old historic buildings were destroyed as well. Look at Dresden, for example.'

'You know you said that most old people in Germany live with their families. Is that really true?'

'Yes, I believe it is. There are such homes, like your Gran is in, but they are mainly for those people who have no family.'

'I can't understand why Mum doesn't take Gran in. After all, she doesn't work, and we've got plenty of room. I'll be off soon, and so will Dan, I suppose.'

'Maybe your mother does not want your Gran to live with her for other reasons. Do they not get on well, for example?'

'Well, not wonderfully well. Mum has never seemed to have much time for Gran.'

They are approaching The Cedars. They sign in, and are conducted to Ida's room. Ida is sitting in her chair. She is wearing her coat and hat. Clearly the staff have prepared her for her outing. Jude had rung up the day before and booked her out for lunch. Kate kneels beside Ida's chair and kisses her. Ida looks at her granddaughter. She strokes her spiky hair.

'Kate, my dear, what have you done to yourself? You used to have such pretty hair when you were a little girl.' Ida seems quite lucid today.

'Oh, it's just the fashion Gran. My fashion, anyway. By the way, this is Christoph, my boyfriend. He's from Germany.'

Christoph approaches and gives a little bow. '*Guten Tag Gnädige Frau. Es freut mich.*'

Ida looks up at him, startled.

'I – I do not speak German any more. Please speak to me in English.'

Christoph is confused. Kate smiles at him.

'Don't worry, Gran doesn't like speaking German. She never has. She won't even speak German to me, and it would have been such a help.'

Getting Ida down to the car is a great performance. However, once at the front door, they are able to escort her, one on each side, as far as the car, where they settle her in the front seat. Christoph gets in the back. Kate thinks this will be best because of Ida's deafness.

'Mum's really looking forward to seeing you, Gran,' says Kate, not entirely truthfully.

'I haven't seen her for so long. She doesn't come and see me, you know. Anna comes and I think Edward came once, but not your mother.'

Kate chats to Ida about the family, her job and her university course. Christoph puts in the odd remark from the back, but Ida doesn't pay him much attention. Perhaps she cannot hear him very well. In about half an hour, they are home.

**

The first thing Jude notices about her mother is how thin she is. The second thing it that her clothes are different; or rather, they are the same clothes but they look different on her; as though she's been dressed in them. Which she probably has, of course. Ida beams when she sees Jude. She wants to embrace her, but she cannot, because she requires assistance to get out of the car. Christoph obliges, lifting her almost bodily from the vehicle and supporting her into the house. They install her in an armchair in the sitting room. Kate fetches her a glass of sherry. Jude has disappeared back into the kitchen, and Kate goes to fetch her.

'Look Mum,' she says, 'I'll finish off here, you go and talk to Gran. It's you she really wants to see.'

Jude dries her hands somewhat reluctantly and goes into the sitting room. It is a vast room, which runs the width of the house. Patio doors give onto the back garden, where the trees and hedges are just beginning to turn to copper and red. They look iridescent in the autumn sunshine. The Indian summer seems to be going on and on. Autumn has always been Jude's favourite season.

99

Unlike the rest of the family, for whom the approach of winter brings with it a sense of loss, she positively relishes the smell of damp in the air, the chill that sets in earlier and earlier in the evenings. Perhaps perversely, it has always seemed to signal a new beginning for her. Maybe it has its roots in the children's return to school at the end of the long summer holidays, giving her a chance to devote more time to the household tasks that she has always enjoyed.

Her mother is seated near the fireplace. She looks lost in the huge chair. Jude had felt a sense of shock when she first saw how she had changed. Now, realising how rapidly she has gone downhill, she feels guilty. Maybe she should have made time to visit her more frequently. She goes up to Ida, pulls a chair near to hers.

'It's good to see you, Mum,' she begins uncertainly. 'How have you been?'

Ida wonders why people keep asking her how she is. What is she supposed to say? She puts out her hand and grasps Jude's. Jude notices that her mother's hand is defleshed, like a claw.

'Jude, my dear girl, why did you not come and see me before? Every day I waited for you, hoped you would come. Why did you stay away?'

'I didn't stay away on purpose,' replies Jude, stung. 'I was going to come. I just haven't had time yet. I've been so busy recently, with the twins home from university.'

Ida sighs. 'Well, my dear, I should have thought you could have found time to come and see you old mother. Anna has been many times, and I have even seen Edward. But you, I really wanted to see, and you stayed away.'

'No Mother, I did not stay away, as you put it. I fully intended to come when the twins went back to university.'

'Well, never mind. Let's forget it. I'm here now. I see you have put weight on again. Are you alright my dear? Are you happy?'

'Happy, Mother? Who is really happy? I am not a young girl any more. I'm a middle-aged woman, and happiness is asking a lot.'

'And Gerry, how are things with him?

Jude looks round, hoping no one can overhear this conversation.

'Things could be better,' she says shortly.

Just then, Kate comes in. 'Lunch is just about ready, Mum. Hugo's here but there's no sign of Dad yet.'

Ida needs to go to the toilet before lunch. Kate and Jude escort her to the bathroom door. Jude wonders if she needs to go in with her, and is thankful when Ida says she can manage on her own. After that, they settle her at the table, and then shout for Dan and Sebastian, who are incarcerated in Dan's room doing whatever they do for hours on end. Eventually everyone is seated. A place is left for Gerry. Jude, Kate and Christoph carry in the plates of food. The conversation is desultory at first. The young men eat with gusto, with no thought for anyone else, but Kate notices that Ida isn't eating. Eventually she offers to help her.

'No thank you dear, I can manage. I'm just not very hungry at the moment,' Ida replies.

'The carrots aren't cooked properly. They're bendy, like rubber,' Dan announces suddenly. 'Did you microwave them, by any chance?'

Kate looks at him, furious. 'For God's sake, is that all you know how to do, carp and criticise? You shut yourself up in that room of yours, and you just expect the food to be ready when you deign to come down for it.'

'Sebastian and I have reached a crucial stage. We can't be expected just to drop everything.'

'Kate, Dan's work is very important, you know,' puts in her mother.

'Oh for Heaven's sake. I keep forgetting that he's saving the planet. Of course mundane things like cooking Sunday lunch have to be done by us lesser mortals.'

Sebastian, changing the subject, turns to Christoph.

'What do you do, Christoph?'

'I work for a shelter for the homeless in Berlin.'

Dan looks up.

'I didn't realise you had homeless people in the land of the economic miracle,' he says.

'It is no longer like that in Germany. We have much unemployment now.'

'I thought your social security was so wonderful that nobody need go without.'

'Well, these people may be homeless for many reasons,' says Christoph mildly. 'Maybe they have no qualifications, or they may be' – he turns to Kate – '*wie sagt man Asylanten?*'

'Asylum seekers,' she supplies.

'Yes, they may be that, as well.'

At this point Hugo makes his first contribution to the discussion. 'Damned lot should be sent back,' he says. It is not clear if he means those in Germany or the ones in England.

'It is not so straightforward,' says Christoph. 'You know, it is written in the constitution; you cannot just send them back. We must process their applications according to the law. I think it is so here, no?'

Kate nods. 'Yes, we have the same procedure.'

'Well, I bet we're softer on them than you,' mutters Hugo. 'They come flooding in here and then, if their application is rejected, they just disappear into the black economy. It makes me sick!'

Dan ignores Hugo. He addresses Christoph. 'Where do they come from, mainly?'

'Very many come from the East, from Poland, the Czech Republic, Albania, Bulgaria. Berlin is the first place they would come to.'

Dan looks thoughtful. 'Well, they must be economic migrants, not asylum seekers. There is no persecution in those countries.'

'Yes, this is partly true. But many have no future in their homeland. Then there are also many gypsies, and they are definitely persecuted.'

'You say it is in your constitution. When was that written?' asks Sebastian.

'After the war. It was written so that the events of the third Reich should not happen again. So that we should not again persecute foreigners. But at that time, nobody could have imagined how big would be the problem.'

Dan turns to Sebastian.

'I find it incredible that Germany has changed from a fascist dictatorship to a model of liberal democracy in fifty years. Can people really change like that?'

'Well, what do you think, Christoph? Do you believe they can?' Sebastian asks.

Christoph shrugs.

'Who knows? We have certainly changed the framework of society. Whether individuals have changed, I just don't know.'

'Do you ever wonder if the same thing could happen again?'

'Sure I do. All my generation do.'

'And what about your parents?'

'My parents were born after the war, like yours.'

'But your grandparents, then?'

'Ah well, yes, that is a different matter. But I guess we do not really want to ask them. But it is the same with your grandmother, Dan. If you want to know such things, perhaps you should ask her.'

For the first time, Dan looks uncomfortable. He glances at his grandmother. It is hard to tell if she is listening to the conversation or not. She is not eating. She is tapping rhythmically on the tablecloth.

'Anyway,' says Kate, 'As Christoph says, German society has changed and, in many ways, it is now better than ours.'

'How do you make that out?' asks Hugo.

'Well, for example, old people are better looked after. Pensions are much higher.'

'And people do not usually put their elderly parents in these homes, like your grandmother. They would stay with their children, if possible. Unless, of course, they are too ill to be looked after.'

Jude has been dreading this. She knows it was just a matter of time before Christoph got onto that subject, but she hoped at least it would not be in front of Ida. Just then, though, the front door bangs and Gerry appears. He has clearly had a few drinks. Without speaking, Jude gets up and goes to fetch his dinner. There is silence around the table. Gerry appears unaware of the atmosphere. He greets Christoph and Sebastian, and walks unsteadily round the table to Ida.

'Well, Ida, how are we then?' He enquires.

'Not too bad, thank you Gerry. And how are you?'

'Oh, never better,' replies Gerry heartily.

Just as Jude is returning with Gerry's dinner, which she has been keeping warm, Hugo gets up from the table and walks out.

After lunch, Ida falls asleep in the chair. She looks small and pathetic in the overstuffed armchair. Kate, Christoph and Jude rustle idly through the Sunday papers. Dan and Sebastian have disappeared again to Dan's room, and Hugo has not reappeared since lunch. Nor has Gerry. Then the phone rings. It is Juliet. She would like to come over and see Gran. She also offers to run Gran home. Jude is pleased. She likes Juliet, and it would be a relief to have someone else to talk to Gran, when she awakes.

When Juliet arrives, about half an hour later, Ida is still asleep. Kate goes out to the kitchen to make tea, and Juliet follows her. She has been introduced to Christoph and found him pleasant, if a touch self-righteous. She is struck by how little togetherness there is in her Aunt's household. Everyone seems to be aggressively doing their own thing. That could, of course, also be said of her own family, except that their separateness seems to be a result of apathy. She likes Kate though, even if she finds her a little immature. She is, after all, eight years younger. They chat a bit, catch up on news, and Juliet asks about Christoph. Kate has apparently known him for about a year and a half, and says she may go and live in Germany when she has taken her finals. Juliet is surprised. She didn't realise the relationship with Christoph was so strong. But she knows that Kate has always loved Germany; and Germans, come to that. She asks Kate how she finds Gran.

'I was pretty shocked when I first saw her,' admits Kate, as she pours the tea. 'She looks so sort of defeated, somehow. She's lost a lot of weight, too. I really don't see why she couldn't come here and live with us. We've got a big house and, really, Mum hasn't got anything else to do.'

'Well, I suppose you could say the same for my parents,' says Juliet. 'But I don't think they'd think of taking her in. It's a big thing for anyone to take on, really. Gran's not going to get any easier to look after; in fact, things will probably get a lot harder. And our parents perhaps don't want to sacrifice the rest of their lives.'

Kate shrugs.

'I can't see it would be such a great sacrifice on Mum's part. After all, she hasn't got a job or anything.'

'But perhaps now that you are all more independent, she might like to get a job, or do some studying or something. Anyway, what I really came over for was to ask you if you would translate something for me.'

'Oh, sure. I'll get Christoph, shall I? He can give me a hand if there are any bits I'm stuck on.'

'Oh – Kate, I'd rather you did this on your own, without Christoph's help, if you don't mind.'

Kate is surprised, but agrees immediately. They go up to her room. Christoph is devouring the Sunday papers in the sitting room, and is unlikely to come looking for them. Kate gets out her dictionary and rolls a joint. She offers it to Juliet.

'No thanks. I don't, actually. Do your parents know you smoke?'

'Good heavens no. They'd go mad. They don't even like me smoking cigarettes. Although, come to think of it, tobacco's much more harmful. Now, let's have a look.'

Juliet explains briefly to Kate where the newspaper cutting comes from. She also tells her about the photograph. Kate is shocked. 'God, I always wondered if there were any Nazi sympathisers in the family. Gran was so cagey about that period of her life. But I must say I never imagined two of them would be the SS!'

'Well, at least he wasn't your grandfather,' says Juliet. 'He was mine, though.'

When Kate looks at the cutting she sees that it is in Gothic script.

'Shit. That's going to make it more difficult.' She studies it in silence for a minute. Then

'Christ,' she says slowly, 'do you realise what this is?'

'Well, I've got a vague idea from the title,' says Juliet.

'New Head of Denazification Programme' translates Kate. 'Mr Ernest McFarlane, 36, has been appointed to the above post. Mr McFarlane from Edinburgh in Scotland, will head a team of American investigators in the search for former members of the National Socialist Party in Vienna. Mr McFarlane's team will seek out and then – deal with? – process – former Party members. Those members that have played only minor parts will be – um – reinserted – into civilian life, but those who have committed heinous crimes will be brought to trial. Mr McFarlane's team is thought to be particularly interested in former SS members who may have been involved in concentration or death camps.' Kate pauses.

After a while, Juliet says

'According to Aunt Anna, Gran's really stressed. Almost as though her fall and the move have brought all these memories back.'

Kate hands the cutting back to Juliet. They decide to keep it to themselves, and go down quickly to see if Ida is awake yet. When they get down, they discover that she is, and that she is very agitated.

'Oh there you are,' says Jude. She is clearly irritated. 'Your Gran's awake, and she's saying that she wants to go back now. The trouble is, I've told them at the home she's staying to tea.' Juliet sits down beside Ida.

'Gran, what's wrong?' she asks.

'Oh Juliet, what time is it, dear? I ought to be getting back you know.'

'But it's only half past three Gran.'

'Yes, but it took a long time to get here. I don't want to get back in the dark. Who's going to take me back?'

'I will Gran. But don't you want a cup of tea first?'

'No, no, I just want to get back now. They might lock the doors, you know.'

'I'm sure they won't lock you out, Gran, but I'll take you back now, if you insist. Is that alright with you, Aunt Jude?'

'Yes, you'd better take her if she wants to go. Really, all that fuss about not seeing anybody, then she wants to go as soon as she's arrived,' grumbles Jude.

'I think it's a common sort of anxiety. Anyway, I'm quite happy to take her now.'

'Can you manage alright on your own?' asks Kate.

'Yes, if you help me this end, I'm sure the staff will help me get her in when we get there.'

They manoeuvre Ida into the car. She is muttering and twisting her rings.

'I might mention that business to Anna. After all, she found the photograph,' says Juliet to Kate in a low voice. She gets into the car. Ida barely responds to Kate and Jude's cheery goodbyes. Juliet waves and drives off into the fading light.

*　*　*

Once the car has disappeared down the long drive, Kate returns
to her room. She is already feeling slightly light-headed but in
spite of that, she rolls and lights another joint. She lies on the bed
and, although the autumnal gloom is creeping in, she does not put
on the light. She has an increasing sense of unreality; Her mind
drifts, her thoughts are unconnected, interspersed with images of
young men in military uniforms. Just then, Christoph appears.
Momentarily, as he stands there in the doorway, he too appears
to be wearing a uniform. As he enters the room, though, she
sees that she is mistaken. He is wearing his customary jeans and
T-shirt. He comes in and sits on the bed, puts his hand on her slim
stomach and strokes it. She asks what everyone is doing.

'There is no one downstairs but your mother,' replies
Christoph. 'She is watching the television.' He takes the joint from
her fingers and drags on it.

'How many of these have you had?' he asks.

'Only two,' replies Kate. Christoph's hand is now under her
T-shirt. It moves up and under her bra, cupping her breasts. Kate
feels languid, strangely unresponsive. Christoph is now undoing
the buttons of her jeans, pulling them down over her hips. His
fingers are now between her legs, inside her pants, touching her
lightly, then moving away again, so that she feels the first stirrings
of desire. Sensing this, Christoph moves on top of her. The joint is
now deposited in an ashtray on the bedside table, and Christoph
moves quickly inside her. Kate has a sudden intimation of a more
violent act of aggression, a violation. She struggles for a moment
but Christoph is either unaware of it, or is too far-gone to care. He
comes quickly, then rolls off her, seemingly unaware that he has

left her far behind. Blood rushes in Kate's ears. She sees images of goose-stepping soldiers, heads all turned to the left, saluting. She can almost hear the sound of marching feet, the roar of the crowd. Then Christoph speaks, and the images disappear.

'*Ich liebe Dich*, Kate,' he says. 'When will you come with me to Germany?'

She looks at him, surprised that he is still there. It suddenly seems to her as though a stranger is lying beside her. She picks up the joint, relights it.

'I don't know. After my finals, I suppose,' she says at last.

Christoph runs his hand through her spiky hair, kisses her.

'Why don't you come now?' he insists.

'No, there are things I need to be sure of first, things I need to sort out.'

'But you will come, eventually?' asks Christoph anxiously.

Now Kate turns to look at him. 'We will just have to see what happens,' is all she says.

CHAPTER 8

Ida is back in her room. She is relieved to be back. Her room is warm and familiar. She wonders now why she felt so compelled to return to it. It was the first time she had been away from the Cedars for any length of tune, and it was a disorientating experience. She knows she could have spent more time with Jude and the family, but the desire to be back in her own surroundings had been overwhelming. Her relief is mixed with regret, though, now. Who knows when she will see Jude again. 'I am too old,' she thinks. 'Nothing works out right anymore.'

Gloria and the girls had been surprised to see her back so soon, but they had said nothing. She has just missed tea, so Kim brings her up some sandwiches and cake. She eats just half a sandwich; she is not hungry. Although it is only half past four, dusk is already falling, reminding her that winter is approaching. The light from the bedside lamp does not penetrate the shadowy comers of the room, creating a mysterious atmosphere. When the staff come in, they usually put on her little transistor radio, presumably so she will not feel lonely. Now it is playing Paganini, softly in the background. Ida leans back in her chair and closes her eyes.

She is drifting off again, into the familiar territory of her childhood. She can remember everything so clearly now. More clearly than before, somehow. All the little details of her life in the flat in the Zieglergasse start to come to the fore again. The winters had been so cold, often with a covering of snow on the ground from November, but Mutti had always made sure at least one room was kept warm. It meant that they had all had to sit together in the evenings, but Ida hadn't minded that. It had been very *gemütlich* – cosy. The other rooms had been glacial, though. The children had had to steel themselves to go to bed. Even the duck down quilts had felt icy when they first got under them, although they soon warmed up. They had had to scrape the ice off the insides of the windows in the morning, and Ida used to get dressed underneath her duvet.

Mutti had been such a clever housewife. Even at the worst moments, there had always been some food on the table – usually cabbage and potatoes, admittedly – and, from time to time, *Leberknodel* – dumplings. Everything had been clean and tidy in the flat, in spite of the shortages. Her clothes, although shabby, were patched and mended until there was almost none of the original material left. In the evenings, when Pappi came home from the paper factory, he would always have a glass of Schnapps before dinner. He was a veteran of the First World War, and they could always hear him coming, dragging his gammy leg along the corridor. Then Mutti would serve the meal.

'Eat slowly,' she used to say to them, 'then you won't feel so hungry.' It didn't make any difference, though – she usually did go to bed hungry.

Mutti used to take in washing to help to make ends meet. Ida helped her, sometimes, folding and carrying the heavy bed linen. On washdays, there would be washing hanging everywhere and the atmosphere was heavy with damp. Ida hated those days. They could never get near enough to the fire, because the washing had to take priority. The flat, though clean, was sparsely furnished. Ida remembers a couple of silver frames, containing family photographs; the subjects posed sedately, unsmiling, staring at the camera. In one of them, her brother Ernst, aged about six, stood to attention between his parents, dressed in a sailor suit. There was also a picture of her older brother, who had died as a baby, in his mother's arms, dressed in a stiff, lace christening gown.

There were occasional visits to her mother's sister, who lived in the mountains. Ida loves to remember these visits. Although there was more snow than in the city, it actually never used to feel so cold. The penetrating chill, which characterised winters in Vienna, was curiously absent, and the sky was often china blue, making the snow sparkle. There was more to eat there, too, as her aunt and uncle used to grow most of their own food, and there was always fresh milk. She and Ernst used to play outside, making houses out of snow, and sliding down the slope outside the chalet on pieces of wood, which they found in the outhouse. Their clothes would get soaked, and their aunt would make them take them off and wrap themselves in lengths of sheepskin while they were dried. There was no shortage of wood for fuel, either. It used to be collected in summer and stacked up to the roof of the barn, ready for winter. This meant that there was always a blazing fire.

Gradually, as Ida reached her teens, things had become more prosperous and, for a while, life was not so hard in the city. She left school at sixteen and went to a secretarial college. These first steps towards adulthood were marred, however, by political strife, which divided the city. At first, it was just scuffles between various groups. Ida didn't like walking home on her own, after dark but later, when she met Horst, he always accompanied her back to her parents' flat. The news of Hitler's rise to power started to filter through from Germany, but it didn't seem to be anything to do with them at first. Gradually, though, the signs of fascism became evident everywhere you looked. Swastikas appeared in the streets or *Juden raus* was scrawled on the walls. After 1938, pictures of the Führer were displayed openly – often proudly – in people's homes. Not in hers, though.

When war broke out, there was much talk of which young men would go first. Her brother Ernst, proud in his new uniform, was keen to go to the front. Her parents dreaded it, though, and so did she.

She dreaded Horst's departure even more. She can see the two young men now, happy and smiling, arms around each other's shoulders. They had always been great friends. They looked so young, only boys. How could they, at twenty-two, envisage the horrors that lay ahead. Ida moves in her chair, draws in her breath sharply in a half sob. Her hands move mechanically along the edge of the blanket on her knee. All the talk then was of *Lebensraum* and the Thousand Year Reich. How could anyone have known where it was all to end, or the nightmare they were all to live through, before peace came? Everyone had seemed so triumphant and full of hope in that year.

Ida remembers the day that Horst left for the front as though it were yesterday. He didn't want to leave her, of course, but he couldn't hide his excited anticipation. She accompanied him to the railway station, which was thronging with young men in uniform, saying fond farewells to their wives or mothers. Ida could hardly hold back her tears. Horst looked very dashing in his uniform; she had never loved him more passionately than on that day of leave-taking, but she had not been pleased when he and Ernst had joined the SS. Horst was off to the Eastern front, and Ernst was to follow later.

A knock at the door breaks Ida's reverie. It is Kim. She draws Ida's curtains and turns her bed down. 'Wouldn't you like to go and watch television with the others in the lounge?' she asks. 'Songs of Praise is on.'

'No thank you,' replies Ida. 'I'm rather tired. I'll just stay here, if you don't mind.'

Kim sees Ida's plate.

'You haven't eaten much. Aren't you hungry?' she asks.

'I had a big lunch at my daughter's house,' Ida replies.

Kim looks doubtful, but picks up the tray.

'Just ring the bell when you're ready to get into bed,' she says.

Ida can scarcely wait for Kim to be gone, to return to her memories. One of the happiest is of Horst's first leave. Ida had saved up her coupons to make a special meal, and they had celebrated with a bottle of Heuriger wine. That first night that they had spent together again had been so wonderful; she had wanted it never to end. She had felt ashamed of the strength of her desire, after weeks of separation, and they had made love repeatedly that night, until both fell into a sated sleep. When the time came for him to leave again, she thought she wouldn't be able to bear it. But the moment arrived; he left, and life went on, grey and monotonous for those left behind.

The Waffen SS were the heroes of the Eastern front at that time, and all the news was good. Paris fell, and it seemed their troops could do no wrong. As time went on, the army spread further East, reaching beyond Poland to the Ukraine and the Caspian. Ida spent much of her free time listening to the victorious news on the radio – and knitting baby clothes. Edward had been conceived on Horst's first leave. When he was born, she had sent pictures of him to his father, at the front, and he had written back, full of pride and love, counting the days until he could see his son.

After that, things started to get very hard. There were endless queues at the shops, and it began to be difficult to find enough food for Edward, especially milk. The course of the war was starting to change, almost imperceptibly at first, and the news was no longer all good. Many Austrian soldiers were killed, and Ida's neighbours were losing husbands and sons. They began to dread the knock at the door. One family, in the same street as Ida's parents, lost three sons. After the defeat at Stalingrad, where Ernst was lost, pride was replaced by fear. Soldiers began to return from the East dull-eyed, injured, often with limbs missing.

Ida suddenly feels immensely weary and a little cold. She rings the bell and, after a while, Kim comes up and helps her to undress and get into bed. She can't stop shivering, though. Kim fetches her an extra blanket and offers to make her a hot drink.

'No dear, I'm all right. I'll warm up now I'm in bed,' she says.

Kim leaves the room and Ida drifts into a troubled sleep. She dreams she is back in Vienna, in an air raid. First there is the low, distant drone, and the sound of the sirens, which always provoked gut-wrenching fear. She knows she must get into a shelter because of Edward. She probably wouldn't bother, otherwise.

The cellar is full of people, huddling together against the biting cold. Edward is crying. He cries almost constantly, either from fear or hunger. So do the other children. The drone is turning to a roar. Ida sits clasping Edward, her face hidden in his siren suit. At last the noise dies away, and the frightened occupants of the cellar stagger outside. Ida cannot believe the scene of devastation that greets her. Jagged sections of building soar out of the blackness, with parts of walls and roofs missing. Interiors are exposed, almost obscenely, revealing the intimate details of bedrooms and sitting rooms. Chairs, beds, pots and pans litter the streets, and tiles are still raining down. There is broken glass everywhere. Ida remembers broken glass before, and wonders if this is retribution for that other time. She hugs Edward tighter and struggles through the mess in the street. Then she sees that human limbs can be seen protruding from the rubble. She turns her head away and walks on. Her street is unrecognisable. Half the houses are razed to the ground, including hers. She stares in disbelief at the space where it used to be. She picks her way through the rubble of her possessions in despair.

Just then, she wakes up with a start. Far from being cold, she is now soaked in sweat. She tries, unsuccessfully, to throw off the extra blanket. It is still pitch black, so she imagines it must be the middle of the night. Her nightmare still feels real. She has not had one like that for years although, at one time, it was a recurring dream that she was homeless, destitute, with Edward to care for. She doesn't know why she has this dream; it never happened. She was never bombed out, although she did spend many nights in bomb shelters.

Now she's wide awake. The quality of the darkness has changed subtly. Now the pitch black is tinged with grey along the edges of the curtains. There are still hours to wait, though, until there are any signs of life. Ida knows she will not sleep again. She doesn't really want to, either, for who knows what dreams may come. She is still not free of the past, though. Now she remembers a specific day, just after the beginning of the war. She had taken a tram, rattling and clanging through the streets of Vienna, to visit her mother. Halfway there, the tram stopped in an unfamiliar part of town. It had broken down, and they all had to get off. There was no relief tram, so Ida set off to walk the remaining distance to her mother's house. Her walk took her along the Sterngasse, with its boarded-up shops and swastikas. Some of the tenements above the closed shops were still occupied, and she saw a truckload of soldiers, dressed in the same uniform as her husband, pull up outside one of them. The men jumped out and started to hammer on one of the doors. When there was no response, two of them put their shoulders to the door and broke it down. Ida walked past quickly, her head bent, and her coat wrapped tightly round her against the biting cold. She could hear barked orders from the soldiers, then the sound of a woman screaming and children crying. The woman's voice followed her clearly; '*Bitte, bitte, nicht die Kinder*,' – not the children.

Ida felt a cold shock run through her. She glanced round once more. The soldiers were pushing people into the truck, accompanied by kicks and blows. One of them picked up a small child, and threw him into the truck after his mother, so that he hit his head on the side. Ida could not bear to look again. She was reminded of the incident a couple of years back, with Mr Reuben's son. She was deeply shocked, and hurried blindly on, before she could witness anything else.

All that day and the ones that followed, she was haunted by what she had seen. She had heard people speak of the Jewish transport, but had just assumed that the Jews were being resettled. Surely, though, it must be more than that, if it was done with such brutality. At that time, she had been three months pregnant, and the treatment of the child affected her deeply.

When Horst next came home on leave, they had their first

argument. She brought up the subject of what she had seen. Horst didn't really want to listen, brushing it off and trying to change the subject. When she persisted, he repeated the resettlement theory. She could not drop the subject, though.

'If they are just being resettled, why is it necessary to do it with such cruelty?' she said. At this point Horst became very angry.

'You do not understand, Ida,' he said. 'These people were the cause of most of the hardships we suffered before the war. We are the superior race. They are *Untermenschen*, as you will come to understand.'

'But even if that were true, why must they be treated cruelly? What about the children? They cannot be held responsible.'

'It must be done. You are a woman, and you do not understand politics. You must take my word for it. Your duty is to keep the home and to prepare for the birth of our child.'

Ida has never heard Horst speak like this before, and she is shocked. When she had told him about the incident with the Reubens, he had seemed sympathetic. Perhaps he has just become hardened to suffering because of what he has witnessed at the front.

She cannot get the pictures out of her head, though, especially as the soldiers had been in the same uniforms as her husband. When he next comes home on leave, he suddenly seems threatening in his dark SS uniform. She thinks about her school friend, Esther, and her family. She had assumed that they had moved away of their own accord but, when she thinks about it, she starts to remember that they had disappeared very suddenly. Where were they all being taken? To the East, people said, always the East. The word began to take on sinister overtones in her mind. She pictured it as a freezing, barbaric place, from whence few returned.

By the time the day staff come in to help Ida to get up and dressed, she is distressed and confused, and starts to struggle with them as they try to help her. Eventually they have to call for help, and she is given a mild sedative. They have long ago given up asking her what she would like to wear. Clothes are just chosen at random, with little thought for colour coordination. Her drawers are full of sweaters, many of which are not hers, but she doesn't care; doesn't even seem to notice. The sedative starts to work; she calms down. For a while she is free of the ghosts. At peace. Her memories, initially anodyne scenes from her childhood, always end up with her trying to make sense of the things that happened; seeking answers to the unanswerable; trying to assuage the guilt.

CHAPTER 9

Anna, Juliet and Kate each find themselves affected by Ida's emerging past in their own way. The story is incomplete, prompting each one of them to speculate as to what may have happened. They are beginning to realise how one's view of self can be changed by the knowledge of one's heredity. Is it just a perception, Anna wonders? She thinks of articles she has read about the progeny of Nazi war criminals. How they have spent a lifetime trying to assuage their perceived guilt-by-birth, attending endless self-help forums to debate the existence or otherwise of inherited guilt.

She remembers in particular the account of Martin Bormann's son, a pastor who, even today, regularly appears on television to describe his childhood memories of his parents as though, by endlessly re-examining the past it can, in some sense, be purged. Now she remembers his account of the shocking tea party given by Himmler's mistress, to which the whole Bormann family was invited. The high point of this macabre fest was the visit to the attic room, to inspect the furniture made of human bones, the stool from a human pelvis, the copy of *Mein Kampf* bound in human skin, all proudly displayed. She shudders. How can a child ever come to terms with such an obscene memory? And yet, her own father's role has been revealed to have been a positive one. A force for good, a hunter-down of the evildoers. But what about her mother's first husband and her brother, who were in the SS? How far was her mother implicated in their actions?

She thinks again about the photograph of the laughing youths. In spite of everything, how poignant to think that within a couple of years they would both be dead. But then, if he had lived, Edward's father might have been hunted down by her own father. She tries to think back to her own childhood, to see if there are any clues there. Of course, Ida never spoke about her early life, when they were children. She also never mentioned how she and Ernest had first met, as far as Anna remembers. She had never thought about it much, at the time.

Looking back, she thinks her family were, in the modern idiom, somewhat dysfunctional. Or perhaps they were just a typical post-war family. In those days, people did not endlessly examine their feelings and analyse their relationships as they do today. But why was Edward so withdrawn? Admittedly, he must have lived through great hardships as a little boy. His personality was – is – almost psychotic, though. Could he have been autistic? Probably, if he had been the child of modern parents, he would have seen a child psychiatrist. In those days, though, people tended to get on with life; accept things. The idea that a solution for everything is possible is a modern phenomenon. Anyway, it's a miracle that he ever got married, she thinks.

There had been other interesting relationships in their family, too. Why, for example, was Ida so fond of Jude, almost to the exclusion of the other two? And why was there such a close bond between herself and her father? Maybe, though, this sort of thing happens in all families. Anna doesn't know. She decides that she would like to go and see Edward, to see what he remembers. He is ten years older than she is, and must remember more. One thing is certain, though. Ida is tormented by her memories now. Something has released the ghosts from her past, and she can think of nothing else.

***

Juliet, too, thinks frequently about Ida's past. She is plagued by thoughts of her grandfather's – and possibly her grandmother's – complicity in atrocities. She wonders how much Ida knew of what was happening; whether she turned a blind eye, or even acquiesced. It's all right for Anna and Kate, she thinks. Anna's father – Kate's grandfather – was above reproach, whereas hers was certainly tainted, if not directly implicated. To what extent she does not know.

At the same time, she thinks of Simon. What if he finds out? Should she tell him and, if she does, how will he react? She is unsure of his commitment, as it is. Perhaps this would give him the perfect excuse to leave her. She thinks of her father, too; wonders why he is so withdrawn. He and her mother hardly speak; are rarely in the house at the same time. Even when she and Amanda were children, he had been cold and distant. With an unpleasant jolt, she remembers that her forthcoming concert tour is only about three weeks away. The one good thing about it is that she will be going to Vienna. She will be able to see at first hand the city where her grandparents lived. She doesn't quite know what she expects to find. She just hopes she will somehow gain some insight into their lives.

Kate, too, has been thinking a lot about her grandparents ever

123

since Juliet asked her to translate the article about her grandfather. Ever since she was very young, she has been fascinated by German language and culture, and when it came to choosing the subject for her degree course, she had no hesitation in choosing German. She has been having some strange dreams recently though. She knows she has been smoking too much dope. Maybe it's because of that. She has one recurring dream. It is peopled by shadowy figures in dark uniforms, but they are not any uniforms that she can recognise. They are driving military trucks through a bombed city. The mounds of rubble loom up in the shadows, on either side of the road. Every now and then the trucks stop, and the soldiers run into a bombed out house. A few minutes later they re-emerge, carrying things, but sometimes they stay in the house longer. She hears a woman scream, then silence. She is hiding in one of the houses, and hears the sound of the approaching soldiers with dread. Just as the truck pulls up outside, though, she wakes up, her heart exploding in her chest, her skin clammy.

Christoph had gone to his meeting and then returned to Germany. She was not so sorry to see him go this time. She feels differently about him after seeing him on her home ground. She has at last noticed the self-righteousness, which other people had pointed out to her. His attitude now seems uncompromising, almost challenging. She, on the other hand, finds herself increasingly without convictions or certainties.

CHAPTER 10

Anna is trying to work. She has a lecture to deliver tomorrow morning and, although she has the majority of her notes from last year, some recent research has been done on the subject, and she needs to insert the extra material at the relevant points. She can't concentrate, though. Every now and then she stops and looks out of the window. She is sitting in the second bedroom, which has been converted back to a study now that Charlotte has gone back to school. The silence in the flat suddenly seems oppressive. It's broken only by the ticking of the clock in the hall.

Tony is away for a few days, on a lecture tour in the States and, up till now, she has been enjoying her own company; catching up on some reading and generally suiting herself, without having to think about preparing meals – never her strong point. This morning, though, much as she tries, she doesn't seem to be able to concentrate on her work. Her mind keeps wandering back to Ida. She knows she should go and visit her this afternoon. She hasn't seen her for over a week and guilt is weighing in, now.

Perhaps she can put it off for another couple of days. Her train of thought completely broken now, she saves the notes she has typed so far and goes into the kitchen to make herself a cup of coffee. Henry is curled up asleep on one of the kitchen chairs. He looks like a fat black cushion. She picks him up and strokes him, but he is grumpy at having been woken up, and struggles to get down. Really, she thinks, the cat affords very little in the way of entertainment value.

When she has made her coffee, she sits at the kitchen table, both hands clasping the mug. For the millionth time, she thinks about the timescale of events in her mother's life. Something doesn't seem to fit, somehow. She decides that she will pay Edward a visit that afternoon, instead of going to see her mother. He must surely be able to shed some light on it. She picks up the phone and dials his number. After many rings, it is answered. There is little surprise in her brother's voice when she announces herself. After establishing that their mother is all right, Anna asks if she can come and see him that afternoon. Now Edward sounds taken aback.

'Um – er – well, yes, I suppose so. What time would you come?'

'About three, if that's all right.'

'Yes, yes. Marion's out until five.'

'I'll see you later then,' says Anna crisply, and hangs up.

***

Edward and Marion live in Dover. It is a long drive for Anna, nearly a hundred miles, and she would normally expect to be asked to stay for dinner, if not for the night. She knows that no such invitation will be forthcoming from her brother, though. She leaves just after lunch. Traffic out of London is heavy but by the time she reaches the M20 coastbound, it has thinned out considerably, and she is able to put her foot down and maintain a steady eighty miles an hour.

The extended Indian summer has at last given way to the dull drizzle of early winter. The days are getting very short now, and the damp gloom lasts until the early darkness sets in. The fine spray on the motorway means that she must keep her windscreen wipers constantly on. The inside lane is a solid stream of lorries, with barely a gap between them. Occasionally, one of them gets ideas above its station, and pulls out to overtake the one in front. Its progress is so slow, though, that all the traffic in the middle lane is forced to slow down to a crawl. Anna glances at the names on the lorries as she flashes past them. They are French, German, Italian, Spanish and many now from Eastern Europe – the Czech Republic, Slovakia, Poland, Bulgaria. All heading for the continent. Once they reach the turn off for the Channel Tunnel, they peel off and the road is almost empty.

The fields stretch out wide and flat on either side of the road, now. Even before you can see the sea, you sense it is there. The horizon seems to melt into a general greyness. Suddenly, over the brow of a hill, the sea comes into view in the distance; a flat, grey, expanse, the same colour as the leaden sky. The road drops down gradually. Seen at a distance, the setting of the town is impressive; the castle dominates the harbour; the white cliffs drop steeply into the sea, and the seagulls scream overhead. The ferries can be seen plying back and forth and, as Anna drives along the sea front, she finds herself behind another contingent of lorries, this time heading for the port.

The spectacular approach to the town belies the reality, however. Once away from the sea front, the mean streets begin. The houses are small and shabby, and the shops are mostly short-term lets, selling cheap jeans and kitchenware. Greasy spoon cafes abound. Dover has suffered from the transience of its trade.

No one now needs to stop here, even for a night, on their way to Europe, and the days when these Kent coast towns welcomed holidaymakers from all over England are long gone. The few hotels on the seafront have an abandoned air.

It has been so long since Anna has visited her brother that she cannot remember exactly how to get to his house. Once on the impenetrable one-way system, it is impossible to retrace one's steps, and she has to go round about three times before she finally recognises her brother's road. Sandgate Street, that's it, she thinks, as she moves to the right-hand lane.

Edward's house is a three bedroomed semi, which, save for a narrow strip of flagstones, opens straight onto the road. The road itself is lined with cars, and Anna has to drive round for ages before she can find a parking spot. She has been mesmerised by her thoughts on the journey down; so much so that she hardly noticed her route. She was mainly thinking about Edward, trying to recall if he and she had ever played together, as children. But no, that's unlikely, she thinks, Edward is ten years older than she is. He would hardly have wanted to play with a baby. He was a shadowy figure at the best of times, hardly participating in family life, shut up in his room for hours.

She knocks on the door with some trepidation. The last time she saw Edward was in the hospital, after their mother's last fall. At least he has made an effort to go and see their mother a couple of times, which is more than could be said for Jude, although she lives the nearest.

Some time elapses before the door is opened. At last Edward appears, and Anna is shocked to see how ill-kempt he looks. He is tall, and used to be well built, but he has lost weight, and has developed a stoop. His clothes appear ill fitting, and there are buttons missing from his cardigan. She follows him down the dark hall to the dingy sitting room to the left of the stairs. The furniture, never very imaginative, she remembers, looks worn and none too clean. They sit down opposite one another, either side of the meagre gas fire. The room is chilly, and Anna wants to keep her coat on, but gives it up reluctantly, afraid of giving offence.

Anna asks him about the family, although she is aware that she has probably seen Juliet more recently that Edward has. She wonders how he spends his time, now that he is retired. He does not appear to have any interests. He had been a teacher in a prep school all his working life, until he retired, about five years ago. Marion still works part time in a florist's; that's where she is now. Eventually, Edward gets round to asking her if she would like a cup of tea. Anna thought he would never ask, and accepts readily. When he leaves the room, she huddles closer to the fire, wondering how to broach the subject of Ida's past.

At last Edward reappears, bearing two cups of pallid looking tea. Anna notices that his hand shakes a little. She suddenly feels sorry for him. He has such a defeated look. Being married to Marion all these years can't have helped, she thinks. Edward should have been with someone who would bring him out of himself. Marion, on the other hand, seems to have made him retreat even further into his shell. Anna takes a sip of tea.

'How do you find Mum? she begins tentatively.

'Oh, well, not too bad, I suppose, considering.'

'Considering what?' asks Anna, acerbically.

'Well, her age, I suppose.'

'How long ago did you see her?

'About a fortnight, I think.'

'And was she – well – compos mentis, then?'

'Yes, no, well, not entirely, actually.'

'Edward, was she talking a lot about the past? I mean, when she was young, in Vienna.'

There is a pause. Edward fumbles for a cigarette, and lights it. He puts it nervously to his lips.

'Yes,' he says slowly. 'Yes she was. She seems almost sort of obsessed with it.'

'Well, that's what I found, too. And the more she talks about it, the more worked up she seems to get.'

Anna puts her cup down.

'Only there's obviously something really upsetting her, but I'm not sure what it is. And some of the things she's been saying just don't seem to add up.'

Anna tells him about the discovery of the photograph and the newspaper cutting. She wonders briefly if Juliet has already mentioned it to her father. Edward's reaction is hard to fathom. He does not seem shocked, or even particularly surprised, but then he is hardly a man to express his emotions anyway.

'Well, Edward,' she presses him, 'did you know that your father was in the SS?'

Edward hesitates before answering.

At last he replies, 'at the time, no. And I never saw that photograph, either. I suppose though, later, when I thought back, I must have guessed. I think many people were, in Vienna, at that time. You may find this hard to believe, but I don't remember him at all. I just remember mother telling me he'd been killed on the Eastern front.'

This is quite a speech, for Edward. Anna presses on before he loses impetus. 'And Ernest, my father, what about him? Do you remember how they met?

Edward shakes his head.

'Well, when was it? How old were you?'

'I honestly don't remember.'

'You were born in 1941, weren't you?

Edward nods.

'So, were you at school when they met?'

'Yes, I think so.'

'At proper school or some sort of kindergarten?'

Edward thinks.

'Well, I don't think there was much in the way of kindergartens then so proper school, I suppose.'

'There's no date on that newspaper cutting, so we don't know when Ernest arrived in Vienna,' says Anna. 'But they must have met just as the war ended, because that's when Jude was born. That would make you about four, so you can't have been at school.'

Edward looks puzzled.

'Well, mother only started working for the American base after I started school. I would have been five or six, and that makes it – what – 1946.'

'But Jude was born before that, in 1945, says Anna. 'So you must be mistaken. They must have met earlier.'

They stare at each other. Anna thinks Edward looks ill. She notices again that his hand shakes as he raises his cigarette. Yet he is clearly genuinely puzzled.

'Do you remember anything of your early life?' asks Anna more gently.

'I remember being constantly cold and constantly hungry,' says Edward. He stares into the fire.

'And what about mother?'

Edward is silent for a long time. Just as Anna thinks he is not

131

going to answer, he says dully,

'I wanted to protect her, but I couldn't. When Ernest came along, it was good. He looked after her – us. He gave us food coupons. Then he took us to England.'

'And what was that like?'

'Grey and dismal, but not so cold, and we did have enough to eat.'

Just then there is the sound of a key in the door. An expression of shock crosses Edward's face. He had clearly not been expecting it. They both look expectantly at the door, but it doesn't open. Then they hear the sound of someone going upstairs, it must be Marion. Anna cannot understand why she doesn't come in, but she doesn't say anything. After a decent interval, she takes her leave of Edward. The events of the past are not mentioned again. Anna reaches for Edward's hand, as she says goodbye, but he recoils from her touch.

As Anna walks away from Edward's house, dusk is already falling. She glances back once and sees Marion staring after her from an upstairs window. For the twentieth time she wonders how her brother and Marion could possibly have produced such normal and, in Juliet's case, talented girls. It really didn't make any sense.

As for her brother, though, she feels that if only one could break through his almost paranoid inhibitions, there is a good kind man underneath. Marion is a different proposition altogether, though. As she makes her way to her car, a gang of youths on the street corner bawl obscenities across the road at their mates. As she passes, one of them spits at her feet. She shudders. How hateful to have to live in this environment. No wonder Juliet doesn't go to see her parents all that frequently.

By the time she hits the motorway again, it is completely dark. She struggles to see in the glare of the oncoming headlights. She finds the unaccustomed concentration exhausting, and is relieved to get home. She goes into her warm, welcoming flat and pours herself a stiff gin and tonic, then she lights some candles. She puts a CD on – the Brahms Requiem. She sits in a chair and closes her eyes. The music fills her head and, for a while, drives all other thoughts away.

CHAPTER 11

The next morning, as Anna walks to the university to give her lecture, she feels renewed enthusiasm in the task ahead. She had got up early to complete her lecture notes. As she crosses Bloomsbury Square, there is a real touch of winter in the air for the first time. Frost glitters on the leaves, and she walks carefully for fear of slipping on the patches of ice, where yesterday's rain has frozen. The murk of the previous day has been replaced by an intensely blue sky. The world seems to have been transformed overnight. The cold air stings her nostrils and makes her eyes run. Just then her mobile rings. She rummages in her bag, surprised. It's unlikely to be Tony. He's probably on his way home by now.

When she hears Mrs Piggott's voice, she experiences an unpleasant jolt of surprise.

'Mrs Simpson? Don't worry, your mother isn't ill.'

All communications from the Cedars start like that. Presumably to allay fears that the worst may have happened.

'We've just got one or two concerns about your mother, and I'd like to have a chat with you,' Mrs Piggott continues.

'Concerns? What sort of concerns?' asks Anna, a slight shake in her voice.

'I'd rather not go into it on the phone if you don't mind. When do you think you might be able to come up and see me?'

'Well, I've got a lecture to give this morning, but I was planning to come and see Mother this afternoon anyway.'

'That's perfect. Shall we say about two then?'

Anna returns her phone to her bag. Her mood is shattered. If her mother isn't ill, what can the "concerns" be? It must be something to do with her state of mind. Something to do with her growing mental anguish.

Anna has always been good at compartmentalising her life and she is able to put the phone conversation out of her mind temporarily, as she delivers her lecture. She decides to give lunch a miss and picks up a sandwich in the canteen, which she eats in the car before setting off for the Cedars.

When she arrives, lunch has just finished, and the stragglers are still making their way out of the dining room towards the lounges. Anna notices that one or two residents are only just being served though and briefly wonders why. An all-pervading smell of cabbage hangs in the air. As usual she gets stuck behind a Zimmer frame, and proceeds at a snail's pace down the corridor. A dishevelled looking old woman appears in one of the doorways in her nightdress.

'Excuse me lady. Have you seen my son? 'E's supposed to come and see me today.'

Anna smiles and shakes her head.

'No, I'm sorry, I haven't.' She's been asked the same question by this particular woman on every one of her visits so far.

How anxious the old are, she thinks. And how unfair that they should be condemned to a state of permanent agitation in this way. She knows from experience that their anxieties cannot be calmed by reasoned argument. It seems they are to be perpetually denied peace in their declining years. She finally arrives at Mrs Piggott's office, but she isn't there. The door is open, but Anna doesn't like to go in, so she takes a seat outside, feeling like a parent who's been called up the see the headmistress because her child has been misbehaving. In fact, the whole experience of her mother being in a home is a reversal of their former roles. Anna is now the parent and Ida the child. Of course, prior to her going into the Cedars there had been an element of that already, but now it is emphasised. It seems ironic that, having had no children herself, she is not, after all, to escape parental responsibility.

After about five minutes, Mrs Piggott arrives, full of apologies. She explains that she has been showing a new resident round. She sits down at her desk and asks Anna to take a seat opposite her. The headmistress/parent image is reinforced. Mrs Piggott has short grey hair and a warm sympathetic smile. Anna feels though that this belies not coldness, exactly, but a professionalism, which enables her to detach herself, so that she doesn't baulk at difficult decisions. Understandable really, she thinks. After all, in a job like this, there must be plenty of those to be taken.

'Well Mrs Simpson,' she begins, 'the reason I asked to see you today is that we've had some concerns over your mother's behaviour recently.'

'Her behaviour? What do you mean?'

'Well, just recently, she has been extremely agitated and confused, and, on occasion, she has been violent towards the staff.

'My mother, violent? I can't believe it.' Anna is deeply shocked.

Mrs Piggott continues. 'She's been struggling with the girls when they try to get her into the bath or to dress her and, in fact, we've had to get the doctor to have a look at her. He's prescribed her some mild sedatives.'

Whilst Anna cannot imagine her mother behaving like that, she does know how agitated she has become recently. She mentions this to Mrs Piggott.

'Yes, it's true; she seems to be extremely worried about something. She's been talking a lot about someone called Horst. She keeps saying she doesn't know where he is, or something like that. Then sometimes she talks in German. But we had a very unpleasant incident at lunchtime today. After I rang you, in fact. I'm afraid to say she hit one of the ladies on her table.'

Anna's mouth almost literally falls open. Her mother hit someone? This cannot be possible.

'I can't believe it,' she stammers eventually.

'Yes, I know, it is hard to believe. And in fact the lady she hit is a bit of a troublemaker. Ivy Johnson, her name is. We were thinking of moving your mother to another table, because there had been some unpleasantness before. It seems they were talking about the war and the conversation became heated.

Albert Smith is on their table too, and he never talks about anything else. I must say, I think Ivy had been provoking your mother, but still, we can't have that sort of thing at the Cedars.'

'Well, it sounds as though Mum was goaded into it,' says Anna, feeling near to tears. 'It's really most out of character. There's no way she would normally behave like that.'

'No, we are aware of that. And hopefully the sedatives should make all the difference. We think your mother is a little depressed, so once we calm her down the doctor may prescribe some anti-depressants. As you say, she has become very confused. I needed to see you though first of all to let you know about the medication, and secondly to let you know that if your mother were to continue to behave violently, we would need to look into the possibility of a transfer to a different type of home.'

Anna cannot believe she is hearing this. Just when she thought her mother was beginning to settle down at the Cedars.

'What do you mean? What sort of place would she be transferred to?' she says, almost in a whisper.

'Well, it would be a care home where the staff are more geared up to dealing with cases of dementia. But let's not jump to conclusions. It's entirely possible that your mother may settle down very well once the sedatives take effect. Several of our residents are mildly sedated and they cope very well.'

Anna feels desolate. She is desperately sorry for her mother. Her mental torment must have been overwhelming to make her act like that.

'Please don't upset yourself too much, Mrs Simpson,' says Mrs Piggott. 'Your mother is quiet at the moment. Why don't you go up and see her?'

Anna tries to smile. She knows there has been a lot in the press recently about the sedation of old people in care homes, but she has to admit that there seems to be little alternative in her mother's case.

Although she still has difficulty in accepting that her mother hit anyone, she realises that it must be true. Mrs Piggott wouldn't lie. She is only doing her job. 'Yes, I'll do that,' she says.

When Anna enters her room, Ida appears to be asleep. She is leaning back in her chair. Her mouth is slightly open and her jaw is sunken. Her breathing is so shallow that for one awful moment, Anna thinks she is dead. Her face is almost devoid of flesh, and her skin is parchmenty, so that Anna has a sudden premonition of what she will look like after death. Once again, she is struck by how emaciated she has become. As she approaches the chair, though, her mother opens her eyes. For a few moments she gazes uncomprehendingly at Anna. She pulls up the other chair and takes her mother's hand.

'Hello mother. It's me, Anna.'

Ida closes her eyes again. Anna rubs her arm, feeling the sharpness of the bone through the wool of her cardigan.

'Mother. Don't you want to talk to me?'

Ida opens her eyes again. This time she looks directly at Anna.

'Hello my dear,' she says at last, rather hoarsely.

Anna notices that for the first time her mother is not rocking or fiddling endlessly with her blanket.

She even smiles.

'I've been having such a strange dream, Anna. I dreamt I was back in the house in the Zieglergasse, where I used to live when I was a child. My mother and father were there, and my brother Ernst. But then some soldiers came knocking on the door and told us that Ernst had to join the army and go to Stalingrad. But he was only a little boy, and my mother was crying, and saying that he was too young to go. But they wouldn't listen, and they dragged him away. I was crying too, and I ran down the passage after them, but it was too late. They had gone.'

'How strange, Mum. Do you often dream about when you were young?'

'Yes. All the time. Mainly about my parents and Ernst, but then sometimes about your father, too.'

'My father? Ernest, you mean?'

'No, not Ernest. Horst.'

'No, Mum,' says Anna gently. My father was Ernest, not Horst.'

Ida is silent for a minute, thinking. Anna hopes she will continue. She is desperate to hear more about her mother's early life. Ida does not acknowledge Anna's correction. Instead she says,

'Your father's personality changed, you know. We were very happy at first, but after he had been away, he wouldn't tell me anything. I know he wasn't allowed to tell anyone any details about where he had been, but he wouldn't even discuss anything with me. In the end he hardly talked to me at all. And there were things I needed to know. When he finally came back, and it was all over, it was too late.'

'But what do you mean, when he came back? He was killed, wasn't he? On the Eastern front.'

Ida seems to recollect herself.

'Yes, yes of course he was killed.'

'But Mum, what about Ernest, my father? When did you meet him?

Ida thinks for a moment.

'After the war. I met him after the war.'

'Yes, but when exactly? How long after the war?

Ida is vague.

'Well, you know, when the Americans came. I met him then.'

Anna makes a sudden decision.

'I went to see Edward yesterday, Mum. I went to see how he is. I haven't seen him for ages.'

For the first time, Ida reacts.

'What? Why did you go and see Edward? What has he been saying to you?

Anna is surprised at Ida's tone.

'Well, all he told me was that he thought you met Ernest later. Once he had started school, which would have been about 1946. But then we thought he must have been mistaken, because Jude was born before that.'

Ida is not mollified.

'But why? Why did you need to go and see him?' she persists.

'I told you, Mum. I just went to see how he's getting on. You know how strange and antisocial he can be.'

'Yes, I do. Poor Edward. It is no wonder. He had so many trials in his young life. I wanted so much to protect him from it all but, in the end, I could not.'

Anna is struck by the similarity of this last comment to what Edward had said yesterday. What had they both wished so badly to protect each other from? She asks her mother; But Ida immediately becomes vague again.

'Oh you know, the hunger, the cold, the bombing. He had no childhood.'

Anna must be content with that.

Just then she remembers the incident at the dinner table, and decides to ask her mother about it.

'It is that dreadful Ivy,' says Ida. 'All the time she is talking about the war. And Albert too. The trouble is, she is so ignorant. She has no idea what it was like for us. No one has.'

'Well, what was she saying about the war?' asks Anna.

'She talks about the Jews. Always the Jews. She says we all must have known what was happening to them. But it is not true, Anna. We didn't all know. We knew they were segregated, treated badly, but the rest? No. At least, I didn't know, until it was too late.'

'And so what happened yesterday?'

'Yesterday she started again. She said that we had done unspeakable things in the war and now I am taking a place here that should be for an English person. And Albert; I thought he knew better, but he agreed with her. Only Grace tried to stop them, but they would not listen. Their voices went on and on, accusing, saying dreadful things. In the end I just wanted to stop the noise of their voices. Don't they know I ask myself the same question every day? They were not there. They cannot know.'

For the first time, Ida is speaking calmly, lucidly. Anna is mortified that her mother must put up with this, day in day out. And yet what is the real alternative? Ida cannot care for herself, and she has no room for her in the flat. If she is honest with herself, she could not contemplate giving up everything to look after her mother full time. And yet, generally, the Cedars has much to recommend it. Ida is warm and comfortable, and provided with three reasonably good meals a day. And the staff are kind. Mrs Piggott is already considering changing her table companions. Perhaps then things will be better.

'I do understand what made you do it, Mum,' she says at last. 'That Ivy sounds like an evil old bat. But try not to react like that again. She's not worth it.'

'No my dear, don't worry, I won't. The doctor gave me some tablets today and already I am feeling better. *Das ist alles nur Traumerei*,' she says suddenly.

'What mother? What does that mean?'

Ida smiles.

'Dreams, Anna. So many dreams,' she says and leans her head back, closing her eyes again. Anna leaves the room quietly.

CHAPTER 12

At the end of November Gerry leaves Jude. There's no row. He just comes home one day and says he's leaving. Then he goes upstairs and packs his bags. Jude even helps him. She fetches his ironed shirts from the airing cupboard and folds them for him. After so many years of packing for his business trips, she does it almost mechanically. She feels no emotion, knowing that whatever sense of connection they may have once had has long gone. It is Gerry who has had the courage to end it though. Jude thinks that she probably never would have. This is her only bitterness. That in the end he was the one to make the move.

When she asks where he is going he hesitates, then tells her he'll be staying with a friend. Jude knows he has another woman. Hugo told her about seeing his father with her that night in the restaurant. She doesn't care; She just wants him to be gone for good. Perhaps later she'll feel differently but, just now, his feeble attempts to gather together what he needs are just getting on her nerves. He walks aimlessly backwards and forwards from bedroom to bathroom, picking up items of clothing and toiletries, then rejecting half of them.

He's all for letting Jude tell the children, but she's not having that. The least he can do, she says, is tell them himself. He says he will arrange to meet them in the next few days to explain the situation. She follows him down the stairs to the front door. He pauses there, suitcase in hand. For the first time he seems lost for words, searching for something meaningful to say. At the very least, the summary ending of a thirty-year marriage seems to require the utterance of an epilogue of some kind. Gerry never had a great way with words, though. Jokes and one-liners were always more his style. In the end Jude takes pity on him. 'You'll be in touch then? Let me know where you're staying? Just in case there's a problem with the children or the house,' she says matter-of-factly. Gerry nods dumbly and walks quickly towards his car, relieved to have got off so lightly. After all, he thinks, there were faults on both sides. Takes two hands to clap and all that.

He puts his case in the boot and as he gets into the driving seat he turns and lifts his hand in a half wave, but Jude has already shut the door. He looks back at the house, and remembers how proud and excited they had been when he had been promoted, and they had bought a house, which they felt reflected his new status. The novelty had soon worn off, though, and he had taken to spending longer and longer away from home, going to bars and restaurants with colleagues and business acquaintances and, latterly, with Lorna.

Somewhere along the way he had lost any connection with his children, too, and this he regrets deeply. Hugo, who resembles him the most, seems to disapprove of him, will hardly speak to him. Kate seems to see through him, to understand him too well, and this makes him feel very uncomfortable.

As for Dan, well, he's in a world of his own, shut up in his room doing God knows what. At any rate something that lesser mortals, and that includes Gerry, will never understand in a million years. He begins to feel hard done by, misunderstood himself. No wonder he was driven into the arms of another woman with a family like that! He thinks of Lorna. How adoringly she gazes at him, hanging on his every word! It makes him feel like a million dollars! Then he remembers how she wants marriage, possibly even children. His heart sinks at the thought of starting all over again. Perhaps he would be a better father second time round. Marriage means divorce, though, and splitting the assets. Jude may be stupid where money is concerned, but once a smart solicitor gets on the case, there's no telling where it will all end. Still, first things first. He must enjoy his newfound freedom while he can.

Once Jude has shut the front door, she is unsure what to do next. The house suddenly seems huge and empty, the silence oppressive. She wanders from room to room. Should she ring someone? Perhaps her sister? But she doesn't do it. They have never been close, anyway. The enormity of what has happened begins to dawn on her. Although she feels no sorrow at Gerry's departure, she suddenly feels very much alone. Although he has not been very present over the last few years, his imminent arrival always hung over the house, making it difficult to plan anything. But all that has changed now. At last he has gone for good! No more corporate entertaining, no more boring dinners at the golf club, no more meal planning or shirts to iron! For the first time in her life, she is a free agent; accountable to no one. If she decides to stay out all night she can (although she doesn't have a clue where she'd go). The sudden freedom seems mind-blowing. The trouble with freedom, though, is that you must be able to use it and, at the moment, this seems to be a daunting prospect.

She wanders into the kitchen and pours herself a glass of wine.

Before she drinks it she raises the glass in a silent toast. To freedom! There is still some light remaining, so she decides to go into the garden. She puts on her old anorak and Wellingtons. The sky is uniformly grey, and a chilly wind gusts in her face, sending her hair flying. The trees are now winter-bare, and the branches point up at the sky like accusing fingers. Dead leaves lie in drifts against the hedges and in the edges of the flowerbeds. The once gaudy displays of dahlias, fuchsias and geraniums are now a tangled brown mess. They have not survived the first frosts. There is much to be done. Jude fetches the rake from the shed and sets about raking the dead leaves together and decanting them into rubbish bags. The work is exhausting but cathartic. After a couple of hours, she has made a considerable difference. Her back is stiff with bending, and she is perspiring.

Although the wind is strong, it is not cold. The light is fading fast now, and she hurries to dump the bags near the house, ready to be taken to the tip. Finally she leans on the rake and looks back at the house. A few lights are on, but no curtains are drawn. Its sheer size is overwhelming. This is not the place to start a new life. If she were to move, the only thing she will miss, she thinks, is the garden. However small her new abode may be, she must have some sort of garden.

***

When Hugo finds out his father has left he is furious and upset. Jude tries to pacify him, to explain that she doesn't really mind, but he won't have it. Jude wonders if he is cross with his father on her account or on his own.

'He'll have to support you, you know. That'll cost him a pretty penny. He won't be able to keep up his champagne lifestyle then.'

She tries to explain to Hugo that, in a way, it has opened up new opportunities for her. She accepts that he'll have to continue to support the twins until they finish at university but, after that, she thinks she might as well move to a smaller house. This one is far too big for her. She even thinks she might get a job.

'But you're not trained for anything,' explodes Hugo.

Jude thinks she might start a course in something and at the end of it, sell the house and move away. Always a keen gardener, she fancies doing a course in garden design. Hugo is amazed to hear his mother speaking so positively. Eventually he goes back to London in a state of self-righteous fury.

Jude is worried about Kate, though. Although term is due to start next week, she has made no preparations for her return to Bristol. She says she needs to carry on working at the Barchester, to get some more money together, but she doesn't go there much. Instead she spends hours in her room, listening to weird music and smoking. Her room is in a state of indescribable squalor. There are heaps of clothes on the bed, the chairs, the floor. Cigarette ends overflow from ashtrays, and a coffee cup lies on its side, having long ago spilt its contents onto the floor. Whenever Jude ventures in, she is struck by a strange smell, which she cannot quite identify. Usually, though, she doesn't go in at all when Kate is in residence. Sometimes, when Kate has returned to college, she goes in and attempts to tidy up a bit. Just so that the cleaning lady can actually clean.

Dan's room, on the other hand, is always immaculate. All his clothes are hung in the wardrobe, and his books and papers are stacked neatly on his desk beside the computer. The difference could not be more stark. For the millionth time, Jude wonders how twins can possibly be so different. She simply cannot understand it. Kate has been eccentric and rebellious since her early teens, whereas Dan was always controlled and outwardly conventional; the model son, in fact. And yet, in spite of her quick temper, there is an impulsive warmth and kindness about Kate that is lacking in Dan. Jude has to admit to herself that Dan can seem selfish and cold.

***

The night of Gerry's departure, Jude had gone to bed early. It is now the next morning and she is unsure whether Kate or Dan returned home last night or not. By ten o'clock, as no one has yet emerged, she pokes her head round Kate's door. There is a familiar hump under the bedclothes. All she can see of Kate is a tuft of black spiky hair and one arm thrown up on the pillow. She decides to take her up a cup of tea. When she enters the room with the tea, Kate is still in a deep sleep. Jude hesitates. Should she wake her?

Although she told Gerry that he must explain his own actions to the children, she suddenly feels that she would like to tell Kate herself. She clears a small space among the cigarette packets and books, and puts the tea down. Then, with a slight shake in her voice, she calls Kate's name. Eventually, Kate opens her eyes and, for a moment, stares uncomprehendingly at her mother. Jude is struck by how dark her eyes seem, how large the pupils are.

'God, it's you Mum. Whatever are you doing here?'

Jude briefly explains what happened yesterday. Kate stares at her in disbelief at first. She has known for a while that her parents' marriage hasn't been good, but she is amazed that things have come to a head so suddenly. She sits up in bed and runs both hands over her cropped head. Her mother sits on the edge of the bed, and Kate suddenly gives her an unaccustomed hug.

'I'm pleased in a way, Mum,' she says. 'At least now you can do something you really want to do. It's a new beginning for you, really.'

Jude is surprised at the perceptiveness of this remark. She would like to ask Kate if there is anything wrong, but she doesn't want to do anything to spoil this new feeling of warmth between them. She decides to leave it for another time.

When her mother has gone back downstairs, Kate gets out of bed to open the window. Then she rolls a joint. She climbs back into bed and leans back against the pillows. As she inhales, the familiar images start to flood into her mind. Recently, she has been reading obsessively about the Nazi period. Some days she has rung in sick and has just stayed in bed all day, reading whatever she has been able to get hold of. The images have filled her head to such an extent that she can think of nothing else.

She has not prepared for her imminent return to university, and Christoph's many letters remain unanswered. Her thoughts drift off again to the now familiar territory; the pre-war Vienna of her grandmother's youth. She pictures unfurled flags with swastikas and slogans scrawled on the walls, all against a background of thumping martial music. Confusion and terror reign. What started out as prejudice has now turned to naked hatred.

The Viennese have suffered first depression, then inflation and joblessness. Now here is a perfect opportunity to become wealthy again. Jewish possessions and property are simply confiscated by the SS. Stolen and given away. Jews now cannot go to the cinema or to concerts. They cannot walk on certain streets. They are no longer allowed to practise law, and are hounded out of the cultural life of the city. There are signs in Jewish shops warning people not to shop there. Christians cannot employ Jews, and Jewish children can no longer go to school. Even the cafes are divided down the middle; one half for Christians and the other for Jews. Young Jewish men are being grabbed and deported! At first, many of them are sent as slave labour to Germany. Later, they are replaced by deportees from other countries and they join the transports to the East. Eichmann is heading a drive to persuade them to leave the country. By the end of 1942, of the 75,000 Jews in Vienna, only 8,000 remain. All radio stations have been taken over by one single channel, pumping out an endless stream of propaganda.

In the face of all this, is it possible that her grandmother did not know what was going on? Kate has also read that the Austrians were considered by Himmler to be particularly suitable as concentration camp guards, and many top ranking SS officials were also Austrian. Kate drifts again into what has become a recurring dream. She is in a bombed out city. Piles of debris fill the streets: there is no electricity, so it is pitch black. The darkness is only broken momentarily by the flicker of a struck match. Pipes protrude from holes in buildings where windows had been. There are soldiers in the streets. They are shouting to each other in an unfamiliar language. From time to time, in the wavering light of a lantern, she can make out the fur on their hats. They wear full-length overcoats, with their trousers tucked into high boots.

Just then, Dan appears in the doorway. He stares at Kate lying on her back, the hand that holds the spliff hanging languidly down towards the floor.

'Kate, for God's sake, what on earth is going on?' he says.

Kate turns her head slowly and looks at him as though seeing him for the first time. She raises the spliff to her lips and inhales.

'I don't know what you mean. As you can see, I'm lying in bed smoking,' she says finally.

'Kate, you've got to stop this. You have to get a grip on yourself. You're blowing your mind with all that shit you're smoking.'

'What's it to you? It's my life and this is what I choose to do.'

Dan looks exasperated.

'Well, it may be your life, but you're ruining it. And what about Christoph? I thought you were so mad about him. Going to live in Berlin, and all that.'

'Well, maybe I've changed my mind, that's all. I can't see that it's any of your business,' replies Kate. 'I don't keep asking you about Sebastian.'

'Sebastian and I are just working on a project, that's all.'

Kate sighs.

'Oh for goodness sake. I don't know why you can't just be honest about the relationship. After all, it's not as if anyone cares. In fact, it's quite cool now.'

Dan folds his lips into a thin line.

'Anyway, it's none of your business,' he says.

'In that case, keep out of mine,' retorts Kate.

Dan gives her a withering look and withdraws.

***

Downstairs the phone rings. Jude lets it ring for a while, not wishing to have to go into lengthy explanations as to why Gerry is not around. At last, though, she gives in, and answers it. It is Anna. She tells Jude about her summons to the Cedars and describes the incident at the dinner table.

'It's not just that, though, Jude. Mum's been going from bad to worse ever since her fall. It's as though it sort of triggered something off in her brain; stirred up old memories. And there's obviously something traumatic that she's either just remembered about or that has just come to the surface. I really need to get to the bottom of it. Then perhaps we can help her to lay the ghost, whatever it is.'

'Yes, well there's something pretty traumatic been going on here, too,' says Jude dryly, when Anna has finished speaking. 'Gerry's gone. He's left me. I imagine he's gone off with another woman, although he hasn't exactly said so.'

There is a silence at the end of the line. Anna is shocked. It is the last thing she has been expecting. Like Kate, she is aware that her sister's marriage was rather shaky, but she's surprised that it's come to this. She also feels a bit guilty. Perhaps she should have read the signs before that Jude was unhappy. She's been so preoccupied with her mother's problems that she hasn't had time for anyone else's.

'That's terrible, Jude,' she says at last. 'Are you all right? Would you like me to come over?'

'No, no, it's fine. Anyway, Kate and Dan are here, so it's not as if I'm on my own. To be honest, Anna, I'm glad he's gone.'

Anna can understand that, and would feel the same, but she's surprised to hear her sister say it. She always felt that the trappings of being married to a rich and successful man were all-important to Jude.

Still, obviously she's changed.

'Anyway,' continues Jude, 'what's all this about mother? You think she's harbouring some dark secret?'

'Well, I went to see Edward, hoping he could throw some light on things,' she says. 'I get the impression that something happened to do with Horst, you know, her first husband.'

Anna suddenly realises that Jude knows nothing about the photograph of the boys in SS uniform, nor has she seen the newspaper article about Ernest. She decides not to go into all of that now.

'During one of my conversations with her, she almost seemed to be saying that Horst wasn't killed at the front, as we'd all thought. But then she sort of retracted it, so I just don't know. The other thing that is very uncertain is exactly when she met our father. Jude – you were born in 1946, weren't you?'

'Yes, on the second of May.'

'Have you got your birth certificate?'

'Yes, of course,' says Jude impatiently.

'And what does it say?'

'Well, it gives my date of birth, of course and the names of my parents, Ida Mullhauser and Ernest McFarlane. Actually that's odd. They weren't married then, were they? Anyway, what is all this? Surely it's all ancient history now.'

'Yes, it is in a way. But there's obviously something spooking Mum.'

Jude really wants to tell Anna about Kate. About how worried she is about her. But she doesn't. It somehow doesn't seem to be the right moment and, anyway, Kate is still in the house. She might overhear the conversation, and then there would be hell to pay.

When the conversation ends, Jude puts the receiver down and sits thoughtfully at the kitchen table. There are still no signs of life from upstairs. She glances at the kitchen clock. Eleven thirty. Obviously Kate does not intend going to the Barchester today. She wonders why everyone, including her own daughter, is so obsessed with Ida's past. Perhaps I am the odd one here, she thinks. I have never even given it a second thought. Perhaps I have been so preoccupied with my own problems that I have just not bothered to think about anyone else.

She tries to summon up her very earliest memories. They are very few. She can remember crying at night in her bed because she was hungry. She can see disjointed images of rubble-filled streets. She also remembers the penetrating cold and the endless gloom. Did she have any toys? She concentrates hard, trying to remember. Ah yes, of course, there was a rag doll which her mother made for her from scraps of material. What was it called now? Hansi or Mimi. Something like that. Whatever happened to it when she came to England?

She remembers one occasion, she must have been about three, she was playing outside the house amongst the bomb craters, and some American soldiers came by. They had said something to her, which she hadn't understood, then they had given her a whole bar of chocolate and gone off, laughing. She had not been able to believe her eyes. It was luxury beyond her wildest imaginings. She had rushed home with it and shown it to her mother. Her joy soon turned to fury, though, when her mother had broken the chocolate bar in two and handed half of it to her brother. In spite of Jude's screams of protest, she was only allowed to keep her half of the bar. Her mother had doled it out, one square a day and Jude can still remember the delicious sweetness of the chocolate as it melted in her mouth. She had never tasted anything like it.

Funnily enough, she also remembers her grandmother, who had come to see them from time to time, bringing extra vegetables and sometimes a heel of bread. She had seemed very old to Jude at the time. She was a thin, nut-faced woman, with deep lines

154

running down either side of her nose to her mouth. Her hair was pure white, and drawn back tightly into a sparse bun. As far as Jude remembers, she had been kind to Edward and herself. Why, then, had her mother never returned to Vienna to visit her?

She also remembers the military plane, which had transported her parents, her brother and herself to England. It had been a huge, noisy machine, full of British troops. She remembers nothing else of Vienna. Her other childhood memories are all of England. It is strange to think, though, that her mother tongue must have been German. She can't remember a word of it now. She wonders how long it took her to learn English, once she arrived in England. She must remember to ask her mother, next time she sees her.

CHAPTER 13

Christmas is just around the corner. Although it is only early December, the shops are already full of a whole array of pointless objects, all wrapped enticingly to encourage people to shop early. The street decorations have been put up, too, and for weeks now Santa has been holding court in his grotto in the shopping centres. Wherever you are, you cannot escape the tinny and depressing jangle of speeded up Christmas carols, alternating with Slade and Brenda Lee. The town centres are filling up with Christmas shoppers, driving round desperately, searching for a parking space. The days are now so short that it is dark by four o'clock. The over-illuminated shops shine like beacons through the gloomy drizzle.

Christmas has come early to the Cedars, too. All the public areas are festooned with decorations and an imposing and elegantly decorated tree stands in the hall, surrounded by gaily-wrapped parcels. The Sunday hymn-singing sessions are now dominated by Christmas carols, and notices have gone out to residents and their families, listing the events leading up to the Big Day.

Ida is largely unaware of all this, though. She sits in her room most of the day, only emerging for meals and occasional visits to the chiropodist or the hairdresser.

Most mornings, Gloria brings Ida's breakfast up herself. She likes to check on her each morning, and to make sure that the tranquillisers are not making her too drowsy. Gloria is a big presence in Ida's little room and, in spite of herself, Ida looks forward to her visits. She seems to bring a breath of the real world – of life itself- into the confined space.

Gloria usually spends about five minutes with Ida, ostensibly chatting inconsequentially but, in fact, subtly assessing her state of mind. On the whole, she is pleased with the way things are going. Ida is definitely calmer and more relaxed. She is still very resistant to the idea of leaving her room and socialising with the other residents, though. Gloria is not altogether surprised. After all, Ida had a dreadful experience with her table companions who, in Gloria's view, could have been chosen more carefully in the first place. Still, that isn't her job. She just has to pick up the pieces when things go wrong. She has worked with old people for so long now that she has a kind of sixth sense about which relationships will work and which won't.

Now she asks Ida tentatively if she will be spending Christmas at the Cedars or with her family. Ida hasn't a clue. She barely knows that Christmas is approaching. Once Gloria has left, though, she starts to think about it. When she was a small child, Christmas was a magical and mysterious time. Until she was about six though, her father had been out of work, and there was no money for anything other than the habitual thin vegetable soup and bread. There was never any meat. Her mother still put out the carved wooden crib though, with the painted figures of the Holy family, the shepherds and the Magi. Ida can remember every detail of those figures, as though it were yesterday. Her father usually brought in a branch of larch, which they nailed to the wall and decorated.

Christmas Eve was always the most atmospheric moment. Lighted candles were placed on the table and they would gather round, perhaps with an uncle and aunt and some cousins, and sing carols. After that there was always a present for Ernst and herself, however little money there was. One year, she remembers, her father had made her a doll's house out of some pieces of wood that he had brought back from a visit to their relations in the mountains. Her mother had made new clothes for her doll. They were so exquisite that, for a moment, she thought the doll itself was new.

Ernst also received presents. One year their father made him a carved wooden engine. He had been ecstatic when he saw it. Later on, when her father started work at the paper factory, they would have roast goose for dinner on Christmas Eve after getting back from church. Mass was always the central point of the celebrations and her mother, especially, made sure that the children prayed especially hard to the Virgin to deliver them from the sins of greed, sloth and gluttony. Not that there was much chance of succumbing to those particular sins, though. In those days, Christmas was a truly spiritual affair. It bore no relation to the orgy of greed and spending that is Christmas nowadays.

Before Ida went into the Cedars, she had become increasingly shocked by the naked commercialism, which starts in mid-November and extends well beyond Christmas to the January sales. She is at a loss to understand how things can have come to this. Surely modern children cannot still have the sense of awe and excitement when it is a foregone conclusion that their every wish will be fulfilled. Their hard-pressed parents often put themselves in hock for the rest of the year to provide the latest designer trainers, games consoles and mobile phones, which their offspring have to have. Far from making people happy, they seem to become more and more miserable as the stress and extra work mount up. Surely people were happier when they had next to nothing, as her family had had when she was a child. Ida sighs. She must be just too old, too out of touch, she thinks. It is all beyond her.

Her thoughts then return to her mother, as they do so often these days. She was so devout, such a good woman, wasn't she? At least, she was a wonderful mother to Ernst and herself. Always putting them first, making sure they had the least stale vegetables and any ends of meat that came their way. And yet, how could such a good Catholic accept the things that came later?

Ida's thoughts move forward now, to the Anschluss. She seems to remember it all more clearly now. It was in March – the fifteenth to be precise. Hitler had entered the city the previous evening, and had spent the night at the Metropole Hotel. She can remember the huge crowd on the Heldenplatz that turned out to welcome the sombre figure in his brown SS overcoat, standing upright in his official car, his right arm raised in the chilling Nazi salute. How the crowd had roared and cheered. Shouts of 'Heil Hitler' came from all sides.

She and Horst had stood mute, though, bemused and uncertain how to react. Horst's commitment to the Party had come later. Then Hitler had made his 'acceptance' speech from the balcony of the Hofburg. Acceptance of what, she had wondered at the time, of Austria's subjugation? He had seized Austria without a shot being fired in anger. The Austrians had been only too willing to be taken over.

That day the shops and factories were closed. Everyone was out on the streets. The lilac was in bloom, and she can still recall the intoxicating smell, and how incongruous it seemed. Clear and unpleasant as these images now are, they are not exactly what is preoccupying Ida. After all, people can be – and were – taken in. But the church! The Catholic Church was not just acquiescent; it was positively enthusiastic in its welcome of the dictator. She remembers her mother's hero, Cardinal Innitzer, giving instructions for the Führer to be greeted by chimes of welcome from the churches, and for swastikas to be unfurled from their towers. After Hitler's speech on the Heldenplatz, he officially received the Cardinal, who spoke of the realisation of the old dream of German unity. After that, he decreed from the pulpit that everyone should declare themselves for the German Empire.

All this her mother had accepted, if not enthusiastically then with unquestioning obedience. Her view was that if her beloved Cardinal said it was all right, then that was enough for her. Ida remembers trying to discuss it with her mother at the time, but she had got nowhere. Already there were things that made Ida feel very uncomfortable about the new regime: the militarism, the acts of aggression, the treatment of certain people. Finally, of course, the Nazis had destroyed faith in anything except the Führer himself. It was the new religion.

Towards the end of that same year, there had been an anti-Nazi rally in the Domplatz. The occasion had been the Feast of the Rosary, and Ida had gone along to see what was happening, hanging around on the edge of the crowd.

The rally had hardly started when brown-shirted Hitler Youth arrived to try and break it up. Immediately there was shouting and fighting and the rally was dispersed almost before it started. Ida and Horst had retreated quickly as soon as they saw trouble starting. All through the early part of the war, when Ida had gradually become more and more horrified by what she saw around her, her mother never wavered in her allegiance to the Church, and continued to attend mass regularly. In fact she and Ida had argued about it. Ida could not accept the fact that the priests seemed unconcerned about the cruelty and persecution that was going on around them. It was only when Ernst was killed at Stalingrad that her mother lost her faith.

It was widely suggested in Vienna that the Austrian troops were sacrificed there to save the Germans and, whether that was true or not, Austrian losses were comparably higher, and Ida's mother believed it. Stories of the horror had filtered back to Vienna, and Ida and her mother pictured the screaming Arctic winds, the white wasteland, endlessly lit by exploding shells and the months and months of darkness. The thought of Ernst, lying fatally wounded in that icy hell was finally more than her mother could bear.

Ida remembers when Horst first came home on leave after Ernst's death. He was shocked, of course, when she told him but considering that he and Ernst had been inseparable only three years before, she was surprised at how quickly he seemed to put it out of his mind. She supposed that he was so used to seeing his comrades dying around him that he had become inured to it.

During that miserable leave, the only thing that brought a smile of real warmth to Horst's face was Edward. He spent most of his time with his son, playing with him and talking to him, telling him things that Ida didn't really approve of. She even found him one day trying to get him to give the Nazi salute and to say 'Heil Hitler.' On that occasion, she had tried to remonstrate with him, but Horst had turned on her, accusing her of being unpatriotic.

'Don't you realise that every day soldiers are fighting and dying to preserve our master race against the barbarian hordes?' he had said. 'Your brother too, died fighting the Russian *Untermenschen*, and you don't want your son to be taught to respect the Führer. I simply do not understand you any more, Ida.'

By this time, Ida had been witnessing the horrors of the SS *razzias* on an almost daily basis. Every day, truckloads of them had been arriving at different addresses throughout the city and dragging people away.

At first they had only taken the young men, but recently they had been taking whole families, old people, children, even babies. She had heard them begging and pleading, but their entreaties had fallen on deaf ears. Mothers often tried to persuade the soldiers to allow their children to stay if they themselves went, but the soldiers just shouted louder, kicking them and hitting them with the butts of their rifles. Little children, screaming in fear, were picked up and tossed into the trucks like ballast. Old people, who couldn't move fast enough, were helped on their way with kicks and blows. The Viennese either crossed the street and walked past, or laughed and shouted words of encouragement to the soldiers. She too had walked past, pretending not to hear or see what was happening. She was afraid. Afraid of what they would do to her or to Edward if she interfered. Again, she tries to raise the subject with Horst, but it is useless.

'These people have undermined our economy for too long, Ida,' he says. 'They were the cause of our downfall. Do you wish to return to the bad old days, when inflation was so high that a single loaf cost 6,000 crowns? They tried to steal our birthright, and now they must pay the price. The Führer is working tirelessly to rid our country of these parasites.'

Ida gives up. It is clear that Horst will not listen to reason on the subject. She tries another tack. Since Stalingrad, there has been the general feeling that the course of the war has changed. The victories that were a feature of the first few years are now few and far between. But it is not so much Stalingrad, horrific as that defeat had been, that seems to have turned the tide. Defeat in the snowy wastelands, thousands of miles to the East, seems less immediately threatening than the rout of Rommel's forces in North Africa and the allied landings in Sicily. Sicily, after all, is Italy, and Italy is their southern neighbour. It all seems uncomfortably close to home. When she says this to Horst, though, he flies into a fury, accusing her of spreading defeatist lies.

'Maybe I am defeatist,' she says. 'Maybe I think that my brother died for nothing, and that you may do the same. And what I don't understand is, why are your troops wasting their time rounding up innocent civilians, when they could be fighting the enemy?'

This time, she has pushed Horst too far. He raises his hand, and hits her with his full force across the face. She gasps and falls to the floor. Edward, who was playing with his wooden soldiers in a corner of the room, lets out a scream and runs to his mother. Ida recovers herself and gets up, picks up Edward and runs out of the house and down the street. She doesn't know where she is going. She is just running blindly, tears streaming down her face. Edward is clinging to her, sobbing.

Eventually, she slows down to a walk, her breath searing her chest. She has no money, so she cannot even get on a tram and go to her mother's house. She realises that she will have to go back home. Neither she nor Edward have coats, and the temperature is below zero. She turns and walks slowly back the way she has come.

As she enters the flat, all is quiet. Nervously she goes from room to room. Horst is nowhere to be seen. She puts some wood on the stove and sits Edward in front of it to warm up while she prepares their meagre supper. After they have eaten, she puts Edward to bed. A couple of hours later, she hears someone at the front door. Horst appears. He comes straight over to her, kneels at her feet and puts his head in her lap.

'Ida, please forgive me. I do not know what came over me. I love you, and I love Edward, and I would do anything for you. When I am at the front, you are all I think about. You must believe me. I cannot excuse my behaviour, but I can give you a reason. The constant fear is something I cannot describe to you. Every day, you wonder if it will be your turn to be shot or blown up by a shell. If it happens to one of your comrades, you are almost glad. It means that you have escaped. This time. And sometimes, some of the things we are ordered to do make my stomach turn. But, if we do not do them, we would be shot. This is why, when you talked of defeat, something snapped inside me. I could not bear to think that all this has been for nothing.'

Ida is silent. Part of her feels desperately sorry for Horst, but that's all. Nothing else. Who knows what he has already done, perhaps to innocent civilians? She feels that she doesn't know anything, anymore. All the parameters of normal, civilised life seem to have been distorted, so that she no longer knows what is right or wrong. Her once beloved husband has become a stranger.

She holds her body stiffly, her head turned away, resisting him. He is silent now, but his shoulders are shaking. She realises that he is weeping. She lowers her hand and places it on his head, and gradually begins to stroke his blond thatch of hair. It feels like towrope under her hand. After a few moments, he lifts his head and takes hold of her hand, kissing the palm, then the wrist, then feverishly right up the inside of her arm to her elbow. She sits passively. Now he is kissing her face, finding her mouth, forcing his tongue between her lips. He pulls her down from the chair, onto the thin matting in front of the stove, and lays her on her back, fumbling to undo the buttons on the front of her woollen house dress, kissing her breasts, running his tongue around her nipples, then moving his mouth down over her stomach. She feels a wave of desire, almost like a pain. He lifts her body to pull off her pants, then pushes her knees apart. She can feel his tongue again, then she feels him enter her, thrusting desperately. She climaxes almost at once, digging her nails into his back and pushing him in harder.

Once it is over she gets up and cleans herself. When she gets back, Horst is already in the bedroom. He has removed his clothes and has thrown himself onto the bed. Soon he is in a deep sleep. She undresses and creeps in beside him. She feels ashamed of her abandon. It is as if his violence of earlier on has aroused her.

She lies for a long time staring into the darkness, listening to him breathing. After a while he starts to move around in his sleep, whimpering, his breathing rapid and shallow. He has been doing this a lot of late. Guiltily she longs for him to go back, so that she can put all of this out of her mind. She feels a pang of remorse when she remembers how, at one time, she dreaded his return to the front, counting the hours they had left together.

The rest of his leave passes off without further incident. Horst seems to have forgotten his outburst of rage, and Ida avoids discussing anything that is likely to cause a row. Just before he leaves, they go across the city to visit Ida's mother. They find her sitting in her flat staring into space. She looks thin, as though she hasn't eaten for days. The flat is cold, too.

Horst fetches some of the remaining wood from the cellar, and Ida busies herself in the kitchen, making broth with a mutton bone she has brought with her. Soon the wood is crackling in the stove. Ida fetches a shawl to put round her mother's shoulders. She continues to stare vacantly into the fire. Ida holds a spoonful of broth up to her lips and starts to feed her. Her mother's lips tremble, and the broth runs down her chin onto her blouse. She doesn't seem to notice. Ida tries to get her to talk, but it is in vain. At last she offers to go and fetch the priest. This provokes a reaction at last.

'No, you must not do that, Ida,' she says. 'I never want to speak to him again, or hear him telling me that my darling boy has gone to a better place. What God can allow a boy to die an agonising death like that, frozen and far from those who love him? I will never set foot in the church again!'

Horst and Ida wait for Ida's father to return from work, and then they make their way home. Horst has one more night left. Tomorrow he must return to the front. On the way home he is unusually silent. Ida knows that he is dreading the next day. She feels pity for him, but none of the tenderness that she used to feel.

They go to bed early to save firewood. The bed is icy cold, and Ida cannot stop shivering. Horst takes her in his arms, warming her with his own body. As he caresses her with his hands and mouth, her body is again in a frenzy of desire. She can hardly hold back her orgasm. Just as she is about to climax, he turns her over and enters her from behind. At the first thrust she comes, arching her back and moaning. Soon after, he too climaxes violently. They both fall asleep almost immediately.

The next morning, Ida helps Horst to pack his bags. When she thinks of the previous night, she is hot with shame. How can she feel so much desire for a man she almost hates? She just wants him gone, now, so that it can't happen again. When Horst has to say goodbye to Edward, he cannot hold back his tears. Ida knows he is thinking that he may never see his son again.

Once Horst has left, Ida's life returns to the dull routine of trying to make ends meet. She spends much of her time queuing for bread and vegetables. If word goes round that the butcher has some meat in, she must join the queue as early as she can. This is not always easy with Edward. Sometimes she leaves him with her mother, and picks up her rations too.

One day, as Ida is leaving her apartment, she sees a movement through the window of the ground floor flat, directly underneath hers. She is surprised, as she knows that the husband is away at the front, and the wife goes out early to do a cleaning job at the hospital. They have no children. Normally, the flat is empty all day. When she looks again, she sees a little girl of about eight. When the child sees her, she moves quickly away from the window. The next day, Ida leaves a bit later, and makes a point of looking quickly through the window. She sees the child again. Again she moves out of sight quickly. This happens three or four times more.

One night, Ida is up with Edward nearly all night. He has measles, and his temperature is so high that he has become delirious, crying out for his father and thrashing about in his bed. She sponges him with tepid water, willing the fever to subside. His resistance is so low through lack of proper food and milk that she is afraid he may die. She mutters the familiar prayers of her childhood, but with little conviction. Like her mother, she has lost her faith. For different reasons, though. The craven capitulation of the church, and its indifference to the sufferings of the men, women and children who are dragged away on a daily basis, have destroyed her belief in God.

When the fever breaks, and Edward is quieter, she moves over to the window and looks out. She sees a shadowy figure entering the flat below, carrying bags of something. Then she knows. The Steinhammers are obviously hiding someone, or more than one person. She is filled with admiration for them, but also with fear for herself and Edward. What if someone denounces them and she is somehow implicated, suspected of being involved. She knows that people are summarily shot for such offences. She is immediately ashamed of the thought. There the Steinhammers are, risking everything, and she is just afraid that their brave act will somehow rub off on her! The least she can do is to go about her business without drawing any attention to the flat below. She wonders if any of the other occupants of the flats have noticed anything.

Apart from herself and the Steinhammers, there are four other families living in the block. Other than saying good morning if she meets them on the stairs, she doesn't really know them. People tend to be suspicious of each other now. They prefer to go home and shut their doors at night. How different it is to the pre-war Vienna, Ida thinks, when everyone went out to coffee houses and concerts, and the sound of music and laughter seemed to fill the city.

After a week or so, Edward is making a slow recovery, and much of Ida's time is spent trudging round the city trying to find milk and fresh vegetables for him. She also visits her mother every day, trying to encourage her to eat and generally to start looking after herself. She wouldn't change her clothes for weeks on end if Ida were not there to remind her, and the once immaculate flat now has an unkempt air.

A few weeks later, as Ida is returning from her mother's, she sees one of her neighbours, a Mrs Rosenfeld, talking to a couple of SS officers at the end of the road. Her heart gives a sickening lurch, but she forces herself to walk past them without quickening her pace. She can hardly climb the stone steps up to her flat, her heart is beating so wildly. All she can think is that Mrs Rosenfeld must have spotted something in the Steinhammers' flat.

All that evening, and the next day, she is in a torment of indecision about whether she should warn the Steinhammers. If she does, she may find she has got it completely wrong; they may not be harbouring anyone at all. Then she would be revealing where her sympathies lay. On the other hand, if she says nothing, the consequences could be too dire to contemplate. She doesn't get much sleep for the next few nights, usually falling into a deep sleep just before dawn, and awaking feeling exhausted and lethargic. However, time passes and nothing happens. Eventually, the problem slips to the back of her mind, and she starts to believe that nothing is going to happen.

Horst is due to come home on leave again at the end of the month. Ida is not looking forward to it. Every day, now, neighbours in the street are receiving telegrams, informing them that their husbands or sons have been lost in battle. Morale is very low. Ida wonders almost dispassionately if she will receive such a telegram. She really doesn't know how she will feel if it happens. For Edward's sake, though, she hopes he will not lose his father.

When Horst arrives, he looks pale and thin. His face is curiously expressionless, and it is only Edward who can coax a smile from him. The first night, Ida makes him a nourishing stew with rations which she has been saving up, and he falls asleep early, exhausted. Ida creeps into bed beside him, trying not to disturb him.

A couple of hours later, they are both awoken by a terrific noise outside. Horst leaps out of bed, grabbing his pistol. Ida makes to go and look out of the window, but Horst pulls her away roughly. They both crouch on the floor. Now there is a thunderous knocking on the door, and the sound of raised voices. Then there is a splintering sound, and they can hear people running around immediately beneath them. Ida is trembling violently. She puts her hands over her ears. They hear footsteps running down the street. Then there is a shot. Now there is a different sound. It is a high-pitched wailing, that makes her shudder. Pulling away from Horst, Ida kneels on the floor and peers through the window. She can see a dark bundle on the pavement a little to the left of the front door.

Another figure, a woman, runs out and throws herself onto the bundle, screaming. Then there is more shouting, and Ida can see Mrs Steinhammer and some other people being pushed into the back of a truck. A soldier goes up to the woman on the pavement and grabs her by the hair. She too is pushed into the truck. The bundle remains on the pavement.

Ida sinks to the floor, her head in her hands, sobbing. When she looks up, she sees that Horst is staring at her, a look of fury on his face.

'Ida, those people below must have been hiding Jews. Tell me the truth, did you know about it?'

Ida hesitates for a second. That moment's hesitation is enough. It tells Horst everything.

'You stupid bitch, didn't you realise what danger you have put us all in? Don't you understand that they would take us all away and shoot us, including Edward, if they thought we knew what was going on?'

Ida looks up defiantly. 'I don't know why you say 'they'. After all, you are one of them, aren't you? You wear the same uniform. You do the same things, I imagine.'

Horst takes a step towards Ida and seizes her arm. He twists it up behind her back so that she opens her mouth to scream in pain. Horst is too quick for her, though, and he claps his hand over her mouth so that no sound comes out. He puts his other arm around her throat and forces her head backwards so that she is unable to breathe. Just as she is about to faint, he pushes her violently to the floor. Then he grabs a blanket from the bed and strides into the next room. She lies motionless for a long time, her head swimming.

At last, as dawn is breaking, she climbs into the bed and falls into a fitful sleep. The next day she is awakened by Edward climbing into the bed beside her, asking for his father. She assumes that Horst must have gone out, otherwise Edward would have seen him. She drags herself out of bed, her limbs feeling like lead, and goes to look out of the window. The bundle on the pavement has gone, and all is quiet. Around midday, Horst returns to the flat. His face is set in a grim expression.

'Where have you been?' Ida asks. 'What happened to the child?'

Horst gestures towards Edward.

'Edward, go and wash your hands for dinner,' says Ida, and Edward gets up reluctantly from his game.

'I have been to the SS headquarters, to ensure that we were not implicated, after your stupidity.'

'Yes, but did you find out what happened to the child?'

'The child was trying to run away. She was eliminated,' he says shortly.

Ida draws in her breath sharply. 'And the Steinhammers?' she manages to ask.

'They will probably be shot or sent to a camp, for harbouring undesirables,' he replies.

After that, Ida and Horst only exchange the most perfunctory of remarks. There is no urgent making-up, as there was after their last fight. Ida feels numb. Horror-struck at what happened in the flat below, and at her own lack of courage. Even when Horst returns to the front, she feels no great sense of relief, just a profound sadness and sense of revulsion.

CHAPTER 14

During lunch that day, Ivy drops dead at the table. There is a sudden loud clatter, as cutlery and crockery fall to the floor. Then there is silence. Ivy has fallen forward onto the table, splattering her table companions with tomato soup. For a few seconds, everyone seems rooted to the spot, unable to grasp what has happened. Then the staff rush forward. Ivy is not large but it takes several of them to lift her from her chair and carry her out of the dining room. When she has been removed, the girls wipe the soup off the front of Albert's shirt. Although Grace has escaped the soup, she is white faced and shaken, and has to be escorted out of the dining room. Albert, on the other hand, appears unruffled, and is able to resume his meal.

'He probably saw worse than that in the desert,' whispers Kim to her friend.

Fortunately for Ida, she is now at a table at the other end of the room, and hardly knows what has happened.

When Ida returns to her room she is sleepy and is about to lie on her bed, when there is a knock at the door. After a few moments it opens, and a tall figure appears in the doorway. She can't make out who it is at first.

'Who is it? Come in. I can't see you properly,' she says,

impatiently. The figure moves slowly away from the door and comes towards her. With a jolt of surprise, she sees that it is Edward.

'Well, Mum,' he says at last, running a hand across the top of his head in a familiar, self-deprecating gesture. 'How are you?'

The eternal question, thinks Ida. 'Still here,' would be the only honest answer. That would upset people, though.

'Alright thank you, Edward,' she replies instead. 'And very pleased to see you.

Come in and sit down. Don't hang around in the doorway like that.' Edward moves awkwardly into the room, finally perching himself on the edge of Ida's bed, while Ida sits in her chair. They chat for a while in a desultory way. Edward seems on edge, his eyes darting around the room, as though he's looking for something. At last Ida understands.

'Do you want to smoke, Edward?' she asks.

'Well, I could do with a cigarette,' Edward admits. 'Only I suppose it's not allowed up here.'

'Probably not, it's never arisen before. But open the window and carry on. I won't tell if you don't.'

Edward is surprised to find his mother almost jocular. She seems much changed from his last visit.

When they have run out of small talk about Edward's family, Ida says,

'I believe Anna came to see you recently. Why was that?'

'Oh, well, you know, I haven't seen her for quite a while. I suppose she just wanted to see how we were getting on,' says Edward vaguely.

'Edward, my dear,' says Ida suddenly, leaning forward and placing a hand on his knee. 'I feel so desperately sorry that your childhood was so – well – traumatic. I feel that it has marked you, and that it has somehow spoilt your life.'

Edward looks surprised. He shakes his head.

'It's not your fault, Mum. You couldn't help the war and all that.'

Ida persists.

'No, but I feel guilty – for all that happened. I was wondering, Edward, how much do you remember of your father?'

Again, Edward shakes his head.

'That's what Anna wanted to know, too. The fact is, Mum, I don't remember him at all. Try as I might, I cannot recall any single thing about him.'

'And afterwards, when Jude was born, do you remember that? There is a slight shake in Ida's voice.

'Well, yes, I remember there being a baby in the house, after we had been on our own. But I don't have any clear recollection of it. Anna wanted to know about that, as well. She wanted to know if I was already at school when Jude was born.'

'Did she really ask you that?' says Ida. 'And what did you say?'

'I don't know why she wanted to know,' replies Edward. 'I told her I simply couldn't remember.'

Ida is silent for a while. 'Well, my dear,' she says at last, 'I expect that is for the best.'

CHAPTER 15

Oxford Street is beginning to fill up with Christmas shoppers. By late afternoon, the crowds of tourists and middle-aged women from the Home Counties are joined by office workers, all determined to start their shopping early. Juliet, too, is shopping early for Christmas. Her rehearsal over for the day, she has decided to make a start now so that, with luck, everything should be wrapped and labelled before she goes away on tour. There certainly won't be time afterwards, because they return the day before Christmas Eve.

She has already purchased presents for her mother, father and sister, and is now looking for inspiration for her grandmother's present. Ida's requirements have been decreasing progressively over the last few years, and now they are almost non-existent. Her world is now reduced to one small room, in which ornaments and gadgets are superfluous. Juliet knows she has nightdresses, slippers and bed-jackets in abundance. She keeps thinking of ideas and then rejecting them. Ida has never eaten chocolates, her eyes are now too poor to read much, and new clothes are an irrelevance.

At last she decides on a personal CD player, thinking it may make it easier for Ida to hear her favourite music. At the back of her mind, though, she wonders if she will ever master the controls. Anything remotely 'technical' seems to defeat people of her grandmother's generation. Still, it's worth a go. The purchase made, Juliet decides to have a cup of coffee. The weather, though damp, is unseasonably muggy, and she is hot and tired. She puts her bags down with relief and orders a cappuccino and a *pain au chocolat*. A bit of an indulgence, but she feels she's deserved it. She glances at the headlines of the paper she's bought, but she can't concentrate. Her mind keeps straying to her forthcoming tour. They are due to leave at the end of the week, and the concert is already sold out in some venues. It is a wonderful concert, and Juliet feels she is playing at the peak of her ability at the moment. Not only that, but the music lifts her spirits and transports her to another place, where there are no fears or uncertainties. Even when she has finished playing, the serenity continues, at least for a while, but gradually the anxieties come sneaking back.

Things seem to have gone from bad to worse with Simon recently. They seem increasingly to be leading separate lives. The play has now started and, understandably, he is completely taken up with it. She hates the idea of going away, of leaving things in limbo, as they seem to be at the moment. By the time Simon gets in, it is usually about one o'clock in the morning. He frequently stays up, pouring himself a drink and listening to music. He says he needs to unwind. She wonders if it is to avoid her. She is usually in bed by then, at least trying to sleep. Her rehearsals start quite early in the morning, and she has to be up by seven to beat the rush hour. They rarely see each other for more than half an hour a day.

Juliet pays for her coffee and picks up her bags. It is beginning to get dark and she is tired. Her feet are aching. She is tempted to get a taxi back to Clapham. In the end though, reason prevails, and she goes for the tube. If she starts treating herself to luxuries like that, she won't be able to pay the rent. This is another thing, she thinks bitterly. She seems to end up paying most of the bills. Admittedly, Simon had previously been out of work for about four months, but since getting the part in "The Merchant", he has been earning as much as she does; yet she still seems to pay.

When she arrives back at the flat, it is drizzling again. At least, she thinks, when she gets to Berlin, she should get some clear crisp weather, rather than this endless murk. Although it is not cold outside, the flat feels chilly and dank. Juliet's spirits are low. She puts on the lamps and lights the gas fire. The thought of another evening on her own is not enticing. Just then the phone rings. It is Anna. Juliet is delighted to hear from her. They have only spoken briefly since they sorted out the house in Latymer Road. Juliet has told her about finding the newspaper cutting, but they haven't had a chance to discuss the implications.

'Why don't you come over and have supper, if you've nothing better to do? She says. 'Simon won't be home till the small hours, and I could do with some company.'

Anna agrees immediately. Tony is away again, this time in Germany, and she is at a loose end. Juliet has a look in the cupboards, and realises that there isn't even the basic ingredients of a meal. She quickly puts her coat on and dashes out to the parade of shops at the end of the road, where she purchases pasta, tomatoes, onion, Parmesan and a lemon cheesecake. She also buys a bottle of Chardonnay.

By the time Anna arrives, the kitchen table is laid, and a Bolognese sauce is bubbling in the pan. Anna opens the wine while Juliet serves the food. They sit down to eat, chatting at first about generalities. Anna thinks Juliet looks tired and strained. She wonders if the forthcoming European tour is putting her under pressure. She knows, too, that Juliet's relationship with Simon isn't always easy. Then she remembers that she has some family news.

'By the way, have you heard that Gerry has left Jude?'

Juliet puts down her fork in surprise. 'Good heavens, no. When did that happen?'

'Well, I rang her last week, and she told me. Actually, she didn't sound particularly upset about it. In fact, I would almost say she seemed relieved.'

'Well, I must say, there did seem to be a bit of an atmosphere last time I was there. You remember, it was when Gran was there for lunch, and I ended up taking her back. I just assumed Aunt Jude was worried about her.'

'Well, Jude seems to have quite positive plans for the future. It may be just what she needs. To be honest, I never could stand Gerry.'

Juliet gets up and starts to clear the dishes. 'How about Gran?' she asks. 'Have you seen her recently?'

'Yes, I have,' replies Anna. 'There was a bit of a crisis at the Cedars, because some old bat was getting at her and she ended up hitting out at her.'

Juliet draws in her breath sharply. 'God, that doesn't sound a bit like Gran.'

'No, you're right. I think she was provoked beyond endurance. Anyway, they've put her on sedatives now, and I must say she seems a lot better. You know, calmer, more lucid.'

Juliet is slightly shocked. She has heard reports of the abuse of sedatives in old people's homes.

'Are you sure that's a good thing?'

'Well yes, in this case I think it is,' says Anna a touch

impatiently. It seems to have removed a lot of the anxiety. You know, the obsessive rocking; all that.'

Juliet nods. She gets the cheesecake from the fridge and pours Anna another glass of wine. Anna takes a sip and puts the glass back on the table. 'I went to see your father the other day,' she says, cautiously.

Juliet looks up. 'I didn't know,' she says, surprised.

'Well yes, I just wanted to ask him what he remembered of the time that Jude was born, and when Mum met my father. He couldn't remember anything much though. It just seems a bit strange to me. Your Dad reckons he was at school when Mum met Ernest, because that was when she started work on the American base, but Jude was born in 1946, which would have made him younger than that.'

Juliet looks at Anna. 'So, what are you saying?'

'I don't know. It just seems odd, that's all.'

Juliet frowns. 'Yes, I suppose it is. How did you find Dad, anyway?'

'I didn't think he looked too good, to be honest. He seems to have really let himself go physically, and he's smoking far too much.'

'I know. I'm really worried about him. Among other things.'

Anna guesses she's referring to Simon, but doesn't enquire further, assuming that Juliet will volunteer the information if she wants to. She changes the subject and enquires about the concert tour.

'We leave on Saturday,' says Juliet. 'And we come back on the twenty-third.'

'It sounds marvellous. Really interesting. Where are you going exactly?'

'Heidelberg, Berlin, Warsaw, and finishing up in Vienna,' recites Juliet. 'Have you ever been? To Vienna, I mean.'

'No, never. I'd really love to go, though. You know, to see where Mum was brought up.'

Juliet has an idea. 'Look, why don't you fly out and join me for the last leg of the tour? You'll have broken up by then, won't you?'

Anna hesitates. 'Actually, that's a brilliant idea. When do you get there, exactly?'

Juliet gets up and goes to fetch her diary. 'We arrive in Vienna on the nineteenth and return five days later.'

'Do you know, I think I might do that. If you're sure you don't mind.'

'Of course not. Obviously we'll be playing in the evenings, but it will be good to have some company during the day. We get pretty sick of each other, you know, when we're together all the time on tour.'

They clear the remaining plates and cups from the table. Anna washes up and Juliet dries.

'Will Simon be joining you at any stage?' asks Anna tentatively.

Juliet shakes her head. 'Oh no, the play will still be running right up to Christmas Eve. I – well, I really wish I wasn't going this time. I've always really enjoyed touring in the past, but we're not getting on that well at the moment. We just seem to be drifting further and further apart.'

Exhaustion and the wine have affected Juliet more than she realises and, before she can stop herself, she is sobbing wildly. Anna is horrified. She dries her hands and leads Juliet to a chair. Juliet cannot stop crying now she's started. Her whole body is convulsed with sobs. The pent-up frustration of the last few months comes flooding out. Anna waits patiently for her to stop.

When the sobs eventually subside, Juliet tells Anna about Simon's apparent lack of interest in her, and how he seems to prefer spending him time with the other members of the cast rather than with her.

'He's terribly tortured about his Jewishness, too. All his family was wiped out, you know. It seems to make him resentful of me, somehow. Of course, now that I know my grandfather was a Nazi, I'm even more aware of it,' she says with a rueful smile. 'Not that he knows that, of course.'

'He can hardly blame you for something that happened over half a century ago,' says Anna gently.

'You may be right,' says Juliet, 'but he's extremely sensitive about his origins.' She smiles suddenly. 'It's all right for you, you know. Your father was one of the good guys.'

Just then the phone rings. Juliet goes into the hall to answer it. The conversation is obviously brief, as she returns in a couple of minutes.

'Simon's staying over at Tristram's place tonight,' she announces. 'It seems they've got an extra rehearsal tomorrow morning, and it's not worth coming home. Why don't you stay here tonight, Anna?'

Anna accepts readily. She's had a few glasses of wine and, anyway, the Northern Line at this late hour doesn't appeal.

'You know, Ju,' she says before they go to bed, 'you really need to have it out with Simon. Tell him the things you've told me, and ask him if you're right to be worried. But don't do it here in the flat. Choose a neutral place, where there are no distractions. And try to do it before you go away on tour.'

Juliet nods. She had already half made up her mind to do that. The trouble is, if she calls Simon's bluff, so to speak, and he decides to leave her, she doesn't know if she could bear it. Would she be able to survive the tour knowing that he would not be there on her return? On the other hand, things definitely cannot go on as they are. As she gets into bed, she thinks that she could never confide in her own parents the way she has in Anna tonight. She falls asleep almost immediately, worn out with the unaccustomed outburst of emotion.

***

Simon's nightmare is taking place in the Warsaw ghetto. He knows it's the Warsaw ghetto, yet it looks strangely modern; rather like the Barbican, in fact. Although there are no barbed wire fences, he somehow knows he cannot get out. He is with his mother. He knows she must be his mother, because people call her Miriam, and that's his mother's name, but she doesn't look a bit like his real mother. Like the Barbican, with which Simon is very familiar, there is a lot of precast concrete, and endless walkways. It is freezing cold, and isolated flakes of snow are falling from a leaden sky.

He is wearing a sort of Dickensian outfit, very ragged, with a deep cap pulled down over his ears. Every now and then he hears shots and sees bodies fall onto the grey, hard-packed snow. He is very afraid. So is his mother. He appears to have younger brothers and sisters, and he must go out and try to find food for them all. This is no mean task. There are no dogs or cats left in the ghetto, except for Minou, their own pet cat. She has managed to keep herself going so far by catching the odd mouse or rat that has escaped the attention of the starving populace. However, his mother decides that the cat's hour has now come. Hungry as they are, he and his brothers and sisters beg their mother to spare her, but she is adamant. When Simon hears the dull thud and hears Minou's screech of anguish, he rushes outside and vomits in the snow. His brothers and sisters are wailing. However, when he smells the cooking meat, his mouth fills with saliva in spite of himself, and he eats ravenously.

Simon opens his eyes and stares into the darkness. He wonders why the words never quite seem to match the pictures in dreams. Familiar people and places look different, and yet you somehow accept them. How strange it is!

As his eyes become more used to the darkness, he realises that he is in an unfamiliar place. For a moment he lies rigid. Then slowly he turns his head. He can make out a shape under the bedclothes beside him. It is definitely not Juliet. Then he remembers. He stayed at Tristram's flat last night. Oh God! What has he done? His mouth is parched and his head is thumping. They must have had a lot to drink. Memories of the previous evening start to filter back slowly. He and Tristram had been drinking champagne – courtesy of Tristram's father, in whose flat he now finds himself. At first they had been going through their parts, then they stopped and Tristram put on some music. Vaughan Williams. One of Simon's favourites. Then Tristram had started telling Simon about his father. He was an actor, too.

He had discovered that his father was gay shortly before going to university. It was when he came back to the flat one day and discovered him in bed with another man. His parents had been separated for a while prior to that, but it had come as a complete shock to Tristram. He had had no idea. His father had been rather successful, playing many of the meatier Shakespearean roles in his time, but was now living in LA with his long-standing boyfriend, doing occasional commercials. It was an odd story, and had obviously deeply affected Tristram. Maybe it had even influenced his sexuality. Simon cannot imagine what it would be like to discover such a thing about one's father. Or even to have a father, come to that. His mother never remarried, preferring to devote her life to her only son. Simon found it suffocating at times, although he is very fond of her.

By the time that Simon realised that there was only one bed, he was so drunk that he could hardly stand up. He nearly passed out on the sofa, so Tristram helped him to bed, undressed him and finally climbed in beside him. Simon debates now whether to get out of bed quietly and leave. He manages to look at his watch, and sees that it is nearly half past three. If he were to leave now, where would he go? He rang Juliet last night to tell her where he was staying, so he can hardly go back home now, and he doesn't fancy walking around the streets of Battersea at this time of the morning. He sighs and closes his eyes. Soon he has drifted off to sleep again.

When he awakes, he is shocked to find Tristram caressing and kissing him. In spite of himself he feels aroused. He turns away, onto his side, but then he feels Tristram's body against his, his penis hard against his buttocks. His hand grasps Simon's penis and, at the same time, he penetrates him. They both ejaculate, almost in unison. Simon cannot believe what has happened. Although he has known for some time that Tristram was attracted to him, and has not exactly rebuffed him, he did not intend for things to move so fast. He feels ashamed. Now Tristram is telling him he loves him. Simon just wants to get away, to be on his own to examine his own feelings.

He extricates himself from Tristram's embrace, and asks where the shower is. He stands under it for a long time, scrubbing himself frenetically. When he comes out at last, Tristram has made toast and coffee. Simon drinks a cup of coffee quickly. He can't face any food. He is embarrassed to catch Tristram's eye.

'Look Tristram,' he says at last, 'about what happened just now. I'm sorry but I don't really know what came over me. I'm not really gay, you see. I've got Juliet and, well, I don't want a relationship with you. I'm really sorry.'

Tristram picks up Simon's coffee cup and puts it in the sink. 'It's OK, I understand. I just want you to know that I love you. I have ever since I first saw you. And if ever you change your mind – well – you know where I am.'

Simon is grateful that Tristram has taken it so well. They walk together to the tube station in silence. Simon remembers his dream. It reminds him of his mother. How disgusted she would be with him. Still, she didn't really like Juliet, either. In fact, he wonders if anyone would ever be good enough for him in her eyes.

***

The rehearsal is soon over. Although Simon plays a major part in the act, it is Clara's role as Jessica that Gerard is unhappy with. She has received some criticism in the press, and he is anxious to make some improvements before there are any more adverse comments. Clara is very depressed, though, and as she and Simon leave the theatre together, she is near to tears. Simon feels a bit sorry for her. It is the first biggish role she has ever had, and she is devastated that she is the one to have been picked out for criticism. Simon can't resist a bit of *schadenfreude* though. Gerard had been very impatient with her while, at the same time, praising Simon's performance, which has made her feel even worse.

'I wouldn't worry about it, if I were you,' says Simon. 'It happens to everyone at some time in their career, even people who go on to become famous.'

Clara sniffs and tries to smile. 'Yes, I expect you're right. It just makes me feel so useless. Especially when he criticises me in front of everyone else.'

'Well, as I said, Gerard is a hard taskmaster, although he's an excellent producer. Come on, the sun's just about over the yardarm, I'll buy you a drink. You need one.'

Clara looks grateful. 'Well, I must say I could do with one.'

As they cross the road together and head towards the pub, Simon catches sight of Tristram out of the corner of his eye. He is walking towards the tube station, looking very dejected. Simon feels a hint of pleasure at this. He likes to play these games, but it scares him when things get out of control, like they did last night.

He goes to the bar and buys the drinks, then he brings them over to where Clara is sitting. She looks so forlorn, almost childlike. He suddenly realises how attractive he finds her. She is slim and gamine, with very short hair. The exact opposite to Juliet who, he now thinks, has an overblown look.

He lets Clara talk, which she loves doing. He has always been a sympathetic listener, dispensing just the right amount of advice when called for. While she drones on, he finds himself reliving the previous night. It now has the quality of a bad dream although, if he's completely honest, when he thinks of their urgent coupling, he feels a vague stirring of desire. What is it with him, he wonders. Most people would be satisfied with a good-looking and talented girl like Juliet. But no, he must be constantly searching for admiration from other quarters. It is the only thing that makes him feel alive. He wonders how he can be attracted to Clara and

Tristram at the same time. And what about Juliet? It doesn't make any sense.

He drags his attention back to what Clara is saying. She has stopped going on about how unfair Gerard has been to her. Now she is asking him if he would like to go with her to see a play her brother is in. Simon realises that she is asking him out, and it is time to call a halt. Life is getting too complicated, although in other circumstances he would have been delighted to take her up on her offer. When he makes an excuse, she looks so crestfallen he almost relents. Perhaps, after all, he will reconsider when Juliet goes on tour. Best to keep things straightforward for now, though.

When they finally leave the pub, it is a quarter to three. Just about time to go home, have a quick shower and shave and come back for the evening performance. He feels tired and hung over, and can think of nothing better than a night off. Still, it is not to be. It suddenly dawns on him that he has not seen Juliet for nearly five days. In fact, he can't even remember exactly which day she is leaving, although he knows it is towards the end of the week. When was it now? He has a feeling it's Friday, but he can't be sure. It'll be written on her schedule, if only he can find it.

With a sudden pang of guilt, he feels he ought to send her some flowers or something. When he gets back to the flat, he goes to the small bureau at her bedside and opens it. All her papers are stacked neatly, and he has no trouble finding the concert schedule. Yes, Friday, as he thought. Just as he is about to put everything back, a small white envelope flutters out of the pile of documents. Intrigued, he picks it up. The envelope is not sealed, so he opens it. Inside he finds the photograph of the two laughing young men. He stares at it for a few seconds. Then he turns it over. 'Horst and Ernst, 1939,' he reads. Horst! Surely that was the name of Juliet's grandfather. In SS uniform! Good God, surely not. He puts the photo carefully back in the envelope and replaces it with the other documents. Then he goes and has another shower. About twenty minutes later he hears the key in the door. When he has shaved and dressed again, he goes into the kitchen, where Juliet is making tea. She looks up, surprised.

'Hi. I didn't know you were coming home this afternoon. Cup of tea?'

'No thanks,' says Simon shortly. 'I've got to go out again in a minute.'

Juliet looks at him. She thinks he seems moodier than usual. 'What's up? Play not going well?'

'Oh, there's nothing wrong with the play.'

'What is it then? You look as if someone just died.'

Simon is silent for a while, then he says suddenly, 'What did you say happened to your grandfather?'

Juliet feels a cold wave of shock run through her. 'He was killed on the Eastern Front. Why?'

'Why didn't you tell me he was in the SS?' he asks.

'Have you been snooping in my things?' says Juliet, angrily.

'I wasn't snooping. I was looking for your schedule, actually, and I just came across this photograph. I suppose you found it when you were going through your Gran's things. Why didn't you tell me?'

'Precisely because I knew this is how you'd react. Anyway, what is it with you? Am I to be held responsible for the actions of my ancestors? I never even knew him. He died years before I was born. Come to that, my father doesn't even remember him.'

'No, I suppose it is unreasonable. I just can't explain how it makes me feel. It just brings it all back, somehow.'

'All what, though, Simon? It all happened years before you were born.'

'Yes, I know,' says Simon slowly. But my mother came to this country with the *Kindertransport*, you know. The whole of the rest of her family were wiped out. Her parents were just able to get her on the transport, and then they were taken to the ghetto, then Auschwitz. It's just too horrible. It's influenced my whole life.'

'I don't see why that has to affect us. I think you're just using it as an excuse, because you're tired of me. You've been cold and distant for weeks. Long before you found that photo.'

Simon is quiet, knowing this to be true.

'Anyway, who's Ernst?' he says at last.

'My great uncle,' say Juliet shortly.

'My God, so it really was in the family. I'm sorry Ju, but I just can't cope with all this.'

'Then you'd better go,' says Juliet quietly.

Simon seems taken aback. He hadn't quite intended things to go this far. He suddenly realises that, of course, it is Juliet's flat, and he really has nowhere else to go.

'I'm not sure that I can find anywhere to go immediately,' he says.

'That's OK,' says Juliet. 'As long as you've gone by the time I come back from the tour. I'll probably stay with Anna till then.'

She picks up her bag and goes out, shutting the door quietly behind her. Simon is left feeling distinctly uneasy. He feels as if a rug has suddenly been pulled out from beneath him.

CHAPTER 16

It is now a month since Gerry left. Jude has had time to take stock of her new situation, and she finds it far from unpleasant. As Gerry needs to realise some capital now that he has new commitments, she has put the house on the market. Although there have been several viewings, she has had no firm offer yet. She is in no particular hurry to sell the house, but she realises that it has to be done sooner or later.

The separation has made very little practical difference to Jude. Gerry was rarely there anyway, just using the house as a pit stop to refuel now and then. Psychologically, though, Jude feels transformed. She feels grown up, at last, in control of her own life, making her own decisions.

She has enrolled on a landscape gardening course, and the people she has met there are the sort of people she probably wouldn't have bothered with in the past. Now they seem more real to her than the smart and moneyed crowd she used to mix with when she was with Gerry. This profound change has made her re-evaluate her past life, too. Now she spends time thinking about her childhood, questioning things that didn't seem to matter before.

As far back as she can remember, her mother seemed to treat her differently from her brother and sister. Arguably the least talented of the three, at least academically, her mother always seemed to be trying to compensate for that. To protect her, somehow. Sometimes, as a child, Jude used to feel that she didn't quite fit in. Her brother was excessively reserved and fairly studious, and Anna was of course the brilliant one, doted on by their father. Perhaps it was just "middle child syndrome", but there didn't seem to be a proper role for her in the family, and that seemed to continue throughout most of her adult life, too.

She had gone more or less straight from her parents' house to marriage with Gerry, never really having a time when she could develop her own personality. Her mother had been good to her when she was a child and Jude knows she has been neglecting her. She resolves to put this right. Now she feels calmer, more able to deal with Ida. Perhaps not wildly happy, but who can expect that? Her only real anxiety is Kate, who went back to university a week late and returned home the following weekend. She has been home each subsequent weekend since then, spending a lot of time in her room or disappearing for hours, God knows where. When she had first gone to Bristol, they hadn't seen her again until the end of the first term, and that is how it had been ever since. Until now.

Dan, on the other hand, went back to Oxford without a backward glance, never even ringing to find out how his mother is. Hugo still comes home from time to time, but he spends the whole time ranting about his father. Jude is not sorry to see him return to London. She realises that it is a measure of her indifference that she feels little rancour towards Gerry, and she is glad.

She is always happy to see Kate, but she wishes that she knew what lay behind her odd behaviour. Jude has just finished showing a youngish couple round the house. In their early thirties, they both work in the city, although the woman says she wants to give up work soon to start a family. Jude tells her the house is ideal for bringing up children. She wonders if this couple will make a better job of it than she and Gerry did. They both seem very keen on the house, praising the garden in particular, and asking who looks after it. She is aware that they are speculating about her circumstances, but does not feel obliged to divulge any personal information. She is relieved when they've gone. Their enthusiasm is no guarantee that they will be putting in an offer. Jude is already beginning to realise this.

Just then, the phone rings. It is Kate. She is at the station and wants Jude to pick her up. Jude sighs when she puts down the receiver, but picks up her coat and leaves straight away. This is the third weekend running that Kate has returned early on Friday evening. Jude wonders if she's skipping lectures, and makes up her mind to ask her when the moment is right. She makes supper for the two of them that evening. Kate is very quiet and doesn't eat much. After they have finished eating, Jude pours herself another glass of wine. She begins, tentatively:

'Kate, please tell me, is there something wrong? Have you got some problem at Bristol? If you have, I'm sure we can sort it out.'

Kate is silent for a while. She takes a sip of Coke.

'No, Mum, there's nothing really. I just feel that there's no point, somehow.'

'No point in what?'

'Well, university and all that. I don't see how a degree in German is going to help me to do anything.'

Jude puts her glass down.

'Well, I would have thought a degree in anything from Bristol is going to help you get a decent job. Surely you're not going to give up now.'

Kate shrugs. 'I can't really see any point in continuing.'

'Kate, I don't understand you. You were enjoying it so much at the beginning. What's happened to make you change your mind?'

'Nothing really. Except that I suppose I've realised that I don't really want a career, as such.'

'What do you want to do then?'

Kate shrugs again. She fiddles with the ring on her Coke can. 'I don't really know. Travel, maybe.'

Now it is Jude's turn to be silent. At one time, she would have flown off the handle if Kate had said suggested such a thing. Now she feels far more tolerant. She even has a sneaking sympathy for Kate. What does it matter, after all, if Kate doesn't fit the stereotype of the middle-class daughter? Just as long as she is happy. But this is just it. She doesn't believe Kate is happy. She starts to clear away the dishes.

'OK, I think I understand,' she says. 'But it's not just that, is it? You don't seem your usual self. You're not ill, are you?'

Kate shakes her head.

'I just keep having these dreams,' she says eventually.

Jude is startled. 'What sort of dreams?' she asks.

'Well, they're more like nightmares, really. I dream that I'm in this bombed out town, and that someone — or several people – are looking for me. More like hunting me down, really. They are wearing some kind of uniform. Anyway, they're after me. Before anything happens, though, I usually wake up. But then I feel really bad for the rest of the day. You know, really tired.'

The recounted dream makes Jude shiver. It seems familiar, almost as though it has awakened some hidden memory. She looks at her daughter. Kate is pale, her eyes are very dark.

'Look Kate,' she says. 'I'm not going to try and make you do anything you don't want to. But please think very carefully before you make any decisions about giving up your course. As for the dreams, do you think you should see Doctor Mason?'

Kate shakes her head vehemently.

'No, absolutely not. After all, they are only dreams.' She gets up from the table. 'I'm shagged. I'm going to bed now, Mum, if you don't mind.'

When she has gone, Jude sits for a long time at the kitchen table. She finishes the rest of the wine in the bottle. Kate's dream does seem oddly familiar, but she can't think why. Perhaps she has had a similar dream herself. As she reflects on Kate's strange behaviour, she suddenly experiences a small shock of recognition. Of course! That must be why Kate is behaving so strangely, and why her eyes seem so dark. She must be on something! Oh God! Why on earth did she not realise it before? She spent half the children's teenage years in a lather of anxiety about drugs and now, just as they seem to have grown up unscathed, it is staring her in the face and she didn't recognise it! It would account for the nightmares, too. Her first instinct is to rush up to Kate's bedroom and confront her, but she makes herself stay where she is. Nothing would be achieved by precipitate behaviour like that, and it would probably only alienate Kate. Best leave it till morning. Jude switches off the lights and goes to bed herself, but it is a long time before sleep comes.

***

The next day Kate is up before her mother. Jude can hardly believe it. She can hear Kate clattering in the kitchen and eventually she comes in with a cup of tea. At least, she thinks, if something good has come out of all this, it's that she and Kate now have a better understanding. By "all this", she means principally Gerry's leaving. Kate looks better today, too. Her eyes seem clearer and the lethargy of the previous evening seems to have gone. Suddenly Jude remembers a paragraph from a drugs information leaflet, telling parents to beware of mood swings! Oh well. Now is clearly not the time to have it out with her. Kate sits on the edge of the bed.

'Mum, have you been to see Gran recently?'

Jude feels a pang of guilt. 'Not very recently, no. I popped in about three weeks ago, but they were having their lunch.' Actually, it had been more like four weeks ago, and she had stayed about five minutes, embarrassed at having to conduct her conversation in front of an avid audience.

'Well, why don't we go this weekend?'

'Yes, all right,' agrees Jude. 'I've a feeling there's something on this weekend. You know, some sort of Christmas celebration. A carol concert or something. They sent us a sheet on the events leading up to Christmas. I've got it somewhere. I'll go and have a look.'

It turns out that there is a Christmas party on Saturday afternoon, and a carol concert on Sunday evening. They decide in favour of the Christmas party, because it will be difficult to talk at the carol concert.

'By the way, Mum,' says Kate. 'What are we doing about Christmas? Shall we have Gran here?'

Jude hasn't thought that far ahead. She thinks the idea is daunting, but realises that her mother can hardly go to Anna's tiny flat, or down to Dover to Edward's house.

'Yes, we could do that,' she agrees. 'But just for the day, though. I don't think I could cope with her overnight.'

***

Preparations for the Christmas party at the Cedars are moving on apace. Both large sitting rooms have been decorated with paper chains and strings of gilt angels. The party is going to run simultaneously in both sitting rooms, as there are now too many residents for just one room. Each has a large tree in the comer, and presents are heaped around the base. A long table has been set up at one end of each, and mountains of mince pies and sausage rolls have been baked. There are bowls of jelly and trifle for those who find crunchier food difficult to eat. Crackers are liberally dispersed among the plates of food.

When Jude and Kate arrive, the residents are already shuffling along the corridor towards one or other of the sitting rooms, and it takes them an age to reach Ida's room, squeezing past the Zimmer frames and walking sticks. Ida is sitting in her chair looking none too pleased. She is wearing a black velvet skirt and a black sequinned jacket. Jude immediately recognises the jacket. She, Anna and Edward had clubbed together, on Anna's instigation, to buy it for Ida's eightieth birthday. She had always admired it, and had been delighted at the time. Now, though, she isn't pleased to be wearing it.

'I don't know what they've dressed me up like this for,' she says. 'Why can't I just wear my old cardigan and skirt?' She says 'vair' instead of 'wear.' It makes her sound very foreign. She has hardly acknowledged Jude and Kate's arrival. Jude wonders if she knows it's them, or if she just thinks it's one of the girls.

'It's for the party, Gran,' says Kate brightly. 'You've got to look your best. Would you like us to take you down now?'

Ida sighs and huffs, but eventually consents to being

197

manoeuvred onto her Zimmer frame by Kate, while Jude hovers helplessly in the background.

'Come on then Gran. Let's go and see what it's all about,' says Kate.

By the time they emerge into the long corridor, most of the other residents have already gone and it is relatively empty, so their progress towards the West sitting room is unimpeded. As they approach, the sound of singing can be heard. The room is very full. Most of the old people are wearing paper hats, although some are sitting in their usual slumped position, seemingly unaware of the activity around them.

The staff are all wearing red Father Christmas hats. Mrs Grimes, the senior care manager, is seated at the piano, and the rest of the staff are gathered round her, singing carols. Some of the younger girls look uncomfortable, clearly not knowing either the words or the tune. One or two of the more compos mentis of the residents join in, while the rest look on with varying degrees of attention. One is tapping the sides of her chair and talking loudly and monotonously to herself.

Gloria sees Jude, Kate and Ida come in and goes to fetch another chair. Ida is installed, and Kate squats on the floor beside her grandmother. Jude perches awkwardly on the arm of the chair. Two of the younger care assistants have dressed up in jeans and cowboy boots, and are now doing a line dancing routine. Kate and Jude clap enthusiastically when it is over. The girls come round with plates of food, and put a sandwich and a mince pie on Ida's plate, which she does not touch.

Then Father Christmas comes round. He is, in fact, Mrs Piggott's adult son, and he does this every year. There is a present for all the residents and a kiss for the women. Ida is unresponsive, appearing to be hardly aware of what is going on, and Jude and Kate find themselves responding for her, almost as you would do for a small child. Jude finds it highly embarrassing. Kate, however, takes it in her stride.

Conversation with Ida is almost impossible because of the general noise level and her deafness. When the party seems finally to be over, they are able to make a quick getaway, as they are nearest to the door. Jude carries Ida's present – talc and soap – and Kate assists her grandmother along the corridor back to her room. Once they are back, Kate helps her to take off her jacket and skirt and put her old clothes on again. This is no easy task.

Again, it is a bit like undressing a child. Ida's arms don't seem to want to bend at the right angle, and Kate struggles for a long time to get the jacket off. Then Ida must be lifted, so that Kate can pull the velvet skirt off and put the other one on. Here Jude helps a bit. When they have finished, they are all panting. Then Ida wants to go to the toilet, so Kate takes her along the corridor, and the whole procedure has to be gone through again.

While Jude is sitting waiting for them to return, she remembers that her mother is unaware that she and Gerry have separated. She dreads the thought of having to explain it all again. Ida is finally back, ensconced in her chair again. Jude sits on the commode and Kate on the bed. Jude tells Ida briefly about Gerry. Ida seems curiously unsurprised. 'Has he got another woman?' She asks directly. Jude is a little taken aback.

'Well yes, as a matter of fact he has,' she replies.

'And is she younger than you?'

Jude nods. 'Yes, considerably,' she says briefly.

Kate looks at her mother in surprise. Up to now she hadn't known that her father had gone off with someone else, although she was vaguely aware that he had had flings in the past. She makes up her mind to ask her mother about it later. So far, she hasn't seen her father since he left, although she is supposed to be phoning him and arranging to have lunch with him. So far, though, she has done nothing about it. She doesn't know why she should have to run after him. Why doesn't he phone her, if he wants to see her?

'Well,' says Ida eventually. 'You are well rid of him my dear. Make sure, though, that you get all that you are entitled to.'

Jude nods. It is sound advice. She fully intends to. For a moment, she wishes she were on her own with her mother. Her mind is crowded with questions about her childhood, which she would prefer to ask in private. She decides to ask them anyway.

'Mum, you know I was wondering about the time we were in Vienna. Before we came to England.'

Ida looks at her sharply.

'I was just – well – wondering if you and Dad had known each other long, before I was born. And whether it was a long time after Edward's father was killed.'

There is a pause. At last Ida says 'What makes you ask? I suppose you have been talking to Anna. I don't understand why she wants to rake up all this ancient history.'

Ida plucks at the buttons on her cardigan. She rocks slightly.

'Well yes, it may be ancient history, Mum,' says Jude bravely, 'but it is after all part of my history, too. I really don't know why I haven't thought about it before. I suppose the older you get the more you want to know about the past – your own past. And there's no one else I can ask.'

'And I suppose you think I'll be dead soon, so you'd better ask me quickly,' says Ida acerbically.

'No, that's not fair. I just never thought of it much when I was younger, but now it seems to matter quite a lot.'

Kate looks at her mother, intrigued. Up to now she has shown no interest in the past. She wonders what has happened to make her suddenly want to know about these things.

At last Ida says, heavily, 'Horst was killed towards the end of the war. I met Ernest, your father, just after the war ended. He came to help the Americans.'

Kate remembers the newspaper cutting, and suddenly realises that her mother doesn't know that they know about Ernest's reason for being in Vienna at the end of the war. Nor that they have seen the photograph of Horst and his brother Ernst in their SS uniforms.

Jude has to be satisfied with Ida's reply. In fact, there is no real reason not to be, although she feels vaguely that Ida has not told her the whole truth.

'Did I speak German then, when I first came to England?'

'Yes, we all did, although by that time I had learnt a little English from working at the American base and, of course, from your father.'

'And how long did it take us to learn English?'

'Oh, very little time. At that age, you know, yours and Edward's, you learn so quickly. In no time you were speaking English better than I.'

'It's amazing that I don't remember any German,' says Jude.

'Well, there was no reason to. Neither your father nor I spoke German to you after we came to England.'

Ida suddenly seems to remember something. She turns to Kate.

'And how is that young man of yours? The German one?'

'He's all right Gran. I haven't seen him since the weekend when you met him. I'm back at uni now, you know.' Kate has a question she would like to ask her grandmother too. She knows it won't be easy, but something is compelling her to ask. She wonders how best to approach it. Ida seems edgy and unapproachable today. Finally she decides to take the plunge.

'Gran,' she say, 'there's something I really need to know.'

Her grandmother looks at her, with a resigned expression, almost as if she knows what is coming next. Kate takes a breath and forces herself to say what's on her mind.

'During the war, did you know what was happening to the Jews?'

The question sounds bald, almost facile, but really there seems to be no other way of dressing it up. Jude is shocked. She cannot believe that Kate has asked such a thing. There is a long silence. Finally, Ida speaks.

'The answer to that is both yes and no. We – I – knew, obviously, that they were having their rights as citizens taken away, before the war. But it didn't happen all at once. It was very gradual, so in a way there was no particular moment when you suddenly thought, I can't put up with this any more. But when that point came, it was too late to do anything about it. At first, you know, they were encouraged to emigrate, and many of them did. But that wasn't easy for them. They had to have all the right papers and money, too. And then the countries they were going to wouldn't take more than a certain number. And we saw some terrible things. Jewish flats were confiscated and just given to Austrian families. All the professional people lost their jobs, and many committed suicide, especially the older people. I even heard that some jumped out of windows, although I never saw such a thing myself.

Ida is silent for a while, twisting her rings. Then she continues:

'We felt powerless at the time, but if we had all got together, we could have done something. Once the war started, many were transported to the East.'

This is what Kate really wants to know.

'So did you know why they were taken to the East?'

'No, I can tell you we did not know. Not till after the war ended, anyway. We thought they were going to labour camps of some kind, but never did we know what was really happening, until afterwards. How could we? How could anyone ever imagine such wickedness? It is simply beyond belief. And then, you know, when we found out what had happened, many people just could not accept it. Even people who had been against the Jews, they could not believe it.'

Kate can believe that. After all, how would people have known? The Final Solution had been kept very quiet. But the fact remains that Ida's husband was in the SS and goodness knows what dreadful tasks he may have carried out. There is a knock at the door and Kim comes in, to ask what Ida would like for supper. Jude and Kate decide that it is time to go home. On their way out, they meet Mrs Piggott in the hall.

'You're Ida's other daughter, I believe?' she says to Jude. 'I just wanted to let you know that we're a bit concerned that your mother isn't eating very much.'

Jude stops, surprised. She is aware that her mother has been looking rather thin recently, but hadn't realised that this had become a problem.

'So what do you think should be done?' she enquires.

'Well, we're trying to find things that she really likes to tempt her, really. And I'm going to get the doctor to pop in and have a look at her. No undue cause for alarm. I just wanted to keep you informed.'

'Yes, well, thank you very much. It's very good of you,' says Jude. She and Kate make their way towards the car in silence; each engrossed in her own thoughts.

***

When Jude and Kate have gone, and Ida is alone again, she carefully wraps her sandwiches in a tissue and pushes them underneath the cushion of her chair. She drinks half a cup of tea. When Kim returns for the tray, she is pleased to see that the sandwiches have gone. She gets Ida ready for bed and helps her in. Ida feels deathly tired after the unaccustomed activity of the day. She thinks back to Kate's question. For years, she has known that this is the one question that everyone has been dying to ask but, until now, no one has dared. She had discussed it with Ernest but since then, with no one. It makes her think of the last months of the war, when Horst had come home on leave less and less frequently. When he did, he looked haunted and deathly pale. By then, no one was getting enough to eat, not even the soldiers at the front.

In spite of the extensive bomb damage, Vienna still looked picturesque in the late spring of 1944. Even now, Ida clearly remembers the beauty of the changing seasons: the golds and reds of the leaves on the trees in the city parks in October and the thick snow on roofs and pavements in the winter. She remembers going for a rare tram ride with Edward that spring, out to Schönbrunn, and walking with him in the palace park, and then down the long Mariahilfer Strasse, the air heavy with the scent of lilac. The tram had clattered home along the Ringstrasse, with its beautiful trees and baroque buildings. On that day, she had felt briefly human again, after the deprivations of the long winter months.

Then Horst came home on his final leave. Although Ida couldn't even find enough food to feed Edward properly, she had managed to scrape together enough coupons to get hold of a bit of scrag-end and some vegetables, with which she made a stew. Horst looked like a ghost. Thin and drawn, he hardly spoke to her and, what was more surprising, paid very little attention to Edward. The child had been looking forward to his father's return for weeks and he couldn't understand it when, instead of taking him on his knee and kissing him, he sat staring into space. In the end, Ida left Horst to his own devices and took Edward out for walks or to visit her mother.

One day she met an old school friend whose husband had served with Horst. Greta had a little girl, about Edward's age, and she invited Ida back to her flat. She made a pot of *ersatz* coffee and she and Ida sat chatting while the two children played on the floor. Greta's husband, Johannes, was home on leave a few weeks earlier, but had since returned to the front. After a bit, Greta went to make sure the door to the landing was closed, and lowered her voice, conspiratorially.

'Isn't it dreadful what's been happening in Belarus?' she begins.

Ida has to admit that she doesn't know what is happening.

'Horst doesn't talk to me. Most of the time he just sits staring vacantly. I can't get him to tell me anything, and he's not even interested in Edward.'

Greta doesn't seem surprised. 'Johannes was very much like that when he came back,' she says, 'and so thin, I couldn't believe it. He was always so well built,' she adds with a touch of pride. 'But on the last night of his leave, he had a few glasses of Schnapps, which we'd kept from before the war, and he started to talk about what it was really like. It seems that whenever they capture a city, they are made to drive all the local people to the outskirts of the town and shoot them. In cold blood.'

Ida is aghast. 'But who? What sort of people?'

'Oh all sorts. Jews, of course, but also communist officials, even teachers. Any so-called intellectuals. Apparently they sometimes have to shoot hundreds of them at a time. Once one of Johannes' comrades said he wasn't going to do it anymore, because he couldn't stand it, so the next thing was they shot him as well.'

Ida stares at Greta. She can hardly believe what she is hearing.

'And the worst thing is,' continues Greta, lowering her voice even more, 'they shoot the women and children too. In fact, they have orders to shoot the children first!'

Ida feels faint. She and Greta look at their own children playing happily on the floor. Has Horst really done that, she asks herself? If he has, no wonder he can't bring himself to play with Edward. She tries to make sense of it.

'But why would they do that?' she asks, 'if the town has capitulated anyway?'

Greta shrugs. 'Who knows? All I know is that it has made Johannes into a different person. And the thing is, he says there is no attempt to hide what they are doing. And it's not just happening in Belarus. It's all over Russia, whenever they capture a town.'

Ida forces herself to finish her coffee. She can't bear to stay chatting with this terrible knowledge inside her. She makes Edward leave his playmate and put on his coat. He doesn't want to go and he starts crying but, for once, Ida is impervious to his pleas. They walk back through the chill, windswept streets. Horst is still sitting exactly where she left him. In spite of the sheer horror of what she has just heard, Ida feels a stab of pity for him. She puts her hand tentatively on his shoulder.

'Horst, what would you like to eat tonight? It's your last evening.' She suddenly wishes she hadn't said that. It seems to underline the finality of it. Horst stares at her, almost uncomprehendingly, and shrugs. She goes to the kitchen and gathers together the ingredients for a thin soup. There is a little black bread and a piece of cheese. Although she feels hollow with hunger, she can't eat, so she sits Edward down at the table with his father, hoping that Horst might take this last opportunity to talk to his son.

While they are eating, she goes into the bedroom to gather Horst's things together for the following day. He is to leave early, on the six o'clock train. As she picks up his jacket, she feels his military papers in the breast pocket. Overcome by a sudden urge to find out if he has in fact been in Belarus, she pulls them out and flicks through them surreptitiously. At first she's not sure where she should be looking. Then she sees it. *Polen*. She knows he's been in Russia, but now he's going to Poland. Thank goodness for that, at least. She reads the name of the place. It means nothing to her. She stuffs the documents back quickly. There is no sound from the next room. She returns to find her husband and son eating in silence. Every now and then Edward looks up at his father, but there is no responding glance from Horst.

Horst goes back for the last time, and the last months of the war grind inexorably on. The bombing raids get worse and worse, and Ida spends night after night crouched in the shelter with Edward. She thinks of going to the mountains with him but, in the end, she doesn't want to leave her mother. Then it becomes just a matter of time until the Allied forces arrive. Ida hasn't heard from Horst for months. Food is appallingly short. They are getting no more than six hundred calories a day, and the population of Vienna is starving. They almost wish for surrender, thinking it cannot be any worse than this.

Then the victorious armies arrive in waves: first the Russians, then the long-delayed arrival of the Western forces in September 1945. All she thinks about from the moment of waking until dropping into an exhausted sleep is getting food. Once the Allied troops are there, everything she or her mother possesses is traded for food. Her mother's prized Persian carpet is exchanged for a vat of cooking fat. Cigarettes become the common currency. By this time, people are leaving the city in droves. Her friend Greta leaves before the arrival of the Russians with her little girl to stay with relatives in the West. Ida has nowhere to go, so she stays put. Eventually, once the Americans establish their base, things get a little better, and food is slightly more plentiful.

There is still no sign of Horst or, indeed, of any of the remains of the Austrian army. It is only much later that they begin to straggle back, spectral and famished. But then news starts to filter through of the concentration camps. At first it is only rumours, but then the full horror is revealed. To start with, people don't want to believe what has happened, but the Americans force the population to watch the films of the opening up of the camps.

Some people are sick; others faint. Ida just feels completely numb. Then news of the death camps in Poland starts to come through, where thousands of men, women and children have been systematically gassed each day. The names become sickeningly familiar: Treblinka, Sobibor, Chelmno, Belzec. As soon as Ida hears them, a shock of recognition runs through her. Sobibor!

That was the name that she read in Horst's papers – his last posting! The thought of what he must have done is almost more than she can bear. The only thing that keeps her going is Edward. If she cracks up, what will become of him?

Her mother is now somewhat recovered, and comes round regularly with food and offers of help. She cannot bring herself to tell her about Horst. Her mother often asks if she has heard from him, and when he is coming home.

At last, one day, Horst appears on the doorstep. He is ragged and filthy and almost transparently thin. Ida stares at him in horror. Edward comes running, shouting '*Pappi, Pappi!*' It seems that Horst hardly recognises him. Ida stands back silently and Horst walks in. She doesn't say a word. For the next few days they live side by side in the house, without communicating. Edward looks from one to the other, uncomprehending. Then, after five days, they come for him. It is early in the morning, just before daybreak. He leaves silently, unresisting. Edward cries for his father. Ida's mother cannot understand what has happened. Only Ida knows.

***

Ida turns over in bed. Her hip is aching dully, and she wants to go to the toilet. She manages to reach the bell by the side of her bed and presses it. After what seems like an eternity, Gloria arrives. Ida blinks as the light from the corridor floods into her room.

'Ida? What is it, darling?'

Suddenly, an overwhelming wave of pure sorrow engulfs Ida. She sobs dryly, but no tears come.

Gloria sits beside her and takes her hand.

'Ida, my dear, whatever is it?' Have you had a bad dream?'

Ida shakes her head. She wishes it were just a dream. At last she says; 'I was thinking back about some terrible things that happened when I was young. You never seem to be able to escape the past. It just seems to seep insidiously into the present, permeating everything; even touching your children, and their children. You're never really free.'

Gloria strokes Ida's cheek.

'Would you like me to bring you something to help you sleep?'

Ida nods gratefully. Gloria helps her to the toilet, and then brings her a sleeping tablet. Soon Ida is in a deep, dreamless sleep. Free, for a few hours, of the torment of her memories.

CHAPTER 17

When Juliet walks out of the flat, she has no idea where she's going. Realising that she will need to pack for the tour, she decides to wait until Simon has left for the theatre and then go back and pick up the stuff she will need. She feels light-headed, almost as though she is going to faint. The cup of tea she had been making never materialised. She has had nothing to eat since breakfast. She goes into a cafe and orders coffee and a sandwich but when it comes she can't eat it. She drinks the coffee though. Then she phones Anna. Fortunately she is in, and immediately agrees that Juliet can stay with her until the tour.

'Are you all right, Ju? Shall I come over?' she asks.

'No, no, it's fine, really. I just need to go back and pack some things when he's gone.' She needs to be on her own for a bit, to think about what happened. Although she's been pretending to herself that things would improve between herself and Simon, she hadn't managed to convince herself. The trouble is, it all happened so suddenly. She can hardly take it in.

All around her, in the cafe, people are chatting with friends and laughing, while she feels as if somebody has just died, the loss is like a physical ache. And yet she knows they were doomed. Simon is incapable of sustaining a long-term relationship with its essential ordinariness. He craves the constant attention that cannot be supplied by one person alone.

There is an edge of anger mixed with her sorrow, though. How could he make out that it is her background that he can't accept? It seems so unlikely that she can't believe it's the real reason. There has to be something else. He must just be tired of her. Recently he's made odd references to her appearance, calling her *Brunhilde*, commenting on how much she resembles her grandmother, as though this were something regrettable. He must have found her attractive at one time, though. But that's typical of Simon, he's never been exactly unwavering.

After about an hour, when she's sure he must have gone, she goes back to the flat. She lets herself in with a feeling of dread. She can feel his presence everywhere. She wonders if, in the end, she precipitated it. Did she, finally, push him out? After all, it was she who said the fateful words. 'You'd better go, then.' They echo in her head now.

Everything now seems pointless. The flat, the packing, the tour. How will she bear it, knowing he won't be there when she returns? Her head is full of him. His haunted expression, his smile, the things he used to say. It had felt so good at the beginning, although there had always been a little worm of doubt. He had seemed elusive from the start. She had never felt completely sure of him. Yet it hadn't prevented her from pursuing him, suggesting that he move in with her – which he did with alacrity.

She tries to force herself to think what she needs to pack, and ends up throwing a random selection of clothes in her bag, sitting down on the bed to cry every now and then. She nearly forgets her schedule, only remembering it at the last minute. Then she sees the envelope. She can't resist opening it, looking again at the photo of the smiling boys. Why had she put it in there, anyway? She'd had some vague idea of using it when she got to Vienna. How, she can't imagine now. She puts it back and packs the schedule, together with her passport. The last thing she wants is to have to come back to the flat before the tour and risk finding him here.

At last the bag is closed. She has a final look round and then walks slowly to the door. Outside, the dying rays of the winter sun light up the windows of the house opposite. The air is beginning to turn chill as night approaches. Her bag is heavy as she walks to the end of the road. This time she feels justified in taking a taxi.

Anna does not cross-question her about what has happened but leaves her alone to settle in. Juliet is grateful for that. She feels bad that Anna and Tony have to move out of their study, but Anna assures her that Charlotte will be home soon, and they would have to move out anyway. The remaining days slip by, with Anna and Tony at the university and Juliet attending the final practices. The day of her departure is soon upon her.

***

Somewhere as gut-wrenchingly beautiful as Heidelberg probably isn't the best place for someone suffering the pangs of a broken romance, thinks Juliet, wryly. Actually, it's not just that it's beautiful, although it is, with its cobbled streets, baroque facades and the castle walls rising ghostly above the glistening Neckar. It's something else, something less definable. Maybe it's the age-old romanticism of the place, with its ancient university and student fraternities. The past seems to be constantly present in the very fabric of the streets and buildings. All Juliet's sense of grief and loss comes rushing to the surface as she walks along the narrow streets to the old market place. A wave of nostalgia sweeps her back to the days of the Student Prince.

They are to play two concerts in the castle itself. Although it is winter, there are a fair number of tourists in the town, mostly Americans. The members of the orchestra have been housed in various small hotels and guest houses, and Juliet finds that she is staying a little way out of town with a very pleasant elderly widow, who lets out rooms in her house from time to time. The house is spotlessly clean, and the breakfast, which is included, is delicious and beautifully presented. There is grey and black bread, various cold cuts of meat, slices of cheese and boiled eggs. The coffee, served in a Thermos jug, is strong but not bitter.

At first, Frau Meyer addresses her in German, confirming Juliet's suspicion that people often take her for a German. She hardly stands out in the crowd here. Frau Meyer is small and neat, her white hair plaited round her head, rather in the style of her grandmother's. Juliet can't help wondering what her experiences were during the war. Of course, she would only have been a child at that time. In the end she plucks up enough courage to ask her if Heidelberg suffered much war damage.

'No, we were very lucky,' replies Frau Meyer. 'We weren't bombed at all, although Mannheim and Ludwigshafen were practically destroyed. It's strange, because although Heidelberg itself is not industrial, we are in the middle of an industrial area. Some say that the Americans avoided Heidelberg on purpose, because they have always loved it so much. I don't know if that's true, though.'

Juliet thinks about this. It's true that the town represents a kind of idealised view of the 'other' Germany, the country of mysterious forests and romantic castles that attracts some people so much.

'And then we received many evacuees during the war from other parts of Germany,' Frau Meyer continues, 'and also refugees after the war ended. And, of course, for many years it was an American base.'

Juliet has the whole day ahead of her, as the first performance is not until the evening. As she has arranged to meet some of her friends from the orchestra for lunch, she decides to spend the morning exploring the town. There is a light covering of snow on the ground, and it is very cold. She is glad she brought her sheepskin coat.

The cobbled main street contains all the usual chain stores and banks but, as soon as she leaves it and wanders into the lanes that radiate from it, she immediately feels that she is in the 'old' Germany again. She crosses the Old Bridge, and pauses to look down on the Neckar below, covered in winter mist. Suddenly she finds herself walking beside a graveyard. When she looks at the inscription, she sees that it is the old Jewish cemetery. There is writing, presumably in Hebrew, below it. She wonders if there are any Jewish inhabitants left in the town.

Lunch is a convivial affair that lasts a couple of hours, and she finds her spirits are lifted, almost in spite of herself. One of the flautists, a young man called Geoff, sits next to her. He is a fresh-faced, slightly gangling young man, a couple of years younger than Juliet. She has always been aware that he finds her attractive. She's never been particularly interested in him but now, after a few glasses of wine, she finds she is getting on with him rather well, and when he suggests spending the rest of the afternoon exploring the rest of the town together, she agrees.

By now, the sun is a great red ball in the sky, sinking lower and lower towards the river. They visit the old university, where she is surprised to find some of the students still wearing fraternity caps. Then they stroll in the castle grounds. They are almost empty. The snow-rimmed foliage stands out against the silvery sky. The silence is profound. As the sun touches the horizon and then starts to sink below it, the whole town seems suddenly transfigured. The castle walls glow red, and the lights in the valley start to flicker on. The sun disappears altogether and, after a while, the moon comes up. Now the castle is lit by artificial light and the moon hangs above it creating a ghostly impression. It is a dramatic spectacle. Geoff takes Juliet's hand, and she doesn't resist.

That evening the crowds start to stream up to the castle early. Soon every seat is taken. The great hall is lit by flaming torches and the light from them catches the sequinned dresses of the women in the orchestra, making them sparkle. The music soars to the rafters, filling players and audience alike with exhilaration.

The next day, their last in Heidelberg, Juliet agrees to meet Geoff for a walk along Philosophenweg, which runs high above the town. More snow has fallen during the night, and they need their boots. The views are breathtaking, and the winter filigree on the branches is exquisite. Juliet finds herself telling Geoff about Simon, although she leaves out the bit about the photograph. Geoff is sympathetic. He has met Simon a couple of times, and knew that while he was on the scene he didn't stand a chance with Juliet. Now things look more hopeful. He knows that he will have to take things slowly though. The second night in the castle brings more rapturous applause. Juliet is sorry to be leaving Heidelberg, and makes up her mind to return, perhaps in the spring.

The next venue is Berlin. This time they travel by train, and Juliet is glad of the opportunity to be alone with her own thoughts. She purposely avoids Geoff, taking a window seat next to a businessman who is engrossed in his sales figures. She stares out of the window as the flat fields rush past, interspersed with small picturesque villages. The stations are, without exception, clean and neat. What a difference from the view from the window of the Dover train, when she leaves London from Charing Cross to visit her parents. Once the grimy backs of the shabby Victorian buildings have petered out and they are into Kent, the stations that fly past are usually bleak and unmanned. What she has seen of Germany so far seems to be relentlessly well laid out and orderly.

So many aspects of life in Britain seem to teeter on the brink of the abyss, scarcely able to cope with the demands of a modern society. The roads, the railways, the hospitals, the schools are all worn out and struggling to accommodate a larger and more demanding population than the one for which they were designed. That pressure doesn't seem to exist in Germany, where such things are modern and purpose-built. Perhaps, though, it is because she lives in London. Maybe she will get to Berlin and find that it is beset by the same problems.

After the euphoria of the concert in Heidelberg, Juliet's pain has returned with a vengeance. She is unable to stop thinking about Simon. She tries to concentrate on her book, but finds her mind constantly wandering back to their last conversation in the flat. What if she had been more conciliatory, had attempted to persuade him to stay, instead of telling him to go in such an uncompromising fashion? She considers sending him a text message, even gets her phone out a couple of times but, at the last moment, thinks better of it.

After about an hour and a half, Geoff walks along from his seat, a few carriages further down the train, and asks if she would like to go with him to the buffet car for a coffee. She agrees readily, anxious now to escape from the endless rhetorical questions she is asking herself, and follows him along the swaying train. It has reached its maximum speed, and the landscape is flashing past so fast that it is no longer possible to distinguish individual features. Once again, she thinks how different it is from the Dover train, which lurches and rattles along at varying speeds, sometimes coming to a complete and inexplicable stop for up to twenty minutes at a time.

They perch on high stools in the buffet car, sipping the hot coffee, as Germany streaks past in a green blur. Geoff can see that Juliet is feeling sad today, but he doesn't press her to confide in him. Instead, he keeps the conversation light and general. Juliet is grateful for this. She has to admit to herself that she feels surprisingly comfortable and relaxed in his company. It is somehow undemanding, in a way that Simon's presence never was.

They discuss the concert and their own performances. Just then, Juliet's phone beeps in her bag. Startled, she takes it out. There's a message from Simon. It consists of just one word. 'Sorry.' Juliet feels colour rushing to her face. What can it mean? Sorry that it's over, or sorry, let's start again? She has simply no idea. Geoff is tactfully looking out of the window. She switches her phone off and decides to think about what, if anything, to reply later. Eventually the train slows down as it approaches Wannsee station.

Once again, the members of the orchestra are scattered between different hotels. Juliet is staying in a hotel called the Kronprinz, on the Kurfürstendamm, Berlin's main shopping street. Her taxi races along at a speed that would be unimaginable in London. There is the inevitable roar and bustle of a capital city. The Christmas lights make an impressive display, both in the street and in the shop windows. The shoppers, hurrying in and out of the sumptuously decorated shops, are dressed more formally than in London. Many of them wear hats and fur coats. Even from the taxi, Juliet is aware of a general air of affluence.

***

The Kronprinz is not luxurious or very modern, but it is clean and comfortable, and well placed for sightseeing. Four or five members of the orchestra are staying there. Geoff is not among them. As they will only be there for two nights, it doesn't seem worth unpacking everything, so Juliet just takes out her overnight things and her concert dress, which she hangs in the cavernous wardrobe.

She has a shower and then lies on the bed for a while in her bathrobe, idly flicking through the channels on the enormous mahogany-encased TV set which dominates the room. She is beginning to remember how much she enjoys the slightly nomadic feeling of being on tour. There's a kind of abnegation of responsibility which makes her feel that she can do pretty much what she likes, as long as she turns up at the appointed time and plays her bit. Her eyes begin to feel heavy and the warmth of the room has its effect on her. When she awakes, it is dark outside and the television is flickering silently. She stretches out her hand to switch on the bedside light, and peers at her watch. It is already quarter to eight. Realising that she needs to eat something if she is to sleep tonight, she hastily pulls on jeans and a sweater and goes down to find out if she can dine in the hotel.

Fortunately, there are a couple of free places at a table, which is already occupied by Julius (clarinet) and Emil (first violin). She is already beginning to realise that German food is rather

219

monotonous. It is nearly always some kind of pan-fried escalope –
pork or veal – or sausage or roast chicken.

Not one of them lingers over the meal. Julius and Emil go to
the lounge to have coffee, but Juliet goes straight back up to her
room. She switches on the TV again, trying to find something
worth watching. There is a discussion, with a lot of serious-
looking, bespectacled men standing round a table, each talking
in turn, an oompah band in a wine cellar and a semi-nude
caper, involving some fat and not very young men and women.
Finally she finds the news on CNN. That's better than nothing,
so she watches for a bit. She is aware that she hasn't yet answered
Simon's text message. She's not sure if she's going to. When she
first received it, it half awakened hope again, and she wishes in
a way that he hadn't sent it. She eventually decides to leave it
unanswered for the time being.

That night she dreams that Mozart's violin sonata in G is being
played in a large and unfamiliar concert hall. The violinist plays
particularly brilliantly. When he stands at the end to take a bow,
she realises that it is her grandfather, Horst. She awakens from the
dream feeling unaccountably troubled.

As she is getting ready to go down to breakfast, her phone
beeps again. She gropes for it in the bottom of her bag, not really
wanting to read the new message. This time it is slightly longer:
'Can you forgive me, Ju? Please answer.' Now the meaning is
unequivocal. As she reads it, she feels her heart leap. He wants
her back! Full of joy and relief she goes down to the breakfast
room, where guests of all nationalities are helping themselves at
the buffet that is placed in the middle of the room. She takes
some fruit and a roll and butter, and pours herself some coffee.
She is amazed to see a diminutive Japanese woman pile her plate

so high that half of it is in danger of falling off.

She sees Julius sitting alone, and feels obliged to go and sit with him, although she would really rather be on her own. She continues to think about Simon's message and, after a while, her initial pleasure starts to give way to indignation. How can he treat her in such a cavalier way? The trouble is, she knows him too well. She knows that he needs the stability of their relationship to enable him to carry on his flirtations, safe in the knowledge that he can always come home to her. And that's another thing. Home! He won't have one, unless he patches things up. How cynical he is! Again, she decides to leave the message unanswered.

Once again, the first day is spent sightseeing. Berlin doesn't have the romantic beauty of Heidelberg, but she finds it vibrant and exciting. After thirty years of stagnation as a divided city, it seems to be racing to make up for lost time, revelling in the huge new challenges that it is facing.

She strolls down the Ku'damm, looking in the beautifully decorated shop windows, then through the imposing Brandenburg Gate and along Unter den Linden, virtually closed to Western tourists for so long. She is beginning to realise that not everyone in Berlin is well off by any means. As soon as she is away from the main shopping district, the people start to look down at heel, needy. Some are selling trifling objects from homemade pitches, others are openly begging. Many of these people are clearly not German at all, but Eastern European: Poles, Hungarians, Romanians.

She has arranged to meet Geoff for tea – or rather, coffee – at the Kranzler Cafe. They sit upstairs, watching the crowds on the Ku'damm and eating slices of *Sandkuchen*.

'My grandmother used to make this,' Juliet tells Geoff.

The concert is to begin that evening at seven thirty. By six Juliet is standing outside the main door of her hotel waiting for her taxi. The cold is intense, although there is no snow yet. It's too cold to snow, thinks Juliet, as she waits, shivering. She can't remember ever experiencing anything like it. It's a numbing, penetrating cold, which makes you long to be back inside – anywhere. Momentarily she thinks of the endless, freezing winters her grandmother must have endured during the war. And then, of course, there was no central heating and probably little in the way of warm clothes. The concert is again sold out and the audience, if not as rapturous as the one in Heidelberg, is enthusiastic.

Afterwards, several other members of the orchestra, including Geoff, come back to the Kronprinz for a drink. The atmosphere is relaxed and convivial. Apart from one or two prickly characters, they are old friends. Eventually the conversation turns to Germany and the Germans.

'It's hard to imagine what it must have been like here at the end of the war,' says Julius. 'By all accounts, it was just a pile of rubble by the time the Allies had finished with it. It makes you wonder how they managed to rebuild it, and so quickly.'

'Yes,' adds Emil, 'and it wasn't just attacked from overhead. When the Russians arrived, they shelled all the buildings that were still standing. What a nightmare that must have been. Anyone who could escape had already done so, and the rest of them, well, it was just too late.'

'Well anyway, it serves them right,' says Julius. 'They had it coming to them.'

'I'm not sure about that,' puts in Geoff. 'It's always the innocent, or relatively innocent, who suffer in situations like that. All the top dogs, the decision-makers, had already got out or committed suicide. It's always the weak or powerless who suffer most.'

Juliet is silent. She is thinking about her grandmother. Wondering, again, what she must have gone through.

'Yes, well, I'm sorry, but they were all guilty of complicity, of looking the other way,' says Julius obstinately. Juliet looks at him. She wonders if he's Jewish. He has that slightly aquiline look. An older version of Simon. Eventually all the rest go to bed, and Juliet and Geoff are left in the bar.

'Another drink?' asks Geoff.

Juliet hesitates. 'Yes, alright, I'll have a brandy,' she says. The drink has made her feel mellow, relaxed. Geoff returns with the drinks. He picks up the conversation again.

'You know, it's all very well to say they deserved it, but surely the women in the maternity hospital didn't deserve to be raped. The pregnant ones, the ones who had just given birth, the nurses, everyone. It's just horrific.'

Juliet nods. 'Yes, yes of course you're right.' Again, she thinks of her grandmother. 'Anyway,' she says, 'that's enough depressing conversation for one night. How about coming to my room for a coffee? I don't think we'll get one here.'

It's true that the barman, a man of about sixty, is ostentatiously putting glasses away and generally tidying up. He clearly wants to go to bed. Juliet hopes he can't understand enough English to have followed their conversation. Geoff accepts the invitation with alacrity. Actually, he can't believe his luck. They pay for their drinks and the barman closes the bar with finality.

Afterwards, Juliet cannot believe she has been so forward. It is most out of character, but it seems to be a kind of turning point for her, a final letting go of Simon. She has relinquished any hope that things might work out for them, and she feels a strong desire to reconnect with ordinary life, to shake off the shackles of her attachment to him. It is only later that she realises that in order to do so, she may be using Geoff. The coffee forgotten, Juliet takes Geoff by the hand and leads him to bed. She pulls him down beside her and they start kissing. She can feel him fumbling urgently with the buttons on the back of her concert dress, and breaks off to take the dress off herself, in case it gets torn. She hangs it up in the wardrobe and returns to the bed. Soon they are both carried away on a wave of desire that is unlike anything Juliet has experienced for a very long time. Geoff is a considerate, if not greatly experienced lover. As she climaxes she experiences a wave of relief that is almost physical, as though she is now permanently free of Simon. Geoff is honest and straightforward in contrast to Simon's evasiveness. She feels somehow restored. She doesn't love Geoff, but they feel good together and the relationship is undemanding, at least from Juliet's point of view.

Geoff had intended to leave before morning, to save any embarrassment, but they both fall asleep. When they awake the next morning, they make love again, more slowly this time, but with even greater pleasure. Juliet decides not to go down to breakfast, and they wait until they are sure that Julius and Emil will have left the dining room.

They spend the day exploring the main sights of the city – the Reichstag, the Olympic Stadium, the Remembrance Church. By four o'clock Juliet has had enough and decides to go back to the hotel to have a rest before the evening performance. She goes back alone, aware of the need to keep a brake on the developing relationship with Geoff. When she returns to her room, there is a third message from Simon. 'Please answer me Ju, I can't bear the suspense.' She knows now what she must do. She texts him straight back.

'OK. Here's your answer. It's over.' Then she turns the phone off and falls straight into a deep sleep, which lasts until the alarm rings at six o'clock.

***

As Juliet and Geoff are leaving the concert hall by the stage door, a tall figure steps out of the shadows and comes towards them. Juliet experiences an unpleasant jolt of surprise. Occasionally, in the past, someone from the audience has hung around for her after the concert, wanting to invite her out for a drink and once, a middle-aged man followed her from venue to venue, trying to get her to come out with him. She looks up warily as he addresses her:

'Excuse me, I believe you are Juliet,' he says in clipped, over-precise English.

Something about his voice seems familiar, and she looks at him more closely. He looks like many young Berliners – long hair tied in a ponytail, various body piercings.

'Yes. Do I know you?' she asks.

'We met once in Chislehurst. You are Kate's cousin, no?'

Then Juliet understands. It is Christoph, Kate's boyfriend. She remembers now that he was from Berlin.

'However did you know I was here?' she asks in amazement.

Christoph shrugs. 'It was not hard, you know. Kate told me that you play in an orchestra and that you will be playing in Berlin before Christmas. I already know the name of the orchestra, so all I have to do is come to the concert and wait outside for you afterwards.'

'Well, it's nice to see you again,' says Kate uncertainly. After all,

225

they only met once, briefly, so she is puzzled that he should bother to look her up. Then she remembers that Geoff is still waiting for her.

She introduces him, and Christoph gives a stiff little bow, which is out of keeping with his eccentric clothing.

'I would like to invite you for a drink,' he says, 'and your friend too, of course.'

Juliet hesitates. Nothing has been mentioned between Geoff and herself about the sleeping arrangements for that night. She sees an opportunity to slow things down a bit. She turns to Geoff now:

'Look, I'll just have a quick drink with Christoph, then I'll make my own way back tonight. I'll call you tomorrow, OK?'

Geoff has to accept it, although he looks disappointed.

'See you tomorrow, then,' he says, kissing her lightly on the cheek.

Christoph and Juliet make their way to the Kreuzberg district, where the streets are full of colourful characters of every hue, and cafes and clubs abound. Music blares out from every doorway. Christoph clearly knows the area well, and heads purposefully towards a bar where the music is more subdued.

Juliet is tired and doesn't really feel like drinking. She has a coffee and a brandy, though. Christoph brings the drinks back to the table and squeezes in beside her on the narrow wooden bench. The bar is full of smoke and all around them people are talking in loud voices and laughing.

'I expect you find it odd that I come to find you like this,' he begins. 'Although, of course, I greatly enjoyed the concert,' he adds hastily, 'especially the Prokofiev.

'Yes, that's my favourite too,' says Juliet equably. She pauses, to allow him to continue.

'The truth is, I really wanted to talk to you about Kate. She's been acting very strangely recently.'

Christoph takes out a tin of tobacco and starts to roll a cigarette.

'We were very close you know and, since a month or so, I do not hear from her. She has gone – you know – cold.' He puts the cigarette to his lips and lights it. Juliet takes a sip of brandy. The effect is almost instantaneous. She can feel it warming her body as it goes down. She's aware that Kate hasn't seemed to be herself recently, from comments made by Anna. It seems she's lost interest in her university course.

'Well, did you know that her parents have split up?' she asks at last.

Christoph looks shocked. 'No, I do not know that.'

'Well, her father left home about a month ago, I suppose. Although, to be honest, he was never very present anyway.'

Christoph looks thoughtful.

'And, you know, she is smoking far too much dope. It is not good for her.'

Juliet has to admit that Kate is rarely to be seen without a joint in her hand, except when her mother is around, of course.

'Also, you know that there have been some family problems,' she continues. 'for example, my Gran is in a home now, and she seems to be going through some sort of mental trauma. Kate was always very close to her, and I think she's been affected by that, too.'

'Yes,' says Christoph eagerly. 'I remember that. I could not understand why she does not live with Kate's mother.'

Juliet looks at him. He's probably about her own age, and yet he seems to see things so simplistically. Does he really not understand the pressures that can exist within a family? She remembers that he worked with the homeless. Surely that must have taught him something! Various strange-looking people come and go in the bar, and many of them greet Christoph warmly.

She assumes that they are his clients.

Christoph is suddenly confiding: 'You know, Juliet, Kate loved Germany above everything but now, somehow, things have changed. At one time she wanted nothing more than to come to Berlin, but now she always makes excuses. She seems – well – detached, as though she is not living in the present any more.'

Juliet thinks that's an odd way to put it, and yet it does seem to describe Kate's state of mind. She suddenly thinks of the photo of her grandfather and great uncle again, and the article that Kate translated. Perhaps this has influenced her, but she can't think why it would.

'Look Christoph,' she says at last, 'you must understand that I don't see that much of Kate. Although I like her, we live very different lives. I don't think I can really help you.'

Christoph looks dejected. For a horrible moment, she thinks he's going to cry.

'No, I understand. I shouldn't have bothered you.'

'It's no bother. I'm just sorry I can't help any more.'

Christoph enquires politely where the tour is going next. When she tells him that the next stop is Warsaw, and the last Vienna, he looks up with interest.

'Ah, Vienna, I believe that is where your grandmother comes from. Have you been there before?'

'No, never,' replies Juliet.

'Then that should be very interesting for you. Kate has no plans to join you?'

Juliet shakes her head. They finish their drinks and go out into the bitter night. The sky is full of stars, and a cold, crescent moon hovers above the buildings opposite. For a moment, Juliet feels disorientated. Christoph walks with her to the nearest taxi rank and makes sure the driver knows where to take her. Then he bids her a formal goodbye. In the taxi, Juliet thinks over the conversation. Perhaps Kate has been more affected by her parents' break-up than she imagined. Or perhaps there is something else – quite different – which has caused her to change.

CHAPTER 18

The sound of the bell drills into Anna's brain. She dreams that she is back in school again, and that the bell marks the end of lessons. She and her friend gather their things together and run joyfully through the school gate. The bell keeps ringing, though, and the sound begins to force its way through the layers of her subconscious. At last it breaks through to the surface, and she realises she is no longer dreaming, and the bell is still ringing. When the phone goes in the middle of the night, it is rarely good news. Her first thought is of her mother. It must be the Cedars. She struggles to a sitting position and picks up the receiver. As she says hello she can feel her voice shaking.

'Anna? Is that you? It's Jude.'

'Jude? My God! Whatever's the matter? Are you alright?'

Anna manages to squint at her watch, which is lying on the bedside table. It's a quarter to three.

'Anna, it's Kate. I can't wake her.'

Anna wonders briefly why Jude is trying to wake Kate up in the middle of the night. She waits for Jude to continue.

'She brought a couple of friends home after the pub closed. You know, that big one she works in. Well, I say friends. They looked pretty disreputable types to me. Anyway, I went to bed and woke up about half an hour ago. It was quiet downstairs, and something just made me go down to see if they'd gone. Well, they had, but Kate was lying on the sofa and she looked really odd. I tried to wake her to get her to go up to bed, but I just can't. She seems to be unconscious.' Anna is fully roused by now.

'Jude, you must call an ambulance immediately. Don't delay. And in the meantime, have a look round to see if you can see what she's taken. They'll want to know. And I'll get straight in the car and come over.'

'Yes, all right. Thanks Anna.'

By this time, Tony is awake and wanting to know what's happening. Anna explains briefly as she gets dressed. She's had enough experience of students at the university to know Kate's probably OD'd on something.

By the time she arrives at Jude's house the ambulance is already there, and Kate is being carried into it. Jude travels with her in the ambulance and Anna follows in her car. The A&E department of the local hospital is busy, even at this time of night, mainly with young men with bloody faces and fists and a few wailing children, but Kate is attended to immediately. She is already beginning to come to, tossing her head from side to side and muttering to herself. Jude turns to Anna, distraught.

'I feel so bad, Anna. I thought she was taking something but I kept putting off tackling her about it. We'd been getting on better, you see, since Gerry left, and I didn't want to spoil that.'

'Talking of Gerry, do you think you ought to let him know? After all, he is her father.'

Anna's reproving tone needles Jude, as it has always done.

'Yes, of course, but there's no need to phone until tomorrow,' she says shortly.

Kate is moved amazingly quickly to a small private room off a main ward. She is making a satisfactory recovery without having to have her stomach pumped. She is muttering incoherently to herself, though. To her surprise, Anna realises she's talking German.

'*Bitte lass mich in Ruhe. Ich habe nur ein bisschen Geld, aber du kannst mein Schmuck nehmen.*'

'What is she talking about?' asks Anna uneasily. 'Schmuck means jewellery, doesn't it?'

Jude shrugs. 'Perhaps she's having one of her nightmares.

Anna looks at Jude. 'What do you think she's been taking?'

'Well, at first I thought she was just smoking pot, but I think this is something different. Those people she's been hanging around with recently. I'm sure they're pushers, or something.'

Suddenly, Kate is gasping for breath, and they have to give her oxygen. She quietens down again. Finally, she falls into a fitful sleep.

The nurse suggests that they go and get a cup of tea. She says Kate is over the worst and should just sleep now. Anna and Jude make their way along the warren of corridors, following the signs to the cafeteria. Although it is by now four o'clock in the morning, the level of activity in the hospital seems almost as high as during the day. The only difference is that the subdued artificial lighting gives the place an unreal feel. Stretchers are still being pushed along the corridors and the medical staff are coming and going.

Only when they look into the wards do things seem relatively quiet, although even there nurses are padding around and a voice calls out every now and then. Eventually they arrive at the cafeteria. The food counter is shrouded in darkness, but there are various machines dispensing drinks and packets of sweets and biscuits.

Jude is looking ashen and exhausted, and Anna tells her to sit down while she fetches a couple of cups of coffee and two chocolate bars. Apart from an elderly woman, they are the only occupants of the room. Anna notices that her sister seems to have given up the constant battle that she used to wage with her weight. Gerry had been critical of Jude's size, and she had always been following some faddish diet or other. Now her breasts and stomach bulge from her tracksuit and her face, always round, is even fuller. Fat women don't wrinkle though, thinks Anna ruefully. She herself couldn't be more different. She is taller than Jude and slim, almost to the point of scrawniness. The only similarity between them is their colouring. Both have fair hair and pale skin. Anna's hair is streaked with grey and Jude's, although previously dyed to a brighter shade of blonde, now has grey roots, which are beginning to show through.

'I just wish I'd picked up on this before,' reiterates Jude. 'I kept hoping that it was just a one-off, and that it would go away but, if I'm honest, Kate hasn't been herself for a few months now. She doesn't want to finish her university course, you know.'

'Really?' says Anna. 'I thought she was so keen on German.'

'Well, she was. But now she says there's no point in getting a degree. Says she wants to travel.'

'Ah well, that's what they all want to do,' says Anna dryly.

'And then she was so keen on that German boy, Christoph, and now we don't hear anything about him any more. And she's reading obsessively all the time about the Nazis. Really, it's most unhealthy.'

Anna is startled. She unwraps a lump of sugar and puts it in her coffee, then reaches for a spoon. She doesn't normally take sugar in coffee but, this time, she feels in need of a quick boost of energy.

'Jude, you know, I ought to tell you, when we were clearing out Mum's house, Juliet and myself, that is, we found something.'

Jude looks up questioningly. 'What kind of thing?'

'Well, we found a photograph. It was of Mum's first husband, Horst, and her brother. They were in the SS, Jude!'

Jude looks incredulous.

'Does Kate know about this?'

'Well, that's just it, yes she does. Juliet told her, and she also asked Kate to translate an article about our father. It seems he was in charge of a team of Nazi hunters.'

Jude draws in her breath. 'Well, why ever didn't anyone tell me?'

Anna looks uncomfortable. She pauses. At last she says 'Well actually, Jude, I suppose I didn't think you'd be very interested. But the thing is, I'm now wondering if the whole thing has been playing on Kate's mind. I know it upset Juliet. She felt that it might affect her relationship with Simon. Especially, you know, as Horst was actually her grandfather. And in fact it did, because they have now split up, and I believe it had something to do with it.'

Anna feels rather ashamed that she had not said anything to Jude. After all, she has as much right to know as any of them. Jude finishes the remains of her coffee. She is resentful that she was the only one not to be told. It's typical of Anna, she thinks. Anna probably thought that she was too shallow and silly to take it in. However, she has to admit that, up until recently, the past had had little importance for her. She herself then wonders if this could have had an effect on Kate.

They return to Kate's ward. The night sister is a diminutive Filipino, whose grasp of English is limited but whose medical knowledge seems to be boundless. Anna is struck by how the entire staff of the hospital seems to be various shades of brown or black, and that they spend most of their time caring for elderly white people. She wonders how the hospitals could be run without them all. As they enter the room, the night sister and a Nigerian registrar are setting up a drip and taking a blood sample. They work quietly and deftly together, hardly needing to communicate verbally at all. When they have finished, the registrar turns to them.

'Which one of you is this young lady's mother,' he asks.

'I am,' says Jude.

'Well, she's going to be all right now. We've just taken some blood samples to make sure her system is clear, and the drip is in because she's a little dehydrated, but she should sleep now. You'll be able to talk to her tomorrow, and anyway, the hospital social worker will want to speak to you and her.'

'Oh, yes, I see,' stammers Jude 'Well, we might as well go home then.'

She takes a tentative step towards Kate and lays her hand on her arm. There is no response.

'I'll ring Gerry in the morning. There's no point in worrying him now,' she says.

Anna drops Jude off at her house and returns to her flat. By the time she's back, Tony is just getting up. Fortunately, Anna isn't teaching that day, so she gets straight into the still-warm bed. Just before she drops asleep, she thinks again about her niece. Has Kate been affected by what she has found out about her family and, if so, why has the effect been so profound? Jude says she'd been having bad dreams, and now she's taken an overdose, although probably not intentionally. She is surprised that Jude now seems to be showing some belated interest in the family history herself. Anna sighs and closes her eyes. Soon, all these unanswered questions drift away, and she is in a deep sleep.

***

About lunchtime the next day, Anna gets a call from Jude to say that Kate is home. They had both had a session with the hospital social worker that morning, and Kate had to agree to attend half a dozen drug counselling sessions. Then she was allowed home. When Anna asks how she is, Jude says she's very subdued, rather embarrassed, if anything, but that otherwise she's OK. Anna thinks of offering to go round to see her, but then thinks better of it. It would probably just add to Kate's embarrassment.

'Her father's coming to see her this afternoon,' says Jude. 'I thought I might make myself scarce. Actually, Anna, I was thinking, if you haven't anything better to do, how about going to see Mum?'

Anna is astonished. Jude's never been exactly keen to go and visit Ida. She agrees immediately, though.

'As a matter of fact,' Jude goes on, 'I've been thinking a lot about what you told me last night. In fact, I can't get it out of my head. Just recently – before yesterday, that is – I've been racking my brains to remember something about my own childhood in Austria, but unfortunately it's very little. I just thought Mum might be able to shed some light on it.'

They agree to meet at the Cedars. By the time Anna arrives, although it's only about three o'clock, the light is already disappearing. It's been one of those days when it's never seemed to get properly light. The Cedars is cheerfully illuminated though, and a brightly lit Santa Claus is pulled on his sledge over the main entrance.

Jude arrives a little late, looking flustered. It seems Dan turned up just as she was leaving. Jude had been surprised to see him. She'd told him about Kate but, knowing Dan, hadn't really expected him to show up. Gerry was already there when Dan arrived. It was the first time the two had met since Gerry left home, and the atmosphere had been strained, to say the least. She'd decided to leave them to it, though. After all, her presence was hardly going to make things any smoother.

As they enter the Cedars the now-familiar smell of cooking greets them. Lunch has just finished and they join the queue of residents shuffling back to the lounges or to their rooms. Anna experiences the usual sense of foreboding. Each time she visits her mother she wonders what state of mind she will be in. This time, Ida is lying on her bed facing the wall. Anna wonders if she's been down to lunch or if she's eaten in her room. Jude, who hasn't seen her since the visit with Kate a couple of weeks ago, is again struck by how emaciated her mother looks. Anna approaches her mother and shakes her arm gently. She feels guilty about waking her, but if they were to allow themselves to be put off each time Ida appeared to be asleep, Ida would never have any visitors at all. Eventually she stirs. She moans softly to herself.

Anna gets the feeling that she does not want to be dragged back to consciousness. However, eventually she turns towards them. When she sees Jude, a smile lights her face.

'Jude my dear, and Anna of course, how nice to see you.'

Ida is helped into a sitting position and a tray of tea is brought in by Kim. The conversation is general at first, mainly led by Anna. She tells Ida that Juliet is now away on tour. The subject of Juliet's split with Simon is avoided, as, of course, is Kate's latest escapade. The niceties over, Jude can contain herself no longer. She has always been more direct than Anna, less afraid of causing offence.

'Mum,' she begins, 'there's something that we – Anna and I, that is – really want to know.'

A weary, resigned look crosses Ida's face.

'Yes, my dear, what is it?'

'Well, we know that Edward's father was a member of the SS and that your brother was too.'

Anna is shocked. She can't believe that Jude is saying this.

'Well,' continues Jude, 'we want to know what he actually did. You know, if he was involved in any of the atrocities.'

Again, Anna is horrified. This 'we' that Jude keeps using makes her squirm with embarrassment. She had thought that Jude's intention was just to ask about her own childhood. Not this. Ida is silent for so long that both the sisters think she isn't going to answer at all.

Then eventually she says, 'Oh yes, my dear, I'm afraid he was. Very much so, in fact.'

Jude and Anna are astounded. They had not expected such a direct answer. They wait tensely for Ida to continue.

'I think you know that he was sent to the Eastern Front almost straight away.'

'Yes,' says Anna, 'you said he was killed there.'

'Well he wasn't,' says Ida shortly. 'He was fighting there for almost the whole duration of the war and, over the years, he must have witnessed some horrific events, because when he came home on leave, he had changed. It was gradual at first then, later, when he used to come home he wouldn't speak to me. He just sat staring into space. In the end he didn't even have any time for Edward.'

'Why do you think he changed like that?' asks Jude.

'Well, I found out from a friend, whose husband was fighting in the same general area, what had been going on. It seems that every time they captured a town, they had to round up the local Jews and dignitaries and shoot them. But it wasn't just the men. It was the women and children too. And this happened over and over again.'

Jude and Anna are silent, stupefied.

Ida goes on in a low voice, 'Although he wasn't against the Jews in the beginning, he must have been exposed to the Nazi propaganda more than I realised, because when I questioned him about things that were happening in Vienna, he became very angry and told me I did not understand. He said the measures were necessary to rid us of the pernicious evil, as he called it.'

'How awful for you, Mum,' says Anna.

'Well, you say that, but then to some extent I was also implicated. On many occasions I turned a blind eye. For example, when the SS came and took away Jewish families, I just crossed over to the other side of the street. You see, as soon as you have children, they are hostages to fortune. That is what I tell myself now. Perhaps though that's just an excuse. Perhaps it is simply cowardice.'

Anna thinks of her conversation with Tony. How do any of us really know how we would act?

Jude finds her voice: 'Did you speak to him about it?'

Ida sighs. 'I tried to, but by that stage we weren't really speaking to each other in a normal way. Or rather, he wasn't speaking to me. The situation had become impossible.'

'It must have been dreadful for you, Mum,' says Anna again.

'Well, I think it was worse for him. In a way I felt sorry for him, although I knew, or rather suspected, what he had been doing. Those men who were on the Eastern Front, when they came home on leave they were like ghosts. It was as though they had had all the humanity knocked out of them. Really, it was appalling.'

'But you told us he was killed,' persists Jude.

'Well, I tell you now my dears, he wasn't killed in the war.'

Anna is taken aback. Her mind races over the possibilities. If he wasn't killed in the war, then perhaps Edward remembers correctly, and Horst, not Ernest, is in fact Jude's father. Jude does not seem to have understood the implication, though.

'Why did you tell us he was, then?' she asks impatiently.

Ida sighs. 'I said that to spare you from the truth,' she says. 'And to spare myself from having to tell people what really happened.'

Anna feels a cold wave of fear run through her. What can be coming next? Jude is staring fixedly at her mother. Ida seems unusually calm now. All the rocking and twitching has stopped, and she is sitting very still.

'If I don't tell someone now, I think I shall go mad,' says Ida.

'Tell us what?' asks Jude.

'Towards the end of the war he came home on leave. He was in an even worse state than usual. Gaunt, silent, terrified. Just before he left, I looked in the pocket of his uniform jacket to see where he was going next. I found a piece of paper with his next posting written on it. At the time it didn't mean anything to me. It was only later.' Ida pauses. She sits very still.

'Well, so what was it?' prompts Jude.

'Sobibor. He was going to Sobibor.'

Jude looks puzzled but Anna's heart lurches. She casts her mind back to the conversation with Tony. He had named the death camps – only four of them – that had been situated in Poland. The only name that had been familiar to her at the time was Treblinka. But Sobibor was almost definitely one of the others.

Pictures of the camps flash into her mind. She remembers how Tony had explained the difference between them and the other concentration camps; how they had been purely killing factories. She shudders, conjuring up pictures of men, women and children running naked into the gas chambers, under the whips of the Ukrainian guards. Clearly, then, not all of those guards were Ukrainian. She vaguely remembers reading something about Stangl, the Commandant of Treblinka. Surely he had been Austrian?

Ida continues, her voice very quiet now. 'After the end of the war, we started to hear about the death camps. Most of us just could not imagine such horror. We knew that the Jews were transported to the East, but we just assumed it was to work camps of some kind. Never, never could we imagine such a thing.'

'So – when did you see Horst after that?' asks Jude.

'He came home one last time. He turned up at the house. I had to let him in, I really had no choice, but we did not speak about where he had been, in fact, I did not wish to speak to him at all. After a couple of days, they came for him – the authorities, you know. They took him away and I never saw him again.'

'So where do you think he went?' asks Jude.

'Well, there were camps for these people; those that had been members of the party or who had committed what they called crimes against humanity. I suppose he went to one of those, but I never found out. I did not want to know where he went.'

Jude and Anna are silent. Anna is thinking again about her own father. He must have been involved in tracking down people like Horst, if not Horst himself. Jude feels shocked and angry at the revelations, Anna merely feels a deep sadness. How awful for Ida, at the end of her life, to live with this burden. It can't be called guilt, because she had nothing to do with it personally. Perhaps guilt by association.

'Mum, look, I'm sorry that we brought all this up. We did need to know but now perhaps we can all put it behind us. There's no need to distress yourself any further.'

Her mother smiles bitterly. 'But that's just it, Anna. I cannot put it behind me. I am an old woman, so I can't look to the future. Usually, the old dwell on the past, but I dare not allow myself to do that either. So, what do I think about to fill in the long hours?'

'But how could you have acted any differently? You had a child to care for and, I suppose, in those days, women's views were of little account.'

By now Ida is looking exhausted. Anna can see that she needs to rest. She helps Ida back onto her bed and sits beside her for a moment, her hand on her mother's arm.

'We'll leave you now, Mum, but I'll be back in a couple of days. Try to get some sleep now.'

Anna and Jude walk to their cars almost in silence. It is now completely dark, and an icy wind has sprung up.

Just before she gets into her car, Jude says 'I hadn't heard of that place, you know, Sobibor.'

'I hardly had either,' says Anna. 'It's just that Tony and I were speaking about it recently.' She explains briefly to Jude what it was, and how it differed from the better-known concentration camps.

Jude blanches. 'I can't believe it,' she says, almost in a whisper. 'Do you think I should tell Kate'?

'I should say certainly not,' says Anna with asperity. 'She's already traumatised by something. It would only make it much worse.'

As she drives home, Anna goes over the revelations of the afternoon. She thinks then of Edward. Even if he professed not to be surprised that his father was in the SS, he would surely be shocked at this. And Juliet, too. She reflects on how a person's actions can have such a long and damaging effect on their descendants and wonders, for the millionth time, how people could allow themselves to be sucked into committing such crimes. Surely a point must come when even an individual like Horst would say to himself 'thus far and no further.' And what about the idea of inherited guilt? She rejects it as being as farcical as the idea of original sin, and yet if heredity accounts for all our characteristics, then surely this as well?

**

When her daughters leave, Ida does not sleep, although she is very tired. She lies for a long time with her head turned to the wall, images of that last ghastly year of defeat running through her head.

The early spring of 1945 had been exceptionally cold and, by then, there was almost no wood or coal to be had, and homes were unheated most of the time, their underfed occupants spending their days and nights wrapped up in all the clothes they possessed underneath thinning overcoats.

Following the long-awaited and dreaded arrival of the Russians, much of the city that hadn't already been bombed was smashed by shelling, and the snow-covered ruins stood outlined against the sky like great jagged ice sculptures. All along the Kärnterstrasse the buildings were reduced to eye level, and smashed tanks lay rusting at the corners of the streets. Vienna's central cemetery could hardly cope with the influx of new occupants, and the iron-hard earth could only be penetrated with great difficulty to create new graves for the never-ending stream of victims of the cold or the guns.

When the first wave of Russian fighting forces finally entered the city, things were not as bad for civilians as people had feared. White flags of surrender were hung out of the windows – rags, sheets, towels, anything that came to hand. In the main, these troops did not behave too badly, and the hard-pressed citizens felt almost relieved that it was all over. Mongol-featured Russian soldiers, with their fur caps and rifles, became an everyday sight in the city, and people soon became used to their presence, although it was wise not to frequent the city centre at night.

Food became, if anything, even harder to obtain. There was no sugar, no butter and rations sank to six hundred calories per day, the lowest level yet. Electricity was scarce and often went out for no apparent reason, plunging the city into darkness for hours on end. Scarce commodities were often traded, such as a bottle of wine for cooking oil, a piece of soap for some salt, and the black market in medicines, coffee, chocolate and cigarettes was rife.

Nearly all of Ida's friends had left Vienna before the arrival of the Russians. Her father had died a few months earlier, finally succumbing to the chronic bronchitis, which was exacerbated by the cold and lack of nourishment. So her mother moved in with her for company for a month or two, and the two women spent much of their time queuing for food, taking it in turns to stand in line whilst the other one looked after Edward.

That spring it seemed that the thaw would never come. One day, sick to death of spending their time queuing for food, Ida and her mother decide to take Edward to the Prater amusement park. As they leave, the snow is sifting down, and helmets of snow adorn the statues on the Ring. The snow makes everything silent.

As they cross the Prater Square, they see the great wheel looming darkly over the ruined houses beneath. They get off the tram and trudge onwards on foot, the snow clogging their boots. At the sides of the street, where the snow is deeper, Edward, who is puny and small for his age, nearly disappears in the drifts. He wails and Ida pulls him out, but his trousers are soaked up to the thighs.

In spite of the desolation, there are a few stalls open, selling thin, flat cakes, and ragged children queue with their coupons to buy them. This is the first time since the arrival of the conquering troops that the wheel has been operating, and Ida's mother has saved enough money to give them all this meagre treat. Ida is reminded of that time before the war, when she and Ernst, long since dead in that other snow, spent a happy day there, courtesy of Mr Rubens. Where is he now? she wonders.

As the wheel mounts slowly, the steel grey of the Danube and the struts of the Reich Bridge become visible. Edward grips his mother's hand, transfixed. Poor child! thinks Ida. What else has he known in his short life but war and hardship? The Prater Park stretches out beneath them, dreary and desolate. As their cabin reaches the summit it stops, and then slowly begins its descent. The iron girders move round slowly and at last they are down. Ida has enough coupons to buy Edward a cake from the stall, and he crams it into his mouth, hardly chewing before he swallows it.

Then they begin the journey home. The sky is leaden, heavy with more snow, and before they reach their apartment, it starts again – driving against them this time on the arctic wind. As the tram crosses the inner city, a few lights can be seen from the bars and groups of young women hang around the badly-lit streets, smoking and chatting. Russian soldiers in great coats and boots stop to talk to them.

By late March, the thaw sets in and the ugly ruins are revealed for what they are. Steel rods and rusting girders protrude from the buildings, and everywhere there is grey slush as people splash through the melted snow. Soon, the only snow to be seen is on the distant slopes outside the city and, in spite of everything, the lilac blooms again amid the chaos, its intoxicating scent filling the ruined streets.

Then the second line of Red Army communication troops arrives from the East and fear again sweeps through the city, and it is well founded this time. It is not until 11 September of that year that the Western forces at last reach the capital, leaving a six-month period when the population is at the mercy of this horde of Mongol-eyed victors.

Ida had not been truthful when she told her daughters that she had never seen Horst again. Edward, five by now, pestered his mother endlessly about his father. He had heard Ida tell a few of her remaining acquaintances that Horst had been killed. Although something seemed to stop him challenging this in front of them, when they got home he asked his mother why she had said that.

'It's not true, is it Mummy? Pappi isn't dead. He came home, but then he went away again with some men. Why can't we go and see him?'

Every day Edward asks the same questions until, at last, Ida gives in. She has no idea where Horst has been taken, but she goes to the US headquarters to make enquires. It is there that she meets Ernest for the first time. The US Army had amassed huge amounts of information about former party members, but were having difficulty interpreting it, so they had enlisted the help of some British personnel who could speak German, under the direction of Ernest.

When Ida appeared at the headquarters, he thought he had never seen such an appealing yet vulnerable woman. He immediately wanted to protect her, and he decided to help her personally to discover where her husband had been taken. Fortunately, they were able to track him down from his army details, and Ida was not obliged to divulge where he was bound for on his last mission. Ernest felt immeasurably sorry for Ida, struggling to keep a home going and food on the table for her child and her ageing mother. He used to give her extra food rations, and sometimes a pair of stockings or chocolate for Edward.

When they eventually located the camp where Horst was being held, Ernest borrowed a military vehicle and drove her and Edward out to it one day. It was situated in the hills outside the city. While she went in, he waited for her in the car. The meeting was not a success. Horst was brought to the hut where the commandant of the camp had his office. When Ida saw him, she thought he looked worse than ever, gaunter and somehow expressionless. She explained to him that Edward had been constantly asking for him, but he spoke little to the child and seemed intent on returning to his quarters as soon as possible. Edward was overcome with shyness at first and then, when he saw that his father had no interest in him, he hid his face in his mother's skirts and wept. Ida felt devastated for the child.

When they returned to the car, Ernest remained tactfully silent, but he soon realised Ida was weeping silently. Edward had stopped crying and was staring out of the window, his thumb in his mouth. Ernest stopped the car and put his arm around Ida. She had never felt so defeated. She leaned against him, the fear and grief of the past years pouring out in a paroxysm of tears.

Ernest kissed her hair and wiped her tears with his

handkerchief. Ida felt safe and protected for the first time in years, and it was a seductive feeling. That evening Ernest came back to the apartment with her and sat playing with Edward, trying to take his mind off the disastrous visit to his father. He chatted to Ida's mother too, while Ida prepared the thin vegetable stew that was to be their evening meal.

Ernest got into the habit of coming round to the apartment in the evenings after work, sometimes bringing some cooking oil or a piece of meat or even a bottle of wine. Ida soon got used to his solid, dependable presence in her life, and so did Edward. Although she often thought about the dreadful things Horst must have done, she and Ernest never discussed it. She knew by that time that Ernest was responsible for processing information about war criminals, but they never talked about his work, knowing that it would cause nothing but pain. She had no idea if Ernest knew what Horst had done, nor did she wish to know.

They spent Christmas of 1945 together. Ernest's contributions made it quite festive, and there was even a wooden sledge for Edward and some dress material for Ida. Early in the New Year, Ernest got Ida a job at the American base, but it did not last for long. It was a peaceful interlude in her life, but it was not to last.

***

Ida is woken from her reverie by a visit from Mrs Piggott. She is startled, and struggles to sit up. 'No, please Ida, don't disturb yourself. I just wanted to have a word with you because the girls tell me that you haven't been eating very much recently. Don't you like the meals here? We could always get you something different to eat, if you would like.' Ida doesn't know what to say.

'I eat all I want to,' she says at last.

'Well we don't really feel that you're eating enough, so we've decided to call on the services of someone to sit with you while you have your meals. She can help you, she'll even feed you if it's necessary, and that way we can really keep a check on what you're eating.'

Ida sighs deeply. It's true that she hasn't been eating anything much for a long time, and she's become quite crafty – pretending to eat and even hiding food on occasion. The thought of being virtually forced to eat is an unpleasant one. All the time she's been getting away with it she felt she had a certain control over her own destiny, subconsciously feeling that it is in her power to end it all, if she chooses. That won't be possible now, though.

***

Anna is surprised to receive a call from Edward the next day. She had had the intention of speaking to him about what Ida had said but apparently Jude had decided to tell him. It is very unusual for Edward to ring any of them so, clearly, the news has had a profound effect on him. Anna feels deeply sorry for him. It must be one of the worst things you could possibly find out about one of your parents.

'You know, Anna, when you came to see me, you asked if I knew my father was in the SS. Well, what I said then was true. I didn't know, but I'm not exactly surprised. I can't remember anything about that time at all, except very general things like the cold and the hunger. But to find out that he was in a death camp, well, that's just too much.'

Edward's voice cracks with emotion. Anna feels helpless,

unable to think of a single thing to say to console him.

At last she says, 'Well you must have been a great comfort to Mum when she was all alone in the world.'

'But that's just it,' cries Edward, 'when it came to it, I couldn't protect her.'

Again, Anna is surprised to hear Edward use this odd turn of phrase.

'But Edward, what could a little boy do to protect his mother?' she asks.

Edward is silent.

'Anyway, Mum seemed almost relieved to have told someone about it,' says Anna. 'Perhaps she will be calmer now.'

'Yes, yes, maybe.' Edward sounds distracted.

'I believe Jude is inviting us all for Christmas this year,' says Anna, changing the subject. 'You'll be coming, won't you?'

Edward hesitates. 'Well, it really depends on Marion but, all being well, yes.'

When Anna replaces the receiver, she thinks again about her mother's revelations. Is it possible that the population of Vienna did not know what was going on in the East? They must have known, or at least have suspected, she thinks. Where did they think all those people were being taken? What about the guards returning from the camps, the visiting wives? Stangl's wife knew from quite early on, she remembers reading that. They listened to the BBC, didn't they, especially towards the end of the war? Perhaps, though, some didn't. Ida certainly sounded sincere. Maybe her mind simply closed down, refused to believe the evidence. All these years in England, perhaps she's convinced herself she didn't know. But then, at that stage, what could they have really done if they had known?

She thinks about her forthcoming trip to Vienna. It is only two days away now. How strange it will be to visit her mother's birthplace at last. Perhaps the city will yield up its secrets. She somehow doubts it, though.

CHAPTER 19

Warsaw is dismal, grey, freezing. Juliet feels her spirits dip as they pull into the station. The city stretches out under a pall of cloud. Although the buildings in the centre are impressive, the Iron Curtain years have left their mark. The bleakness of the weather has its part to play, too. Berlin, although cold, had been crisp and invigorating. Here, the cold seems to penetrate her very bones, making her shiver and huddle into her coat. Thank goodness they are only here for one night.

There is another factor, though, which is making her feel decidedly gloomy. She feels compelled to visit the site of the ghetto, and the thought of this sharply recalls memories of Simon. All of his family had been there, and none had survived. He used to dream about it frequently and disturbingly, thrashing around in his sleep and then waking up, panting and whimpering. On those occasions she would hold him until he calmed down and eventually fell asleep again. He used to tell her that his dreams took different forms, but always he knew it was the ghetto.

When she first told him she was coming to Warsaw, though, he hadn't reacted particularly. Perhaps by then he had other things on his mind. The concert is to be that evening, and the next day they move on to Vienna so, if she is going to visit it, it must be this afternoon.

Geoff insists on coming with her, although she would rather go alone. At first it looks indistinguishable from the rest of the city, with its busy streets and thundering traffic. When they realise how small an area it actually covers, though, it is almost impossible to imagine nearly half a million people crammed into it. On the northern edge, near the Ostbahn – the East station – is the Umschlagplatz, the collection point where the selections were made, with its memorial representing a freight train, its doors open. It is unbearably poignant.

Juliet imagines the inhabitants of the ghetto being shoved into the cattle cars and transported east in conditions of indescribable squalor. Of course, they were the "unproductive" ones, the sick, the old, children, those who had not been quick enough to provide themselves with forged work papers. And then the journey! Pitch black, no toilet facilities, no water, no food for days! The stench, the screaming of the children, the desperation of the mothers, the dead and the dying. Each time the train drew to a stop, the desperate hands reaching through the slats, the pleas for water, mostly unheeded.

Geoff is busy reading the inscriptions.

'They were mostly transported from here to Treblinka,' he announces. 'That was one of the death camps, wasn't it? It was on the eastern border of Poland. Jesus, listen to this! Seven thousand were deported a day, in sixty carriages. It's unimaginable! And before the deportations started, a hundred thousand had died of starvation or disease.' Juliet is silent, appalled. Again, she thinks of Simon. Geoff's eagerness is irritating her. To him it must just seem like ancient history but somehow, to her, it seems much more personal.

As they walk round the busy, normal-seeming streets, she

tries to conjure up the micro-universe that had existed within this confined space. All the normal institutions had been represented. There were factories, schools, theatres, newspapers, hospitals, soup kitchens, clinics, pharmacies and homes for the elderly. All making use of the various talents of the residents and overseen by the ill-reputed *Judenrat*.

Afterwards, the question was asked how Jews could select their own people for the gas chambers. The classic response was always that this selection had to be made in order to save some lives and yet, in the end, everyone went, even the *Judenrat* themselves.

She thinks then about her grandfather. Thank God at least he wasn't in Poland. At least he had nothing to do with the deportation to the death camps in the East. Feeling thoroughly shaken, she returns to the hotel with Geoff. Seeing how distressed she is, he puts his arm around her, assuming she is merely affected by the bleak atmosphere of the place.

After the concert he comes to her room. She is glad of the human contact, but her desire has left her and they just lie huddled together in the huge mahogany bed. Later, she dreams about her grandfather again. This time he is in the ghetto in his SS uniform, giving orders for the inmates to be herded into the cattle trucks. She wakes in a cold sweat, her heart racing.

CHAPTER 20

Anna is getting ready to fly to Vienna. She plans to see Ida once more before she goes; she has been anxious about her since the last visit. Mrs Piggott has rung her to say that she is proposing to bring in some outside help to encourage Ida to eat. Anna is consumed with guilt at the very thought of it. Surely she should be the one helping her mother to eat. But the time! She would have to be there three times a day. It is simply impossible.

As her flight is in the evening, she decides to go and see her that morning. She arrives just before lunch. A quick glance into the dining room tells her that Ida is not there, so she goes straight to her mother's room; there are no Zimmer frames this time blocking her path. All their owners are having lunch. When she arrives at Ida's room, she sees she is seated in her usual chair and an unfamiliar young woman is holding a spoonful of soup to her lips. Ida obediently opens her mouth. Anna is not sure if she should come in or disappear. Perhaps her arrival will put Ida off, stop her eating. Just then, the young woman looks up and sees her.

'Oh look Ida, you've got a visitor,' she says brightly.

Ida turns her head slowly. Her eyes are dull. Anna almost wishes she hadn't come. She has to go in now, though. She enters the room and perches on the bed.

'Look, I'm sorry, I didn't mean to disturb my mother's lunch,' she apologises.

'It's quite all right. We're doing pretty well, aren't we Ida? Just the pudding to go now.'

She picks up a bowl of jelly and cream and proceeds to feed it to Ida, who accepts a couple of spoonfuls but then clamps her jaws resolutely.

'All right then, Ida, that'll do for now,' says the young woman.

When she has gone, Anna moves into her chair.

'Mum, I just came to tell you that I'm going away for a few days.'

'Where are you going?' Ida's voice sounds hoarse; it seems to be an effort to speak.

'I'm going to Vienna. Juliet's there, doing her concert, and she suggested I should pop over and see her.'

A flicker of life crosses Ida's face. 'Vienna! Fancy that.'

'Mum, I wanted to ask you where you used to live, so that we could go and see it, and tell you what it's like now.'

'Zieglergasse. That's when I was a child.'

'But later, Mum, when you were married, where did you live then?'

Ida's eyes seem to grow misty. 'I don't remember,' she says, at last.

'Just try, Mum. Was it in the city centre?'

'Yes, I think so. It was near my parents' apartment. I can't remember the name of the street.'

Anna changes the subject, resolved to come back to it when Ida is more receptive.

'How have you been, Mum, since I saw you last?'

At first, Anna makes no reference to what Ida told them last time, and nor does Ida herself.

'They make me eat now. This woman comes every mealtime

and sits with me and feeds me. Really, it is too much. I just cannot eat so much food. You must tell them, Anna.'

'Well, Mum, it's for your own good you know. You were getting much too thin.'

'What does it matter if I'm thin? It is neither here nor there. I won't be here much longer.'

Anna is distressed. 'Please don't say that, Mum. You know we love you and we don't want to lose you.'

'Do you? Do you really? After the things I've told you?'

'Of course we do. We hate to see you distressed.'

Ida seems to be fading away before Anna's eyes. Each time she leaves her, it is a wrench. She wonders if she will see her alive again. Just as she is leaving, her mother speaks again.

'Albertgasse, that was it. Near the railway station.'

Anna makes a mental note, determined to look it up later. She kisses her mother and leaves quickly.

***

Anna has to be at Heathrow by five o'clock that evening. Her flight departs at seven and arrives in Vienna a couple of hours later. She already has the name of Juliet's hotel, and they have agreed that she will get a taxi straight there when she lands. Juliet will be playing that night and will meet her at the hotel later on.

Anna has managed to pack all she needs into a small travel bag, so she won't have to wait to collect her luggage at the other end. Heathrow is crowded with people going away for Christmas, and Anna struggles to find a seat while she waits for her flight to be announced. She has brought with her a guide book and street plan of Vienna, and she studies this now while she is waiting. She soon locates Albertgasse. It is not far from the centre. She doubts though that any of the old buildings will still be there.

She feels a tinge of excitement at the thought of visiting the place that she has spent so long imagining over the years, but it is mixed with an indefinable sense of apprehension. In truth, she doesn't know what she expects to find there, or how she will feel. She just knows that the trip is necessary, to lay some ghost or other. Juliet had rung the previous day from Warsaw. She had sounded glum, and Anna supposed she was still despondent after her break-up with Simon.

The flight is on time, and they land at Vienna International Airport just after nine o'clock. Anna is able to get a taxi almost immediately. The waft of freezing air which meets her as she leaves the well-heated airport gives her a shock. Juliet had warned her about the cold, and she is well wrapped up in an old sheepskin jacket, long boots, hat and gloves, but her face, the only part of her that is exposed, soon begins to feel numb. The night is cloudy, and there are no stars. It is trying to snow. Anna is pleased to get into the warmth of the taxi. She gives the driver the name of the hotel; the Kaiserin Elisabeth.

Although she had been prepared to try out her German, there is no need. The taxi driver speaks perfect English, even asking her about the weather in London. She checks in and takes her bag to her room. Then she goes back down to the bar to wait for Juliet.

Sipping a glass of red wine, she looks round at the other guests. The hotel is full, mostly with tourists who are probably there for Christmas, but there are also a few businessmen, having a drink with their clients. She does not have to wait very long.

Soon Juliet arrives, her face flushed from the cold. Anna thinks she looks pretty and animated. Quite different from what she expected, after their telephone conversation the previous day. Juliet is laughing at something the young man with her has said. She looks round for a second, then catches sight of Anna. The two women hug each other, then Juliet turns to her companion, taking off her scarf and gloves.

'Anna, this is Geoff. He's playing in the concert, too. He's a flautist, and a very good one.'

Anna shakes hands with Geoff, taking in his fresh complexion and dark, rather unruly hair. She notices that he can't take his eyes off Juliet.

'I'm very pleased to meet you,' she says. 'I can't wait to hear the concert. I'm booked for tomorrow night. That's right, isn't it Juliet?'

Juliet nods. 'Centre, front row, no less,' she says.

They sit down and more drinks are ordered. At first the conversation is general. Juliet and Geoff talk about the places they have seen so far, and Anna listens with interest. She becomes aware that Juliet and Geoff are more than friends. She's surprised, remembering how devastated Juliet had been at Simon's leaving. She's very pleased though. She has known for a long time that Juliet's relationship with Simon was ultimately a destructive one. Now Juliet is asking if there is any news from home.

'Well, I haven't seen your father,' says Anna, carefully, 'although we have spoken on the phone.'

Ever since Ida's revelations, Anna has been debating whether or not to tell Juliet. Whatever she decides, though, now is clearly not the time. She does tell Juliet briefly about Kate, though. Juliet is shocked.

'I knew she was smoking a lot of pot,' she says, 'but I didn't think things had got that bad. Oh, that reminds me, you know her boyfriend, Christoph? Well, he turned up a couple of nights ago, outside the concert hall in Berlin. I was so surprised. I'd only met him for a few minutes, you know. Anyway, he wanted to ask me about Kate. Said she's been behaving really oddly recently. I got the impression that she's gone off him, big time. But he seemed to think it's because he's German or something. But I can't believe that, because she was always so keen on Germany.'

Anna looks thoughtful. 'Certainly Kate seems to be going through some kind of trauma,' she says. 'Maybe it's to do with her father leaving.'

Juliet shrugs. 'Could be, I suppose. Look Anna, I'm done in. I think I'll go to bed now, if you don't mind. Shall we meet at breakfast tomorrow?'

'Yes, fine. About eight thirtyish?' Anna wonders if Juliet and Geoff are sleeping together. Perhaps her arrival is an unwelcome intrusion. She decides to ask Juliet later if she would prefer it if she goes sightseeing alone. She realises that she is very tired, too. The couple of glasses of wine have gone to her head, and she sways slightly as she stands up. She says goodnight to Juliet and Geoff and tactfully goes off to her room on the first floor, leaving them to follow in their own time.

***

When Anna awakens the next morning, everything seems strangely silent. She gets out of bed and goes to the window. The sight that greets her makes her gasp. The few sparse snowflakes of the previous evening have turned into a thick, obliterating blanket. The window ledges of the buildings opposite have several inches of snow on them, and there are great wedges of snow perched on the roofs of the cars parked below. And it is a silent world that she looks out on. The everyday sounds of the city are muffled, and all that can be heard is the scraping of spades as the hotel employees attempt to clear a path in front of the hotel. One or two intrepid people are trudging through the snow in high boots.

Anna glances at her watch. It is early, only six thirty. However tired she was the night before, she seems incapable of sleeping much later than six these days. It must be something to do with her age. She thinks of Charlotte, who will sleep until midday if undisturbed, and yet her mother, although frequently dozing during the day, complains bitterly of being unable to sleep at night. She decides to read for half an hour and then have a leisurely bath.

In spite of the outside temperature, the hotel is overheated, and she decides to leave off the layers of jumpers she has brought with her until it is time to go out. Just before eight she rings Tony. He is working at home this week, taking the opportunity to spend some time with Charlotte, who is home for the holidays. Then she goes downstairs to the dining room. Juliet and Geoff are seated at a table by the window. Anna notices that Geoff is holding Juliet's hand across the table. When he sees her, he quickly removes it.

Part of the Stephansdom can be seen from the windows. Its spire soars dramatically above the snow-covered roofs. The snow has stopped falling now and there is a break in the clouds. Anna is amazed to see how the city seems to have come to life since she first looked out of her bedroom window. The traffic is now moving, albeit slowly, and even the trams are clattering along. People are on their way to work. She supposes that snow like this must be a common occurrence here. People are geared up for it.

The breakfast is good, served by waitresses whose command of

English is excellent. Anna is introduced to a couple of musicians from the concert. When they have finished, Geoff gets up from the table.

'I'm going to leave you two to explore the city by yourselves today,' he says. 'I'm going to listen to the concert in the Augustinerkirche with Toby. It's Haydn today. Sounds pretty good.' Anna thinks that the Augustinerkirche sounds slightly familiar, but she can't think why.

'Heavens, don't you want a break from music?' exclaims Juliet. But Anna realises that Geoff is probably being tactful, leaving the two of them some time together. When he's gone, Juliet asks Anna what she would like to do.

'I see you've got your guidebook. Shall we do the really touristy things first?'

Anna smiles. 'Yes, that's fine, although goodness knows how easy it will be to get around in this snow.'

'Well, we had a fair bit of snow in Heidelberg, but it was amazing how quickly they cleared the streets. Although I don't know if the Praterstern will be operating today.'

They fetch their coats and scarves and venture out into the crisp, cold air. Juliet is right. The city seems to be operating at full steam already. The chink in the clouds has become bigger and a shaft of sunlight sends needles of light shooting off the snow. They head for the cathedral first. It looks breathtaking in the snow, the sunlight glinting on the golden ball on the spire. There are already quite a few people about. Anna is surprised to be accosted every few minutes by students dressed in eighteenth century garb, trying to sell her tickets for the various concerts and operas that are to take place over the Christmas period. Not a word of German is to be heard, and the square itself and the roads running off it are full of the kind of shops to be found on any British high street: Marks and Spencer, Laura Ashley, Tie Rack and, further on, the exclusive designer shops – Gucci, Armani and Prada. She can't help feeling disappointed. Really, they could be in any city, anywhere in the world.

They move off towards the Hofburg, where Juliet's concert is to be held that night. The architecture is stunning: classical statues juxtaposing the art nouveau/secession style architecture. But the city seems curiously soulless; the Mozart connection is milked for all it is worth. Toy Town, set in a Habsburgian time warp, thinks Anna, disappointed.

'Let's be real tourists and take one of those Fiakers,' suggests Juliet. 'They look fun and at least we'll be sure to see everything, and we'll be out of the snow.'

Anna readily agrees. Her feet are already numb from plodding through the snow, which is still deep on the pavements. They drive through the Hofburg in the open horse-drawn carriage, and down the Ringstrasse, with its grandiose buildings, including the State Opera and then on to the Secession House. The white building looks positively grey against the pristine snow, but the sun glinting off the golden ball on the top makes it look as though it were on fire. Anna thinks how innovative it must have appeared for its time. She catches sight of a slab of marble beside it, and is amused to see the words 'fucking neo-liberals' inscribed on it. She wonders how long that has been there.

The ride lasts about an hour in all, and when they get down, Juliet suggests a coffee. They aren't far from the Demel Cafe, which Anna has read about in her guidebook.

'It's supposed to be famous for its Sachertorte,' she says.

Many of the customers turn out to be Japanese tourists.

They obviously have the same guidebook. However, in the large and airy art nouveau conservatory at the back there are quite a number of well-dressed Viennese.

'Don't order cappuccino unless you want half your cup filled with cream,' warns Juliet. After a scrimmage at the cake bar to get a ticket for the much vaunted Sachertorte, Anna and Juliet settle down to enjoy their coffee. The Sachertorte turns out to be dry and tasteless.

'Well, what do you think so far?' asks Juliet.

Anna hesitates. 'The buildings are very impressive,' she says at last. 'It seems to have lost its character somewhere along the line though. I suppose I'm looking for some sign of the romantic, pre-war Vienna; you know, glistening, deserted streets, that kind of thing, or spies hiding in gloomy corners, left over from the Cold War. What's left, though, is a kind of Mozart theme park, full of Japanese tourists. I suppose, in truth, we've simply left it too late.' Juliet nods. She's seen the Third Man too.

'So, what shall we do next?'

'Well, I'd quite like to see the old Jewish quarter and the Praterstern, if there's time.' She hesitates. 'Actually, Juliet, there's something I really ought to tell you. I'm afraid it's not very palatable. It's something Mum told Jude and myself after you'd gone on tour.' The smile leaves Juliet's face.

'Oh no. Not more horrid revelations about my awful antecedents!'

Anna nods. 'I'm afraid so. I did wonder whether to say anything, but I think you've a right to know and, anyway, I'd like to do a bit of digging, if there's time.'

Juliet waits in silence. Anna explains briefly about Ida's conviction that Horst was sent to work in one of the Polish death camps towards the end of the war and how, on his return, he was sent to a camp for ex-party members.

'She never heard from him or saw him again after that.'

Juliet is aghast. Involuntarily she thinks of Simon again. Then she remembers the dream she'd had last night. She tells Anna about it.

'I was feeling really depressed after going round the ghetto,' she explains. 'That was just before I rang you. And then that dream. It's so strange. 'I'm just wondering if we could go and find the street where she used to live,' says Anna.

***

They find the Albertgasse without too much difficulty. All the buildings are clearly post-war, except for one large house at the end which dates from about the turn of the century, and which could have been an apartment block at one time. It seems to be offices now. Anna pushes the outer door and they go in. The interior is dark and cold. A flight of oak stairs runs up at the end of the corridor. Small plaques bearing the names of various companies are affixed to the doors on either side of the corridor. Anna turns to Juliet.

'This could have been it, you know. It's about the right date.'

Ida's spirit is almost palpable in this humbler, more traditional part of the city, and they both feel it. Anna is moved. She imagines her mother as a young woman, trudging the snowy streets, pushing an infant Edward in his pram. Then she thinks of the fear they must have felt for the knock on the door in the night, the military motorcades, the brutal evictions. She shivers.

'What if we could find a relative or something,' says Juliet uncertainly. 'What was his surname?'

'Mullhauser,' says Anna. 'Edward was given the name McFarlane when they came to England'.

'Do you think that's a common name?'

Anna shrugs. 'I've no idea. We could try the public records office or something of the sort.'

They decide to have lunch and work out some sort of plan of action. They don't have much time. Juliet has to be back at the hotel by six to prepare for the concert that evening. After that, there's one more full day, and then they fly home in the afternoon of the day after. After a warming lunch of goulash soup, they decide to try the public records office, back at the town hall.

'Does Dad know about this latest development?' asks Juliet suddenly.

'Well yes, actually he does. Jude decided to ring and tell him the day after we spoke to Ida.'

'How did he take it? I mean it's a pretty devastating thing to find out about your father. Or your grandfather, as far as that goes,' she adds bitterly.

'I don't really know, Juliet.'

Anna changes the subject, and asks Juliet about Geoff.

'We just get on really well.' Juliet brightens up. 'He's so uncomplicated, after Simon. But I don't want things to get too heavy. I'm just not ready for that.'

Anna is not sure that Geoff feels the same way, but she says nothing. They take the tram back to the town hall and are directed to the archive department. Unfortunately, though, there are quite a few Mullhausers, and they don't have enough information to go on. They are looking for possible brothers or sisters, having decided that Horst himself might not appear on any list as he spent a long period of time in a camp.

'They'd be pretty ancient by now, if there are any. If only we had at least an initial to go on,' says Anna.

Just then, Juliet has an idea. 'I know, let's ring Jude and get her to go and ask Gran if Horst had any brothers or sisters.'

Anna is doubtful. Knowing Jude, she thinks it unlikely that she will drop everything to go off to question Ida.

'Well, we could give it a go,' she says.

When the phone is answered, it is not by Jude but by Kate. Apparently Jude is out at one of her gardening classes. Kate sounds completely recovered.

'Kate, I'm here in Vienna with Juliet. Actually, we're trying to find out a bit about some of your Gran's family.'

'Vienna! Oh how fantastic. I wish I was there with you.'

'Yes well, we've come to a bit of a dead end. We need to know if your Gran's first husband, Horst, had any brothers or sisters and, if so, what their names were.'

'Oh I see. Well, I could go and see Gran and ask her if she remembers.'

'Could you really? That would be fantastic. It's a bit urgent, actually. If we're going to do anything about it, it would have to be tomorrow.'

'No problem. I'll go this afternoon. I haven't got anything else to do, and it's about time I saw Gran again. I'll give you a ring if I find out anything useful.'

Juliet and Anna are cold and tired by now, and decide to return to the hotel to wait for Kate's call. When she gets to her room, Anna lies down on the bed and falls asleep almost immediately. When she wakes up it is dark outside, and her phone is ringing insistently. She fumbles for it in her bag. It is Kate.

' Aunt Anna, it's me. I've been to see Gran.'

Anna feels the usual thrill of apprehension at the mention of her mother.

'How was she?'

'Well, OK I suppose. Actually she didn't look that great. But she did give me the information you need. Apparently Horst had a brother and two sisters. The sisters were older than him – Annaliese and Marie Louisa – and the brother was younger – Frederik Georg.'

'Oh that's brilliant, Kate! Well done. Did your Gran ask why you wanted to know?'

'Not really. I tried to sort of disguise the question as much as possible. You know how upset she gets. So what are you going to do now? Try to track them down?'

'Yes, that's the general idea.'

Anna remembers that Kate doesn't know any more about Horst except that he was in the SS. Unless Jude has chosen to tell her as well, of course. Anna hopes not. Kate is disturbed enough as it is without that. She thanks Kate again and rings off, promising to let her know if they find anything out.

She looks at her watch and sees that it is already six thirty. Time to get ready for the concert.

***

The next day Anna goes back to the public records department early. Although she had greatly enjoyed the concert, she was completely exhausted by the end and had gone up to bed early, leaving Juliet and Geoff and some of the other members of the orchestra in the bar. She and Juliet have agreed to meet at eleven in the Museum cafe.

No more snow has fallen today, but the sun is not out, and the air feels damp and bone-chillingly cold. Armed with some initials and approximate dates of birth, Anna feels more hopeful. The tedious form filling must be gone through again, although she is certain that the severe looking young woman behind the desk must recognise her from yesterday.

This time, the search is easier. She goes back to the year that Ida was born and searches a few years either side of it. Eventually she finds the names she is looking for. 1914: Anneliese and 1915: Marie Louisa; both deceased. She feels a stab of disappointment. There is just Frederik Georg to go now. There he is – 1918 and still alive! What a find!

She copies down the address with shaking fingers, then she glances at her watch. Quarter to eleven already. Hurriedly she leaves the building and decides to hail a taxi. She arrives at the Museum cafe just as the church clock is striking eleven. Juliet is already there, sitting on one of the red leather seats and looking at an old music score. She looks up and smiles as Anna comes in. Anna unwraps her scarf and sits down opposite her.

'Any luck?' asks Juliet eagerly.

'Yes, I think so. The two sisters appear to be dead, but the brother is still alive. I've got his address. Look, it's Gluckstrasse 13.'

They order hot chocolate with cream and Anna gets out her street plan. She soon finds Gluckstrasse. It's in the same part of the city as Albertstrasse, where they were yesterday. As they drink the chocolate, they chat about the concert. Anna is full of praise for Juliet. It had been a magical night.

The Hofburg had looked wonderfully romantic in the snow in the light of a full moon. It had been a glittering occasion and

Anna had been glad she had brought a long dress. Anything less would have looked out of place.

'And you're right about Geoff, adds Anna. 'He certainly is a very talented young man.'

'Yes.' Juliet looks thoughtful. 'I know he is. He'll go far. I just wish he wasn't so – well – smitten. It's crazy, isn't it? Simon would never pay me enough attention, and now that I've got someone who's really keen on me, that doesn't suit either.' She sighs.

'Human nature, I suppose,' says Anna. 'And remember, he did catch you on the rebound. That's always dangerous.'

'Yes, I know,' says Juliet. 'I just feel mean, as though I've been using him.'

'Well, I shouldn't worry. He'll get over it. Anyway, you haven't finished with him already, have you?'

'Oh no, nothing like that. I'd just like to cool it a bit, that's all.'

Then Juliet tells Anna about Simon's text messages.

'Simon always wanted what he hasn't got,' she says wryly.

They leave the cafe and get a tram back to the area they were in yesterday. Gluckstrasse turns out to be a narrow street, lined with old, double-fronted houses, obviously now flats. They find number 13 without too much difficulty. There is an intercom on the door with faded names listed beneath. Herr F Mullhauser is one of them and they press the bell. There is no response. They press it again. After a while, Juliet suggests pressing the bell to the flat next door.

'*Wir suchen Herr Mullhauser,*' says Anna, on hearing the receiver having been picked up.

'*Er ist nicht mehr da,*' comes a woman's voice. '*Er ist im Altersheim.*' He's in a home. '*Momentmal, ich gebe Ihnen die Adresse.*'

After a few moments, a stout, middle-aged woman appears. She hands them a piece of paper.

'*Das ist seine Adresse. Bitte.*'

Anna takes the proffered piece of paper.

'*Das ist in der Nähe von Grinsing.*'

They thank the woman and walk back down the street.

'Grinsing. I think I've seen that on the map,' says Anna. 'It's a fair way from here.'

'I think we're going to have huge problems because he probably doesn't speak English. And anyway, goodness knows what sort of state he'll be in.'

They stare at each other. They've come so far and now it seems hopeless.

'Well there's nothing for it,' says Juliet resolutely, 'We'll have to enlist Geoff's help. He speaks German.' She takes out her mobile and rings him. After a few moments of low conversation, during which Anna tactfully moves away, Juliet turns back to Anna. 'It's fine. He's coming. He's going to meet us at the hotel in about half an hour, and then we can get a taxi out to Grinsing.'

Anna is relieved. She could not bear to have come so far and then go home without seeing Fredrik. But she admits to herself that it could be awkward.

The thing that strikes Anna first is how small the home is compared to the Cedars. Small and individual. The door is opened by a grey-haired woman in a white pinafore. Geoff steps forward:

'*Wir möchten gerne mit Herrn Mullhauser sprechen.*'

The woman looks surprised.

'*Sind Sie vielleicht Verwandte?* Are you relatives?'

'*Nein – eigentlich ja.*'

The woman stands back and they troop through. Anna

immediately notices that there is no underlying smell of urine, as there is at the Cedars. Hardly surprising as there only seems to be five or six occupants. It is bright and clean, with large picture windows offering views of the surrounding pine forest.

They are told that Frederik is in the garden having his daily walk. In spite of the snow he is out there today, as usual. They go out through the back door and into the garden. It is quite extensive, rising in terraces, which are linked by small flights of steps from which the snow has been meticulously cleared.

'*Er kann gut Englisch*,' says Frau Schulze, the housekeeper, as they prepare to mount the steps to the part of the garden where they can see a tall, spare figure, only slightly bent, making his way along one of the paths with the help of what looks like an Alpenstock. As they approach him, Anna takes the initiative and introduces them all. At first he looks suspicious.

'Who are you? What do you want?' he asks.

Anna explains who they are, and that they are relatives of a kind.

'But you're not blood relations, are you?' Geoff asks Juliet quietly.

'Well, Anna's not, but I'm afraid I am,' says Juliet. Then to Frederik:

'I'm your great niece. Your brother, Horst, was my grandfather.'

A look of incredulity crosses Frederik's once good-looking face, and he totters slightly, grabbing the alpenstock for support. Then, to their horror, he bursts into tears. Anna takes his arm.

'Shall we go back inside? Then you can sit down and we can explain properly.'

They make their way slowly back through the snow. Frederik's room is twice the size of Ida's. It is elegantly furnished, with matching curtains and a featherbed cover. On the polished wooden floor there are a couple of Chinese rugs. Frederik is settled into his armchair and more chairs are brought for the visitors. By this time, he has recovered his composure.

'How did you find me?' he says at last, hoarsely.

'Well, Juliet is a violinist in an English orchestra and she is in Vienna on a concert tour. We thought we would try to find out if we have – well, if there are any relatives here.'

'A violinist? Just like Horst! I can't believe it. He was a wonderful musician. You should have heard him play!'

Anna and Juliet look at each other uncomfortably.

'I cannot believe it,' he repeats. 'I thought I had no living relatives in the world.

At last, Anna says: 'My mother – Juliet's grandmother – is Ida.'

'Ida! She is still alive? Did she ask you to look for me?'

'Well no, not exactly.'

'Ida was always very unforgiving.'

'She is very old and frail now,' says Anna. 'And she seems to be haunted by some memories of the past. Things to do with your brother, Horst.'

Frederik's face clouds over.

'Poor Horst. Things turned out so terribly badly for him. When he was put in the camp – by the Americans, you know – Ida would not go and see him. Well, I believe she went once and took Edward, but the visit was not a success.'

At this point, Geoff tells Juliet he will wait for her outside, as there is obviously no language problem. Juliet is rather relieved. Who knows what further revelations may be forthcoming. She sits beside Frederik and takes his hand. She experiences an odd surge of warmth, almost love, for him.

'Did you go and see him then, in the camp?'

'Oh yes, I went several times, right up until the end.'

'The end?'

'Yes,' he looks surprised. 'Didn't you know? He died in the camp.'

'Well, I suppose we assumed he must have done, but we didn't know the details.'

'He was found dead one morning. He had hanged himself by his belt from the bars on his window.'

Frederik suddenly sounds very tired. Anna and Juliet both draw in their breath sharply. For a while, Frederik is silent, then he continues:

'He couldn't take any more, you know. He had seen so many dreadful things.'

'Did Ida know of this?'

Frederik shrugs. 'By this time she was being courted by someone from the American Intelligence Unit. Poor Horst was forgotten.'

Juliet says: 'Uncle Frederik, we don't want to make you drag all this up again. It's just that we need to know, I suppose.'

He puts his hand on her head and strokes her hair.

'It's all right my dear. I can promise you none of us has ever been allowed to forget the things that happened in those troubled times. And, as for your grandmother, well I don't blame her really. She had a right to some happiness, both for herself and for the boy. But has anyone ever told you, you look just like her?'

Juliet smiles and nods.

Anna says: 'I must tell you, one of the reasons my mother is so distressed is that she believes he was being sent to Sobibor towards the end of the war.'

Frederik gives her a penetrating look.

'No, that's not what happened. Although it might have,' he says slowly.

'What do you mean?' asks Juliet.

'It is true that he was due to be sent there, but just at that time it was closed down. They knew they were losing the war then, and they didn't want to leave any evidence, you see. The whole place was razed to the ground, I believe. They planted trees where the gas ovens had been.'

Anna notices the use of the word "they".

'So what did happen then?' asks Juliet.

'They changed his posting at the last moment. He was sent to the Balkans to help to suppress an uprising there. "Operation Wolkenbruch" it was called. It was just after Italy capitulated. They were sent there to fight the partisans.'

Juliet feels a wave of relief.

'Thank God he wasn't at Sobibor, anyway,' she says.

Frederik looks at her sadly.

'No, he wasn't at Sobibor,' he says briefly.

Anna is afraid they are tiring him. She changes the subject for a while, and tells him about the rest of the family.

'So, Ida had three children, finally,' he says. 'Edward was the only one I knew.' He shakes his head. 'That poor child. He lived through some terrible times. So then Ida met her Scotsman,' he continues.

'That must be your father,' he turns to Anna.

'Yes, that's right. I was born in England, but my sister Jude was born in Vienna.'

Frederik looks surprised. 'You have an older sister? And when was she born?'

'1946.'

Frederik looks thoughtful.

'So anyway Uncle Frederik,' says Juliet, 'if my grandfather was not sent to Sobibor, why did he commit suicide? I know he was in the Party, but surely then he wasn't involved in any of the atrocities.'

'Well *mein Liebchen*, it's a long story, and one you may wish you had not asked to hear.'

Just then, there is a knock on the door and Frau Schutee comes in with coffee and Sandkuchen. It is four o'clock. When the coffee has been poured and the cake cut, Frederik begins his story.

'You know, I have forgotten many things since, but the events of those years are etched into my memory. I am three years younger than Horst. He was always more interested in politics than I was. I was keener on sport. The first time I realised what was happening was when Hitler marched into Vienna and the crowds went mad; cheering and shouting *"Heil Hitler."* Afterwards, you know, they all said they had not wanted it but believe me, at the time they certainly did.

It was just after that that Horst joined the Party. When war broke out he was sent straight to Poland. As you know, that campaign was quickly successful, and when the conquering troops came home on leave, there was a general sense of euphoria. Horst went back to the Eastern Front almost straight away. When he came home on leave subsequently, we often used to meet up, either just the two of us or with Ida as well. He used to recount his exploits at the Front and we would listen admiringly.

We had some very good times in those early days of the war, going out to cafes or dancing. Sometimes I would bring a girlfriend and we made up a foursome. Everyone in Vienna seemed elated then. The city was so animated; full of soldiers home on leave from the Front and their wives or girlfriends. Although I hadn't really been interested in the war up till then, I suppose I became infected with the general sense of excitement, and I began to think of joining up myself. I was still too young though. At that time there were no shortages in Austria and the victories just kept coming.

I particularly remember the spring of 1940, just before the fall of France, Horst was home on leave, and I hadn't yet been called up. Spring had come unexpectedly early that year, and we had a few days when there was real warmth in the sun. One afternoon Horst, Ida and myself took a stroll in the Stadtpark. We sat outside, listening to a small orchestra playing Strauss waltzes. It was lilac time, and the smell was intoxicating. I remember thinking, if only things could stay like this forever.

Ida was expecting Edward, and they were both happy and excited. It wasn't to last, though. As time went by, Horst became quiet and withdrawn. When Edward was born, he almost seemed like his old self for a while, but then he became surly and uncommunicative again. He and Ida were not getting on too well, and I felt sorry for Ida. In fact, I even tried to have a word with him about it myself, but he jumped down my throat. And if anyone dared to make a light-hearted joke about Hitler – well – he used to go mad, telling us that the Führer understood everything better than we did, and that he was going to lead us to a glorious future. Some such rubbish, anyway. I soon learnt never to discuss politics with him.'

Frederik pauses and takes a sip of his coffee. Then he resumes his tale: 'I was called up in the summer of 1941, just in time to be sent to Russia. Ida's brother Ernst was called up just after I was. He was a few months younger me. He was sent to Russia too, although he was in a different division. I was in the 44th infantry.

To start with, things didn't seem so bad, although I must say that I had a sense of foreboding right from the start. Most people, though, had high hopes of victory. Of course I didn't see Horst, the campaign was so vast, but I knew he was there too. He was an officer by then.

'At the beginning it was very hot, sometimes up to 40 degrees. That brought its own problems with it, of course. There were thousands of flies, and many of us had chronic dysentery. "The Russian sickness", we called it. Then there were the dust storms, and always the Russians would attack us at night. We had to move forward constantly, and that made it very difficult to care for the sick and wounded.

Our tanks rolled on and on and somehow, even in summer, we all felt a kind of unexplained fear of the steppe. It was so vast, stretching beyond the horizon, towards Asia; always taking us further away from home. It was beautiful sometimes, though.

In summer the vast fields of sunflowers all turned their heads towards the sun and, in the evening, the sky would be streaked with pink and gold. Then we would sit reminiscing about home as the shadows lengthened. The vastness of the distances made us all feel homesick, and home took on a dreamlike quality as leave became rarer and rarer. Eventually we were about 2,000 miles from the frontier.

Then the days started to shorten and we had to start to dig in for winter. Everyone was afraid of the approaching winter, but nobody wanted to speak of it. The vastness and the cold seemed to consume us. First the temperature dropped to minus 20, then eventually to minus 40. We had to dig bunkers to shelter from the cold, but first we had to light fires to make it possible to dig.

We knew in our hearts we could never defeat the Russians,

the country was simply too huge and too cold. Our clothing was unsuitable too. Our boots were too tight, so we used to wrap our feet in paper to avoid frostbite. We even stole clothes and boots from the Russians – either from prisoners or from the dead. It was about this time that I heard that Ernst had been killed. When his mother received the news, it nearly killed her. She was told he died fighting for the Fatherland but, in fact, he died of frostbite, which had turned gangrenous. Not a pleasant death.

'Anyway, the Red Army was better equipped than us; they had white camouflage suits, so we simply couldn't see them approaching, and some of them were on skis. About that time, there was an appeal at home for more warm winter clothing for us, and they did send fur coats and skis, but it was too little too late.

The Red Army used to ride into battle on Cossack ponies, and they would attack us at night with no warning. There was death everywhere. Bodies lay heaped in the drifting snow. We were terrified most of the time, and far from home. Remember, I was only nineteen. Eventually we were encircled and the rest, as everyone knows, is history.' Frederik pauses. Juliet and Anna are silent. Then Anna says:

'Yes, I suppose we do know the facts, but to hear it from someone who was actually there is just amazing.'

Frederik looks gratified. Then a shadow crosses his face.

'But then, all the time – I mean from the beginning of the campaign – we kept hearing rumours about what was going on behind the front line. People said that in the wake of our forces, Jews and others were being systematically rounded up and shot.

Horst was in one of those SS units. He told me afterwards – after the war finished, that is, when he was in that camp – that people were taken to the forest, where they were made to dig graves and then they were lined up, naked, and shot. It wasn't just Jews, of course, there were partisans and Gypsies and communist officials as well. The "Jewish Bolshevik conspiracy", it was called, to justify what they were doing, I suppose. He told me that as time went on it got harder and harder to do. He said they found they needed to get drunk before they could do it. There was always plenty of vodka for that purpose – stolen from the local villagers.

There were various atrocities that he witnessed or, indeed, took part in. A Jewish orphanage was discovered, and all the occupants were shot; villages were burnt, that kind of thing. They called it "collective measures". There was one particularly horrific incident – Frederik's voice falters, he almost stops speaking – 'Horst told me this during my last visit. It seems they'd reached the banks of the Don and they were clearing out a village — rounding up the inhabitants. Ammunition was running low, apparently. So, to save bullets, they threw the babies into the freezing river, knowing that the mothers would jump in after them. Nice and economical, wasn't it?' Frederik pauses. At last he says: 'So, you say thank God he wasn't at Sobibor, but you have to ask yourself, how was that any better?'

Juliet clears her throat. 'When you saw him, years later in the camp, did you ever ask him why he didn't just refuse to do it?'

'That's what all the young people say. Yes, I did, as a matter of fact. He said the whole thing had simply gone too far, they were in too deep. There wasn't one particular point when you could say "enough is enough". And they were afraid of disobeying orders. I think I said to him then "well, why didn't you just take your own life?" and he replied that they were all anaesthetised. He did repeat, though, that none of them wanted to do it. They had to get drunk first. Then, Horst said to me "but you did awful things, too. You killed people." And I remember replying "yes, that's true". But there is a line to be drawn. Whatever my comrades or I did it was, at least, connected with the war, even if we sometimes went too far and, believe me, it happened. Russian civilians were turned out of their houses. People were shot for giving food to escaped Red Army prisoners, and then the prisoners themselves were frozen and starved.'

'Mum always said Horst was silent and depressed when he came home on leave,' says Anna. 'It's hardly surprising, is it, in light of what you've told us.'

'What do you think makes a man do things like that?' repeats Juliet. 'Why didn't they just rebel and refuse to do it?'

'You would need to have lived through those times to know the answer to that,' replies Frederik. 'It was a different world then. People were more patriotic, more obedient: less individualistic, perhaps. Many of the Wehrmacht officers were anti-Nazi, but they were afraid; some might say craven.'

'So what happened to you in the end, Uncle Frederik?' asks Juliet.

'Well, the Russians broke through the centre of the Kessel, as we called it, the encirclement, and that was really the end of the Sixth Army. I told you, didn't I, that I was in the 44th Infantry Division. We'd more or less given up by then. Many prisoners had been taken, and they were giving a huge amount of information to the Russians. They were using it for propaganda, to tell us (as if we didn't know) about food shortages and numbers of casualties.

Those last few days were like hell on earth. Piles of frozen corpses everywhere. The ground was too hard to bury them, even if we'd had the strength to do it. The wounded were lying in the snow. My fingers were so swollen with frostbite that I couldn't pick up my gun. At one point, the wind was so strong that the bare steppe was exposed, even though it was the middle of winter. Our defences were totally smashed and we were at the mercy of the enemy and of course the cold. So many were deserting every day. I'll never forget the sight of my dead comrades. They lay all around us in the snow. The minute they died their bodies froze stiff; they were twisted and grimacing. I suppose you could say I was lucky.

I received a hit in the leg, and I knew if I didn't get it treated I was finished. I was too weak to have any resistance. The frostbite would get in it. Anyway, I was lying in the snow, and a supply Junker landed near me. I thought I'd have no chance of getting on, because I couldn't walk and the walking wounded were already rushing to the planes. As luck would have it, the pilot turned out to be an Austrian – from Linz – and he took pity on me and got me on board. That was the end of the war for me. I got back to Vienna and I was never fit for active service again – thank God.'

'And Horst, what happened to him?'

'Horst was never in the Kessel. He was in the SS support group, and they eventually made it back to the frontier. Then, as you know, he finished the war in the Balkans.'

Anna and Juliet are silent. Juliet looks at her watch. It is already five thirty, and it is quite dark outside. Snow is beginning to fall again. She knows she must go and get ready for the last performance of the concert. Somehow she can't bring herself to move, though. She is mesmerised by Frederik's story. She has one last question for him.

'Did you know what was going on behind the front line?'

'Yes, of course. We all knew. It was common knowledge. We

didn't know about individual cases until afterwards. But what could we do? The whole situation was so appalling. Yes, the atrocities were completely unnecessary, irrelevant, even. But those kinds of moral judgments were a luxury. We were fighting for our lives. Less than a kilometre away from our encampment, Russian prisoners were being thrown into barbed wire encirclements on the steppe with no shelter. They were left to freeze or starve. Is there any real difference?'

'Yes, I think there is,' says Anna slowly. 'Bad as it was, they were men at arms. It was a war situation. The rounding up of those others – civilians – wasn't.'

Now they really have to go. There are tears in Frederik's eyes as they get up to leave.

'Will you tell Ida I'm still here? She's the only one left who could even begin to know what it was like.'

Juliet kisses him. She promises to pop in tomorrow, before they leave. Anna shakes his hand. They drive back in the taxi almost in silence.

The next morning Juliet goes back to see Frederik. Anna doesn't want to go. She decides to go to the Praterstern instead. She wants to be alone to think about all that Frederik told them. Her route takes her through the Naschmarkt area, which is full of Turks and Arabs selling exotic spices and vegetables. The Praterstern was built at the end of the last century and, by today's standards, it is unimpressive. Hardly a competitor for the London Eye, Anna thinks. The whole area is a little seedy, like most permanent funfairs, but it is nonetheless evocative of the 'old' Vienna in a way the other sights have not been.

There is a short queue which moves quickly. Each cabin holds about twenty people and, as they rise, the snowy vista of the city spreads out beneath them, the Danube steely grey in the distance. Her mother's city, she thinks. The scene of such powerful events in the last century. She tries to imagine life then. How different it must have been. There was no luxury of choice – moral or otherwise, just a hard struggle for survival. How depressing it all is. How can we ever understand how people felt then, what pressures weighed upon them to make them act as they did? She of all people, a historian, should know that. Juliet of course, being young, sees everything in black and white. 'Why didn't they just refuse?' she had said. It makes her think of her conversation with Tony. Who knows how we would act in a given situation? Her cabin reaches the ground.

She walks slowly back through the park. The temperature is slightly higher, and the sky is leaden. It looks like more snow. She makes her way to the tram stop. There is just time to have a quick coffee, then she must meet Juliet and the others at the hotel, ready for the return flight to Heathrow.

CHAPTER 21

When Kate received the call from her Aunt Anna she was trailing around the house feeling tired and lethargic, yet bored. She feels vaguely envious when she thinks of Juliet and Anna in Vienna. Why couldn't she have gone with them? Yet she knows she couldn't really have done so. It is taking a surprisingly long time to get over her overdose. Her mother has been anxious, fussing, questioning her about her friends. In fact, that fatal night, she had brought home some regulars from the Barchester. They had given her some stuff which they said was kosher, but it couldn't have been. Or else it had reacted badly with something else she had taken earlier. Fine friends they turned out to be. Clearing off like that when they saw she had already passed out. If her mother hadn't come down when she did, God knows what would have happened. She probably wouldn't be here now. She's still having the nightmares: not every night, but every so often. Are they a result of the stuff she's been smoking? She's not sure.

The house is unnaturally quiet. Her mother has gone off to her gardening class and she has the place to herself. Although Dan is down from Oxford for Christmas, he's at Sebastian's. No surprise there, then! She hadn't wanted her mother to tell him about her escapade, but she had. Said he needed to know, although she couldn't see why. He'd greeted the news with a world-weary 'what did you expect' sort of attitude, as she knew he would.

Her father, on the other hand, who'd come over the following day, had seemed surprisingly concerned. He'd stayed quite a long time, asking her why she'd done it. As if she knew! Perhaps he had a guilty conscience about leaving them. He'd also told her he'd lost his job. That piece of information was for her ears only, apparently. Her mother was not to be told on any account. She'd thought he looked strained, older. When she asked him about Lorna he'd seemed embarrassed. It turned out she was only twenty-nine. Years younger than her own mother and not that much older than she was. Kate had wondered at the time if she'd be wanting to have a baby soon. That was what usually happened when middle-aged men went off with younger women. Her father had seemed strangely loath to leave.

Her mother had gone to see Gran when he arrived and he had stayed with her until the sound of the key in the lock signalled her return. It was only then that he had got up reluctantly and kissed Kate before he left. Just before he left he dropped an envelope onto the sofa beside her. When she opened it she found it contained a Christmas card and a £50 note.

'Don't spend it on anything silly,' he said meaningfully. Kate thought that he probably couldn't really afford it if he'd just lost his job. Still, it would come in very handy. Once he'd gone, Kate wondered if he regretted his decision to leave.

Hugo was due back home for Christmas in a couple of days' time. He, of all of them, had taken his father's departure the hardest, and refused to be in the house if he was going to be there.

When Jude returned from seeing Gran, she was very quiet. Kate asked her what was wrong, and she just replied that she was tired and that visiting Gran was always a bit of a strain. Another letter had arrived from Christoph a couple of days before. Kate's heart had sunk when she read it. He was proposing to pop over to England for a few days over Christmas and was planning to come and see her. Kate hopes it won't be on Christmas Day, and wishes he would just take the hint and disappear.

Her mother would not be best pleased, as the number of people who were expected seemed to be growing by the day. There was their own family of course, minus her father. Then there was Gran, Aunt Anna with Tony and Charlotte and Uncle Edward, possibly Aunt Marion with Juliet and her sister, Amanda. No doubt Sebastian would also turn up during the course of the day. And now Christoph, too. She and her mother really needed to start making a shopping list, and to go up in the loft for the decorations.

In one way, Kate is quite pleased to receive Anna's phone call because it gives her something to do. She wonders what she and Juliet will discover, if anything. The weather is damp and miserable. It is trying to rain. Kate wonders why it never snows in winter any more. When she was a child there was always a snowfall at least once a year. Nowadays it just seems to be endlessly wet. The car park at the Cedars is unusually full and she eventually abandons the car on a bend in the drive. Her mother would have a fit, but Kate's attitude to parking, and to driving for that matter, has always been cavalier. As she approaches Ida's room, she can hear a voice calling out repeatedly:

'*Bitte, bitte, ich brauche Hilfe. Ist jemand da?*'

As she enters the room, she is shocked to see Ida on all fours between the bed and the commode.

'Gran! What are you doing? Let me help you.'

Ida lets out a faint moan. Kate rings the bell and then tries to lever her grandmother up off the floor. Although her Gran weighs practically nothing, Kate is terrified of breaking her ribs; they feel so brittle – so close to the surface. Fortunately, just then, one of the girls arrives in answer to the bell. She and Kate soon manage to get Ida back into her chair. She is flustered and panting, but seems otherwise unhurt.

'What were you trying to do, Ida?' asks Joanne.

'I wanted to use the commode, but I must have lost my balance.'

'How many times have we told you, you must ring the bell for one of us to come and help you.'

'Yes I know, I know. But sometimes I ring and nobody answers.'

Joanne expertly helps Ida onto the commode. One more indignity, thinks Kate. Her grandmother now cannot even go to the toilet in privacy. Once Joanne has emptied the commode and gone, Kate sits down on the lid. She takes her Gran's hand.

'Are you feeling OK now Gran? Please don't do anything like that again.'

Ida smiles weakly, her chest still heaving. 'No, all right my dear. I'm not hurt – really.'

Again Kate notices how frail and thin her grandmother has become.

'Now tell me, my dear. What news do you have for me? How is your mother?'

'Mum's OK really, Gran. Since Dad left, she's really come into her own, somehow. She's joined a gardening class and she seems more relaxed than I've seen her for a long time.'

'Poor Jude. She always was so vulnerable. And then she didn't have the mental resources of the other two.'

Kate hadn't thought of it like that, but she realises that it is probably true. Her mother has spent most of her life pursuing the idea of a wealthy middle-class lifestyle. But somehow it never seemed to make her happy. Now that the rug has been pulled out from all that, she seems finally more content.

'And you, my dear. Are you happy?'

Kate stops short. Only her Gran would ask a question like that.

'Well Gran, I've been having some strange dreams recently.'

She explains the dreams to Ida. When she has finished, Ida remains silent for a while. At last she says:

'And how long have you been having these dreams?'

Kate tries to remember.

'Well, a couple of months, I suppose.'

Ida shakes her head. 'How, strange, how strange,' is all she will say.

Then Kate remembers the main purpose of her visit. She doesn't want to ask Ida outright about Horst's family, so she tries to think of an opening gambit. She decides to talk about her own brothers, and then to lead the conversation round to brothers and sisters in general. She tells Ida that Hugo has been particularly hurt by their father's leaving.

'He seems so angry, somehow, and yet – goodness knows – people get divorced every day.'

'And what about Dan?' asks Ida.

'Well, he hardly seems to have noticed that he's gone. He's so taken up with some project he's working on with Sebastian.'

Ida thinks about this for a moment.

'Dan's not really interested in girls, is he?' she says suddenly.

Kate is astounded. Once again, her grandmother's perceptiveness has caught her off guard.

'No, you're right Gran. He's not. But Mum just doesn't seem to know.'

'Perhaps she doesn't want to know,' says her grandmother.

Kate has to acknowledge that this is probably the case.

'What about you Gran?' she says. 'You just had one brother, didn't you?'

'Yes, Ernst. He was killed in the war, you know. We got on really well on the whole, and I was devastated when he died. But he was always my mother's favourite. I knew that from an early age. When he was killed, she seemed to lose her reason for living, at least for a while.'

'Did your first husband know him?'

'Oh yes. They were great friends. In fact, Ernst was the best man at our wedding. And of course they shared a love of music, and would play together for hours. Just like your cousin Juliet. She has inherited their talent,' she says with a touch of pride.

'And did Horst have brothers and sisters who were also musical?' puts in Kate quickly.

'Well, his sisters played the piano rather well but Frederik was always more interested in sport. He was a charming boy,' says Ida wistfully. 'It seems like only yesterday that we were sitting in the park listening to the Stadtkappelle playing Strauss waltzes; and yet it must be – what – over sixty years ago.'

Ida sighs; engulfed by a wave of nostalgia for that sunlit time when life had seemed full of promise and evil was an unknown concept. It's funny how nostalgia – *Heimweh* in German – so much more descriptive – can make you feel as if you are drowning. *Heimweh* actually describes her feelings better. A longing, not just for another time, but for another place – for home. Is Vienna then still her spiritual home, in spite of everything? She remembers someone saying once that nostalgia is really mourning, not for another time or place, but for one's lost youth.

Kate has the information that she needs. It is easy now to check the relative ages of the siblings. There is a knock at the door and Kim comes in, with a pot of tea and two cups. She and her grandmother drink the tea together and then Kate leaves, reminding Ida that it is Christmas in a few days' time, and that she is invited to Bromley. Kate will pick her up.

Ida smiles. 'Yes, my dear. I shall look forward to it.'

Once in the car, Kate dials Anna's number and tells her what she has found out. Then she drives back home through the suburban streets, still crowded with Christmas shoppers.

CHAPTER 22

There is something about Christmas Eve that is better than the day itself. Children haven't understood this yet, but adults know it to be true. Anticipation ranks highly among life's pleasures. The longed-for event itself is invariably something of a let-down. How is it that this is still the case, so many years after the lesson has been learnt and relearnt? The pleasure of anticipation dies slowly but it does, finally, die. The rite of passage to true maturity is not just to accept disappointment but, positively, to expect it. Ida knows this. Anna also believes it to be true.

She unpacks her case. Fortunately, this year there is little to be done, as Christmas Day is to be spent at Jude's. She, Tony and Charlotte are planning to have a Christmas Eve dinner tonight, and then to exchange presents. The trip to Vienna and the meeting with Frederik are still occupying her thoughts. She wonders if she should make a special trip to the Cedars today, to tell Ida what she has learnt, or the more palatable part of it at any rate, or whether she should leave it till tomorrow. Finally, she decides to leave it. In spite of the horror of the things Frederik told them she can, in all honesty, tell her mother that Horst was never at Sobibor. That much is true. What does it matter now if the things he did were equally dreadful? The main thing is that Ida should have some peace of mind for what remains of her life.

By the time Tony and Charlotte return from their last minute shopping trip, Anna has laid the table and the chicken is roasting in the oven, filling the small flat with an appetising smell. Tony opens a bottle of champagne and they are ready to open the presents. Charlotte is still excited, even though she is thirteen now, and rips the paper eagerly from the iPad mini they have bought her. Anna and Tony have bought each other books, which they chose together a month or so ago.

After they have eaten, Charlotte goes to her room to listen to her music, and Anna and Tony remain at the table, finishing their wine, while Anna tells him everything that happened in Vienna. He listens in silence. Anna tries not to leave anything out. When she has finished, Tony finishes his glass of wine and leans back in his chair.

'What a horrifying story, but how fascinating, somehow, to hear a first-hand account of the Russian campaign. I suppose it's no worse than other atrocities one has heard about but, in a way, when someone one knows, or even knows of, is involved, it seems that much worse. I presume you won't tell your mother any of that.'

'Oh, good heavens, no. I'll just tell her that Horst was never at Sobibor, which is the truth. I must admit, though, that the whole business has left me feeling very gloomy. I just can't seem to get it out of my mind.'

Anna gets up to clear the dishes. Tony comes up behind her and puts him arms round her waist.

'Anna, it all happened light years ago. It's ancient history. You must try to forget it now.'

That phrase 'ancient history' again. Maybe it is, but it's her

293

family's history and anyway, she's a historian, and she knows that its history that makes us what we are.

'Yes, I know,' she says at length. 'But unfortunately ghastly events tend to have repercussions on successive generations.

***

Whatever the weather is like in the town, the cliffs above Dover are often swathed in a blanket of sea mist. Today is no exception. When Edward had left home in his ancient, rattly Ford Anglia, a wintry sun had been breaking through the clouds but as soon as he reaches the headland, he has to put his lights on. Now the air smells damp and salty. Through the mist, the foghorns of the ferries can be heard, although the boats themselves are hidden from view.

Edward has come out early to walk Buster, their Highland Terrier, and also, if truth be told, to avoid Marion, who has worked herself into a fury about the proposed visit to his sister Jude's. Edward has never really understood Marion's antipathy towards his family. But then, Marion doesn't much like her own family, either, or her colleagues or customers, come to think of it.

Edward gets out of the car and puts Buster's lead on. If he decides to go chasing after a rabbit or something in this mist, he doesn't fancy his chances of ever finding him again, and the thought of going home without him is too dreadful to contemplate. Although Marion has little time for people, she is besotted with the dog. Edward secretly rather dislikes Buster. He is yappy and bad tempered, just like his mistress.

Edward now fumbles in his pocket for his cigarettes and pauses for a moment to light one, his head averted from the breeze that has sprung up. He follows the path that runs along the edge of the cliff. There are few other walkers about today. After all, it is Christmas Eve, and the weather is inclement. As he walks, he finds that he is thinking yet again about his early childhood. Try as he might, he cannot conjure up any image of his father, nor can he hear his voice. All he can remember is his mother telling him that his father is about to come home on leave, and his feeling of excited anticipation at the thought of it, at least in the early days.

Later on, his mother always seemed tense and anxious when he was due home. Hardly surprising he thinks, in retrospect, considering what Ida must have known, or at least suspected. Occasionally he remembers playing with other children; usually the children of his mother's friends, or other children living in the same apartment block as themselves. Most often, though, he was alone. Not exactly left to his own devices, because his mother was always there, but solitary.

He also has fleeting memories of his grandmother. She, too, was quiet and sad. He knew that her son, Ernst, had been killed, and that that was the reason. He used to look forward to her visits though. She was fond of him and, when she was having a good day, she would tell him stories about when she was a little girl in the mountains. As he plays through these scenes in his mind, some other memory, something he can't quite reach, floats frustratingly close to the edge of his consciousness and then recedes again. Each time this happens, a wave of nausea comes over him and he starts to shake.

This time, the effect is particularly violent. He grips the dog's lead tighter and stands still for a moment until it passes. The mist is beginning to lift slightly now, and he can make out the grey expanse of sea below him. The edge of the cliffs is only a few feet away. For the millionth time he imagines stepping off the cliff and floating down into oblivion. Never again having to endure the feelings of fear and self-loathing that spring up, unbidden, whenever his thoughts take this turn. How easy it would be and yet how hard! What is it that holds him back? Certainly not Marion. Possibly his daughters, although they have their own lives now, and his relationship with them has never been particularly close. His mother? Maybe it's because he can't bear to inflict more pain on her. Surely the worst thing imaginable must be to outlive one's own children.

When he is able to consider things more objectively, he realises that he also needs to know what it is that has so destroyed his life. He is sixty-three years old, fast becoming an old man himself, and yet he still cannot exorcise these feelings.

He turns and starts to walk slowly back towards the car. The mist has almost gone now, and the cloud before his eyes is beginning to lift too. He thinks about tomorrow. He will probably have to go to Jude's on his own, although it is likely that Juliet and Amanda will also be there. Mother too, of course.

He remembers one of the last Christmases in Vienna, after his mother had met Ernest. There had been good food, and even presents, something which had been unheard of during the dark years of the war. For the first time, Edward had felt safe and protected, and he knew that his mother was safe now too. Ernest's presence had been a warm and comforting one. He had even made his grandmother laugh! He wonders briefly how she must have felt when what remained of her family decamped to England. He doesn't remember her ever visiting them here, and his mother certainly never went back to Vienna.

He sighs. There are so many unanswered questions. He installs

Buster in the back seat, and turns the key in the ignition. After a few unpromising splutters, the engine jerks into life and he sets off for home.

***

The Merchant of Venice is a sell-out for weeks to come, but there are always a few seats reserved for friends and relatives of the cast. The play has received rave reviews, with special mentions for Simon and, of course, for Shylock himself. The Christmas Eve matinee is the last performance before the four-day break.

Simon has been feeling odd, out of sorts, recently. The thrill of Tristram's devotion and Natasha's doe-eyed admiration now seem curiously meaningless. Instead of going to the pub with the rest of the cast after the performance, Simon has been going straight home and to bed. He moved out of the flat in Clapham a week or so after Juliet left, and is now staying with his mother in Golders Green.

Juliet's departure, or rather her dismissal of him, has left him feeling strangely bereft. At first, he couldn't believe she meant it, but when she subsequently rebuffed his messages, he was forced to accept that he has lost her. The words of the Joni Mitchell song echo through his head: 'You don't know what you've got till it's gone.' It just about sums him up.

His mother is pleased that he's no longer with Juliet, he can tell. She never did like her; she wanted him to marry a nice Jewish girl. He realises now that Juliet represented security for him and, now that she's gone, he feels adrift, rudderless. It is true that he is now free to play the field, to indulge in any adventures that he likes but, strangely, he no longer wants to.

At least his gloom hasn't affected his performance. When the play ends, the audience are on their feet, and there are so many encores that he just wishes he could go home. After the final curtain has dropped, he is making his way back to his dressing room, when Tristram stops him. 'Simon, did you see Juliet in the audience? She was in row two.'

Simon stops dead.

'Are you sure?' He looks searchingly at Tristram.

'Yes, quite sure. She's pretty unmistakable.'

Tristram is aware that Simon and Juliet have split up, and is convinced that it is over him.

Simon can't decide whether to rush round to the foyer to try to intercept her, or to go and clean off his stage makeup first. Eventually he decides on the latter course of action. After all, she may have already left, and he can hardly chase down the street in doublet and hose. He is hurriedly cleaning off his makeup when there is a tap at the door of his dressing room.

'Come in,' he calls, and suddenly Juliet is standing there in the doorway. She looks different, somehow, older yet more attractive, less needy.

'Hello Simon,' she says evenly.

'Ju! What are you doing here?'

'I came to see the play, of course.'

Simon is speechless for a moment. When he finds his voice, he says: 'Wh – what did you think of it?'

'I thought it was brilliant. You, particularly, were brilliant.'

This is said coolly, without flattery.

'Well, I'm glad you came, although I must say I never expected to see you.'

'Your friend spotted me straight away,' says Juliet.

'What? Oh Tristram, yes,' says Simon uncertainly. 'Look Ju, do you fancy going for a drink or something?'

'Yes, why not. Only not that pub that all your mates go to. Somewhere quiet.'

Simon thinks for a moment. 'How about the George, then, on Old Street? You know where it is, don't you?'

Juliet nods. 'I'll see you there in twenty minutes then.'

Simon hurriedly removes the rest of his makeup and changes out of his costume. All the time he is speculating as to Juliet's motives. Is he forgiven, or did she just come to the play out of curiosity?

When he arrives at the George, he spots her at once. She is sitting at a table a little way from the bar, a glass of red wine in front of her. She looks calm, self-possessed. Simon gets himself half a lager – he's not normally much of a drinker – and sits down opposite her.

'So, how did the tour go?' he begins.

'Oh, the tour. It was very interesting, as a matter of fact,' she says enigmatically.

'You went to Warsaw, didn't you?'

'Yes, that's right.'

The words are left hanging in the air, both thinking of the ghetto, neither voicing it.

'And then Vienna?'

'Yes.'

'Your grandmother comes from there.'

'Yes.'

'Did you – I mean – did you go and see where she lived, or anything like that?'

'Oh yes. Aunt Anna joined me, and we did quite a bit of

investigating. It's a remarkable city.'

Juliet doesn't seem inclined to elaborate further.

'Ju, about what happened,' Simon begins desperately. 'I never meant for it to go that far. I've missed you so much.'

Juliet raises her eyebrows.

'Have you really? You surprise me.'

'Yes, well, I mean it. When you left, it made me realise how much I need you.'

'Well, I've always been aware that you "need" me. That was never really the question.'

'Well, what is the question, then?'

'Oh,' says Juliet vaguely, 'love, I suppose.'

'Well I do. Love you, I mean.'

Juliet sighs. How ironic life is. All those years when she would have given anything for him to say that and to know that he meant it, as she knows he means it now. But it's too late. It's as though, all this time, she's been wearing blinkers and they've suddenly been removed. The haunted air, the ambivalence, now just seem like weakness and immaturity. He certainly seems immature compared to Geoff, although he's several years older. But, in spite of all this, she knows she is going to take him back. She feels that their destinies are irrevocably bound together, and the things she has learnt recently have only served to underline the fact. From now on, Simon is to be her act of contrition, her atonement, for her family's dreadful history. She cannot leave him now. She puts her glass down and gets up from the table.

'Come on,' she says, 'let's go home. You can ring your mother in the morning.'

He looks at her in amazement, then meekly gets up too.

***

Jude and Kate are at the supermarket early on Christmas Eve. List in hand, they plough through the crowds of shoppers, throwing mounds of vegetable and fruit into the trolley. The turkey, ordered last week, has already arrived. Kate insisted on asking all the guests to bring some item from the list: chocolates, Christmas pudding, mince pies, although Jude was not keen.

'It makes sense, Mum,' she says. 'Now that Dad's not here we're no better off than anyone else.'

Jude has to concede that this is true. Although they've had a couple of offers on the house, they are waiting for the asking price and, in the meantime, it is expensive to run. Unlike Kate, Jude is unaware that Gerry has lost his job. She is beginning to realise how much she dislikes Christmas. The expense, the interruption to normal life, the forced gaiety. Still, it has to be got through. The queues at the checkout are enormous, even though it is still only nine thirty. When they have finally loaded the bags into the back of the car, they decide to stop at Starbucks to revive themselves, before the ghastly business of unloading the shopping again and putting it all away.

Kate gets the two cups of cappuccino while her mother lowers herself onto one of the red leather sofas. Her face is pink with exertion, and wisps of hair are falling onto her face. Kate, on the other hand, couldn't look more different. She is positively gaunt, and her face is unnaturally white against her black hair.

Jude is thinking about her mother, as she so often does recently. Ida's account of Horst's activities seems to have stirred something within her. It is making her rake through her early memories, searching for some kind of trigger.

Kate is wondering what, if anything, Juliet and Aunt Anna have discovered in Vienna. Last night she had the dream again, only this time it was a little different. She shivers as she recalls it, her hands clammy. She is alone in a house. It is dark. There is no light, even from the street outside. She has bolted the doors but there is one door at the back she has forgotten to lock. The only sound comes from the radio on a table in the corner.

Suddenly, she hears a noise from the back door. She feels herself stiffen with fear. She realises the back door is not locked. Footsteps are coming down the passage now. They are not stealthy footsteps, but loud, clattering ones. The swish of material can be heard. She reaches out her hand to switch off the radio, but the owner of the footsteps know where she is. She shrinks back into a corner of the room. The door opens and she can feel an alien presence in the room. She hears a voice calling her name, urgently. 'Kate, Kate, what's the matter?'

Gradually, memories of the dream fade and she realises where she is. Her mother is repeating her name, anxiously. 'Sorry Mum, I was miles away. What were you saying?'

'It doesn't matter. You look so sort of stricken though, are you sure you're alright?'

'Yes, perfectly,' says Kate, brisk now. 'Come on, Mum. We'd better get this lot home.'

They unpack the shopping and prepare the vegetables for the following day. That evening, Kate is to start work at the Barchester again. It promises to be a riotous evening – ticket admission only – and Jude isn't keen on her going.

'It'll be fine, Mum, don't worry. I'm hardly going to do the same daft thing again.'

'No, it's not that. It's just that you don't seem strong enough yet.

I know what these places can be like.'

In fact, Jude doesn't really know what they're like at all. She's never been to the Barchester, and would be shocked if she did. When Kate has left she goes into the sitting room. The curtains are still undrawn, and the night outside is very black, very silent.

She picks up the paper and tries to read, but she can't concentrate. It falls onto her knees, and she finds herself staring out into the dark. She thinks about how much her life has changed in the last few months. The things she took for granted have changed irrevocably. She is now separated, soon to be divorced, and her days in the house the children grew up in are numbered. It is as though she is no longer the person she always thought she was. She feels rootless, without a past. It is an odd feeling, not altogether unpleasant. She pours herself a glass of white wine and draws the curtains.

Soon it will be Christmas Day, her first without Gerry. She wonders briefly and incuriously how he will be spending it. No doubt with the lovely Lorna. She yawns. She really doesn't care. Her thoughts then move on to her mother again. She is the one person who has always succeeded in making her feel uneasy. And yet she is aware that she has always been her mother's favourite. She really cannot think why. After all, Edward was the one who went through so much with her in Vienna, and Anna was always the perfect daughter, clever and capable. It is all very bizarre. She gives up trying to make sense of it all, and decides to have an early night, ready for the onslaught tomorrow.

CHAPTER 23

Ida's hip is aching again, the pain running right down her leg this time. Pain is a funny thing, she thinks. Just when you're absolutely sure that the problem is in one particular area, it suddenly moves to somewhere completely different. This pain in her leg, for instance, she hasn't had it before. And why should it be in her leg at all? It's nowhere near her pelvis. She tries to turn over in order to transfer the weight to her other side, but it's no better. She debates whether to ring the call bell, or to try to stick it out until breakfast time.

Today is Christmas Day. There'd been a general air of excitement about the place yesterday that even she couldn't miss. The girls had decorated their hats with tinsel or bits of holly, and some were wearing Christmas pudding earrings or brooches. At about ten o'clock in the evening, when everyone was in bed, they'd come round to each room, singing carols. Ida was glad to see them enjoying themselves. They were so young, some of them barely more than schoolgirls. They'd been chattering about what they hoped to receive from parents or boyfriends. Ida knew they didn't have much spare cash. Christmas was obviously an important time for them.

Ida can just about remember a time when it was important for her, too. Not any more. Now nothing is important except perhaps for this pain in her leg to stop. When you get old, your horizons shrink, imperceptibly at first, then faster and faster until eventually your life is bounded by the four walls of your room, often in an old people's home. Your memories, of course, know no such boundaries. They gradually expand until the most distant ones, those of your earliest childhood, become clearest. It's odd really, she thinks, in youth and middle age those memories are fuzzy, vague. She supposes it must be because then, day to day problems occupy you, pushing other things to the back of your mind. The funny thing is, though, nobody thinks it will happen to them. She herself would never have imagined that she would end up in a place like this, her life reduced to one small room and her memories.

She struggles to look at the clock on her bedside table. Six o'clock. Only another hour and a half to go till the girls come round with breakfast. Not that she's hungry, but at least it will mean a change of position. She manages to drift into a fitful doze, and awakes groggy and bleary-eyed, as Gloria comes in with her breakfast.

'Merry Christmas, Ida darlin'!' she says, and kisses her.

'Merry Christmas,' replies Ida weakly.

When Gloria has gone, Ida drinks half a cup of tea and pushes the food around a bit on her plate. As it's Christmas, the woman who is employed to feed her is not there. Ida is relieved to have a holiday from the constant jolly exhortations to 'eat up, there's a good girl.' The fact is she is never hungry now. Kim and Jo come to get her up and wash her. Kim knows there's no point in asking Ida to choose her clothes, so she expertly selects a velvet skirt and blouse which she considers fitting for the occasion.

'You're going to your daughter's today Ida, aren't you? You

make sure you enjoy yourself.'

'Yes, thank you dear. And when are you going to be able to go home?'

'Oh, we're on till just after lunch,' says Jo.

'And then what are you going to do?'

'Well, first I'm going to my boyfriend's house, and we're going to swap presents. Then he's coming over to have Christmas dinner in the evening with my Mum and Dad.'

As she talks, Jo's face flushes with excitement, and her eyes sparkle.

'Kev says he's got me a lovely present. I keep trying to find out what it is, but he won't tell me.'

'Perhaps it's an engagement ring,' says Kim, grinning.

'Oh I don't think so. Although, you never know.'

'Well, my dears, I hope you have a lovely day,' says Ida.

Kim thinks Ida's a really nice person, really considerate. Some of the old bats are so crabby, but Ida is usually grateful for what they do for her, especially now she's on the tablets. Once Ida is washed and dressed, the girls sit her in her chair to wait for Kate. She won't be here for about two hours, but Ida is used to sitting and waiting, or just sitting.

For some reason, she is thinking about Ernest today. What a good man he was, and what a support he had been throughout her life, especially when they first met, but afterwards as well. He only died – what – six or seven years ago, and yet he seems such a shadowy figure, far less clear than people who died years earlier – her mother, for example. Much as we try, we cannot hold onto the dead, she thinks. They retreat from us, inexorably, into the shadows.

Poor Ernest, perhaps he deserved better than her. He should

have been someone's first choice, not second best.

Just then, Gloria pops her head round the door.

'Ida, I just came to tell you that the priest is here, just in case you was wantin' to see him. I know you don't usually, but seein' as it's Christmas.'

'No, thank you. I'll just wait here for my granddaughter.'

'Just as you like darlin'. Have a nice day.'

'Thank you Gloria. You too.'

Ida wonders how long it must be now since she last went to church. She reckons it must be about sixty years! When she stopped going, it was because she could no longer accept that a benign God could allow horror on such a scale. She knows all the counter-arguments, about free will and so on, but she cannot reconcile them. What about the children? Did they need to be sacrificed so that men could be taught the error of their ways? It makes no sense to her. She looks at the clock again. Another hour until Kate is due.

***

Anna has half a mind to go to church before going to Jude's. She could just fit it in if she went to the ten o'clock service, but she knows Tony won't come with her. He is a confirmed atheist, although she would describe herself more as agnostic. In spite of herself, she is drawn to the formulaic rituals of the church, the archaic language of the service. The musty, incense-laden atmosphere gives her a feeling of spirituality, which she can find nowhere else.

Objectively, though, she cannot really accept any defined idea of God. The idea of a force for good is an easy one to accept,

307

but it is not Christianity. For that, you must accept all the tenets of the Bible, and that she is unable to do. Oddly, her mind is running along the same lines as her mother's. She thinks about the dreadful things that Frederik told them. In the end, she decides against going. Although Tony would not say anything, she would feel his disapproval of her hypocrisy. She puts on the radio instead, and listens to the carols from King's while she gathers together the things they have promised to take to Jude's.

***

Juliet hasn't slept much. Simon, on the other hand, is in a deep sleep, his breathing regular. Juliet looks at him with an overwhelming sense of resignation. He is so neurotic, so complicated. Is it his background? It seems strange, because he has never personally experienced any of the things that seem to obsess him so. But nor has she, yet she too feels oppressed by the past. She knows she would be better off with Geoff, yet she also knows that Simon is her destiny, somehow. Poor Geoff! How badly she has treated him!

Just then, Simon stirs. He turns over and looks at her, as though surprised to see her there. Then he smiles.

'Ju! It's really you. For a moment I thought I was dreaming.'

'Yes, it's me. Merry Christmas!'

'Merry Christmas! What a lovely Christmas present, having you back.'

Juliet smiles wryly.

'So, tell me about your trip.'

'Well, what do you want to know?'

'Oh, you know, everything. How the concert went, what the places were like you visited.'

'The concert couldn't have gone better. We had a full house every night, and people seemed to love it, especially, perhaps, in Heidelberg and Vienna.'

'And how about Warsaw?' There's a slight catch in Simon's voice.

'Well yes, it went down well there, too.'

'And did you do any sightseeing?'

'You mean did I go to the ghetto. Yes, we went there.'

'Who's "we"?' asks Simon immediately.

'A friend from the orchestra and myself,' says Juliet evenly.

'And you and this friend, what did you think?'

'It was quite simply horrible. Of course, it's just part of the city now, but you can feel what happened there. It's as though it's impregnated the fabric of the place.'

Simon is silent for a moment.

'You should go there yourself sometime. It might help to lay a few ghosts.'

'I don't think I could ever bear to do that. And when you went to Vienna,' he goes on, 'did you find out anything about your Gran's life?'

'Yes, we did. We found her brother-in-law, Frederik, in an old people's home.'

'Good heavens! How amazing! And had he been in the SS too?'

'No,' says Juliet shortly. 'He fought at Stalingrad, though. It was pretty horrific.'

Simon pauses. 'Look, Ju,' he says eventually, 'I know I was completely out of order before you went away. I can't blame you for stuff your grandfather did – or may have done. I know that now. Just the same as I can't be constantly thinking about what happened to my relatives. We're a new generation, and it's a new century. We can't let our lives be tainted by all that.'

But Juliet can't shake off the feeling that she is and always will be tainted, as he calls it. She nods, though.

'Yes, you're right. We've got to get on with our lives.'

He leans over and kisses her, affectionately, but without passion. She feels no passion, either. Again, she thinks of Geoff.

'I'm going to my aunt's house today. Gran will be there and all the family. What plans have you got? I expect you could come too, if you wanted. Or have you arranged to see your mother?'

'Mother will be expecting to see me sometime, but I don't think she'll mind if I go in the evening.'

'Fine. I'll just give Aunt Jude a ring to tell her to expect both of us.'

She jumps out of bed and puts her dressing gown on. She feels depressed by the inevitability of it all. Her strike for freedom did not last long. Wearily she picks up the receiver and dials her aunt's number.

***

Edward can't believe it! Marion has decided to come with him to Jude's. After all that she said about his family, he truly expected her to stay at home, but that morning she appeared in the kitchen early and even, grudgingly, made him a cup of tea. For years they have slept in separate rooms, and sometimes days go by when they hardly see each other, only occasionally meeting on the stairs or in the hall. Today, though, Marion has dug out her tweed suit, and has put on a blouse with a floppy bow at the neck. It is clear she is intending to come. Edward's heart sinks.

'I thought you had quite made up your mind you didn't want

to come,' he says mildly.

'Well, I don't want to, but I suppose it's better than sitting her on me own all day.'

Marion speaks with an unpleasing southern twang. Edward had been vaguely embarrassed about it when he had been teaching at the college, and afterwards immediately ashamed of himself.

'Very well. We'd better get going then.'

He goes to the cupboard to collect the box of crackers and the mince pies that he has agreed to take.

'What's that then?' asks Marion.

'Jude asked everyone if they would make a contribution, as there will be so many of us.'

'Huh!' Marion sneers. 'I should have thought your posh sister could have managed to provide lunch for us. That fancy house and those stuck-up kids of hers.'

'Well actually, Marion, things aren't so good for Jude now. Gerry's left her, and she's going to have to sell the house.'

'Is that so? Well, welcome to the real world! I suppose she may have to actually get a job now.'

Edward says nothing. He walks Buster to the end of the road, then they get in the car and pull out into the one-way system. The weather is cold but bright. Yesterday's fog has completely dissipated, even on the headland.

As they join the motorway, Marion says; 'Who else is going to be there, then?'

Edward runs through the list of guests.

'I'm not sure about Amanda, but I know Juliet's going. Have you heard from her, by the way?'

'Not a thing,' replies Marion.

Amanda is their older daughter. She's a social worker in London, and rarely comes down to Dover to visit her parents.

'They both seem to see more of the rest of your family than they do of their own parents,' says Marion sourly.

'Perhaps it's because you don't exactly make them feel very welcome.'

'Well, I like that! What about you, always moping about the place smoking.'

Edward has to admit to himself that this is true.

'Look Marion, let's have a truce, just for today. We don't want to spoil everyone's Christmas with unnecessary arguments, especially not Mum's.'

'Your mother never liked me, anyway. Nor did the rest of your family. Not good enough for you, that's what they thought. Makes me laugh, though, with a past like theirs.'

'What do you mean?'

'Oh, you know perfectly well. All Nazis, the lot of them, if you ask me.'

Edward freezes. Where on earth has Marion got that from? He would have dismissed it as vicious gossip if recent facts hadn't come to light.

'That's just nonsense, Marion,' he says weakly. 'And anyway, what do you mean, they're all Nazis? You can hardly accuse my sisters, or your own children of that, surely.'

'All tarred with the same brush, I say.'

Edward thinks this is rich, coming from someone who never stops ranting about the groups of asylum seekers who constantly roam the streets of Dover, with nowhere to go and no money to spend. He guesses she probably doesn't even understand that xenophobia was one of the main tenets of Nazi philosophy. As far as she's concerned, "Nazi" is just a term of abuse, which will do as well as any other to insult his family. They continue the drive in silence.

Eventually, Edward switches on the radio. The poignant notes of a Mozart violin concerto fill the car. He doesn't know why the music is so familiar, but he seems to remember someone playing it, over and over, when he was small. It must have been his father. It couldn't have been his uncle Ernst, because he was killed early on. How strange that he cannot remember the man himself, but he can remember the music! It moves something within him, making him feel unutterably wistful.

***

As Jude expected, Kate got in from the Barchester very late. Consequently, at ten o'clock on Christmas morning, she is still in a deep sleep. Fortunately, the vegetables have already been prepared, and all Jude has to do is put the turkey in the oven to cook slowly. The previous evening hadn't been as peaceful as she'd imagined it would be. Dan and Hugo had arrived within about an hour of each other and, unusually, both were in the mood to chat. Greatly relieved that they had both already eaten, Jude fetched a bottle of wine. They soon finished it and then opened another. Hugo wanted to know all about the sale of the house. He was still in a lather of rage about his father. Looking at him, Jude couldn't help thinking how much he was beginning to look like him. Even at twenty-three his hair was beginning to recede and his waistline was thickening.

'I suppose he's still with that woman,' he says aggressively.

'Well yes, I think so,' replies Jude.

She suddenly wonders if Hugo is actually jealous of his father.

'And is he really going to make you sell the house?'

'Well, it makes sense, Hugo. It's far too big for me now. You've already left, and Kate and Dan won't be here forever.'

'I'm planning to move up to Oxford permanently after my finals,' says Dan. 'Sebastian and I have a chance to start work on a new project funded by the university.'

'That's marvellous, darling,' says Jude.

'Yes, It's a fantastic opportunity. But what on earth is going on with Kate, Mum?'

Jude sighs. 'Well, she's definitely given up her university course.'

'Good God!' says Hugo, 'I didn't know that.'

Before she can stop him, Dan has told Hugo about Kate's overdose.

'Well, I can't say I'm surprised,' says Hugo. 'It's probably all down to Dad's behaviour.'

Jude doubts it, but she says nothing. She thinks how self-righteous both her sons are in their own way. It's almost as though she has to justify everyone's actions to them.

In the morning, Kate finally surfaces about eleven.

'God, sorry Mum. You should have woken me. What shall I do?'

'It's OK, Kate. I think it's all under control. You could lay the table, though. And you're going to pick up your grandmother, aren't you?'

'Yes, definitely. I'll do the table, then I'll leave in about an hour.'

Just then, there's a knock at the door. Kate and Jude look at each other. Surely the guests aren't arriving already. Kate is wearing an ancient T-shirt and her hair is standing on end.

Are you expecting anyone yet?'

Jude shakes her head. 'No, the rest of the family are coming about one.'

She goes to open the door. On the doorstep are Sebastian and Christoph.

'Hi,' says Sebastian. 'It's OK, we didn't come together, we just met at the gate.'

'Good morning Mrs Fairbrother,' says Christoph, formally.

'Well, hello both of you. Come in.'

Jude calls Dan and Kate. Sebastian disappears upstairs with Dan, and Kate is left staring at Christoph.

'Kate, I had to come. You did not answer my letters.'

He takes a step towards her. Jude retreats tactfully into the kitchen.

'Christoph! Were you in England anyway, or have you come specially?'

'I had a meeting two days ago, but I thought I would surprise you on Christmas morning.'

Surprise? More of a shock, thinks Kate. Still, it's Christmas, the season of good will and all that, and she can hardly turn him away. She makes him coffee and finishes laying the table. Then she goes and gets dressed. When she comes down, Christoph is in the kitchen, talking to Jude. As she appears, he breaks off what he was saying.

'Right,' says Kate brightly. 'I'm ready. Let's go and get Gran.'

***

Jude is in a panic. She counts up. She was expecting ten people to lunch altogether and now, suddenly, it looks as though there will be fourteen. Juliet had rung earlier to ask if Simon could come. She had been a little surprised. She'd understood from Anna that Simon was no longer on the scene but, of course, she'd had to say yes. Then there was Sebastian who, admittedly, she'd half expected, then Christoph, whom she definitely had not. Finally, there's Amanda, Juliet's sister. She'd rung last night to say she was coming too. Well, thank God she'd got a large ham to eke out the turkey. She's done mountains of potatoes, but fourteen people! And the young men eat so much! Oh well, they'll just have to manage.

By half past one, everyone has arrived except Edward. Hugo has gleefully raided what remains of his father's cellar, and has opened six bottles of vintage champagne. The atmosphere is convivial. Everyone is clinking glasses and wishing each other Merry Christmas. Ida is ensconced in her habitual armchair near the fire. She too has a glass of champagne in her hand, but she doesn't seem to be drinking it. Anna is talking to her. Although she needs to raise her voice, there is such a hubbub that no one else can hear what she is saying.

'Mum,' she says urgently. 'You know I told you I was going to Vienna. To meet Juliet.'

Ida is looking confused. Her eyes are rheumy, as she peers round the room. Anna wonders if she actually knows where she is. She lays her hand on her mother's arm.

'Mum,' she says.

Ida turns to look at her daughter. Anna feels she now has her full attention.

'I have to tell you something important.' Ida blinks and peers anxiously at Anna. The wave of pity that Anna feels runs through her whole body. Ida looks so small and out of things, as though everything is now beyond her.

'When I was in Vienna,' she repeats, 'I found Frederik, your brother-in-law.'

Ida stares at her. 'Frederik? Who is Frederik?' she says at last.

'Mum, you know, Horst's younger brother. He's still alive, and he's living in a residential home, a bit like the Cedars.'

'Frederik,' repeats Ida. 'He is still alive?'

'Yes Mum, I told you. We had a long chat with him. He asked about you, of course. I think he was very fond of you.'

'He was a sweet boy.' Ida stops for a moment. 'In the end though, we fell out. I can't remember why, now.'

Anna remembers Frederik telling them that he had continued to visit Horst at the end whereas, by that time, Ida had washed her hands of him.

'Anyway, Mum, the really important thing is, he told me that Horst never was at Sobibor.'

Ida stares at Anna. She grabs her hand.

'Never at Sobibor? But I don't understand. I saw his ticket. He must have been going there.'

'No Mum. Frederik was quite definite. He said he was sent to the Balkans, to fight the partisans.'

Ida's face seems to crumple, and her eyes fill with tears.

'Thank God,' she says. 'Thank God.'

Anna doesn't elaborate. She had never, in any case, had any intention of telling Ida anything about Horst's other activities.

'I just thought you might like to write to Frederik,' she suggests. 'He was so interested to hear about you. I can help you, if you like.'

'Yes, I'll do that, Anna. Poor Frederik, we had such good times, the three of us, until it all started to go wrong.'

Anna squeezes her mother's arm and moves away.

She is amazed to see Simon. She goes over to Juliet. Juliet has been slightly dreading this moment.

Before Anna can say a word, she says, 'Yes, yes, I know what you're going to say. As you can see, we've got back together again.'

Anna is incredulous. 'But why, Juliet? I really thought you'd got over all that. And you were getting on so well with Geoff.'

'Yes, I know. It's hard to explain. It seems to be something to do with going to see Uncle Frederik and, before that, the whole trip I suppose, and the Warsaw ghetto.'

'How do you mean?'

'I just feel that – well – I've found out so many terrible things recently, about my family, I just needed to do something to make up for it.'

'You mean you've got to make it up to Simon because of what your grandfather might have done?'

Juliet nods. 'Yes, I suppose so.'

'But none of it's your fault. You don't have to sacrifice your whole life. All that may have happened back then, it's nothing whatsoever to do with you. You don't have to atone for anything.'

Juliet looks stubborn. 'Even so, it's something I feel I have to do.'

Just then, to Juliet's relief, Kate comes up to them. Anna remembers she knows nothing about their visit to Uncle Frederik. She feels guilty about it. Kate, after all, had gone to the trouble of going to see Ida to find out if Horst had any brothers or sisters. She and Juliet tell Kate the gist of what happened, leaving out the grisly bits. Kate's eyes are unnaturally bright.

'I'd love to go and see him. He sounds really sweet.'

'Yes, he certainly is. And he has some amazing tales to tell.'

Anna thinks Kate is looking very thin and pale. She wonders if she has fully recovered, but doesn't like to bring up the subject in front of Juliet.

Christoph finds himself standing on the edge of the group. Kate is deep in conversation with her cousin and aunt. Suddenly a voice beside him says 'Hi. I don't think we've met.'

He looks round and sees a dark, good-looking young man, with very intense grey eyes. Christoph is not quite sure how he should introduce himself. It seems presumptuous to say that he is Kate's boyfriend as she, quite evidently, does not see him as such. In the end, he says he's a friend of Kate's from Berlin. Simon raises him eyebrows.

'Berlin? Fascinating. My name is Simon. I'm Juliet's partner. Do you know her? The blond girl, Kate's cousin.'

It is Christoph's turn to be surprised. The last time he had seen Juliet she was with someone different. Someone from the orchestra, if he remembers rightly. He doesn't say anything, though. He just nods.

'Have you been to Berlin?' he asks, as an opening gambit.

'No, never. In fact, I've never been to Germany. I'm not sure that I could.'

Christoph looks at him guardedly. He thinks it's an odd thing to say. Could he be Jewish?

'Oh well, I think you would be pleasantly surprised. German society is very open now, you know.'

'So I've heard. I'm not sure that people change that much, though, even if "society", as you put it is so open.'

Christoph is saved from countering this by Tony, who comes to ask Simon about the play. He slips gratefully away and joins Dan and Sebastian, who are helping themselves liberally to the champagne.

'Hello, my friend.' He addresses Dan in a way that has always irritated him. 'And how is the project going?'

'Oh, pretty well. In fact, we're nearing completion, aren't we Seb?'

Sebastian nods. He remembers Christoph from the family lunch just before Dan's father had left.

'And how is your work going? You're involved in some kind of charitable work with the homeless, if I remember rightly.'

'Yes, indeed. I suppose if I were to say that it's going well, it would imply that we have now housed them all but, I'm afraid, that is far from the case. They still keep coming in hordes.'

'And what happens when all the available housing is taken?' enquires Dan.

Christoph shrugs. 'I really don't know. The government would either have to build more social housing, outside the city, or they would have to stop the flow of immigrants from the East.'

'What, create a sort of fortress Germany?' says Dan sarcastically. 'Surely that wouldn't do.'

'It might have to happen,' says Christoph, without rising to the bait. 'After all, most other European countries have restrained, no, restricted immigration.'

Sebastian nods in agreement. 'It seems the only possible thing to do. Services in the so-called host countries are vastly overstretched as it is. And there's a groundswell of public feeling against them. Far better to help these people in their own countries, I say.'

After Dan's obvious antagonism, Christoph is grateful for Sebastian's objective comments, even if he does not totally agree with them.

Jude has been checking on the meal, turning down various pans of boiling vegetables, transferring the turkey to the heated trolley and making the gravy. She comes into the sitting room now, taking off her apron and trying to smooth down the bits of hair that are wilfully escaping from her bun. The kitchen is very hot, and she can feel sweat rolling down beneath her armpits. She sees that her mother is sitting by herself, still clutching an almost full glass of champagne. She realises she hasn't spoken to her yet since Kate brought her. She goes up to her and kneels beside her chair.

'Hello Mum. Aren't you going to drink your champagne?'

Ida looks surprised to see that the glass is still in her hand. Obediently she takes a sip. She smiles at Jude.

'I hope you're not working too hard, my dear.'

'No, it's OK. Kate's been helping me, and it's all under control.'

'Jude, Anna has just told me the good news,' says Ida.

'What good news?'

'Well, apparently Horst was never at Sobibor. Frederik told her.'

'Who's Frederik?'

'He's my brother-in-law. When Anna was in Vienna, she went to see him.'

'I didn't know. She never told me anything about any brother-in-law. Honestly, sometimes I wonder if I'm a member of this family or not.'

Ida gives her an odd look. Just then the doorbell rings. Jude gets up and goes to answer it. On the doorstep are Edward and Marion. Her heart sinks. Oh, surely not Marion! That makes five people she wasn't expecting. She forces herself to smile, though, and kisses Edward. As she goes to kiss Marion, she turns her head away.

'Well, this is wonderful,' she hears herself saying. 'The whole family is together at last. And I believe lunch is just about ready.

***

Jude soon realises there's no way everyone is going to fit round the dining table. It would have been a tight squeeze for ten. For fifteen it's impossible. Tony and Christoph carry the kitchen table into the dining room and set it up at one end of the room, near the glass doors which open onto the garden. Fortunately, the room is big enough to take it. They have a bit of a struggle to find enough cutlery, but they manage in the end, even though it's not exactly matching.

After they had got back from the supermarket yesterday, Kate had got the Christmas decorations down from the loft. The house really looks festive. There is a large tree in the corner of the hall, and Jude has cut branches of holly from the garden, which, this year, is covered in berries. They are all aware that this will be the last Christmas in the house they have lived in for so long. Jude wonders where she will be this time next year.

Kate, Christoph, Dan, Sebastian and Charlotte sit at the smaller table. The others squeeze round the big one. Ida is put at the head, between Anna and Jude. Edward is next, then Marion. By this time the champagne has done its work and the atmosphere is animated. Everyone is very hungry. Hugo produces several bottles of Meursault and a couple of Fleurie. Jude had given up the idea of doing starters; there simply weren't enough plates. Amid the general chat and noise, Ida seems isolated. She toys with the food on her plate. Anna glances at her uneasily. She wonders if she should attempt to feed her. It hardly seems appropriate here, though.

'Come on Mum,' she leans over to her. 'See if you can eat just a little bit.'

Marion is seated opposite Juliet. She leans across the table now.

'Well, Juliet, you haven't told us about your tour. I suppose everyone else knows all about it. I expect I'm the last to know, as usual.'

Juliet looks up, startled.

'Well, I've only just come back, Mum. I haven't really had a chance to tell anyone about it yet.'

'Your Aunt Anna went with you, though, didn't she?'

Edward wonders where this is leading. He knows there's no point in trying to shut Marion up. When he's tried to do that in the past, it has only made her worse.

'Yes, Anna joined me in Vienna. She'd never been there, and she wanted to see where Gran was brought up.'

'I'd have thought she'd have wanted to draw a veil over that,' says Marion, nastily.

'Marion, please,' says Edward.

'What do you mean "please"? I'm just asking about Juliet's trip, that's all.'

By this time, they have the attention of the whole table, except for Ida, who continues to move the food around her plate abstractedly. Anna has a sinking feeling. Christoph, Simon, Sebastian and Dan look up with interest, sensing an altercation.

'I should have thought no one would want to go digging up a Nazi past. No one in their right mind, that is.'

Kate looks across at Christoph. She can see he's taking it all in. Simon takes a gulp of wine and glances at Juliet. He wonders if he should somehow come to her aid. But what would he say? And anyway, it's just the sort of thing he was saying to her a few weeks ago. What Marion is saying is, in essence, the truth.

'Well, since you ask. the fact is that we did find a relative of

Gran's. Her brother-in-law. He's a nice old man, really interesting.'

Edward is astonished to hear this. Jude thinks there seems to be some kind of inner circle in this family, from which she is excluded.

'Oh really?' says Marion. 'Was he a Nazi as well? As well as your grandfather, I mean.'

There is a deathly silence around the table, then Juliet says quietly, 'No, he wasn't a Nazi.'

Anna steals a furtive glance at her mother. She seems completely unaware of what is being said. Tony changes the subject, asking Jude what her plans are with regard to selling the house. The general conversation resumes, although it is a little muted now. By the time lunch is finished, darkness is already falling. Ida is beginning to look anxious. She taps on the table, and asks Kate several times what time it is.

'It's alright. Gran. It's only half past three. They know at the Cedars that you're staying out for tea. We'll get you back before bedtime, I promise.'

'Alright dear.' Ida doesn't look entirely convinced. 'Did I see your young man from Germany here?' Kate looks uncomfortable.

'Yes, Christoph's here. He's not exactly my young man any more, though.'

Ida looks puzzled. She cannot comprehend how often the young change partners nowadays. When she was young, you met someone, you got married and that was that. Or, at least, that was that if a war didn't intervene. She herself had remarried, but many of the girls she was at school with who lost their husbands in the war remained widows for the rest of their lives. There were not enough men to go round.

After lunch, Dan and Sebastian disappear upstairs. Kate puts the TV on and the younger ones start watching some inane game show in the family room. Tony, Anna, Jude and Edward scrape the plates and start to stack the dishwasher. Marion is nowhere to be seen.

'I'm sorry about Marion,' begins Edward. 'I just don't know what gets into her.'

'Well, never mind,' says Anna. ' At least, I'm sure Mum didn't hear any of it. That's the main thing.'

'I have to say, Anna, I don't know why I wasn't told about this Uncle Frederik person,' says Jude. 'Did you know about him?' she asks Edward.

'No, I can't say I did.'

'Well, I think you might have told us. First we hear some ghastly story from Mum about a concentration camp and then, suddenly, you and Juliet have dug up some uncle we didn't even know existed.'

'Well, obviously I was going to tell you, but I haven't exactly had much time. It's good news, actually. Uncle Frederik told us that Mum got it wrong. Horst was never at Sobibor.'

Edward is washing the glasses and placing them upside down on some kitchen roll.

'What I don't understand is what made her think that he was there in the first place' he says.

'Well, apparently, he wasn't even in Poland. His last posting was somewhere in the Balkans. Fighting partisans.'

'He and Frederik were in the Russian campaign,' goes on Anna. 'Of course, it wasn't exactly a picnic, and some pretty dreadful things happened, but at least he wasn't involved in anything worse.'

They are all silent for a while. Then Edward goes outside for a smoke and the rest of them adjourn to the sitting room. By now it is completely dark. A few overhead lights are on, but the curtains remain undrawn. The room has a bleak, over-lit appearance. Ida is back in her usual chair. Again, Jude is struck by how small she has become, how insubstantial. She puts some lamps on and draws the curtains, wondering why no one else ever thinks of doing this.

Marion is seated in one of the other armchairs. She is not making any attempt to talk to Ida. The others come in. At first, the conversation is desultory. Everyone is feeling well fed, languid. Juliet thinks fleetingly of Uncle Frederik, wishing he could be there too. At least they are a family; he has no one. Anna is thinking how like her grandmother Juliet is; same wide brow and pronounced cheekbones. She knows she and Edward are alike. They are both tall and spare and have the same wide, curving mouth. As for Kate, she doesn't look remotely like anyone, not even her twin brother. Marion's thoughts are obviously running along the same lines.

'It's funny, isn't it?' she says. 'You don't look nothing like any of the others, Jude.'

Anna realises it's true. Jude is somehow a completely different shape from the others. She has a round face and a round body. She has a vaguely peasanty look, whereas the others have thinner, more ascetic features. Jude shrugs. She has always felt different from the others. Then Marion turns her attention to Ida. She calls her nothing; not Mum, not Ida. She repeats what she has just said. 'Jude's nothing like your other two, is she? You wouldn't really think she was from the same family, would you?'

Edward is just about to remonstrate yet again with Marion when suddenly he experiences a blinding flash of recollection. He utters a cry, and half gets up from his seat, then falls back down again, covering his face with his hands. He feels as though a blindfold has been torn away from his eyes. All these years he's been carrying this knowledge within him. It's been eating at his inner self, like a cancer. And now he knows! Something Marion said, some chance remark, has triggered it. The pictures flood into his head, blindingly clear.

He is a small boy – four or five – and he is sitting on the floor in the corner of a room. His heart is beating so much that he thinks his chest will explode. It is dark, but there are chinks of light coming from somewhere. A terrific noise is coming from the street outside; men shouting, women screaming. There is the clatter of boots on the cobbled street and the rumble of an engine. His mother has told him to stay as quiet as a mouse. He knows that she is also in the room, sitting in the dark, away from the window. He wants desperately to go to her, but she gestures to him to stay where his is.

Just then the noise gets much closer. He can hear the door downstairs opening, and then the sound of booted feet running up the stairs. Voices are raised in a language he can't understand, then the door of the room bursts open and three or four figures enter. A powerful beam of light sweeps round the room.

For a moment, Edward is dazzled by it, then the beam moves on and picks out his mother. What follows next is confused yet horrifying. His mother is screaming and Edward puts his hands over his ears. The blood is beating behind his eyes. He is aware that there is a lot of shuffling around in the other corner of the room. He knows his mother is being hurt. He wants to go to her but he cannot move, and she has told him to stay where he is, whatever happens.

After what seems like an eternity, the figures stand up, doing up their greatcoats, laughing. Then they are gone. His mother is completely silent. He thinks she must be dead. A wave of fear sweeps over him. What will he do, here on his own? After a while, though, his mother starts to move. She is whimpering. He crawls over towards her and, for a long time, they sit huddled together in the dark. His mother's clothes seem to be in disorder, and her skirt feels wet. At last, she struggles to her feet and they both go to bed. When Edward wakes up the next morning, his mother is still asleep, her head buried beneath the bedclothes.

Anna comes over to where Edward is sitting. She kneels beside him and puts her arms round him, in an unaccustomed gesture. He does not resist.

'Edward,' she says, urgently. 'Edward, what's the matter?'

Edward sobs. He is shaking. So that is it. Now he knows. He knows why he always had the feeling that he had let his mother down somehow, did not protect her. He gets up and staggers towards his mother.

Ida looks up, uncomprehending. She is aware that something dramatic has happened. Edward sinks to the floor and clasps his mother's knees.

'Mum,' he says. 'Mum.' His voice is hoarse. 'I'm so sorry. Please forgive me.'

Ida stares at him. She puts her hand on his thinning hair.

'Forgive you, my dear? For what?'

'I – I couldn't protect you. I couldn't save you. I wanted to but I couldn't.'

Ida's face is beginning to register what Edward is saying.

'Edward my dear. Don't distress yourself. You were a child. All this time, I hoped you did not remember. But, in the end, perhaps it would have been better if you had.'

The others are watching this scene with incomprehension. At last Jude speaks.

'Edward, what is it? What couldn't you save Mum from? Please tell us what it is you've remembered.'

Edward sits back on his heels and shakes his head. He makes a strange figure. An elderly man with thinning grey hair, kneeling in front of his mother in such abject despair. Finally, it is Ida who speaks, calmly:

'Edward witnessed me being – attacked – by Russian soldiers. He was only a little boy and I couldn't protect him from that horror.' Anna's inside seems to melt, as a cold wave of shock runs through her.

Her mother must have been raped! And Edward – he would have been about four; it would have been at the end of the war, 1945, when the Russians held Vienna and before the Western allies arrived. Jude, too, is thinking fast. She looks at Anna. They are both, for once, thinking the same thing. Horst had not been home for months. Ida herself said she did not see him again after the end of the war. Ernest was not yet on the scene. He only arrived in the September of 1945. Anna is thinking all this through logically.

Jude's reasoning is vaguer but, still, she has a gut feeling which is hard to deny. Her voice trembles as she speaks:

'So, Mum, who is my father?' she asks.

Her mother looks at her with an expression of immense sadness.

'I don't know my dear. One of the three of them. One thing is certain though, it was neither Horst nor Ernest.'

Jude gives a little scream. 'Oh my God! I can't bear it!'

She gets up and rushes from the room. Anna and Tony look

at each other in consternation. Then Anna gets up and goes after Jude. Just then, Kate comes in. She stops short in the doorway, taking in the scene.

'What on earth's the matter? Why did Mum go rushing off like that?'

For a moment, Anna doesn't know what to say. Then she makes a quick decision.

'Kate, your mother's just heard some upsetting news. Come with me and I'll explain. Then we can go and see her.'

Once the initial shock has subsided, Edward feels a curious sense of calm and relief. He takes his mother's hands.

'I'm so glad I know now, Mum. It explains so many things I've felt throughout my life. Sometimes I thought I was going mad.'

'I know my dear. When I realised you'd blocked it out of your mind, I probably should have told you, but the moment never seemed to be right.' Ida too feels a kind of relief. 'I just feel so dreadfully sorry for poor Jude. What a thing to find out.'

'Well, you did the very best for all of us, you and Ernest.'

Ida nods sadly. 'Yes, poor Ernest. What a thing to take on. The wife of a member of the SS, pregnant by a Russian soldier! He was always so good to us, though.'

Then Edward turns his attention to his wife.

'As for you, you evil bitch, I hope you're satisfied. I never intend to listen to your poisonous tongue again.'

Marion looks taken aback. 'But Edward, I only said what everyone else was thinking.'

'Oh no you didn't. No one was thinking anything of the kind. You just wanted to stir up trouble. But I'm pleased, really. It's made me see you for what you really are.'

Tony gets up and leaves the room. He feels he has already

heard more than he should. He goes into the kitchen where he finds Juliet preparing tea. He explains what has been going on in the sitting room.

Juliet is horrified. 'Oh, poor Dad! How dreadful! And Aunt Jude. And Gran! I really believed that we'd heard the last of all these horrors.'

Meanwhile, Anna is unsure what she should do about Kate. Her first instinct had been to tell her everything, but then perhaps Jude would not want that. She's just not sure. She's gone too far now, though, she'll have to tell her.

For a moment, Anna thinks Kate is going to pass out. Her face is ashen, and she starts to sway, so that Anna grabs her arm. She steers her towards the bottom of the stairs and sits her down. Shocking as the revelation is, she's taken aback by Kate's violent reaction. For a minute, Kate doesn't speak.

At last she says 'The dream. This is what I dream. Night after night. I thought it was happening to me, but all the time it was Gran! Oh God! This is the weirdest thing that's ever happened to me.'

Anna remembers Jude telling her that Kate had been suffering from nightmares, though she'd had no idea what they were about. Finally, Kate seems to gather her strength:

'I must go to Mum,' she says.

'Shall I come with you?' asks Anna, uncertainly.

'Yes, of course.'

They go into Jude's bedroom. She is lying on the bed facing the wall. Kate goes up to her, but Anna hangs back.

Jude's head is spinning. She feels as if her past life has been lived on a false premise. And yet, in a funny sort of way, she's not completely surprised. She has had the odd feeling for some time that she is not the person she believed she was. At first, she just thought it was all tied up with Gerry leaving. Then she started to feel it went further back than that. In truth, since she was born, she has always felt herself to be an outsider. Perhaps that is why her mother has always seemed to favour her. She must have been trying to make it up to her.

'Mum.' Kate lays her hand on her arm. 'I'm so sorry. What a dreadful shock for you.'

Jude feels numb. 'It's just – a thing like this – you know, it makes you rethink everything. Who am I? I don't know any more.'

'Yes, I know,' says Kate.

After a while, Jude says 'I suppose the same thing applies to you too in a way. And to Dan and Hugo. Who are we? I suppose we'll never really know.'

Anna hesitates in the doorway. She wants to go to her sister, but she feels that, somehow, she won't be well received. Jude has always rather resented her. Now she'll probably be even more bitter.

She moves unwillingly towards the bed: 'Jude, my dear, what can I say? I'm so sorry.'

'What can you say? What can anyone say? I'm just not who I thought I was, that's all,' says Jude dully.

Anna thinks back to the time when she first started to wonder about the dates in Ida's life. She knew there was something that didn't add up. Ernest must have come on the scene later, when Ida was already pregnant. So all three of them have different fathers!

Suddenly, she remembers Ida. Everyone has been so concerned with Edward, and then Jude, but it is Ida, after all, who has had to live with this knowledge. She leaves Jude's bedroom and goes slowly back downstairs to the sitting room.

Ida is still in her chair. The fire has almost gone out, leaving the remaining logs glowing a dull silver in the hearth. As she approaches her mother, she sees that her head has fallen to one side and she is sleeping, her mouth slightly open, her breath barely moving her chest. Each time she sees her mother now, she checks automatically to see that she is still breathing.

Just then Edward comes back into the room, taking a cigarette out of the packet and putting it to his lips. He shrugs apologetically.

'It's too damn cold to smoke outside,' he says.

Anna smiles. 'I suppose we ought to think about getting Mum back,' she says after a pause.

'I think Juliet volunteered for that,' says Edward.

'If – you know – you need to, you can always stay with us for a while,' says Anna. Edward nods.

'Thanks. I might just take you up on that,' he says.

CHAPTER 24

Ida is back in her room again, within the familiar four walls. Her bedside lamp is on, throwing a circle of light onto her clock and her water jug. The rest of the room is in shadow. The girls who were on duty this morning are presumably in the bosom of their families, but the night shift will be on soon, ready to undress her and put her to bed.

How simple and uncomplicated life is here. No one asks her any awkward questions except, perhaps, to see whether she has eaten her dinner. She has to admit that she is relieved to be back in this place that she has begun to think of as home. At first, she just enjoys the comforting warmth, and lets her mind drift off, to nowhere in particular. After a bit, she begins to focus on the events of the day.

Poor Edward! He had been so upset. And Jude! That secret that she has guarded so closely all her life, has suddenly and inexplicably been exposed. How? By whom? She can't remember. It was the final ghastly event of her life in Vienna but, in a way, it was the least significant. She had been attacked – and raped – by Russian soldiers, but then so had so many women: those who had not managed to get away. And Jude was the result! Poor defenceless Jude, who had never quite fitted in, and who had not asked to be born.

Surely the best thing had been to do what she had done: just get on with it. She remembers most of it clearly. Only the actual rape is a blur, but her feelings afterwards are not. At first she'd felt defiled, guilty. Couldn't stop washing. All the classic things. But it had passed, eventually, and when she began to feel the new life within her, she had felt a surge of love for the growing child, which she could not easily explain.

The conquering troops had arrived from the East in the spring. The lilac, like mauve lanterns, hung from the walls that were still standing, its perfume filling the air. The population of Vienna feared and dreaded the arrival of the Mongol hordes but, in fact, they had not proved as terrifying as expected.

The first wave was fairly well disciplined and, providing one did not venture into the city at night, they posed no great threat. Time passed, and the Viennese waited and waited for the arrival of the Americans. They expected them at any moment, but they did not come. Instead, the second wave of back-up troops arrived from the steppes and, between May and September 1945 the citizens were at their mercy.

Every night Ida and Edward would shut themselves in and turn off the lights. It proved no defence in the end. Her assailants finally came in August, and the following month the Allies arrived and, with them, Ernest. By the time she met him, she was already pregnant, although she didn't know it. After a month or so, when the signs were unmistakable, she tried to break off the relationship, but Ernest was persistent and, in the end, she gave in and told him what had happened. Instead of running away, as most men would have done, he wanted even more to protect her.

When Jude was born the next spring, when the lilac was once

more in bloom, his name was put on the birth certificate and when his assignment was completed, they all went to start a new life in England. The family clearly finds it deeply shocking, but they cannot understand that, in those days, there were so many horrors going on, so much torture and death, that it somehow didn't seem to matter so much. At least she wasn't dead. Nor were the children. That was more than could be said for many families. The thought that Horst had been involved in atrocities and murder seemed to her much less easy to bear.

Just then, Gloria arrives.

'Good heavens! Don't tell me you are still on duty,' says Ida.

'I'm going home soon. Just as soon as I've put you to bed. Did you have a nice day darlin'?'

'Well, let's say it was a very revealing one.'

Gloria turns down the light until it is just a faint glow. Ida yawns. She sinks down into the softness of the bed. Her eyes close, and she feels herself drifting, drifting…